WESTERN

Small towns. Rugged ranchers. Big hearts.

The Rancher's Secret Daughter

Jennifer Slattery

His New Companion

Jill Kemerer

MILLS & BOON

THE RANCHER'S SECRET DAUGHTER
© 2025 by Jennifer Slattery
Philippine Copyright 2025
Australian Copyright 2025
New Zealand Copyright 2025

First Published 2025
First Australian Paperback Edition 2025
ISBN 978 1 038 95395 7

HIS NEW COMPANION
© 2025 by Ripple Effect Press, LLC
Philippine Copyright 2025
Australian Copyright 2025
New Zealand Copyright 2025

First Published 2025
First Australian Paperback Edition 2025
ISBN 978 1 038 95395 7

MIX
Paper | Supporting responsible forestry
FSC® C001695
FSC www.fsc.org

Published by
Harlequin Mills & Boon
An imprint of Harlequin Enterprises (Australia) Pty Limited
(ABN 47 001 180 918), a subsidiary of HarperCollins
Publishers Australia Pty Limited
(ABN 36 009 913 517)
Level 19, 201 Elizabeth Street
SYDNEY NSW 2000 AUSTRALIA

Printed and bound in Australia by McPherson's Printing Group

The Rancher's Secret Daughter

Jennifer Slattery

MILLS & BOON

Jennifer Slattery is a writer and speaker who has addressed women's and church groups across the nation. As the founder of Wholly Loved Ministries, she and her team help women rest in their true worth and live with maximum impact. When not writing, Jennifer loves spending time with her adult daughter and hilarious husband. Visit her online at jenniferslatterylivesoutloud.com to learn more or to book her for your next women's event.

Books by Jennifer Slattery

Restoring Her Faith
Hometown Healing
Building a Family
Chasing Her Dream
Her Small-Town Refuge

Sage Creek

Falling for the Family Next Door
Recapturing Her Heart
Christmas on the Ranch
The Rancher's Secret Daughter

Visit the Author Profile page at millsandboon.com.au.

Two are better than one; because they have a good reward for their labour. For if they fall, the one will lift up his fellow: but woe to him that is alone when he falleth; for he hath not another to help him up.

—*Ecclesiastes* 4:9–10

This novel is dedicated to those holding tight to hope amid a storm of disappointments.

Acknowledgments

Thank you to Amanda and the Two Rivers Vaulting Club in Freemont, Nebraska, for allowing me to watch you all in action and for answering my plethora of questions! Thank you also to Rebecca Lowe and Christina Rich for helping to ensure I handled autism accurately and compassionately. I want to thank my daughter's friend Luke Monhollen, farmer's kid and former horticulture researcher with NASA, for answering all my pasture-related questions asked through my daughter. Finally, I want to thank my sweet friend Shelley Brooks for pre-reading this story to help me make it better.

CHAPTER ONE

CHARLOTTE MURPHY PARKED between a silver pickup and a rusted, beat-up two-door and pulled out her phone. Still no response from Whole Peace Wellness Center. Had she and her sister made a mistake partnering with the organization? At the time of their arrangement, operating under a parent company—one that, as a nonprofit, already knew the ins and outs of managing a charitable organization—had seemed like the best plan. And she and her sister needed the monthly support they'd promised, now more than ever. The problems with their property seemed to grow by the day, most of them expensive.

Father, did we hear You wrong regarding moving to Sage Creek, Texas?

With a sigh, she dropped her cell into her purse and stepped out into the hot, mid-June sun. Talk radio pouring from a passing vehicle mingled with the twang of country music from the nearby diner. A couple emerged in her peripheral vision. She tensed with recognition, then released a breath. The man wasn't Xavier Shaw. Nor, upon direct glance, did he resemble her ex-boyfriend at all, other than his cowboy attire.

Her reaction over a potential sighting all but guaranteed she'd make a fool of herself were she to encounter him. But she couldn't stay hidden on her new ranch indefinitely, as appealing as that idea was.

If only she hadn't left back when they'd been dating, not that her mom and dad had given her any choice in the matter. Their greatest fear: that locals would discover their daughter's pregnancy and judge them. Oblivious to Charlotte's pain and confusion, they'd sent her to live with her older sister, Rachel, and brother-in-law until her delivery. Had she chosen adoption, as they'd demanded, she probably could've returned after her senior year.

But the moment she held sweet Gianna in her arms, Charlotte knew she could never let her go.

That choice severed her and her parents' relationship.

Where would she and Xavier be now, had she stayed?

Fighting against the mounting anxiety these thoughts always evoked, she squared her shoulders and strode toward Nuts, Bolts and Boards Hardware Store. The bell above the door jingled as she entered, and a gust of cool air smelling of wood and oil swept over her. The woman behind the cash register was busy helping another customer, with two others waiting in line.

Charlotte scanned the signs above the nearby aisles. Where might she locate drain snakes?

She was heading toward plumbing when a male voice called her name. She turned around and locked eyes with Xavier, standing beside his best friend, Jason, who'd called out to her. This couldn't be happening. Xavier's blue eyes widened before narrowing into a hint of a scowl. Obviously, he wasn't any more thrilled to see her than she was him, only for entirely different reasons.

Unlike her, she assumed, his heart no longer bled for the love they'd lost. That she had shattered. His rigid stance suggested bitterness had replaced any affection he'd once held for her. She probably would've felt the same if he'd disappeared the way she had.

Standing at least half a foot taller than her five-foot-five frame, he was even more handsome and muscular than she'd remembered. His brown hair, streaked with golden highlights, peeked out from beneath a beige cowboy hat, and his broad shoulders and chest muscles seemed to strain against his V-neck T-shirt.

Forcing a nonchalant smile, she stepped forward. Her gaze flitted from him to his best friend, then back to him. "Hello."

Widening his stance, he gave one firm nod.

"When'd you get back in town?" Jason's cheerful tone and broad grin indicated he was clearly oblivious to the tension invading the space.

"Ten days ago."

"Visiting your folks?"

Of course Jason would press for information. Then again, all of Sage Creek would find out about her and her sister's circumstances once they started marketing their program.

She shook her head. "Rachel and I purchased a plot of land out on County Road 385." Unfortunately, the property hadn't been tended to in a decade, if not longer. That was precisely why she and her sister had been able to afford the place. But they'd also underestimated the necessary renovations and overestimated their ability to make them.

Thankfully, they'd have help from Whole Peace Wellness.

Xavier angled his head. "Didn't Rachel's husband manage events for some big-city hotel? Did he trade that in for hobby farming?"

"They got divorced six months ago."

"Sorry to hear that." The glimmer in Jason's eyes contradicted his words. Obviously, his crush on Rachel, five years his senior, hadn't lessened. "Did they have kids?"

Her gaze shot to Xavier as a jolt of electricity zinged through her. The odd look he gave her suggested he'd noticed her moment of panic.

How would Xavier respond, if he learned her secret, knowing she'd robbed him of nearly six years with the most precious gift God could provide? He'd hate her and maybe even fight for custody. At the least, he'd want paternal rights. That would completely upend her autistic daughter's world, which their recent move had made chaotic enough.

She inhaled slowly in an attempt to suppress her anxiety. "Rachel has a daughter. Age five. She's autistic."

Xavier's features softened. Was he thinking of his sister, JoEllen, who was also on the spectrum? "Has the move been hard on her?"

She released a breath. "A bit."

"Dude." Jason flicked Xavier's arm. "You could give them some tips. How about the four of us talk things out over a bite at Wilma's?"

Was the guy seriously trying to use Gianna's discomfort to snag a date with Rachel?

Xavier shook his head. "I'm sure the ladies know what they're doing."

Charlotte didn't share his confidence. But neither was she looking to share a meal with her first—and only—love.

"So, what're y'all planning on doing with the land?" Jason asked.

She explained their plans for an equine therapy program. "We've got a lot of renovations to make. We've hired someone to build us an indoor arena. His prices were great. His communication, not so much."

"Who is it?" Xavier asked.

"The guy's name is Drew Mason."

Xavier's immediate wince, quickly covered with a more stoic expression, made her nervous.

Jason's phone rang. He glanced at the screen and rolled his eyes. "I need to take this." Answering, he walked outside, leaving Charlotte alone with Xavier.

"So…" Why did she feel the need to initiate small talk? To show that she could behave like an adult? To act like her stomach didn't flutter whenever Xavier's eyes met hers? "You still working for Happy Trails Dude Ranch?"

She could still envision the joy on his face the day he came home from a two-week camp hosted at the popular vacation sight. Although he'd expressed little enthusiasm for the religious aspects included by Trinity Faith's youth leader, he'd developed a passion for all things horses. Soon after, he spent most weekends mucking stalls in exchange for riding time. The facility owner had hired him the following summer.

That was one month before their one-year anniversary as a couple and the day he'd first told her he loved her.

Sadness shadowed his smile, as if he were reflecting upon similar memories. "Run my own ranch now. Train horses."

"That's wonderful." She meant it. It felt good to know he was living his dream, even if she was no longer part of it. "How long have you been doing that?"

"Almost long enough to make a name for myself." He chuckled.

Did that mean his business was struggling? She wouldn't be surprised. Considering this was horse country, he probably faced significant competition. It took time to build the reputation needed to sustain a business like his.

Thankfully, she and her sister didn't share a similar challenge. Based on their research and feedback from their parent company, theirs would be the only equine therapy program in the county.

"Any of your clients competing in the fall festival?" The event was known to draw quality talent from across the South.

"A couple."

"That's exciting."

"They don't need me much outside of the training arena. That gives me time to focus on my equestrian vaulters."

She raised her eyebrows. "You've got a club?"

As a teen, the idea of doing acrobatics on a cantering horse had appealed to her. Everyone had expected her to do well based on her experience with gymnastics and cheerleading. She might have, too, if not for her pregnancy, sudden move and the lack of parental support that followed.

He slipped a hand in his pocket. "A team of ten."

"How often do they compete?"

"Not as frequently as they'd like." A hint of the boyish smile that used to quicken her pulse—and, unfortunately, still did—emerged. "They're hoping to make it to nationals next year."

"Wow. That's impressive."

He seemed to stand a bit taller. But then he shrugged nonchalantly. "It's been fun." He glanced about as if trying to locate his friend. "I best go buy us some fish bait."

"Right. I should get going, as well." Grateful for a legitimate reason to excuse herself from the man who was stirring conflicting emotions within her, she darted off in search of the plumbing aisle.

She stopped in front of a shelf of drain snakes and breathed deeply to slow her racing pulse. Maybe if she remained in this spot long enough, Xavier would leave before she went to check out.

She scanned the products' lengths and prices. With their financial challenges and upcoming expenses, everything seemed expensive.

If only she knew which item to buy. With a huff, she left to track down the worker she'd seen upon first entering the store. Hopefully that wouldn't lead her directly into Xavier.

She found the guy in the paint section helping a mother with two young children locate primer. While waiting, she responded to a text from her sister regarding an equine therapy workshop she wanted to take. Yet one more painful but necessary expense.

Hopefully, the wellness center would reimburse them.

"May I help you?"

She glanced up to see the worker, Ken, based on his name tag, standing in front of her. "Yes, please." She relayed her problem.

"First thing you'll want to do is remove your stopper. Should screw off easily enough. Might find your clog right there, attached to the underside of your drain. Course, you'll want to look further down using a flashlight. Clean out whatever you can see. And reach."

She grimaced. "That sounds lovely."

He chuckled and continued to explain next steps, if the one previous didn't solve the problem. "If the water still won't go down, you'll probably need to call a professional."

"Okay, thank you."

With a nod, the guy sauntered toward the back of the store.

"Hey."

She turned to find Jason standing a few feet away. Xavier wasn't with him. "I wasn't trying to eavesdrop or anything, but I couldn't help but overhear. Sounds like you've got your work cut out for you."

"Not exactly my favorite Saturday morning activity. But if it keeps us from calling a plumber..."

"How about I stop in and take a look? Attack the problem with some good old elbow grease. Often, that's all these things take. Pretty sure I could figure it out."

"Oh, no. I couldn't ask you to do that."

"You didn't. I offered." He grinned. "Heading that direction anyway."

She bit her bottom lip. It'd be nice to have help, especially some they didn't have to pay for. "I'd appreciate that."

At least Xavier wasn't coming, because based on her reaction during their awkward reunion, she clearly wasn't over him.

And he just as clearly was completely over her.

XAVIER CLIMBED INTO his truck as Charlotte stepped out of the hardware store with her purchase. She'd always been the most beautiful woman around. He used to love to run his fingers through her long, auburn hair, noticing the copper streaks glimmering in the sun. And how her green eyes had danced with amusement whenever he acted playful, only to deepen with adoration a moment later.

He'd often told her he'd give her the world, if he could. To which she'd reply, "But all I want is you."

Until she didn't.

Shaking the thought aside, he snapped on his seat belt and started his truck. "Ready to go see what's biting?" He turned on the radio, tuned to country music.

"Let's go." Jason drummed his hands on the dashboard. "See if we can't catch enough to invite the boys over for a good old fish fry."

Xavier laughed. "That might be a touch ambitious. But we can always supplement with hot dogs and baked beans."

"Perfect feast." He glanced back as they turned onto A Street, heading out of town. "Charlotte and Rachel. Never thought I'd see those two again."

That would've been his preference.

"Sad to hear about her sister, though. Her getting divorced and all."

Xavier quirked a brow. "Are you, now?"

"For her, yeah. Being a single mom ain't easy. And on a ranch, besides?" He gave a low whistle. "Speaking of, I told Charlotte I'd stop by on our way to fishing. See if I can't help them with a water problem."

Xavier's grip tightened around the steering wheel. "You what?"

"We're passing right by there." He paused. "Oh. You're still bitter about your breakup."

He scoffed. "Hardly." He'd never been the type to hold a grudge. But he wasn't exactly keen on his buddy learning the truth—that the woman who'd stomped on his heart still caused it to accelerate.

Apparently, some habits were hard to break. Thankfully, he retained enough common sense to keep the wayward emotions her encounter stirred in check.

He sensed Jason watching him, likely with that annoying smirk of his. "I wasn't looking to spend my off-day playing handyman, is all."

"Won't take long."

They crossed the railroad tracks, an old, covered bridge and a stream at which they'd spent many lazy Saturday afternoons catching crawfish. Charlotte and a few of her friends had come on occasion. That had usually resulted in exaggerated antics from his buddies while the girls they were chasing after feigned annoyance.

Inevitably, he and Charlotte would slip away to wander along the bank or onto a worn footpath. They'd talked about everything from unusual ice cream flavors and upcoming tests to locations they hoped to visit one day.

While he'd never expected that they'd actually travel the world, he had assumed, wherever they landed, they'd be together.

Jason slapped his thighs in a rhythmic tempo. "You think the kid's dad is still in the picture?"

"'Spect so." Nearing Mr. Lee's old place, Xavier slowed and turned onto a dirt road riddled with potholes. He surveyed the barren and slightly charred land on either side of them and shook his head. "I'd forgotten about the wildfire that roared through here last August. These pastures won't be grazeable for some time. Hope Charlotte and Rachel accounted for that."

"And that they got a good deal on this place."

"That's probably why they moved out here."

"You think Mr. Lee swindled them?"

"Don't know." Although, he wouldn't be surprised. The fact that the sisters hired Drew Mason suggested they hadn't exactly analyzed their options or read the fine print, figuratively speaking. Either that or they'd been foolish enough to think steep discounts didn't come with a cost.

Regardless, that wasn't his responsibility, or Jason's. Although he had a feeling his buddy would act like it was. Some men tried to impress ladies with candy and flowers. Others, like Jason, found ways to flex their biceps.

Xavier had no intention of getting roped into his buddy's attempts to impress Rachel. He had his own problems to deal with, like keeping his ranch from tanking.

Yet, here he was, pulling up alongside a maroon four-door with a dented fender. He recognized Charlotte's green station wagon, cockeyed, in the shade of a large oak. Her parking hadn't improved over the years.

She and her sister stood on the porch talking. Nearby, a child with blond, shoulder-length hair sat cross-legged, engrossed in something, he couldn't tell what.

Charlotte glanced up as he stepped from his vehicle.

For a moment, he froze, pulled to a simpler time when a tank of gas and an afternoon with the person he loved had made him feel beyond blessed. Like the envy of every Hill Country cowboy.

When she left, he thought his heart would never mend. He'd spent many sleepless nights begging God to bring her back.

Now she was here, but it was too late. He had no desire to reopen the wounds time had finally healed.

CHAPTER TWO

CHEST TIGHT, CHARLOTTE hovered near her daughter as Gianna lined her paper dolls along a plank in the porch. If left undisturbed, the child could spend hours adding pieces of clothing in a particular order or constructing a multileveled home from cardstock and other supplies Charlotte kept on hand.

This was one of Gianna's obsessions for which Charlotte was grateful. The familiar activity, amid a deluge of change her daughter didn't understand, soothed her.

It had also been one of the most successful pre-meltdown diversions Charlotte had found.

She eyed Xavier, trying to read his body language as he listened to Jason mansplain to Rachel about proper horse care.

Gianna bore a strong resemblance to her father. Same blond hair, oblong face and expressive eyes, more radiant than the ocean. The way she frowned when absorbed in something mirrored the expression he'd exhibited countless times. Plus, her condition, fragile X, was genetic, and not seen in Charlotte's family history.

Until now.

"I love your vision and what y'all have planned for this place." Jason gestured toward the scorched and neglected property. "Once I get your bathtub draining, maybe you can give me a tour."

So he could see just how dilapidated the property was and how foolish they'd been to purchase it?

"What about fishing?" The deep crevice between Xavier's brows said he didn't want to extend this little meetup any longer than Charlotte did.

Jason shrugged. "What's another ten minutes?"

Rachel pulled her auburn hair back in a handheld ponytail then released it. The action often indicated her long-trained people-pleaser was battling her desire to speak frankly.

"I'm sure there'll be other opportunities." Rachel softened her refusal with a soft chuckle, another behavior birthed from their hypercritical upbringing.

A frown lengthened Jason's features before fading behind a smile. "Yeah, of course." He turned toward the house. "Shall we?"

"Absolutely," Rachel said. "And again, we cannot thank you enough." She led the way inside.

Charlotte glanced at Gianna, reluctant to disrupt her happiness.

Then again, there was no reason she had to. Not yet, anyway. Their diligently followed schedule would dictate a transition soon enough.

Besides, Charlotte's presence in the bathroom wouldn't help Jason unclog the drain any faster.

She knelt beside her daughter, focusing on her carefully arranged figurines to decrease her awareness of Xavier standing a few feet away. She could sense him watching her. Probably Gianna, too.

Charlotte would breathe easier once he left.

Except he chose to remain outside. Then he excused himself, adding distance between them, to make a call.

Leaning against the driver's side door, legs crossed at the ankles, he looked relaxed, almost bored.

As if her presence had no effect on him.

Clearly, he'd gotten over her. The realization left a pit in her gut.

Over the years, she'd tried hard to talk herself out of loving him. She'd even convinced herself that she'd succeeded. But sitting here now, with the man who'd once occupied all her dreams for the future, she now recognized how skilled she'd become at suppressing her emotions.

A brisk breeze sent some of Gianna's carefully arranged paper dolls fluttering across the porch.

"No. No. No." The child scrambled after them.

Charlotte hurried to help before her daughter became overwhelmed. "It's okay, Gianna. They're all here. Look."

"They're messed up now." Hands behind her head, elbows pulled close to her ears, she rocked.

"We can fix them." Charlotte kept her voice soft and calm. "Where would you like the mama? Here?" She pointed to a spot beside the father figure.

"Yes, please." The tension slowly seeped from Gianna's frame as Charlotte helped to reposition the dolls. Soon, her daughter was once again absorbed.

With a relieved exhalation, Charlotte settled beside her.

"You're really good with her." Xavier's deep voice startled her.

She looked up to find him standing at the bottom of the porch stairs, watching her.

"Thanks." His encouragement meant a lot, and not just because he spoke from a place of understanding.

"My mom's talked about how she regrets not being more patient with my sister when she was young. Says she wishes she would've better understood her difficulty dealing with change. Or busy places. Or simply surviving our sensory-loaded world."

"That was a different time."

He nodded. "The mid-eighties, back when a whole slew of autistic people went through the school systems undiagnosed."

"How's your sister doing?"

"Better. She works as a janitor at Sage Creek High. Under Mr. George."

"That's wonderful. JoEllen still live at home?"

"Yep. Likely always will, least until…" He gazed past her, probably thinking about the reality that haunted every family member of an autistic person—who would care for their loved one once their parents passed?

Thankfully, JoEllen had Xavier.

The alarm on Charlotte's phone, set to ensure she didn't unnecessarily disrupt her daughter's schedule, chimed.

"Gianna." She waited until she knew she had her daughter's attention. "It's snack time."

Gianna paused as if considering this. "And iPad?"

"Sure." She stood and turned to Xavier. "Can I get you a glass of sweet tea or a cup of coffee?"

Had she really just invited him in? Yet, not doing so would've seemed as rude as disrupting her daughter's schedule would've been disastrous.

He rubbed the back of his neck, obviously looking for a reason to decline.

"A shot of caffeine sounds great." He ascended the porch steps and followed her inside.

She scanned her living room, grateful that her daughter's need for order allowed for an uncluttered sitting area. To help Gianna gain a sense of control during a highly triggering time, they'd folded packing paper and stacked it, with boxes, along one wall. They'd also placed stickers on the containers with her belongings and tried to pattern her new room as closely as possible after her old one as they unpacked.

Gianna immediately found her iPad and hunkered down in her favorite beanbag, set in a corner with numerous other familiar items arranged into her "safe place."

"Have a seat." Charlotte motioned to the green-and-white-striped couch.

Xavier complied.

She dashed into the kitchen to make a fresh pot of coffee. While it brewed, she searched her brain for potential conversation starters.

She hadn't felt this nervous around a man since…well, since Xavier had asked her out. She'd stumbled over her words, and he'd responded with the same cool confidence he'd displayed this afternoon.

He later told her he'd been so nervous he'd feared he'd become a blundering idiot.

Maybe he wasn't as nonchalant around her now as he seemed.

Or maybe she simply wished that was the case. Then she wouldn't feel like the only one fighting old memories.

A few moments later, she loaded a tray with two steaming mugs, juice and apple slices for Gianna and a plate of chocolate chip cookies for all.

Turning toward the living room, she stopped at the sound of Xavier's smooth voice.

"That looks like an interesting game. What's it called?"

"Creatures of the Wild."

"How's it work?"

"You create biomes, like rainforests, oceans and places for animals to live. You need to have the right climate. That means what the weather is like for a long time. A desert can get really hot when the sun is shining and cold at night because they do not have clouds to hold the heat in. More than two hundred and fifty different types of butterflies live in the Sonoran Desert."

A slight smile tugged on his mouth. "Really?"

"Yes." She continued parroting facts acquired from countless library books and hours of documentaries.

"Interesting." His voice radiated tenderness.

"Yes. Do you know about the queen butterfly?"

"I don't."

"It looks like a monarch, but it is not." She explained the differences.

"I see." He asked her more questions, allowing her to regurgitate yet more information gathered over the past few years.

Charlotte's heart squeezed at the genuine interest conveyed in his tone and how easily he drew Gianna in.

A wave of anxiety followed. While she longed for her daughter to connect with her father, every encounter increased the risk of seeing her secret exposed. Recognizing this only increased her guilt.

If she and Gianna were the only ones affected, Charlotte might even come clean. But she'd promised her sister she wouldn't. Rachel said she had too much to lose. Charlotte would never take the child away from the woman Gianna believed to be her mother. Yet, she and Rachel both knew, their lives could drastically change were Xavier to learn the truth and fight for custody.

Although Charlotte had assured Rachel he'd never do that, Rachel's divorce had left her distrustful. Neither of them had thought her ex could betray her as he had.

Shoulders squared, Charlotte strode into the room with a smile she hoped disguised her inner angst. She set the tray on the coffee table and handed him a cup. "Still like it black?"

"Yes, thank you."

She eyed the adjacent recliner, which felt entirely too close to his position on the couch, and sat. "Help yourself." She motioned to the cookies. "Baked today."

He took one.

An awkward silence followed.

She hurried to fill it. "So, how've you been?"

"Good. You?"

"Busy, as you might imagine." She forced a laugh. "Turns out, we don't know as much about raising horses as we'd thought." More accurately, they'd discovered there was a big difference between training one's horses for personal use and preparing them to work with autistic children. "What about you? You still competing in the rodeo?"

He'd been great at steer roping and bronc riding.

"Working more behind the scenes now. Focusing on horse training and riding lessons. And my equine vaulting club."

"I always wanted to get more involved with that. Back when we were kids."

"From what I remember of your balance beam routines, you would've been terrific."

He'd come to a lot of her meets, and she'd attended most of his football games. "Maybe I'll add that to my bucket list."

Another stretch of silence.

He shifted and looked about. "When'd you and your sister move in?"

"Ten days ago. As you can probably tell, we still have a lot of unpacking to do."

"How's Gianna handling the move?"

Exhaling, she raked a hand through her hair. "Better than expected, but it's been a challenge. Everything we've been dealing with on the property hasn't helped. We've realized there's a lot more to renovating a ranch than we'd thought. I worry we've gotten in over our heads."

One cookie finished, he grabbed another. "So long as you hire competent help, you'll be fine."

She nodded as if that was their plan. Unfortunately, they'd barely had enough money to buy the place and move in.

And if they failed? Not only would they lose their newly purchased ranch, but they'd fall so deeply into debt they'd be paying off their massive loan until the day they died.

"I'm sure y'all talked through the logistics," he said. "Showing my ignorance here, but I didn't realize there were enough children in Sage Creek on the spectrum to sustain something like this."

Regardless, they needed to make this work, for Gianna's sake. Charlotte would do anything to help her thrive. Besides, they'd prayed about this. Despite how things appeared today, she chose to trust God to work everything out.

"You thought of widening your target?" he asked. "Including at-risk teens or troubled families?"

She clicked her pinkie and thumb nails together. "Long term, we want to make this a vacation spot for families who find touristy places challenging."

Xavier watched Gianna play her game. "Your sister got full custody?"

"Yeah."

"Her dad live close?"

She tensed as the subject once again veered dangerously close to the child's birth. "New Mexico."

"Must be tough."

"Rachel's ex, Russ, was never that involved." Charlotte had always suspected he resented her and Gianna, especially when he and Rachel couldn't conceive. Their infertility had softened Rachel's heart and embittered his.

"Because she's on the spectrum?" The sudden edge in his tone reminded her of how protective he'd been of his sister—and anyone with disabilities who experienced mistreatment. She'd always loved that about him.

"He'd probably deny it, but I'm sure that was part of it."

"Your sister must have felt pretty alone. She's blessed to have you."

Charlotte smiled. "We make a great team." She wasn't sure what she would've done if not for Rachel. She probably wouldn't have finished high school. Worse, she might not have chosen to keep the greatest gift God had given her outside of salvation. "Plus, our brother lives in San Marcos. That's another reason we moved here, to be closer to family."

"Does he have children?"

"A son, aged nine. Daughter's seven."

"They on the spectrum?"

Her chest tightened. He was thinking of the genetic connection, which meant his thoughts could easily travel the one direction she was trying to keep him from. "No."

"I imagine your parents are thrilled y'all are here. They still in the area?"

"Yes." They lived one town over, in the same home where she and Rachel had grown up and were no longer welcome. Their mom and dad had barely spoken to Charlotte or her sister since they'd defied their wishes.

They'd never met Gianna.

While Charlotte ached to reconcile, her still-wounded heart was reluctant to initiate contact. The rejection she'd received during her crises had felt devastating enough. She wasn't sure she could take watching her daughter experience the same thing—by adults who were supposed to cherish her.

As they should've Charlotte, as well. Nothing she'd done had been enough to capture their affection. Back when she became pregnant, she'd allowed her fear of losing her relationship with her mother to dictate her actions.

That had cost her the man she loved.

If only she'd stood up to her mom sooner, maybe she and Xavier could've built a family together.

Now it was too late.

CHAPTER THREE

HEARING RACHEL'S AND Jason's approaching voices, Xavier fought the urge to spring to his feet. He'd often worried about how uncomfortable he'd feel being around Charlotte once again. He should've been concerned with how dangerously pleasant their conversation would be. His head could list numerous reasons why he'd be wise to keep his distance.

But the way his pulse escalated whenever their eyes met proved he'd need to keep a tight rein on his heart.

Rachel and Jason entered the living room talking about feed prices, which sat at all-time highs.

Thanking Charlotte for the snack, Xavier stood, ready to leave.

Unfortunately, Jason sat in the now empty space on the couch. "That stinks about your moldy hay. Dude did you dirty."

Xavier looked from him to the women. "What happened?"

Charlotte sighed. "When we purchased this place, Mr. Lee said he had enough hay stored in his barn to feed our horses through the winter. We didn't realize until after closing that the roof leaked."

His jaw tensed. "That weasel." Most folks in Sage Creek acted with high integrity, but every community had a low-life looking for someone to swindle. Two out-of-town sisters must've seemed an easy mark.

Sadly, it appears they had been.

"A buddy of mine owns a contracting business," Xavier said. "He might-can help you out at a decent price. Want me to call him?"

Seemed callous not to offer. Besides, Drake Owens would appreciate the recommendation.

Charlotte's eyes turned misty. She opened her mouth to respond when her phone rang. She glanced at her screen and her expression brightened.

"Hello, Mr. Carrington." She exchanged a look with her sister, who appeared equally encouraged by the call. She listened for a moment. "We won't be needing a gym membership anytime soon, that's for sure. Speaking of repairs, we've hit some unexpected expenses."

His response must have concerned her, because her face fell. She began rubbing her collarbone.

Brow furrowed, Rachel inched closer.

"I don't understand." Charlotte's pitch heightened. "We need that money."

Why did the distress in her voice stir a gut-level reaction within him?

He was simply feeling compassion for two women who had obviously landed in a difficult situation, and, based on Charlotte's conversation, stood to lose crucial funding.

Call ended, Charlotte slid down the wall to the floor, dropped her phone beside her and kneaded her temples.

Rachel sat beside her. "What'd he say?"

"They're dissolving the Wellness Center and terminating our support. Due to insolvency."

"All of it?" Rachel's face blanched.

Blinking as if fighting tears, Charlotte nodded. "What're we going to do?"

"We have to sell."

"We can't." Charlotte looked at Gianna, who remained focused on her game. "We wouldn't have enough for the Realtor's fees. Or to pay back the loan we took out to build the arena."

Xavier frowned. "Don't y'all have a contract or something?" Surely, they wouldn't have purchased this land otherwise.

"Yes!" Charlotte sprang to her feet. "I'll get it." She dashed out of the room and returned with a stapled document. Flipping through the pages, she walked to the table.

They followed.

Reading aloud, Rachel traced the words with her finger. "Either party may terminate this contract by written notice if the other party becomes insolvent…" She pressed a fisted hand to her mouth.

"In other words, the Wellness Center found a loophole," Charlotte said.

Rachel sighed and raked a hand through her hair. "What about the horses? How will we feed them? Or pay for their boarding while we wait for our pastures to grow back?"

A heavy silence, other than the upbeat melody of Gianna's game, filled the room.

"I've got an idea." Jason turned to Xavier. "You've got plenty of space on your ranch."

He blinked. That'd mean increased time with Charlotte, something he had zero intention of doing. "I don't think—"

Jason raised a hand. "Hear me out. You need a vaulting coach, right?"

"Yeah, but—"

He faced Charlotte. "With your years of gymnastics experience, you probably know a thing or two about flips and tricks. Seems you two could work out some sort of trade."

Xavier sighed. He would've jumped on the idea, had it been anyone else. "I don't know."

"Weren't you complaining the other day about not being

able to find anyone competent and affordable? Especially with your first paid gig coming up? Seems y'all don't have many options."

Xavier hated to admit it, but Jason was right. He couldn't work with his vaulting girls like they needed while tending to all the other details related to the event. Not without neglecting his already struggling horse-training business.

He scrubbed a hand over his face. "Okay. I'll do it." He looked at Charlotte.

Her frown suggested she wasn't thrilled with the idea, either.

Releasing a breath, she nodded. "That'll help. A lot. Thank you." She paused. "But we need to give the stables thirty days' notice."

"You already paid for next month?" Xavier asked.

She shook her head. "We've been waiting for our support check. I'd been calling the Wellness Center to find out why we hadn't received it. Now I know why I never heard back."

"How many horses y'all got?" Xavier asked.

Charlotte raised four fingers. "At the Millers'."

"Katey and Jon are friends of mine," Xavier said. "They're about as kind as they come. Explain what happened. Pretty sure they'll cut you some slack. Might even let you out of your deal."

Charlotte bit her bottom lip. "Would you come with me?"

"That could help," Jason said.

He was right, and she and Rachel were in a bind. That meant Gianna needed help, as well. That girl had experienced numerous life-altering transitions in a short period. He thought back to when the pipes in his childhood home had burst. JoEllen's reaction when insurance had placed his family in a hotel had nearly shredded his heart.

He would've done anything to help her feel safe but hadn't known how. At eight years old, there hadn't been much he could do.

There was now.

He offered a gentle smile. "I can do that."

His life was becoming more entangled with Charlotte's by the minute.

Maybe if he reminded himself often enough of how he'd felt when she left him, he wouldn't fall into that dark place yet again.

AFTER CHURCH THE next morning, Charlotte resisted the urge to pace the living room while waiting for Xavier to pick her up. She probably should've forgone her second cup of coffee.

Rachel watched her primp her hair with a frown. "I'm nervous about you spending time with Xavier."

That made two of them. "Don't worry. I won't divulge anything."

She didn't look convinced. "I know how deeply you loved him, and your grief when you moved in with me."

She was probably remembering all the times Charlotte had bemoaned not having him involved in her pregnancy or with her in the delivery room. How he had occupied her dreams for nights after.

She gave herself a mental shake and shifted her thoughts to their ranch. "I refuse to let this destroy our dream. We'll figure something out. When I get back, let's brainstorm ways to fund our program now that we've lost the support of the Wellness Center."

Rachel nodded. "I promised Gianna we'd plant some pipe vines and passionflower vines at the gate after lunch. To attract butterflies. Plus, they'll make this place look more inviting."

"Great thinking." She loved all the creative ways her sister kept her daughter engaged. "Eventually, I'd like to re-stain the porch, as well."

The low hum of an approaching engine and the sound

of tires on gravel spiked her pulse. She took in a long, slow breath to quiet her increased jitters.

She crossed the room to where her daughter knelt, carefully smoothing, folding and stacking packing paper removed from yet another emptied box.

Charlotte squatted to eye level. "Gianna?"

She looked up, made eye contact, then looked away.

"Remember when I told you I'd be leaving for a bit?" She'd learned long ago the importance of explaining and reminding her daughter of every schedule change.

"To move the horses from the Millers' stables to Mr. Shaw's."

"Correct. When I get back, everything will return to normal." She gave her a hug and promised to help her build with her plastic pipes and marbles set later.

"After Mama and I plant a habitat for the butterflies."

"Yes, of course." Grabbing her purse, she rummaged around for her lip gloss, then stopped. This wasn't a date, nor should she care how she looked.

Her days of capturing Xavier's attention were long gone.

She reached for the door. "Pray for favor." If today went well, they could save a lot of money—money they simply didn't have.

She stepped outside as Xavier approached the porch.

He seemed to hesitate, then tipped his hat. "Morning."

Seeing him standing there, wearing dark jeans and a teal T-shirt that accentuated his muscular frame and his blue eyes, stalled her breath. "Hey. I really appreciate you doing this."

"No problem." He led the way to his truck, behind which he'd attached a tall, six-horse trailer.

She surveyed the shiny black-and-silver aluminum structure. "Our horses are going to think they're stepping into an equine spa."

"I know it's bigger than we need, but my smaller one only holds two." Displaying the same cowboy manners that used to leave her weak-kneed, he opened and held her door. "Brought this in case things go our way today."

His use of *our* almost made her think he was invested in the outcome, which was ridiculous, of course. He was simply showing kindness to a fellow Sage Creek resident. That was something for which this town was known.

"Smart." Thanking him once again, she climbed in.

He nodded, strode to the driver's side and slid behind the wheel.

His familiar smoky, rosemary-sage scent filled the cab, merging with a faint aroma of leather and earth.

"I called my friends this morning to let them know we're coming." Country music flowed from the radio as he shifted into Drive. "Wanted to make sure they wouldn't be elbow-deep in chores or anything. That we'd have a chance to talk with them."

"How'd they respond?"

"Gracious, as expected."

The low-lying sun streamed through the windshield as he turned onto the two-lane highway leading to town on the left and a long stretch of ranches and farmland on the right. Rows of corn gave way to golden wheat crops waving in the breeze and pastureland dotted with longhorn cattle.

"I hope this isn't cutting into too much of your day."

He cast her a sideways glance, sitting close enough for her to see the silver specks in his eyes. "Don't have anything pressing until after lunch. I'd already canceled vaulting practices for the rest of this week."

"I take it you weren't expecting your coach to leave?"

"Not so soon. Said she and her husband were moving but that she'd stay until after the Fourth of July event. When I learned he'd already been transferred—he works for the railroad—and left her and the kids here alone, I worried she'd change her mind."

"Do you ever coach the team?"

He gave a slight shrug. "I can, but…"

"You've got a ranch to run and horses to train."

He flashed the smile that used to cause all the teenage girls to swoon—Charlotte included. "Something like that. Plus, I'm working on a rebrand. I've got a meeting scheduled with a marketing guy from Austin. He's going to redesign my website, help me create flyers and ad copy. Stuff like that."

"Sounds expensive."

"Doesn't come cheap. But it sure beats the alternative."

"Which is?"

"Letting Performance Equestrian drive me out of business."

They turned onto a long gravel road and passed a yellow, single-story farmhouse with chickens wandering free in the yard and a child playing tug-of-war with a golden Lab.

"More trainers than horses?" she asked.

"More like one outfit making grand promises and trying to undercut the rest of us."

"That stinks."

He turned at the Millers' entrance marker. "I've been specializing in dressage. Hoping that'll help me stand out."

"Is that why you started your vaulting club?" She didn't have a lot of experience with the sport, but she remembered many of the horses perfected their tempo and consistency through dressage training.

He nodded. "And why I agreed to the Fourth of July deal. Sage Creek's patriotic celebration has always drawn quite a crowd from all over the county. The mayor expects an even bigger turnout this year. Figured that'd be great promotion."

He wound his way through a canopy of mature oaks with gnarled branches draped with moss, past a field of horses and tall grass left fallow.

"My horses are in the second set of stables." She pointed to a long rectangular building west of an outdoor arena.

He nodded and parked beside the brick farmhouse with

navy trim, a tin roof and wraparound porch. "Figured we'd visit with my friends over lemonade first."

That was something else she loved about Sage Creek. People prioritized relationships and tended to connect on a personal level before talking business. Where she grew up one town over, everyone seemed out for themselves.

Maybe that was why she'd spent so much time on this side of the railroad tracks.

That and because she wanted to be with Xavier.

Katey, a short, stocky woman with black pixie-cut hair, strode toward them wearing jeans, a pink tank top and well-worn boots.

"Hello." She grinned as she greeted Charlotte with a handshake and Xavier with a hug. "Feels like I haven't seen you in ages." Motioning for them to follow, she climbed her porch steps. "We need to have you over for dinner soon. The kids miss you." She turned to Charlotte. "They adore him."

His smile indicated he felt the same. "I'll never turn down a home-cooked meal." Entering the house, he removed his hat and placed it on the entryway table. "Thanks for taking time to meet with us."

"Absolutely." She invited them to sit on a suede couch in the living room, then excused herself to get refreshments. She returned with a cheese, vegetable and crackers tray, followed by three filled glasses.

As Katey chatted pleasantly, Charlotte took in the framed photos decorating the walls. One captured four generations of women, clearly related. In another, a good thirty people, from seniors to infants, stood smiling on a white sandy beach.

Blue-, yellow-and white-checked curtains adorned an expansive window with views to a large yard bordered by thickly clustered trees. A rock and flower garden, with two chairs and a circular table, occupied one corner and a wooden playground another.

Charlotte longed to create such an inviting space at their

ranch, with trellised vines to attract butterflies and honeysuckle to draw hummingbirds. Gianna would love it.

"So, Charlotte." Katey's voice cut through her wandering thoughts. "I must say, I admire what you're trying to do."

Her face heated as she realized she'd completely lost track of the conversation. "Thank you."

Katey smiled at Xavier. "And I understand why you feel personally invested in the mission. You've always been a champion for the autistic community."

He stabbed a black olive with a toothpick. "I think it could do a whole lot of good."

She nodded. "We need more resources for those with special needs and their families. Will you bring your sister, once it's up and running?"

"I'll mention it to my folks. Although my friend here has a few hurdles to jump over first."

His shifting the conversation to why they'd come tightened Charlotte's stomach. *Please, Lord, soften Katey's heart. We really need a break.*

They'd experienced more than their share of problems.

She felt like she was asking for a handout. They'd barely begun the discussion, and already she sensed shame rising within—yet another remnant of her mother's emphasis on outward appearances.

Thankfully, Xavier carried most of the conversation.

Listening, Katey's eyes filled with compassion. "I can't imagine how discouraging that must've been. How can I help?"

Charlotte once again relied on Xavier, who not only had a close relationship with the woman but also spoke with the confidence Charlotte lacked.

"I know it's a big ask, but is there any way you can release the ladies from their agreement? Without penalties?"

Fiddling with her bracelet, Katey gazed ahead.

Charlotte refused to squirm.

Or bite her nails.

Or jiggle her feet.

Xavier sandwiched a slice of cheese between two crackers and popped it into his mouth.

Outside, voices approached, then drifted past.

Katey exhaled. "Okay. I can do that. I've got people waiting for stalls, anyway." She narrowed her gaze, first on Charlotte, then on Xavier. "Just don't go bragging about this."

Charlotte could've hugged the woman.

He held up his hands, palms out. "Our lips are sealed."

"I assume from that trailer you brought y'all would like to pick them up today?"

Charlotte pushed on her thumb cuticle. "If possible."

The front door opened, and a tall blond man in a green ball cap entered. "Sorry to interrupt." He looked at Katey. "Ma'am, Mrs. O'Brian's here and wants to talk to you about feed."

"Tell her I'll be with her shortly." She turned back to Charlotte with a warm smile. "Give me a moment to print out a cancelation contract."

Fifteen minutes later, they'd signed the document, Xavier had pulled the trailer to the appropriate stables, and they were walking out with Charlotte and Rachel's horses. All four seemed relaxed until Xavier attempted to lead Champ, Charlotte's tan and white-splashed paint, onto the lowered ramp. The gelding balked and pulled back.

Charlotte took the rope in one hand and ran her other down his forehead. "You're okay, buddy." She looked at Xavier. "Maybe he's freaked out by the size?"

"Anything's possible."

Twenty minutes later, they'd managed to load two of the horses, but Tucker, Rachel's brown-and-white appaloosa, and Champ wouldn't budge.

Charlotte frowned. "I don't understand why they're being so difficult."

He scratched his jaw. “Did you have any issues on your drive to Texas? Any of them fall in the trailer?”

“No.”

“Make any sudden stops?”

She started to shake her head, then stopped. “Wait. Yeah. Once, when a guy at a four-way stop pulled out in front of us.”

“Were you driving fast?”

She nodded. “But we were back far enough that Rachel didn’t brake hard. More like a tap to slow us down.”

“That could’ve spooked them. Horses have a persistent fear memory. Might take some time for these boys to feel comfortable in a trailer again.”

How many more problems would she and Rachel have to overcome? If not for Gianna, she’d consider quitting. Declaring bankruptcy, letting the bank foreclose on their property and finding a low-stress nine-to-five somewhere.

But she wouldn’t make her daughter move again, and certainly not within such a short time span.

Unfortunately, if they hit many more difficulties, they might not have a choice.

She faced the distant hills to hide the tears stinging her eyes.

“Hey.” Xavier placed a warm hand on her shoulder. “It’s going to be okay.”

The tenderness in his voice nearly undid her.

She would not start crying in front of him. Taking a deep breath, she counted to three, and faced him. “Now what?”

Adjusting his hat, he stared off at the horizon.

He smiled. “I’ve got an idea.”

“Okay.”

“I’ll take these two to my ranch. Then I’ll come back, and we can ride the others there.”

“On the highway?”

“For a bit, yeah. But trails connect much of the land between here and my place. We can travel on those.”

The tension in her stomach lessened. "I don't know what I would've done, had I come here alone."

He grinned. "Good thing I'm here, huh?"

In terms of helping solve her current problem, yes. But in regard to her obviously vulnerable heart, no. She feared the more time they spent together, the less she'd manage to suppress her wayward emotions.

And that she was only one adorable grin from telling him everything.

CHAPTER FOUR

XAVIER WAITED WHILE Charlotte mounted her horse, fighting against memories of all the times they'd gone riding while dating. Some women wanted to go to fancy restaurants, but not Charlotte. She'd once said galloping through an open field was the most romantic outing he could plan.

One evening, he'd decided to top that and had invited her out on a clear, starry night. While horses grazed nearby, they had lain on their backs and searched for constellations. He'd made a few up, just to hear her soft laugh. Later, she'd fallen asleep, her head resting on his arm as an earth-scented breeze swept over them and tickled his cheek with her hair.

"You ready?"

Her voice refocused Xavier's attention off the past he had no intention of repeating.

"Yep." He grabbed the reins and directed the horse to the gravel road exiting the property.

The clip-clop of hooves behind him indicated Charlotte followed. When they reached the country highway, he glanced back "How are these beauties with passing vehicles?"

She offered a smile that left him nearly as unsettled as hitting asphalt. "They'll be fine. Besides, I rarely see much traffic out here."

True. But there was always that one driver who seemed oblivious to speed limits or safety. Regardless, they didn't have much choice. At least they'd reach the trails soon enough.

With one firm nod, he led the way along the shoulder, thankful he didn't hear the hum of approaching engines.

The fact that he felt nervous now triggered concern for the sisters' equine therapy program. Seemed to him they'd need confident horses that followed directions and didn't easily spook. He could train out those behaviors, but he and Charlotte's lives were becoming entangled enough. They didn't need another point of connection.

Neither would he allow special needs kids to engage in a potentially dangerous scenario, not if there was something he could do to prevent that. Besides, families needed what Charlotte and Rachel wanted to offer.

Might do his sister good, too. If Charlotte and her sister didn't get enough autistic clients, they could probably expand their services, maybe even offer it to folks with PTSD.

They continued onto a dirt trail shaded by a canopy of wind-stirred branches. Tufts of grass and bursts of red, blue and yellow wildflowers sprouted between the thick tree trunks.

"You sure we should trespass on someone else's land?" she asked.

"This property belongs to family friends. Their son, Drake Owens, helped coach my football team."

"I remember him. Brown hair shaved on the sides. Slightly crooked nose."

He nodded. "Broke it roughhousing the night before a big game. I think it was against your school." She'd grown up one town over. "And still they creamed y'all."

She laughed. "A pity loss, I'm sure."

Her teasing tone, and the banter that felt all too similar to past playful conversations, ignited emotions he fought to suppress.

Exiting the woods, he cleared his throat. "We'll cut through this pasture to another set of trails."

"You know the people that own this land, as well?"

"Yep. Parents of one of my riding students. Nice folks. They won't mind us cutting through."

"Seems you know about everyone around here." She came alongside him, her long wavy hair bouncing on her delicate shoulders, her cheeks sun-kissed.

He averted his gaze. "The horse community's pretty tight-knit."

"Hard to break into?"

He couldn't answer that, as he'd known most of these people since before he first sat in the saddle. But while some small towns tended to distrust outsiders, Sage Creek residents were known for their gracious welcome.

"Well, you did grow up among the competition." He chuckled.

"I *did* date Sage Creek's star quarterback."

Her statement caused his jaw to clench.

Either she noticed his tense expression or felt equally uncomfortable by the mention of their shattered relationship, because thick silence followed.

He'd always expected they'd build a life together in a renovated farmhouse on a quiet stretch of land. She'd crushed that dream, and his trust, when she'd left him with a broken heart and unanswered questions regarding what went wrong.

He was half-tempted to ask her, but her response wouldn't change anything.

Safer option—talk about her program. "What's next for you and Rachel? Regarding your equine therapy goals?"

She huffed. "Figure out how to fund it all. We thought we'd have a licensed psychologist on staff, paid for by Wellness Center. Now…" She sighed. "I don't know how we can afford that. Or taking care of everything we need to get our business up and running, let alone sustain it while we build our clientele."

"Y'all thought about hosting trail rides and birthday parties?"

"That's a great idea! We don't have a large treed area, but we've got some. We'd planned to clean the trails up anyway. Cut back the branches, smooth out the major potholes, that sort of thing."

That was a lot of physical labor for two women who weighed maybe two bucks and change combined. Part of him wanted to offer to help.

The part that'd lead him straight into another heartache.

"This way." He motioned to another trail.

Winding through county land, they passed the lake where they'd spent countless summer afternoons swimming and tossing Frisbees with friends.

Another stretch of silence threatened to turn awkward.

He glanced at her to find her watching him.

A spark of mischief lit her eyes. "Remember when we used to race across the field behind Happy Trails?"

He grinned. "Hmm…" He leaned forward in his saddle and gave a gentle squeeze with his legs. The horse bolted forward into a full gallop.

"Hey! Cheater!"

He glanced back to find Charlotte gaining on him with a radiant smile, wind whipping through her silky hair. Nearing the next patch of trees, he eased the horse to a stop.

Charlotte reached him a moment later, face flushed, eyes bright.

Looking more beautiful than the day she first captured his attention—something he previously would've deemed impossible.

He cleared his throat. "You need to head back to your place once we get your horses settled?"

Her eyes widened. Did she think he wanted to ask her on a date or something?

"If not, I thought I might-could give you a brief orientation to my vaulting program and show you around the place."

She bit her bottom lip. "I try to maintain a predictable and well-communicated schedule for Gianna's sake. But considering nothing today has gone according to plan..." Her soft laughter sounded slightly sarcastic. She pulled her phone from her back pocket, glanced at the screen and frowned, gazing up ahead. "When do you think we'll reach your property?"

Leading them through a canopy of trees, he checked the time, as well.

Had two hours really passed since he picked Charlotte up that morning? "Another thirty minutes at most." At least, that was his hope. He'd never ridden this route before, nor had he realized how many twists and turns these interconnected trails contained.

"Have you given much thought as to when you'd like to start coaching?" he asked.

"Well, considering you've already begun your part of our agreement..." She tucked a windblown lock of hair behind her ears. "I need to talk to Rachel. And alert Gianna to the adjusted schedule. But I can pop over for a bit tomorrow. She's used to me working on the ranch each morning, so me coming to yours shouldn't be a problem."

"My mom used to write big upcoming changes on an erase board."

"We do something similar. We mark adjustments on the calendar, then have Gianna count down the days. She loves numbers and patterns, so to her, it's like a game."

"Until it's time to adjust?"

She smiled. "Exactly."

"I hope our arrangement won't cause too much trouble." He'd witnessed enough of JoEllen's autistic meltdowns to understand the importance of stability and predictability.

"We'll make it work. How often does your team practice?"

"In the summer, five mornings a week. We switch to afternoons come winter."

Her frown suggested this was a mite more than she'd expected. After all, she had her own ranch to run.

"We could probably reduce that a day, so long as the girls increase their at-home conditioning workouts. Not sure I want to suggest any less than that with how soon our event's coming up."

"How well do they know their routines?"

He scoffed. "Considering they haven't landed on one yet…"

"You're kidding, right?" Her tone indicated that was her hope.

"Unfortunately, no. My former coach choreographed something—well within the girls' capabilities—but one of their moms convinced them they needed to up their game. To 'debut with a bang,' as she called it. She's gotten my vaulters confused."

"You don't think they can increase their skill level in time?"

The answer to that largely depended on Charlotte's coaching competency, how quickly she learned each athlete's strengths and weaknesses and how well the girls adapted to a new instructor.

Expressing those concerns wouldn't build her confidence any.

He rubbed the back of his neck, searching for the best response. "It'll be tight."

"I take it you don't want to force them to perform the original?"

He released a heavy breath. "I was leaning that way…"

"Before you realized you'd be bringing me on board?"

He cast her a sideways glance, grateful her face showed no signs of offense. A mite concerned, maybe, and justifiably so. Not only was she embracing a new role, one that was practically foreign to her, she was also potentially stepping into a battle of wills fueled by one of the most intense helicopter parents he'd yet encountered.

"I'm just wondering if they'll adjust better, the more control I give them."

And if Charlotte's gymnastics experience didn't transfer to equine vaulting?

He studied her for a moment. "You've coached before, right?"

Her expression turned sheepish. "Professionally?" She shook her head, then offered a soft, almost apologetic laugh. "Don't worry. I understand what brings out a team's best."

An evasive response if he'd ever heard one. Was this arrangement of theirs a mistake? He was putting his club and reputation as a riding instructor on the line, and placing himself at risk. Considering their history and how devastated he'd felt when their relationship ended, she was the last person he needed hanging around his stables.

When it came to Charlotte Murphy, he didn't trust his heart.

Unfortunately, he needed her as much as she did him. That fact left him feeling even more unsettled than the thought of arriving at the Fourth of July event unprepared.

CHARLOTTE FOLLOWED XAVIER over a horse-dotted hillside to a wide gray building with green trim adjacent to an outdoor arena. A large barn anchored the field that stretched between two opposing tree lines. Beyond this, a gravel road extended to a single-story, rustic ranch with a covered porch, dormer loft and metal roof glimmering in the sun.

She gazed that direction. "That your place?"

"Yep."

"Impressive."

"You expected a shack?"

He dismounted.

She did the same. "Just didn't realize you'd become so domesticated is all." She laughed, hoping he'd catch the teasing lilt in her voice.

The smile lines crinkling around his often-intense eyes assured her he had. "Drake, the assistant football coach I mentioned a while ago, owns a contracting business. Sent his crew dirt cheap to help me build it."

"That was nice of him."

He nodded. "I've pitched in for him when he was on a tight deadline and one of his guys got sick or pulled a no-show. Said he was happy for the opportunity to pay me back, although they always paid me a fair wage. Then again, we're pert near family."

"I remember that being a big part of the football culture."

He nodded and led the way into the stables, the clip-clopping of hooves on the concrete merging with the sounds of nickers and neighs.

"Put your horses in our quarantine area near the back. It lets out to a small paddock." Her alarm must've shown on her face because he added, "Not that I think they're sick or anything. Katey and Jon's facility is as healthy and clean as they come. But that's our biggest stall. Figured they'd do best if kept together, especially with the anxiety they exhibited this morning. And this being their third home in less than two weeks."

"How long do you think it'll take them to feel comfortable here?"

"Every horse is different. Honestly, I'm more concerned about the trailer incident than the change in location."

"But that shouldn't be a big deal, right? Considering we'll be running our program at our place?"

"So long as they don't develop a nervous disposition, yeah."

"They could do that?"

"It's been known to happen."

She sighed. "High-strung horses paired with sensory-sensitive children who feel anxious themselves doesn't seem like the best scenario."

"Might not be as much of a hindrance as you think."

"How so?"

"Isn't the horse's tendency to mirror people's emotions one of the things that make equine therapy so beneficial?"

She grinned. "In helping them self-regulate, absolutely." He'd always been great at seeing the positive. How many times had he turned one of her surly moods into fits of laughter when they'd been growing up? And he'd always made her feel as if her dreams, even the most fantastical, were within her reach—and that he'd do anything in his power to help her achieve them.

Standing here now, on the cusp of what, at times, seemed like a nearly insurmountable goal, felt much too familiar.

Reminding herself of why she and Xavier could never again have anything but friendship, she focused on getting Champ and Tucker untacked and situated—rather than focusing on the handsome and kind cowboy standing so close she could feel the warmth radiating from him.

After the horses greeted one another with nose bumps and gentle snorts, Honey, Charlotte's quarter horse, led the way into the open paddock.

Xavier hung the coiled lead ropes on hooks outside the stall, then dusted off his hands. "Up for a brief tour?"

"Absolutely." She surveyed the yellow-pined walls, the thick ceiling beams and the large window above the entrance door. "You mentioned how clean Katey and Jon's facilities were."

"You didn't think so?"

"Oh, I did, until I came here." She smiled. "Compared to yours, theirs seems messy."

He chuckled. "Thanks. I like to make a good impression with prospective clients. I do some boarding, although my passion—and bread and butter—is training. That and teaching riding lessons."

They passed a wall decorated with numerous ribbons, at least half of them blue.

Charlotte read the notations. "Texas Dressage, first place. Third at the Regional Championships. Placed at state twice. Looks like your program does well."

He nodded, his mouth quirking toward a grin. "I've had some great riders."

"And they clearly had a great instructor."

He averted her gaze with a slight shrug. "I enjoy what I do." He stopped at a door to their left. "This here's where I store extra vaulting equipment."

He opened the door to reveal a well-organized storage area containing pads, mats of varying shapes and sizes and some hand weights. A standing mirror stood along one wall and a few spring jackets hung on a closet rod anchored in an adjacent corner.

She eyed a pile of clothes, knee and ankle braces and grips like she used to wear in gymnastics. "I'm guessing this doubles as a changing room?"

He chuckled. "That, too."

She studied a series of papers tacked to the wall. The first, labeled "Mounts and Dismounts," provided diagrams and instructions for proper form and how judges scored the skill. The next sheet expanded on "the basic seat," and the following on what they termed a "flag." This was equivalent to a kneed scale in gymnastics.

"I'll need to memorize these." She motioned toward the documents.

"For sure."

"But the moves don't look that complicated." She used her phone to take pictures.

"I'll get you copies. I have all this displayed on a corkboard in our indoor arena, too."

"Perfect. Do you know what drills your former coach led the girls through?"

"Planks for sure. Handstands, with and without handles. Push-ups. And cardio, which they hate."

"I'll have to up my game. I can't remember the last time I intentionally broke a sweat."

"You're thinking of competing?"

She smiled at his teasing tone. "Not exactly, but I know from experience I'm more apt to gain their respect, and trust, if I can execute the moves I teach. Besides, I could use the exercise."

"You look plenty fit to me."

Her eyes widened, and pink seeped up his tan neck.

He cleared his throat and began tidying a stack of folded blankets near the door.

She found his shyness endearing.

And dangerous, as was his nearness in this confined space.

Thankfully, approaching footsteps averted their attention and sent him back into the stable aisle.

She followed to see a short, boxy woman strolling toward them.

"There you are." The lady's tone revealed confidence. Her attire—gray boots, maroon capris and matching top—indicated wealth and accentuated her curvy yet toned frame. As did her chin-length hair, highlighted and lowlighted with various shades of blond.

Charlotte felt a hint of pleasure upon seeing Xavier's frown, and the tight smile with which he quickly covered it. Despite this woman's obvious elegance, she wasn't someone he enjoyed spending time with.

The fact that this brought Charlotte such comfort warned her to better guard her heart.

Would every encounter stir up memories—and the longing for a do-over she was fighting so hard to squelch?

CHAPTER FIVE

CHARLOTTE GLANCED AT XAVIER, catching a sigh as he tipped his hat at the beautiful woman that now stood before them. Was there a story behind his frustration?

"Ma'am." He turned to Charlotte. "This is Nadia Wolfe. Her daughter, Morgan, is one of my vaulters." He introduced Charlotte.

Was this the mother who was pushing for a more complicated routine?

Nadia initiated a handshake. "Welcome to Sage Creek. What brought you to our lovely town?"

Charlotte shared a little about her plans.

Nadia raised her eyebrows. "Interesting. I'd love to offer my expertise." The woman's voice took on the tone of a professor. "Unfortunately, I must allocate my time elsewhere." She faced Xavier. "That's why I'm here. I wanted to speak with you about Samantha leaving."

"Okay."

"I know the girls will miss her. And I'm sure that puts you in quite a pinch."

"I'm not worried. God saw this coming and accounted for it, before opening the door for us to perform."

Nadia nodded. "Indeed, which leads me to my proposition."

Visibly stiffening, Xavier widened his stance and crossed his arms. "Oh?"

Why did Charlotte enjoy seeing his obvious irritation with this woman?

This wasn't middle school, nor did she have any right to feel territorial in regards to Xavier.

Nadia lifted her chin. "You know I was on the equine vaulting team in college. Helped carry us to nationals."

His flat expression indicated he wasn't impressed. "I remember."

"You also know I'll do whatever I can to see this club succeed."

"I appreciate your commitment."

"Which is why I am prepared to step in as coach." She smiled as if she'd just promised to carry the team to the 2032 Brisbane Olympics.

Charlotte tensed. Was she about to get displaced? How would that affect her boarding arrangement?

Xavier's eyes widened before smoothing back into an unemotional expression. "I appreciate the offer, but I've already filled the position."

"Oh?" The woman frowned. "Anyone I know?"

"Charlotte has agreed to take on that role, starting immediately." He placed a hand on her shoulder.

The familiar warmth of his touch nearly countered the unease created by Nadia's pointed glare.

"I see." The woman looked like she'd bit into a rotten lime. "What are your qualifications?"

Charlotte blinked. "Excuse me?" She shot a gaze to Xavier, comforted by his protective scowl.

Nadia pursed her lips. "I'm not trying to be rude, but as a concerned parent, I like to remain informed."

Charlotte swallowed. "Yes, of course. I competed in gymnastics from age four until—" her unexpected pregnancy and sudden move "—the summer before my senior year. Division one."

Nadia's frown deepened. "And your equine vaulting experience?"

Hands cold despite the mid-eighties temperature, Charlotte forced herself to maintain eye contact while searching for a reply that would reveal competency she far from felt.

Thankfully, Xavier responded for her. "Charlotte is an exceptionally gifted athlete well trained in body mechanics and with a passion and nurturing demeanor I'm confident will ensure the girls thrive."

Nadia scoffed. "Nurturing? The vaulters don't need coddling. They need someone with drive who will push them hard. Bring out their best, now especially."

Xavier's chest expanded with his deep breath. He exhaled slowly. "I understand your concern, but I've made my decision."

Jaw slack, the woman looked from him to Charlotte, then back to him. "You'll regret this, I assure you."

Charlotte feared she'd created a battle and angered someone that likely held pull within the horse community. The thought churned her stomach.

With a huff, Nadia stomped off, stating Xavier was making a huge mistake.

Shaking his head, Xavier turned to Charlotte. Compassion softened his features. "Sorry about that. She can be quite… exhausting."

"Do you think her daughter will quit the club?"

"Doubt it. Mrs. Wolfe is too obsessed for that."

"Seems her last name's quite fitting."

He chuckled. "No truer words. I must warn you, she'll probably become more demanding and opinionated. She doesn't respond well to the word *no*."

Charlotte rubbed her collarbone. "In Sage Creek less than two weeks, and I've already made an enemy."

"She's just jealous. And entitled."

That didn't make her feel any better, although his support did. It meant a lot that he'd taken up for her.

Too much, actually.

She was here to do a job, to act like a professional, for the sake of her and Rachel's program and all the children and families they'd help.

Squaring her shoulders, she focused on paying attention to ranching details—and not Xavier—during the rest of her tour.

They walked past a washer and dryer, horse blankets piled on the ground and what looked like a small break area with a table, two chairs, fridge and microwave. He picked up a backpack from the floor. It was decorated with flowers, rainbows, smiling suns and butterflies.

He unzipped it, peeked inside and shook his head. "Tatiana, one of my dressage students, will need this. She's in summer school and is *not* thrilled about that. Come to think of it, she probably left this here on purpose."

"An excuse not to do homework?"

He chuckled and eyed the backpack again. "You probably assumed this, but you can bring Gianna here. I'm sure she'll want to see your horses. She might enjoy watching the vaulters, as well."

"I appreciate that."

She loved the opportunity to reduce her time spent away from her daughter—and that she could expose her to something new. But that would also increase the child's encounters with Xavier, and the potential that he'd see himself in her. Charlotte's secret could unravel in an instant. Then she'd destroy the partnership she and Xavier had formed—a collaboration she desperately needed.

More than that, she hated to think how Xavier might respond, were he to learn she'd kept him from his daughter.

XAVIER STUDIED CHARLOTTE. Her words and body language contradicted one another. She was probably concerned with keeping an eye on her niece while coaching the girls. Or maybe she worried about seeming unprofessional. Still, she had to know him well enough to recognize he wouldn't offer something he'd later hold against her.

Then again, their breakup had caused him to rethink a lot of beliefs he'd once held regarding her and their relationship. Maybe she'd done the same.

Not that he'd given her cause. She was the one who'd left. Unless he'd done something to drive her away?

Rehashing past wounds wouldn't help either of them now.

"About your horses." He rested his hand on his belt buckle. "I've got some time this week. Mind if I work with them?"

Her brow furrowed. "You don't think they're ready for equine therapy?"

"That's not it. Just want to make sure they don't turn anxious on you. With their recent transitions and all."

"I'm thankful for the offer, but—"

"This isn't charity, or an act of kindness." Although he had to admit, a part of him *did* want to make her life easier.

The part of him he was trying hard to suppress.

But he couldn't exactly call their arrangement fair. He was simply offering a couple of empty stalls and grazing privileges on land he had more than enough of. She, on the other hand, would be devoting hours to training his vaulters.

"Consider it payment for coaching. And my way of compensating you for the drama you might soon face. From Mrs. Helicopter Mom."

She laughed. "You make the job sound so appealing."

"Just keeping it real."

"Guess every team's got at least one Mrs.—or Mr.—Wolfe."

"Sadly." He shook his head, then glanced past her. "What do you say we finish that tour I was giving before we got so unpleasantly interrupted?"

"I'd like that." She accompanied him toward a side door that was propped open. Sunbeams formed a slanted triangle on the concrete. "First, back to my horses. I'd love if you'd work with them—so long as you allow me to help with your event planning."

Stepping outside, he faced her. "I would greatly appreciate that. When I accepted the Fourth of July gig, I hadn't realized all it'd involve. Or how many times city officials would want to meet to discuss things."

"Sounds intense."

"It'll be the county's biggest Independence Day celebration ever, and with all the veterans in Sage Creek, they wanted the shindig to go well. As do I, of course."

"Have you ordered uniforms?"

"Haven't figured out how to cross that bridge yet. A couple of the girls don't have a lot of money. I know they already feel insecure about that. Don't want to shame them."

"I love your heart. I'll make sure to keep costs low."

"Have you seen the uniform catalogs lately?"

"If they're anything like those for gymnastics, I can imagine. But I have faith."

He raised his eyebrows.

"You're surprised?"

"About?" He needed to practice his stoic expression, especially if he and Charlotte were going to be working together. Otherwise, the emotions he was fighting would overtake his heart *and* his face.

"I'm a Christ-follower now. There's something about having a chil—" Her eyes widened. "Chili-pepper niece that helps a person see their need for God."

He chuckled. "That's a nickname I haven't heard. But as to your conversion—if you're the praying type..."

"I am. And I'll be asking God to bless the girls and your club."

"I'll do the same for you and your program."

She raised her eyebrows. "Does that mean you're a believer now?"

He smiled. "Yeah. Surprised?"

"A bit. Considering how opposed you seemed to religion back in high school."

"We all have to grow up sometime."

She laughed.

Her phone rang. She pulled it from her pocket and looked at the screen. "It's Rachel. Can you excuse me?"

"Absolutely."

She moved to a series of benches along the wall to their left. Although he couldn't hear her words, her body language indicated a problem. As if those sisters needed any more of those.

Call over, she returned, and the defeat in her eyes stirred his compassion and provoked a desire to fix it—whatever *it* was.

"Everything okay?"

Her posture deflated with her exhale. "Our contractor pulled another no show."

"Ouch."

"I don't know what we'll do if he doesn't finish the arena. We took out a loan, which means we'll be held accountable for completing what we promised. I guess we're getting what we paid for?"

"He underbid everyone else?"

"Notably. Only now, he's trying to raise his price. He's claiming an increase in material costs. Is that legal?"

"Unfortunately, yeah. Up to ten percent without property owner's approval. More than that, he'd need your consent."

"That man feels like a tangle of problems. At this point, I'd much rather fire him and go with someone else."

"That can be tricky. Your contract got a termination clause?"

"I'm not sure."

"You'll want to check. If you decide to let him go, you'll

need to prove sufficient cause. Document everything. Otherwise, he can put a lien on your house until you pay whatever y'all initially agreed upon."

"Even if he's not the one to finish it?"

"I've seen it happen." With Drew in particular. Xavier wondered if that was part of his shady business plan—drag things out and make every step so frustrating, the property owner gave up and hired someone else. Then strong-arm them to pay for hours of labor never spent and supplies never used.

Hopefully, Xavier was being too cynical.

Her shoulders drooped. "My sister and I were so convinced God was leading us here to Sage Creek to launch this program. Now I'm wondering if we heard Him wrong."

"Obstacles don't always mean closed doors. Could be preparation for something amazing up ahead. Like training drills before the national championships."

She laughed. "Spoken like a coach."

He smiled. "That's your role now."

Did that overwhelm her, on top of everything else she was dealing with? He was half-tempted to release her from her obligation, except then his help really would be charity, something she'd never go for. Plus, it'd further muddy a relationship he needed to keep professional.

Besides, he needed her help. As much as he hated to admit it, or land in what felt like an increasingly precarious situation, he wouldn't let his vaulters down. They'd worked too hard for him to fail them now.

He'd simply limit his interactions with Charlotte, and remind himself, often, of their past and how she'd proclaimed her love one day and left the next.

Tour completed, he walked her back to her car. "Hopefully I didn't keep you tied up too long."

"I appreciate you taking the time."

The breeze swept over him, carrying her soft floral scent. Steeling himself against a surge of unwelcome emotions, he opened her door for her. "It was my pleasure." He hated the truth in that statement. "Hope you and Rachel can get everything worked out with D.M. Exteriors."

She frowned. "Me, too." She slid behind the steering wheel and snapped on her seat belt. "When should I plan on being here tomorrow?"

The reminder accelerated his pulse, alerting him once again of his need to better wrangle his rogue emotions. "The girls start trickling in around nine forty-five. Practice runs from ten to eleven thirty. Some like to stay after to work on the barrel and whatnot, but you can send them home. I know you've got things to take care of on your ranch."

"I'll talk to Rachel—and see how Gianna's doing. But I'd like to stick around, if possible. Get to know the girls a bit. Start earning their trust." She bit her bottom lip. "You think Mrs. Wolfe will show up?"

"I'd say count on it."

"Lovely."

The vulnerability in her eyes, and knowing the toxicity she'd soon encounter, provoked his protective side. She used to joke that he'd fight off shadows if he thought they spooked her. To which he'd respond, "And bring you the moon and stars while I'm at it."

The look she gave him in return had always made him feel like he'd scored the winning touchdown during the biggest game of the season.

Man, was he in trouble.

Lord, show me how to build a working relationship with that woman, without moving toward another heartache.

CHAPTER SIX

MONDAY MORNING, CHARLOTTE woke earlier than normal, partially to help with chores before heading to Xavier's. But first-day-on-the-job jitters had also propelled her out of bed.

She wasn't sure what made her most anxious. Taking on a position for which she basically had zero experience? Gaining the trust of teenagers? The thought of encountering Mrs. Wolfe—and her going off on Charlotte in front of the team? Or doing her best not to disappoint Xavier, the man who still stole her breath whenever his blue eyes landed on hers?

She entered the house through the mudroom, shucked off her boots and followed the scent of bacon and maple syrup into the kitchen.

Rachel stood at the stove stacking pancakes onto a plate. "Perfect timing. Catch sight of Pumpkin's kittens?"

"Nope."

The stray started coming around shortly after they'd moved in, growing less timid with every bowl of cat food left on the porch. She disappeared for a couple of days, then resurfaced with a much smaller and sagging belly.

Charlotte set glasses on the table. "Where's the munchkin?"

"Either getting dressed or lining up her stuffed animals."

That was one of her rituals. Each night, she'd tuck them

into her bottom shelf-turned-cradle. The following morning, after donning one of four identical T-shirts, she'd position her animals on her windowsill facing outward. Only then would she emerge for breakfast.

They'd learned the hard way not to disrupt or rush her routine, even when—especially when—they were running late.

Movement in Charlotte's peripheral view caught her attention, and she turned to see Gianna enter with her iPad.

"Good morning, sweet pea." Charlotte greeted her with a side-hug. "Sleep well?"

"I'm hungry."

"Good news." Rachel flashed a smile and brought the pancakes and bacon to the table. "Because I made your favorite."

And about the only thing Gianna would eat for breakfast.

Gianna smiled, bounced on the balls of her feet, and flicked her fingers.

"Would you like orange juice?" Charlotte grabbed a pitcher from the fridge.

"Pink cup, please." Gianna sat at the table and immediately started playing her game.

Charlotte pulled her daughter's favorite tumbler from the cupboard, filled it and carried it over. "Remember what we talked about last night? About me leaving this morning?"

Rachel brought over their week's schedule, written on a magnetic erase board kept on the fridge.

Gianna glanced at the color-coded blocked times and nodded. "You are going to work. With big kids. But not here. Somewhere else."

"Correct," Charlotte said. "I won't be back until after lunch."

"Then exploring."

"Yes." She released a breath, grateful the conversation had gone so well.

"Let me know how the horses are handling their new home." Rachel filled two mugs with coffee, handed one to

Charlotte, then sat across from her. "I don't expect any difficulties. But—"

"I want to see Tucker." Gianna said. "And Champ and Honey and Whisper."

Xavier had encouraged her to bring her daughter. "How about I take you when I get back?"

"No. We're going exploring."

"After."

"No. We visit the horses in the morning. After chores."

Charlotte took in a slow, deep breath to quiet her frustration. Carefully maintaining a schedule was as challenging as it was necessary. The slightest disruption could prove quite upsetting to Gianna, especially with all the other changes she'd experienced.

With more still to come.

Charlotte checked the clock. If they left now, Gianna could spend time with the horses before vaulting practice started.

Not counting the drive home, then back.

She leaned toward Rachel to whisper, "If I take Gianna to Xavier's this morning, could you pick her up? Like, say, at nine thirty-five?" That'd allow a ten-minute cushion, should her daughter need extra coaxing when it came time to leave.

Rachel glanced at their schedule and nodded. "We can head to the library from there."

Charlotte grinned. "Go team sisters." She turned to her daughter, ensured she had her attention, then explained the new arrangement. "How does that sound?"

"Okay."

Thankfully, Gianna finished her breakfast and got out the door without delay or complication.

On the drive to Xavier's, Charlotte carefully described what they might encounter and reiterated their plans, emphasizing the need for cooperation once Rachel came to pick her up. This probably wasn't the wisest move, her first day on the job. But she didn't feel right triggering a tantrum she wouldn't be around to deal with.

And Gianna did much better overall when she was able to see the horses.

They arrived at Xavier's to find him in the stables, pushing a wheelbarrow filled with dirty wood shavings.

"Hey there." He donned an easy smile. "I see you brought a helper."

Gianna stood a bit taller, her demeanor revealing how important she deemed her endeavor. "I'm going to groom Tucker and Champ and Honey and Whisper. I brush the dirt out of their hair. Dirt is bad for their skin. They could get sores."

"I see." He matched her weighty expression, contradicted by the mirth in his eyes. "Then it's good you came."

He'd always treated others with dignity, even those most people discounted. In high school, his deliberate defiance of petty social lines had seemed courageous.

Gianna gave a firm nod. "Yes. Where are the horses?"

"This way." Abandoning his chores, he turned toward the back of the stables.

"We don't want to interrupt you." Charlotte was here to help, not steal time from him. "I can take her. Thank you, though."

"I'm ready for a break, anyway." He smiled at Gianna, who matched his steps as he headed toward where he kept her horses.

Charlotte followed close behind.

"How are your biomes going?" he asked. "In your *Creatures of the Wild*?"

He'd remembered the name of her game?

"Good."

"Have you added any butterflies?"

"No." Gianna paused. "Mom and I planted flowers to attract the pipe vine swallowtail. It's black, and blue, with orange dots."

"Sounds beautiful."

"Yes. Birds don't like to eat them because they taste bad."

"Great news."

"Yes."

As they neared the last stalls, Charlotte and Rachel's horses whinnied and extended their heads over their gates.

"Looks like they've missed you," Xavier said.

Gianna nodded. "Yes. They like to see me. I take good care of them."

"I'm sure you do." Making a clucking noise, he unlatched the gate and slid inside. His body filled the opening and formed a barricade between horses and child.

Once the horses stepped back, he turned around and made eye contact with Gianna. "Stay where they can see you. And approach slowly."

"I know. Never go behind a horse or make loud noises. Loud noises spook them, just like me."

"That's right." He scratched Honey's withers. "Hey, girl." He glanced back at Gianna. "This little lady seems ready for some loving. Shall we start with her?"

"No. Tucker. Then Champ. Then Honey. Then Whisper. Whisper's last."

"Sounds like a plan."

Charlotte held Champ by the halter while Xavier guided the other horses out to their paddock. Then she watched, moved, as Xavier patiently waited for Gianna to complete her fifty brush strokes on the first side.

"You know this could take a while, right?" Charlotte asked.

He chuckled. "I'm beginning to realize."

"I'm sure you have plenty to take care of. You don't have to stay."

"What if I want to?" The almost paternal way he looked at Gianna suggested he spoke truth. This endeared her to him and twisted her insides.

She'd always said her bond with Gianna was God-given.

Was Xavier feeling the same pull? If so, that would be yet one more thread potentially leading to her secret unraveling.

"THREE DOWN. ONE to go." Xavier motioned for Gianna to move back, turned Honey around and released her to graze.

Charlotte's phone rang. She glanced at the screen and answered. "Hi. You here?" Listening, she frowned. "Great. Okay. Keep trying and buzz me again if you're able to get it running."

He moved toward her. "Everything all right?"

She sighed. "That was Rachel. I drove her car here and left her mine. The brakes squeak and bother Gianna."

"Understandable."

"Rachel was going to pick her up, so I could focus on practice. But my car won't start." She kneaded her forehead. "I should've known this might happen. It's been driving rough for a while. This was *not* how I wanted to start my first day on the job."

He waved a hand. "I'm not worried about it. Bring Gianna to practice with you."

"You sure?"

"Yep. We can set up a play area for her in the corner. I'll grab some computer paper and markers. Might even be able to find and print some butterfly activity pages. And scrounge up some colored pencils."

She quirked an eyebrow. "You keep those on hand?"

"To entertain the littles while their older siblings ride."

"Smart. And thank you."

"Yep." He followed them into the stable aisle, latched the stall gate behind them and walked them to the indoor arena. "Going to be a hot one today. Practicing in here will keep complaining to a minimum." He chuckled. "And help you keep a close eye on your princess."

He was glad he'd thought to set up the equipment the night before. At the time, he'd chided himself for this, worried it was yet one more sign that he was still much too attached to Charlotte. Now he wondered if maybe the Good Lord had nudged him in that direction to keep Gianna's morning running as smoothly as possible.

She sure was a cute kid. The way her tense posture had relaxed the moment she began interacting with the horses increased his desire to help Charlotte and Rachel. How many children would experience connection, and temporary reprieve from their often-unrelenting anxiety, through their program? While speaking hope to exhausted and discouraged parents?

An image came to mind of his mom and dad at the kitchen table, arguing over how best to help JoEllen, knowing their options were few. While much had changed, many families within the autistic community still encountered more obstacles than opportunities.

Strolling back through the stables, he glanced at his full and waiting wheelbarrow, mentally sifting through his remaining morning chores, and dashed into his stable office. Numerous documents and sticky notes cluttered the folding table that doubled as his desk. He needed to get back to one of his students who wanted an extra lesson this week. They had a dressage competition coming up—youth championships—and felt unprepared. He understood how an extra session, peppered with honest yet liberal praise, could increase her confidence.

If only his day had more margin.

He reviewed the week's to-dos, instantly feeling the weight. He was scheduled to start working with a new mare on Wednesday. They'd previously sent her to a guy who claimed to use gentle training but left owners with "resistant," also known as traumatized, horses. Logic had told Xavier, quite loudly, not to add yet another responsibility to his already loaded shoulders, but his compassion for the animal won out.

He should probably call the cultural committee to tell them about his coaching change.

Charlotte. She and Gianna were waiting on those pages he'd promised. He wiggled his computer mouse to jolt it from sleep mode and searched the internet for activity pages related to butterflies. Grinning, he clicked on cutout patterns for winged paper dolls with butterfly-styled clothing.

Two of Gianna's passions, merged.

Interesting how attached he felt to that kid after such a short period. Probably because she reminded him of his sister.

And because she held a special connection to the woman he once loved?

He snorted. No. Those days were deader than the fire-scorched pastures that had caused their lives becoming entangled once again.

Professionally, of course, which was precisely how their relationship would remain.

He clicked Print, drumming his fingers on his desk as if doing so would accelerate the process, then snatched the pages from the tray. He grabbed a box of colored pencils and broken crayons from the nearby shelf and searched for a pair of scissors. Items in hand, he hustled back to the arena, arriving slightly out of breath.

He stopped a few feet from the calisthenics area to watch Charlotte with the girls. They were doing piked sit-ups while she stood in front of them counting. He scanned the wooden benches, lined end to end, along the adjacent wall. Gianna paced in front of them, repeating something he couldn't make out.

Thankfully, Helicopter wasn't there. Yet.

Making eye contact with Charlotte, he offered an encouraging smile, raised his items, then approached her niece.

"Gianna?"

She stopped and looked his way. "Coloring pages?"

"Yep." He set everything but the papers on the bench, then

showed her those one at a time. As expected, her eyes brightened when she saw the paper doll patterns.

She clapped her hands, flicked her fingers, then clapped again. "Those are for me."

"That's right." He gave her the sheet and scissors. "Would you like me to show you how to cut them out?"

"No, thanks." She carried her things to the bench, stretched out on her stomach and began cutting.

He turned to see Charlotte watching him with a look of admiration that sent a wave of warmth through his chest, followed by a burst of caution.

Clearing his throat, he ambled over. "Looks like y'all are off to a great start."

"After some bargaining, yes."

"Oh?"

"Apparently, they don't do calisthenics on Mondays."

"Really, now?" He gave the girls a pointed look, receiving sheepish smiles in return. "Sounds like what they were really saying is that they want double. To prepare for their routine and all."

They groaned, and Peyton, the most vocal of the bunch, planted her manicured hands on her hips. "Do we have to?"

"If it were up to me, yeah. But your coach can trump that. If she chooses." Seemed a good opportunity to establish Charlotte's authority while potentially endearing their hearts toward her.

Two actions that could prove necessary, should Mrs. Wolfe try to sabotage both.

The girls sprang forward and bargained for leniency. They'd work extra hard, would stay focused for the remainder of practice. One of them even offered to bring her homemade cheesecake.

"Well, now." Amusement brightened Charlotte's eyes. "Make that strawberry, and you have a deal."

"Yay!" Cheering in unison, they jumped up and down.

"So long as you also remain on task for the remainder of our time."

They immediately turned serious, their posture slightly stiff.

"Now that you're all warmed up…" She faced Xavier. "Do they normally practice on a horse?"

"Oh. Right. I forgot to bring Dolly out. Give me a minute."

He darted off and returned with the mare to find Charlotte and the girls talking about their routine for the upcoming program. Of course, they were pushing for Helicopter Mom's ideas. She'd convinced them they needed to "dazzle" everyone to launch themselves as a performing group, and that her suggestions were the only way for them to do so.

After patiently listening, Charlotte turned to him. "Thoughts?"

Scratching his jaw, he shifted toward the girls. "That sounds like quite a leap from where you're at now."

Mandi, a petite blonde who typically had more sass than sugar, frowned. "You don't think we can do it?"

He and Charlotte exchanged glances. This decision felt challenging on a couple of levels. Not only would the suggested moves require the girls to experience significant growth, but he needed to see Charlotte's competency as well. It was one thing to perform backflips on a balance beam—she'd excelled at that.

Could she effectively coach the girls, as well? And would they trust her guidance?

"I completely understand your hesitation."

He tensed at the familiar voice behind him. Taking in a slow breath to hide his frustration, he faced the woman who seemed intent on causing him continual grief. "Ma'am."

Couldn't Mrs. Wolfe see how her meddling negatively affected the girls, leading to questions and doubts when they most needed to feel confident and unified?

"Xavier." She offered a stiff, close-lipped smile, which disappeared entirely when her gaze shifted to Charlotte. "I can only imagine how daunting this all must feel, with your lack of experience and all."

The girls had probably already heard Mrs. Wolfe's complaints. She'd probably gone home to rant to Morgan the other day, who'd then repeated everything to the others. Morgan wouldn't have done so maliciously. Xavier couldn't say the same for her mother.

That she was causing a ruckus on Charlotte's first day made minding his manners near impossible.

He glanced at Charlotte, his intense reaction to her wounded expression triggering immediate regret. Apparently, his response to seeing her in pain hadn't lessened much over the years.

As soon as the Fourth of July event ended, he needed to invest serious time into finding another coach. And helping Charlotte and Rachel resurrect their fire-scorched pastures, because this arrangement was growing more dangerous by the day.

CHAPTER SEVEN

PULLING ONTO XAVIER'S RANCH, Charlotte glanced at Gianna, who was absorbed in her iPad. Despite the schedule disruption, yesterday had gone relatively well.

At least, as far as her daughter was concerned.

Charlotte had expected Mrs. Wolfe to show up at some point, and to make things tense. She hadn't anticipated the open challenge to her coaching abilities—in front of the girls. Although the teens hadn't become defiant after the woman's insinuations, they had behaved differently. More distrustful, and when she'd only begun to build rapport.

A night of fretting over the incident had turned the encouragement she'd felt, when Xavier had immediately jumped to her defense, to worry. His taking up for her would probably fuel Mrs. Wolfe's resentment. If only Charlotte could think of a way to turn her enemy into an ally.

With a sigh, she parked near the east entrance to the arena and faced her daughter. "Remember what we talked about. First, we'll see the horses."

Gianna nodded. "I'll groom them. Tucker, then Champ, then Honey, then Whisper. Whisper is last."

"Correct. After that, we'll go to the arena, and you'll work on your paper dolls while I coach the girls."

Thankfully, Charlotte had found more patterns online. Gianna had finished the ones Xavier had printed the night before. The activity had kept her occupied while Charlotte watched a series of equine vaulting videos.

However, Gianna had become agitated at bedtime, reminding Charlotte and Rachel of the need to keep her schedule as predictable as possible. Not an easy task, considering the circumstances. But hopefully, they'd all settle into new rhythms soon.

Once again, they entered the stables to find Xavier mucking stalls. He vacated his chores as quickly as before to join her and Gianna.

"Turned the horses out this morning." He brushed Tucker's front mane aside. "Brought this guy in a few moments ago."

He remembered Gianna's grooming order? The fact that he was acting like an attentive father—to his daughter—churned her gut. How would she feel if the situation were reversed, and she was the one deceived?

Forgive me, Father. But I don't know what else to do.

"You okay?" Xavier was watching her with a furrowed brow.

She forced a smile. "Just thinking." About secrets, dishonesty and a heart increasingly burdened with guilt.

Holding Tucker's halter while Gianna counted out her brush strokes, he frowned. "Sorry about yesterday. It's high time I had a more direct conversation with Mrs. Wolfe."

The bagel and coffee Charlotte had eaten earlier sat heavy in her stomach. "Won't that upset her more?"

"Unfortunately, but I'm pretty sure she's heading that direction, no matter what I say. That woman's more stubborn than a well-fed mule."

"Wonderful." Her shoulders slumped. "And if the girls revolt by week's end?"

"So long as you're consistent and fair, they'll do all right.

They want to perform well on the Fourth even more than we want them to."

"It's interesting how different Morgan is from her mom. The girl's so quiet."

"I think her mother intimidates her."

"I picked up on that. Mrs. Wolfe seems to have unrealistic expectations for her daughter."

He nodded. "Pushes her ten times harder than any coach—any decent one—ever would. I worry she'll cause the kid to hate the sport entirely."

"That'd be so sad." Unfortunately, she understood the pain caused by a critical parent. Especially during the teen years, when teens most needed assurance and support.

"Speaking of practice pleasantries—" he chuckled "—you make any decisions regarding their routine? Because you'll want them working on it as soon as possible."

"I've got some ideas. A compromise of sorts."

"Excellent. Let me hear it."

"I know Morgan's mom is demanding she add a back walk-over and a backward handstand dismount." This, of course, made the others want to increase their difficulty levels, as well.

He huffed. "Right. Because learning one new move isn't challenging enough. When they should be in the polishing and perfecting stage."

She nodded. "I figured I have three options. Put my foot down and make them stick with the choreography you suggested yesterday." Considering that was, apparently, a step backward from what they'd been working on with the previous coach, they hadn't liked that idea. Although she could understand why Xavier wanted them to present something he knew they could execute. "I could concede to their wishes."

He frowned. "Not happening."

"Or, I let them all choose one new exercise to learn, and give them two days to do so."

"I don't know." He scratched his jaw. "I get your thought process, but completing and nailing a skill are very different things. As this is our first paid gig, we need to be at our best."

"What if they need to demonstrate their competency to you and get your approval? I'll emphasize that they work on the new moves after practice, so they're still able to sufficiently prepare for the event."

Lines etched in his forehead, he gazed past her. Releasing a breath, he looked at her again with a nod. "I can live with that."

"Wonderful. Now to convince the girls." And Mrs. Wolfe, because if that woman wasn't happy, she'd make sure the vaulters weren't, either.

Thankfully, Morgan's mom didn't show up until the end of practice, after the girls had already agreed to Charlotte's terms. As the woman stood there, watching her daughter attempt her handstand dismount on the mechanical horse, the teens either forgot or chose not to disclose their arrangement.

Based on the nervous looks they shot one another, Charlotte assumed the latter.

Hopefully, that meant they found her suggestion fair. They also might've feared, should they or Mrs. Wolfe force the matter, Charlotte would renege and enforce Xavier's previous suggestion. Regardless, she was grateful not to experience another morning of drama.

Forty-five minutes later, two of the teens left, neither closer to mastering their new skill. The others trickled out shortly after until only Morgan remained, along with her mother, unfortunately, and she showed no signs of letting her daughter leave anytime soon.

Thankfully, Gianna remained engrossed with her iPad. Charlotte had tucked it into her duffel in case Xavier agreed to her plan and she and her daughter needed to stay late. But she'd never anticipated being here this long.

Morgan looked beyond fatigued—and discouraged. She

was obviously trying hard to please her mom, only to receive a firm "Again" in return.

As her coach, Charlotte's job was to nurture and inspire, and, in this instance, intervene when someone worked against those goals.

In the least quarrelsome way possible.

Squaring her shoulders, she stepped forward. "That's enough for today." She maintained eye contact with Morgan, intentionally ignoring her mother's fiery glare. "You've worked incredibly hard. I admire your grit." Hopefully, the affirmation would counter some of the insecurities that came from growing up in such a harsh environment.

Mrs. Wolfe crossed her arms. "Are we taking too much of your time?"

Charlotte winced inwardly at the woman's biting tone but kept her posture straight. She faced her with a firm but amicable expression. "I stayed willingly. But practice is over now." She turned back to Morgan. "I'm sure you're starving. You've burned a lot of fuel this morning."

The teen glanced at her mom, who looked like she was preparing for a battle.

Booted footfalls approached. "Everything all right here?"

Tension seeped from Charlotte's shoulders with her exhale.

She was frustrated, though, at how much she needed Xavier at this moment. Whatever aid he provided in the short term could further hinder her ability to gain her team's, and Mrs. Wolfe's, respect.

Scripture said harsh responses ignited tempers whereas gentleness calmed them.

Charlotte inhaled through her diaphragm so her nerves wouldn't cause her voice to tremble, and briefly explained the situation—without attack or accusation.

Xavier nodded and offered Morgan a compassionate smile. "I admire your drive. But we don't need you pushing yourself into an injury. That could knock you out of the game for weeks." His eyes narrowed as he looked at her mom.

A tense moment stretched between them.

Mrs. Wolfe huffed. "Come on, Morgan. I've got errands to run, and you've got chores."

Charlotte held her breath as the two exited the arena.

She massaged her temples. "While that wasn't how I wanted practice to end, I can't say I'm surprised."

"Wish I knew how to speak sense into that woman. For Morgan's sake."

"I'll be praying for us both." Another biblical promise she was learning to trust—the Holy Spirit would provide perfect guidance. And, hopefully, keep her from doing or saying something to exacerbate things.

Gianna glanced up, abandoned her iPad on the bench and hurried over. "My turn?"

"Remember, you ride on Wednesdays and Fridays," Charlotte said.

"No. On that." She pointed to the mechanical horse.

Xavier smiled. "I knew you were a little athlete."

"It's almost lunch, sweetie." Her daughter didn't need another schedule disruption.

Charlotte walked to her duffel bag and pulled out a printed copy of the day's routine and a plastic toy clock with moveable hands. "Right now, it's eleven forty-five. We eat at twelve."

Gianna nodded. "Yes. With my pink cup. Then we will go exploring."

"That's right." Time spent in nature always soothed the child.

Brow furrowed, Gianna studied the cardio station. "Tomorrow?"

Charlotte mentally sifted through the rest of their week. Thankfully, she and Rachel left open slots in Gianna's chart to allow for the unexpected. Although this helped her adapt, it didn't guarantee she wouldn't have a meltdown.

"You said she rides on Wednesdays?" Xavier asked.

Charlotte nodded.

"So, you'll be coming here anyway, right?"

"True."

"When about?"

"After supper. Seven thirty." She and Rachel had started using the horses as bargaining to get Gianna to eat her vegetables. "Do you typically leave the equipment out?"

"During the summer, yeah."

"You wouldn't mind if she used them tomorrow evening?"

"Nope." The easy smile that always elevated her pulse returned. "I might join you."

Her eyes widened. "Oh, you don't have to do that."

"I know." His cell rang, and he glanced at the screen. "I best get this. See you tomorrow."

"Twice," Gianna said.

He chuckled, his gaze capturing Charlotte's. "Yeah. Looking forward to it."

Was that directed at her? She wasn't sure how to process that.

More likely, he was simply growing fond of Gianna.

That left her equally touched and unsettled. Would their interactions ever get easier, or would her gut always feel like she was being tossed about and turned upside down?

XAVIER DASHED INTO the house to make a sandwich and refill his tumbler with sweet tea, then hustled back to the stables. He arrived to Leila's stall shortly before his next student. After guiding Hazel, the blue-eyed eight-year-old, on how to get the lesson horse tacked up, they proceeded to the arena.

There, he helped her into the saddle and her feet into the stirrups. "Sit tall now. Elbows at your sides. Thumbs on top of the reins." He guided her into the proper position. "Good."

Hazel's wide-eyed grin revealed two missing teeth. She wore her long, blonde hair pulled back into two braids.

"Remember how to tell her to move?"

She nodded and gave Leila three little kicks, the first couple too soft to register. The third spurred the horse forward.

"Excellent."

Another wide grin.

He made eye contact with her mom, who was leaning against the fence railing, as he passed.

Veronica's smile was nearly as wide as her daughter's. "You're so good with her. I can't believe how relaxed she is."

Last week, the girl had been so frightened he wasn't sure he'd get her into the saddle. By the end of the lesson, she'd been reluctant to get off.

"I knew she and Leila would become great friends." He gave his horse a pat. "Isn't that right, kiddo?"

Hazel's braids bounced against her shoulders with her head bob.

"I'm so glad the Reyes recommended you," Veronica said.

She was as pleasant as her little one was cute. A refreshing contrast to his frustrating encounter with Mrs. Wolfe. Although Charlotte had handled herself well, he'd picked up on her nervous tells. Her deep breath, and the slow way she blinked before speaking. The slight lift of her chin and barely noticeable quaver in her voice. And how she'd practically deflated with obvious relief as the snarly woman stomped away.

If he didn't figure out how to deal with Helicopter Mom soon, she could drive his only coach away.

That wouldn't be so terrible, considering the emotions Charlotte churned within him, except that he and his team needed her help. He hadn't realized how much he'd used bitterness as a shield until it'd started to crumble.

Could he find a comfortable medium between walling himself off and falling in love? Again?

A friendship built between two mature and very busy adults, whose lives were becoming increasingly intertwined.

He released a sigh.

"Did I do something wrong?"

He glanced up to see Hazel studying him with a furrowed brow. "What? No, not at all." *Focus.* Veronica wasn't paying for him to become distracted by thoughts he should immediately toss out, not expand upon.

With determination, and the help of an annoying pebble in his boot, he was able to maintain his focus for the rest of the lesson and the two that followed. By the time he finished his evening chores, he'd managed to push her from his mind entirely.

Until his phone rang and Charlotte's number flashed on his screen.

A smile emerged unbidden, then flattened. Was she calling regarding what had happened today? Wanting to talk about the situation without her niece present?

He answered. "Hey. You need something?" He winced. The question was as blunt as it was rude.

"Um…approval?" Her soft laugh eased the tension in his jaw and assured him he was overthinking things. Another sign that he was becoming too emotionally entangled with her.

"For?"

"I had an idea to address your uniform concerns. A way to cut costs."

"Okay?" He liked the sound of that, especially considering he'd already used the girls' team fees to pay for the equipment needed to run the club. Rather, to contribute to the vaulting simulator, which had cost thousands of dollars. Expense aside, that had been one of his best investments in terms of training his team and ensuring their safety once atop the horse.

"I saw something on Trinity Faith's Facebook page about their quilting club. From what I read, the group's quite philanthropic."

"True. They're always making blankets and what-not for one organization or another. Last Christmas, they sent nearly three hundred to orphanages in the Ukraine."

"That's amazing. And based on my conversation with Lucy Carr, who leads the group, I'm not surprised."

"Yeah?" That woman had blessed more lives, locally and globally, than anyone could count.

"She needs to talk to the other ladies. Get their agreement. But she's confident they'll make the uniforms for us. We just need to take care of the fabric."

"Seriously?" He exhaled a chuckle. "How much'll that cost?"

"I recommend we go with Lycra." She relayed the details she'd found, along with how many yards she anticipated needing.

"Did they say they could get this done in time for the event?" Uniforms were something his former coach was supposed to have taken care of. Sadly, she'd been so consumed with moving prep that she'd failed to complete numerous important tasks.

"Lucy didn't see any problem with it. The real challenge will be ensuring the fabric arrives in time. Do you have ideas for colors and design?"

He scrubbed a hand over his face. "I might-should've asked the girls for input."

"That probably would've resulted in too many suggestions, along with Mrs. Wolfe's forceful opinions."

He laughed. "Good point. Think you could come up with something patriotic?"

"Sure. I can work on that this evening. Then maybe we can go over my ideas together? I know I'll already be at your place tomorrow—twice. But Gianna has speech therapy at one. Downtown. We could meet at Wilma's while she's in her session. Assuming you won't get sick of me, that is."

Despite her playful tone, her words hit deep, headlining a truth he wanted to deny. Their interactions triggered a deeply buried part of him to want more.

The part that insisted on replaying old memories he was trying, unsuccessfully, to slam the door on.

Yet he still found himself accepting her invite—when he most needed to reduce their interactions. They needed to work together on the biggest event in his club's short history.

Not only was he growing hopelessly attached to her niece, a child who tugged on his heartstrings with enough force to leave him baffled. But if he continued as things were, he'd soon fall again for the only woman he'd ever loved.

Something hard-earned experience and common sense would never allow.

CHAPTER EIGHT

THE NEXT MORNING, Charlotte entered the cardio area anxious to share choreography ideas she felt certain matched the girls' competency levels. Unfortunately, three hours of Mrs. Wolfe's biting comments and harsh demands deflated her enthusiasm.

As he had the day prior, Xavier arrived near the end of practice. Only this time, he came to decide which of the girls, if any, could add their new skill to the performance. All but three realized they were shooting too high and left.

Morgan's crestfallen expression indicated she felt similar, but her mom showed no signs of relenting.

"All right, y'all." Xavier's firm but kind voice halted Morgan's movement mid-handstand. "Let's see what you got." He made eye contact with her and her two remaining teammates. "Who's first?"

Morgan shot a nervous glance to her mom before gazing at her feet, shoulders hunched.

Charlotte hated to see the teen look so defeated. She'd give her a hug if she didn't think that'd further aggravate Mrs. Wolfe and worsen the situation for her daughter.

"I stink." Jayda, a short girl with red hair styled in a pixie cut, stepped forward. "But I'll go. Brownie points for effort?"

She shot Xavier a sheepish grin. "As in literally, like, a plate of gooey chocolate goodness."

"If that motivates you, I'm sure we could work something out."

She nodded, keeping her lack of baking skills to herself.

Jayda attempted a back walkover, fell off the mechanical horse, then tried again. After her third failed attempt, she shrugged. "Least I'll get chocolate."

Laughing, Peyton came forward. "My turn." She nailed her tech roll and sprang off the apparatus with a fist-raised cheer.

"Nice!" Charlotte gave her a high five. "I vote that's a yes."

"Agreed," Xavier said. "Way to go!" He turned to Morgan, who had shrunk further within herself. "Want to give it a shot?"

"I guess."

"As my gymnastics coach used to say, success is doing your best, regardless of results." Although Charlotte maintained eye contact with the teen, she directed her words at the mother.

Not that she expected them to leave much of an impact.

Morgan gave a barely noticeable nod and mounted the mechanical horse. Her nerves and exhaustion worked against her. Her muscles visibly trembled before quickly giving out.

After her fifth fall, Xavier stepped forward. "You are by far the hardest-working teen I know." Kindness softened his tone. "That grit'll take you far. Believe that." He placed an arm around her shoulders, his gaze hardening as it shifted to Mrs. Wolfe—his warning clear.

Surprisingly, the woman didn't push back. Instead, she strode to the bench area and grabbed her purse. "Gather your things, Morgan. I'll be in the car."

That poor kid.

After they left, Gianna bounded over to Charlotte. "My turn?"

Charlotte shook her head. "Remember our agreement?"

Her daughter frowned and dropped her gaze. "Tonight."

"Correct. Let's get you fed." She faced Xavier, the image of his tenderness toward Morgan fresh in her mind. He'd always been kind to the hurting or mistreated. And quick to notice.

He'd always managed to pry her feelings out of her—and to listen without judgment. She never had to pretend around him.

"Hey." Xavier bumped her shoulder with his, sending a jolt of electricity through her. "You bummed about Morgan?"

That and thinking of all she'd lost, thanks to her inability to stand up to her own critical parents. "Seeing her mom squash her like that?" She sighed. "Yeah. But Peyton killed it."

He grinned. "That she did. Would you believe she used to be the most timid of the bunch, reluctant to try anything unless she knew she could excel at it?"

"Really?"

"Yep. That's why her mom wanted her to join the club. To help her daughter learn to take healthy risks."

"You're great at what you do."

"What are you, saddle dust?" He gave her another shoulder nudge, initiating the same reaction. "We're a team."

She smiled. "Speaking of, I best get the munchkin home for lunch. See you at Wilma's. And I'll bring some designs I've sketched out."

"Can't wait to see them."

With a brief wave, she followed Gianna, who was already exiting the building.

An hour and a half later, she walked into the diner in which she and Xavier had eaten countless burgers, milkshakes and baskets of fries. Often at a discount, because the owner had found them "simply adorable."

Thankfully, the woman's granddaughter now ran the place, so there wouldn't be any comments about her and Xavier together once again. Charlotte was equally grateful that Gianna had gone with her therapist without protest. Of course, the promise of using Xavier's vaulting equipment this evening had helped.

Arriving at the diner early gave Charlotte far too much time to overanalyze her new relationship with Xavier.

Their *working* relationship. Friendship at best, and that was precisely how it needed to stay.

Why, then, had she felt the need to touch up her makeup, spritz the frizz from her hair and change into one of her favorite summer outfits?

Because she didn't want to run around town looking raggedy, especially considering she and Rachel were trying to build a business.

She frowned, no more convinced with that rationalization than her concerned and inquisitive sister had been when Charlotte first made the claim. Each morning as she drove to Xavier's, she'd been determined to keep things professional. Only to have her heart rebel the moment she stood in his presence.

Or watched how sweet he was with Gianna.

Squelching the thought, she wiped her clammy hands on her shorts and focused on her uniform sketches. Each design incorporated elements pulled from the city's event webpage. Would Xavier notice and appreciate her attention to detail?

The bell above the diner door chimed.

"Hey there, stranger." Sally Jo, Wilma's granddaughter, approached Xavier with a coffeepot in hand. "Let me clean off your table for you."

"I'm meeting someone." His smooth voice sent a nervous flutter through Charlotte's midsection.

What was wrong with her? She was a grown woman, and his employee no less.

Straightening, she swiveled to greet him with a smile. "I appreciate you taking time for this." She almost felt like they should shake hands, if only to establish a clear boundary for this get-together—at a place that held far too many memories.

He slid into the booth across from her. "I should be thanking you." He donned that boyish grin that used to cause all the teenage girls to swoon.

Charlotte included.

She cleared her throat and focused on her first sketch, a simple, long-sleeve uniform with a solid red top, blue bottom and a sash of white with the club's name in gold lettering.

Sally Jo approached holding an order pad and pen. "Y'all know what you want?"

Xavier indicated for her to go first.

"Their burgers still as amazing as I remember?"

"Best in the state by far."

"Then that's what I'll have. Extra pickles, please."

Xavier ordered a meat loaf sandwich topped with cheese and onions, sweet tea and a basket of fries.

Charlotte raised her eyebrows. "Looks like your appetite hasn't changed over the years."

He chuckled. "Thought we might-could share the fries."

Just like old times.

The longer she sat across from the most attractive, honest and hardworking cowboy she'd ever met, the more defiant her wayward heart was apt to become. And the weaker her determination to fight it.

What had she been thinking suggesting they meet here, at one of their most frequented dating hangouts?

Obviously, she hadn't been. But she needed to start, before she fell too deep for logic to pull her back to safety.

XAVIER COULDN'T TEAR his gaze from Charlotte's face as she discussed her designs. She was practically giddy with enthusiasm.

It looked good on her. Real good. Her cheeks were flushed a radiant pink, and the delight dancing in her emerald eyes made them even more captivating. Her lavender blouse brightened her peachy complexion, and the honey streaks in her auburn hair shimmered beneath the ceiling lights.

She'd always been the most beautiful woman around.

Taking a swig from his tea, he slid closer to the wall to add distance between them. "You said Gianna has speech therapy?"

She nodded. "As you know, she's highly verbal. But she needs help with basic communication skills. She tends to misuse language, and misunderstand what people say."

"Especially if they use metaphors."

"Exactly."

"I wish those resources had existed when my sister was young. In Sage Creek, I mean. Could've helped her socially, and probably reduced a lot of frustration for everyone."

"It's not too late for her to start."

"Is it expensive?"

"Thankfully, her insurance covers it." Rachel had enlisted Gianna in a Medicaid program for special needs kids.

"That's awesome."

"It's been great for her. Thankfully, she likes going."

"How's she handled the schedule change from vaulting practice?"

"We've had a few challenges, but we've muddled through."

"I imagine she doesn't want to stay home with her mom?"

"Rachel's going to be taking an equine therapy workshop in Houston three days a week. Starts tomorrow, in fact."

"She's not certified?"

Charlotte shook her head. "Technically, you don't need to be to run a program, but we'd originally planned to have the help of a psychiatrist from a nonprofit."

"The wellness center?" He remembered from their phone call.

"Yeah. With that partnership dissolved…" She released a breath. "We debated Rachel getting certified as it's a bit expensive. She's a licensed social worker and all. But we're hoping this will add credibility."

"Tough decision."

"As to Gianna adapting to me coaching, it helps that she loves horses. Being around them calms her."

"They tend to have that effect." He picked up a sketch of a full-body leotard. "This is nice." Wide red-and-white diagonal stripes decorated three-quarters of the uniform and a thick band of blue covered the left arm and shoulder. "Although could get a mite hot."

"True. And would require more fabric, which would raise the price per."

He nodded and studied a design with a tank top and shorts that extended to midthigh. "This isn't bad." It was half-blue, the rest a gradient that began in deep red and ended with white sprinkled with small gold stars.

Sally Jo delivered their food, lingering to admire Charlotte's artwork and ask about the vaulting program. "I heard your club was providing the main entertainment for the Fourth. Other than the fireworks, of course."

No pressure there. "The marching band will be performing, too."

She shrugged. "They do for every celebration, football game and parade. They're great and all, but acrobatics on horses? We've never had that before. Knowing you, I'm sure it'll be beyond cool."

His gaze shot to Charlotte. Sally Jo's comment had clearly freaked her out.

He felt an urge to give her hand a gentle, reassuring squeeze. Instead, he flashed the waitress a confident smile. "We're just happy for the opportunity to introduce the community to the sport."

And, if things went well, to garner more clients.

Thinking about that didn't exactly lessen his stress level.

Sally Jo started to leave, then turned back around. "I almost forgot. Ask Nadia if she still needs music suggestions."

He frowned. "For?"

"The routine she's choreographing. I know this all hit her—

and you—by surprise. I really admire her for agreeing to lead on such short notice, especially considering how busy she already is."

"What all did she tell you?" He squirted ketchup onto his plate.

"Just that your old coach moved away earlier than expected, and that she was stepping into that role."

"That's incorrect."

"Oh. Did something happen?"

What was the most God-honoring way to answer that question? He wasn't comfortable bashing Mrs. Wolfe, but neither did he want false information to circulate unchallenged.

Maybe she'd spoken with Sally Jo prior to his agreement with Charlotte.

Sally Jo waved a hand. "I'm sure it wasn't personal. She's involved in so many things. I don't know how she manages everything."

Correcting Sally Jo's assumptions would only initiate a conversation he wasn't comfortable having.

His phone rang, and he glanced at his screen. "Mind if I take this? It's Steward Long, from Sage Creek's Recreation and Planning Department."

"Absolutely," Charlotte said.

Sally Jo nodded and left to clear dishes from a recently vacated table.

With a nod of thanks, he tapped the green phone icon. "Afternoon."

"Hello, sir. How are you doing this fine afternoon? Got time to talk through some things related to the Fourth?"

"I'll check." He pulled his cell from his ear and navigated to his calendar.

He had three lessons scheduled, including a free introductory session with a lady who'd recently adopted an older mare from the local rescue. He had a feeling that one could turn into a training gig, after. The rescue did a great job of making their horses rideable, but the neglect and abuse many suffered prior often led to long-term issues.

His afternoon was tight, and he'd committed his evening to Gianna and Charlotte. That was a promise he intended to keep. "Unfortunately, I'm booked from noon on."

"How about in the morning?"

During vaulting practice? He'd planned on staying close in case Charlotte needed anything—or Mrs. Wolfe came and threw another fit. But they'd settled the routine debate, and everyone knew what they needed to work on. Still, he'd feel better if Charlotte had one more day, with him nearby, to settle in.

He placed his palm over the mouth of his phone. "Think you can manage practice without me tomorrow?"

Charlotte bit her bottom lip and wrapped both hands around her water glass. With a deep breath, she nodded. "Absolutely."

"You sure? Because if you're not ready…"

"Need to stand on my own sometime. After all, that's why you hired me. What's the worst that can happen?"

Her almost imperceptible wince the moment she voiced the question suggested her thoughts traveled in the same direction as his. Most challenging scenario? Mrs. Wolfe showing up and making a stink.

But hovering over Charlotte would suggest he doubted her ability to manage the girls and their parents.

He returned to his call. "I'm free between nine and eleven."

"Let's pencil that in. I'll shoot you a text if that doesn't work for everyone. Meet in the school cafeteria?"

"I'll be there." Call ended, he set his phone aside and focused, once again, on Charlotte. "Sorry about that." He glanced back at her sketches. "What else you got?"

Her next drawing thrust him back six years to the first time he'd watched her perform. "I know where you got the idea for this one."

She furrowed her brow, as if clueless.

"Your gymnastics meet in San Marcos."

Her eyes widened. "Oh." She laughed. "I can't believe you remembered that."

Had she forgotten? Then again, they hadn't known each other well at that point. But the moment he saw her standing in line at the concession stand, he'd felt compelled to get to know as much about her as possible. So, when she'd casually mentioned an upcoming competition, he'd invited himself to come.

"That was technically our first date," he said.

"I'm not sure I'd call it that, considering we drove separately, you sat in the bleachers and I stayed with my team. We didn't even talk until…" Her gaze faltered, and she offered a sheepish smile. "After I botched my dismount and stumbled headfirst into the leg of the balance beam. Making a fool of myself in front of everyone."

"Nah. You earned everyone's respect, with how you picked yourself up, posed for the judges and went on to nail your bar routine."

"That's almost verbatim what you said back then. When you caught me in the back hall, sobbing like a two-year-old."

The affection in her eyes pulled him back to the moment when he'd first determined to never let her go. He'd naively believed if he swept her off her feet and treated her well she wouldn't walk away.

His wishful thinking had only made their breakup more painful.

Discarding the thought, he shook his head. "Your reaction wasn't childish. More like the emotions of a teenager whose mom had criticized her in front of her friends. When you needed her encouragement."

"And a shoulder to cry on, apparently."

He'd been more than happy to offer his and would've held her the rest of the night, had he been able. Although that might not have been the precise moment when he fell in love, he'd been close.

What might've happened, had he not attended her meet that day, or followed her into that quiet hallway?

Sure, he would've missed out on the happiest year of his life. But he could've saved himself a lot of heartache, too.

While there wasn't anything he could do about the past, there was plenty he could do about where he sat, figuratively and literally, today.

Only problem was, he found himself as reluctant to get up and walk away now as he had been on that day he'd first held her in his arms.

CHAPTER NINE

THAT EVENING, XAVIER hurried through his chores to ensure he'd have time for a quick bite and shower before Charlotte and Gianna arrived. Standing in front of the bathroom mirror dressed in a fresh T-shirt and jeans, he reached for his aftershave then frowned.

What am I doing?

Barreling toward heartache, that's what.

He'd been foolish to think he could build a friendship with Charlotte without becoming emotionally entangled—with her and her adorable niece. But what choice had he had? He'd needed a vaulting coach, and she'd needed boarding for her horses.

He huffed. No matter how he tried to frame it, he couldn't deny that he enjoyed spending time with them both.

Did Charlotte feel the same?

If so, did that mean they could try again, and actually create something that'd last?

Was he ready for that? Not just to build a relationship with Charlotte, but with her niece, as well? Because he'd spent enough time with them both to realize they were a package deal.

Rachel was blessed to have a sister like Charlotte. He

couldn't imagine how hard it would've been, after her divorce, to raise Gianna alone.

He could be the doting uncle. Every kid could use more of those, right? Someone to bring them candy, take them mudding and fishing and what not. Or, more fitting, butterfly catching and horse riding.

The idea brought a smile, which widened at the prospect of Charlotte accompanying them.

What if God was offering him a second chance at love? What if that was why He brought her back, allowed her land to catch fire, and him to lose his coach?

Dare he entertain such a possibility?

God, I trust You, and if this is how You're leading, I'm all in. But if it's not, douse the fire that beautiful woman is stoking within me, because I'm not strong enough to resist the pull she obviously has over me.

A seed of hope enlarging within, he finger-combed his hair and slipped into the kitchen to gulp down a can of stew and two glasses of sweet tea. After pouring more into a tumbler, he strolled through the living room and grabbed his hat on his way out.

Patches of blue poked through thick, fluffy clouds, their lumpy shadows drifting across the ground. A gentle breeze carried the scent of burning brush from his neighbor's ranch. In the pasture, two fillies frolicked about in the field while the rest of the herd lazily grazed.

He paused near the gate to watch Charlotte and Rachel's horses. As he'd expected, they'd assimilated well with the others, and seemed to have settled into their new surroundings. But Tucker still acted skittish, especially when he heard clanking. That didn't bode well for getting him back into the trailer anytime soon. Although, Xavier still had plenty of time to work with him before the fire-scorched land at Charlotte's was ready for him.

That also meant she'd be spending more mornings and evenings over here. Some might take that as evidence of God's grace. Maybe the good Lord heard all those prayers Xavier had offered when she'd left.

Maybe what he'd interpreted as a no had simply been a divinely orchestrated delay. And with her and her sister owning a property, Charlotte had plunged her roots into the hill country and wasn't likely to leave again.

Unless they went bankrupt and sold their place.

His phone rang. He pulled it from his back pocket and glanced at the screen. Marlene, one of his longest-standing clients.

He answered. "Ma'am. What can I do for you?"

"Hello, Xavier. How are you? Staying busy, I imagine?"

"Working hard or hardly working. Not sure which."

She initiated small talk for a moment, then released a heavy breath. "You know I've enjoyed working with you over the years. I've learned so much, as has Blue."

"Glad to hear it."

"And you know I adore you as a person. Which is why I'm reluctant to say... I need to cancel my lessons."

He winced. Was she struggling financially? "If you need a break or to cut back to once a week—"

She paused. "What I mean is that I've found another instructor."

Her words settled heavy in his gut. "I'm sorry to hear that." And not only because of the lost funds, although that hurt. It stung to think she found him inadequate and felt someone else could do better.

"I wish you well."

In other words, end of conversation. "You also."

He scrubbed a hand over his face.

Call ended, he slipped his phone back into his pocket and grabbed a halter and lead rope from the tack room, then entered the pasture from an empty stall. Beauty, one of his most gregarious boarders, immediately trotted over.

She was likely looking for carrots, a habit her owner had long established.

Xavier laughed. "Sorry, girl. No treats for you." He scratched her withers, then approached Tucker. "Hey, bud." He held out his hand, knuckles up, to let the gelding sniff him, then gave him an affection pat. "Let's get you inside. Your owners will be here soon."

After securing the horse in his stall, Xavier occupied his time tidying up the outside aisle.

He paused mid-step, a jolt of anticipation shooting through him at the sound of an approaching engine. Taking a slow, deep breath, he deposited a pile of hay and dirt into a nearby wheelbarrow and set his broom and dustpan aside.

Gianna entered the stables first. Charlotte followed close behind in boots and riding pants that brought him back to their old days of galloping across fields. She wore her hair pulled back with a few wavy strands framing her face, which flushed a soft pink when her eyes met his.

Realizing he'd been staring, he cleared his throat and averted his attention to Gianna, who wore a blue T-shirt decorated with colorful butterflies.

"Hey, I recognize that one." He pointed to a brown butterfly with orange markings and large eyespots. "Common buckeye, right?"

"Yes. How did you know that?"

"I read some of the papers I printed out for you."

Gianna gave one firm nod, as if she found his response reasonable and expected. Charlotte, on the other hand, looked at him like he'd just presented the child with a priceless and unexpected gift.

Her obvious admiration caused him to stand a mite taller. Seemed she always had that effect on him. Made him want to be a better man.

"Shall we?" He motioned toward the end of the aisle where Tucker waited in his stall.

Gianna marched that way with the seriousness of a rancher tending to a wounded foal.

Acutely aware of Charlotte's nearness, Xavier fell into step beside the child. "I'm guessing you know a bit about the buckeye?" Interesting how he enjoyed pleasing the girl nearly as much as he did her aunt.

The admiration, dare he say adoration, that filled Charlotte's eyes whenever he engaged Gianna assured him that his insect discussion accomplished both.

"Yes," Gianna said. "I know a lot about most butterflies."

"Figured as much. Think you can teach me some?"

Frowning, she cast him a sideways glance. "You said you read the papers you printed."

"Yeah, but that was only a paragraph or two. Plus, I tend to be forgetful when it comes to facts."

"Not me."

He pressed his tongue to the roof of his mouth to keep from chuckling. Gianna was something else. And pricked at his desire for a family. "Exactly. So, what can you tell me about the little guy?"

Pulling at her shirt, she glanced down at the image. "She's a girl. She has rounder wings than boys do. They're bigger, too."

Betsy, a retired jumper he'd purchased a few years ago, neighed as they passed.

He gave her neck a quick scratch. "I see. Any other important differences?"

"They lay eggs. The boys don't." She continued relaying facts, stopping once they reached her horse. With a little bounce, she turned to him with a bright-eyed grin. "Tucker first."

"Yep." He handed her a brush, and, making eye contact with Charlotte, opened the gate. "What time do y'all need to head home?"

Charlotte chewed her bottom lip, likely gauging the consequences of disrupting the child's bedtime schedule. "We're still…"

She was probably hesitant to mention something he might've forgotten, not that her niece would've.

"Vaulting practice?" he said. "Yes, ma'am."

Rubbing at her collarbone, she studied Gianna. "We should probably leave by eight forty-five."

"That should give us a good forty-five minutes to groom and go for a quick ride before heading to the arena. Shall I round up Champ while y'all take care of things here?" He would've preferred to stay, indefinitely, but not enough to risk causing problems for later.

Charlotte's soft smile warmed him from chest to limbs. "Absolutely."

Stepping outside, he gazed upon his pasture, remembering the dreams he'd once held of buying a plot of land and building a ranch and home—for her. Of the two of them sitting on a porch swing, sipping coffee in the morning, laughing over a home-cooked meal in the evening, and ending the night chasing the setting sun on horseback.

Although he hadn't thought much about kids back then, Gianna was a joyful addition who already occupied a firm place in his heart.

Might be too soon to bank on, considering he'd prayed less than half an hour prior, but so far, God didn't seem to be dousing his feelings any.

Then again, the Lord hadn't kept him from falling for her the first time either, and look where he'd landed.

CHARLOTTE WATCHED XAVIER amble away with conflicting emotions. She hated to admit how much she looked forward to an evening with him. The way his face lit up upon seeing her and Gianna made her think he felt the same.

Would he be open to giving their relationship another shot?

A bigger question—if things between her and Xavier became serious once again, would she have the strength to keep his daughter a secret? She feared the guilt might destroy her.

Truth be told, she had a half a mind to tell him everything. He'd hate her for it, as would Rachel. Not to mention, the revelation, and whatever action he chose to take after, could shatter their daughter's world.

Fretting about him, their past or their nonexistent future would only make their partnership all the more challenging—and emotionally unnerving.

Forcing a levity in her voice she in no way felt, she joined Gianna in her counting. "Forty-eight. Forty-nine. Fifty."

"Other side."

Nodding, she nudged Tucker to take a step back as the child rounded to his left shoulder.

She glanced out to the pasture where Xavier stood talking with Champ—and in no hurry to bring him in.

Her former therapist would say she was overthinking things and making herself miserable in the process. *"What might it look like if you practiced simply being present?"*

Currently, that would look like enjoying time with her daughter while she was relaxed and in her happy place.

Charlotte ran her hand over Gianna's head, grateful her daughter wasn't averse to touch. "It seems Tucker missed you."

"He probably wants to go riding. Horses need exercise."

"I agree."

"And grazing. That's why they're here. But only until our grass grows back."

Everything, it seemed, hinged on that. Hopefully, they could survive that long. Although they didn't need to worry about boarding and feed costs, she and Rachel still had a sizable mortgage to pay, ranch to renovate and arena to build.

As soon as they cleaned up their property, they could start booking trail rides and birthday parties. If only she and Rachel could devote more time to that area. Coming twice a day to Xavier's wasn't helping her schedule.

Or her determination not to fall in love with the man who still accelerated her pulse whenever his blue eyes captured hers. Or engaged *his daughter* with the most endearing combination of tenderness and strength.

As if she'd ever stopped loving him in the first place.

He'd make someone an amazing husband. Great father, too.

It stung to think what could've been, had she told him about Gianna.

"Y'all ready for Champ?"

Xavier's deep voice startled her.

"Yes," Gianna said.

Charlotte cleared her throat and, echoing her daughter's response with a nod, led Tucker out.

Grooming done, they decided to try the vaulting prior to going riding so they could end their visit with an activity known to soothe Gianna. "Hopefully, that will accommodate for the change in schedule," Charlotte said.

He nodded. "I totally understand."

She knew he did, in a way many people didn't, and the shared connection drew her to him.

How different he was from the man Gianna had come to know as father. Whereas Rachel's ex had always seen the child's quirks and preferences as a nuisance and frustration, Xavier seemed to view them as opportunities to express affection.

Attachment he clearly already felt, made all the more evident by the patient attentiveness with which he led Gianna through warm-up exercises in the cardio area.

After a series of stretches, leg lifts and knee push-ups, which he did with her, he stood and brushed off his hands. "Let's start with a basic seat." He turned to Charlotte. "Coach, would you like to demonstrate?"

She smiled. "Absolutely." She enjoyed the sense of togetherness she felt—almost as if they were a family.

Which, technically, they sort of were.

Would every interaction remind her of what she was withholding from him?

Breathing deep to squelch her reemerging guilt, she swung a leg over the mechanical horse and sat with her posture straight and arms extended.

"See how her shoulder, hip and ankle are all in a straight line?" He traced his hand down her side, sending a flutter through her midsection. "And notice how she keeps her toes pointed."

"Okay." Gianna said. "My turn now?"

He laughed. "Sure thing." Once Charlotte dismounted, he helped Gianna into the saddle, then guided her into the proper position. "Excellent. You're a natural."

Gianna beamed, then studied him. "What do you mean?"

Initially, his face registered confusion, followed by a look of comprehension. "A natural is someone who learns something quickly."

"Oh. Yes. Mom says I'm a good student. Because I pay attention when she teaches me things. Unless it's something boring."

Laugh lines added depth to his masculinity. "Makes sense to me. You ready for me to turn on the horse?" He motioned to the apparatus beneath her.

Her eyes widened. "What will happen?"

Charlotte stepped forward. "Do you remember seeing the girls on it? How it moved beneath them?"

She nodded.

"It'll feel a lot like riding Tucker," Xavier said. "We can start out slow. And stop it if it feels uncomfortable."

Charlotte released a breath, grateful he understood the wobbly balance between too much and too little sensory stimulation.

That was yet another reminder of the amazing father he'd be to Gianna, if given the chance.

Brow pinched, Gianna stared at the handles clasped firmly in her grip, her posture stiff. Keeping her gaze locked, she nodded, and Xavier turned the simulator on the lowest speed.

Before long, Gianna visibly relaxed and seemed to be enjoying the movement. That made sense, considering how calm she felt atop Tucker.

After they let her ride a bit longer, Xavier and Charlotte led her through some safety exercises, then returned to the stables. Then, with Honey contentedly munching hay in her stall, they'd saddled up the others and were trotting through a fallow field, Charlotte on Whisper, he on Champ and Gianna astride Tucker.

Comfortable in the saddle, and thankfully wearing her helmet with minimal fuss, Gianna repeated a silly rhyme learned from her equine therapist back in Arkansas—the woman who first turned her and Rachel on to the idea.

Riding beside Charlotte, Xavier chuckled. "She's certainly found her happy place."

"That she has." She gazed across the countryside, taking in rich earthy air, the lush pasture dotted with vibrant wildflowers and the blue sky streaked with wispy clouds. "Being here in general."

His expression indicated her words hit him as deeply as this whole evening had her. As hooves pounded a rhythmic melody beneath them, she found herself fantasizing about what it might be like for the three of them to unite as a family. First, gathered around the dinner table, discussing their day—their goals and their struggles. Followed by riding side by side as dusk began to summon the moon and stars.

"I like having her here," he said. "Both of you here."

An intensity filled his eyes that made it near impossible to look away. She understood his unspoken invitation, and his words echoed her heart's deepest longing. How easy it would be to rekindle what, clearly, had never truly died during their years apart. To feel his arms around her once again, hearing him promise to never let her go.

Until he learned the truth. As much as she ached to receive his love, she knew she'd never recover from his hatred.

At least she was keeping a friend.

But what if they could be more? Either way, she was withholding a secret. As things stood now, she was keeping his daughter from him, as well. Could she allow herself to love him, unhindered, and receive his love in return, without yielding to the guilt that urged her to tell all?

Was that wrong, sinful, for her to even consider?

CHAPTER TEN

THURSDAY MORNING, GIANNA awoke in a mood. Her discomfort grew when she learned they were out of vanilla yogurt. Charlotte must've accidentally grabbed peach—the kind with chunks. The child couldn't handle the mixed texture. She'd also suddenly decided she hated fruit, which wouldn't help her digestive issues. Then she'd spilled orange juice on her newest butterfly activity pages. It had taken a good thirty minutes, and some strategic bargaining, to calm her down and get her out the door.

As a result, they arrived at Xavier's with little time before the vaulters began trickling in.

"Remember, you can groom Tucker and Champ now, and Honey and Whisper after practice." She'd relayed this to Gianna numerous times on the drive over, hoping to prepare her for the schedule change. Unfortunately, explaining that her behavior had caused the disruption wouldn't help.

"No thank you." Frowning, Gianna fisted her hands at her sides. "First Tucker, then Champ, then Honey, then Whisper."

"Correct. The order will stay the same. We're just adding a break in between."

"No thanks."

"We talked about this." Charlotte kept her tone steady and calm.

"First Tucker, then Champ, then Honey and Whisper."

Time to appeal to the child's sense of fairness by initiating a negotiation. "How about this? If you divide the grooming, *like we discussed*, you can use the vaulting equipment afterward."

Gianna's pinched brow relaxed as she considered this. She gave one stiff nod. "Okay."

Tantrum avoided.

The tension seeped from Charlotte's shoulders with her exhale. "Great. Let's go see how the horses are doing."

Xavier popped by as Gianna was just finishing with Tucker. "Hey." The effect his easy grin had on Charlotte only seemed to increase with every interaction. "You ready to ride solo today?"

"Absolutely. Figure the worse that can happen is the girls throw a fit, and I've had plenty of experience with those."

He chuckled. "Imagine you have." He turned to Gianna. "And how's my favorite vaulter doing this morning?"

The child lifted her chin, clearly encouraged by his praise. "I groomed Tucker. Next is Champ. Then we're taking a break so Aunt Charlotte can coach the big girls. Then it's my turn."

"Nice. Wish I could stay and watch." He made eye contact with Charlotte. "I'm not sure how long this shindig will last. Don't 'spect it'll be quick, though. Not with the mayor, cultural committee and the Chamber of Commerce president all coming together. And likely each with ideas on how the Fourth of July deal should run."

"And I thought nailing down a vaulting routine was challenging."

"Guess all that drama Mrs. Wolfe kicked up helped prepare me for today's hubbub." He laughed. "As they say, the Good Lord's always working, setting us up for whatever lies ahead."

The reminder that God always equipped people for the assignments He gave brought her peace. And determination, because it meant that God had not only given her everything she needed to handle whatever she might encounter today. It also promised that He would use her most uncomfortable moments to craft her into the woman able to fulfill His plans for her tomorrow.

She smiled. "I'll be looking forward to hearing all about it."

"I'll give you a call. If you've already left before I get back, that is."

She immediately thought of all the times he'd spoken those very words, back when they were together. Each time he dropped her off after a date or whatever else they'd been doing, he'd end his goodbye with a promise to call her. Inevitably, they'd end up talking late into the night about nothing and everything.

A wave of sorrow over all they'd lost swept over her, followed by a hint of hope for what they seemed to be building.

She smiled. "Sounds good."

She watched him saunter off with the same confident swagger that used to accelerate her pulse—and still did—then shifted her attention to Gianna. Thankfully, the time with the horses was helping to soothe whatever funk she'd woken up in.

She also honored their agreement, allowing them to make it to the indoor arena moments before the girls arrived. Charlotte's stress decreased yet another notch when Morgan arrived without her mom, and noticeably more cheerful and energetic.

Poor girl probably felt like a penned animal finally let loose.

For the next two hours, anyway.

Charlotte hated to think what the teen's home life was like. Actually, she had a pretty good idea. She knew all too well the constant anxiety that came from living with a critical parent. Such environments created a constant sense of inadequacy.

Maybe that was why God brought her here—because she understood, and hopefully, by His grace, could leave a positive impact on the girl.

Father, soften Mrs. Wolfe's heart toward her daughter. And show me how I can speak life and encouragement to counter the soul-crushing negativity.

With a renewed sense of purpose, she spent the rest of the morning looking for reasons to praise each teen. Their increased enthusiasm in response reminded her of the power of encouragement.

Maybe she had more coaching in her than she'd realized.

She waited for Mandi to finish her turn on Dolly, then gathered the girls together. "I'd like you each to work on your swing forward, getting as much height as you can while landing softly in the seat."

They nodded, and Peyton waved an arm in the air. "I'm up."

After a few shaky attempts, she nearly extended into a handstand.

Her triumphant grin widened Charlotte's smile. "Excellent. Great job of keeping your legs straight and pointed." She paused to let her encouragement sink in. "Now, try again, staying tight in your core."

"Peyton! Peyton!" Mandi started to clap and chant, and soon the others joined in.

Charlotte's gaze shot to Gianna, who was pacing, face scrunched, with her hands over her ears. "Quiet."

Mandi's wide-eyed response indicated Charlotte's tone came out harsher than she'd intended. She quickly countered with a soft smile. "I didn't mean to snap. Just want to save our eardrums."

"You're so old." The teasing glint in Mandi's eyes contradicted her eye roll.

Charlotte laughed. "Ancient enough to remember VHS and cassette tapes existed." This initiated lighthearted banter that helped restore a sense of fun to the practice. By the time they shifted to dismounts, the teens were a perfect blend of focused and relaxed.

Take that, Mrs. Wolfe.

She frowned. Since when did she engage in such juvenile thinking? She was acting as if she had to prove herself, and giving the woman way too much power over her emotions in the process.

Besides, Charlotte's competency would be demonstrated at the Fourth performance.

Her stomach turned queasy as she mentally ticked down the days. The girls were doing great, but they still had a ways to go before they'd be performance ready.

Would Xavier regret asking her to coach the team? The thought of disappointing him left her feeling jittery and uncertain.

While the teens took a brief water break, Charlotte flipped through her binder in which she kept printed documents detailing vaulting exercises, moves and guidelines. She'd lead them through drills next, then they'd cool down and she'd send them home.

"Ms. Murphy?"

She turned to see Morgan at her side, her expression timid. "Yes?"

"I know you and Mr. Shaw already decided on our routine and everything. But I was kind of wondering if I could, like, maybe stay after today to work on my back walkover on the mechanical horse?" Her gaze faltered. "I kind of promised my mom I would."

Charlotte resisted a sigh, although her frustration must've shown on her face, because the teen quickly added, "Not to change anything in the program or anything. Just so I don't lose progress, you know?"

Charlotte glanced at the time on her phone, then to Gianna, who was engaged with her iPad. They were supposed to be done for the day. "For fifteen minutes. But after that, I need to close up the arena." She couldn't get into the habit of consistently extending practice, not when she was trying to establish routines for Gianna.

Neither did she want to build unsustainable expectations in her vaulters.

Morgan grinned. "Yay! Thank you!" She jogged to a purple backpack and pulled out her cell, likely to text her mother.

Hopefully, that meant the woman wasn't planning on showing up until they finished.

After asking Mandi to cool down Dolly and tie her to the hitching post in the tack area, Charlotte gathered everyone for drills. The girls groaned and shuffled over with slumped shoulders.

She laughed. "I know you're tired, but I also know you're super pumped for your performance and want to be as strong as possible. Arms out. Core tight." She demonstrated. "Lift your right leg, knee bent, thigh and hip at ninety degrees. Reach up as you breathe in, focusing on your posture, and hold it for a count of ten."

Loud, pulsating music emanated from outside the arena.

Mandi squealed, and, hands clasped, bounced on the balls of her feet. "Bobby's here."

"No way." Haiven's eyes widened. "Are you two a thing now?"

Mandi shrugged with a coy smile. "He's picking me up."

"Think Chet is with him?"

Before she could respond, a husky-boxer mix came barreling into the arena. The girls giggled, as alert to the dog as they were to the three teenage boys that came strolling in after. Slapping their thighs, they each called out the animal's name, which escalated the dog's near-frantic enthusiasm.

Charlotte shot a glance at Dolly, thankful the visitors hadn't arrived while one of the girls was practicing her compulsories. One of them could've been seriously hurt—the dog, as well, had he darted under the horse's hooves.

That was precisely why she needed everyone to know that this was not a place to roughhouse. "All right, now." Stepping forward, she reached for the dog's collar.

He darted away and straight toward the benched area where Gianna had resumed her pacing.

"No!" A jolt of adrenaline propelled Charlotte forward.

Not fast enough. The dog jumped up on Gianna, and she fell backward into the sawdust. Hercules began licking her face as, panicked, she tried to fight him off.

Charlotte yanked the dog off, straining to hold on to his collar as he continually lurched forward.

Gianna sprang to her feet, still screeching, and ran out.

"Sorry, ma'am." The tallest of the boys, and presumably Hercules's owner, squatted beside her and took the dog.

Biting back an angry retort, she whirled around to face the girls. "Stay off the equipment until I get back."

Chest tight, she raced out of the arena in search of Gianna. The midmorning sun stung her eyes as she scanned the horizon. Where might she have gone? She wasn't near their car. Charlotte jogged to the house. Her daughter wasn't on or beneath the porch, or in the yard. The property and treed land beyond provided far too many places for a frightened girl to hide.

"Gianna?" Hands cupped around her mouth, Charlotte ran to a rickety shed standing in the shade of a massive oak tree. The dingy window was closed, as was the padlocked door, and the shaded area behind the structure was vacant.

Lord, help me find her.

Surely Gianna wouldn't have gone too far or climbed up to a loft or anywhere dangerous. Most likely, she'd found a dark, quiet place to hunker down.

Right?

Would she have gone to see Tucker and their other horses? Charlotte hurried back in that direction.

"Gianna? Sweetie. Everything is okay." Speaking loudly

enough to be heard, she struggled to keep the panic from her voice.

Xavier. She needed to let him know what had happened so that he could come supervise the girls. She shot him a quick text. By the time she reached the back stalls—finding them empty—he still hadn't responded.

Then she remembered his meeting with the Fourth of July planning committee. Would he have silenced his phone, knowing she'd be coaching the girls?

If he trusted her to manage things while he was gone, yes.

How would he feel knowing she'd taken off during practice? Once he learned why, he'd probably understand, but that didn't mean he wouldn't change his mind regarding their arrangement. But surely, having grown up with an autistic sister, he'd recognize more than anyone the difficulty of her situation.

While he might want to accommodate her, out of kindness, he had a program to run—and parents to whom he needed to report.

Like Mrs. Wolfe.

The woman could arrive at any moment—to find the team unsupervised. The pit in Charlotte's stomach expanded into nausea.

She sucked in a deep breath and released it slowly. All this fretting wouldn't help her find Gianna any faster. Regardless of how anyone else responded, Charlotte needed to focus.

And if she lost her job and boarding for her horses?

Then she'd trust God to have a plan, because she refused to believe He'd bring them here to fail.

Passing overgrown blackberry vines tangled around wire trellises, she came upon an abandoned, fenced henhouse. The gate stood open. She ducked inside and poked her head into the cool, dark interior. Vacant.

Shielding her eyes, she gazed with a sense of dread toward the wooded area she and Xavier had ridden through. Gianna could easily get turned around in there and end up lost, or wandering onto the highway.

Her throat felt scratchy, her lungs tight. Thoughts jumbled by mounting fear, she glanced back toward the arena and surveyed the land once again. This time, she noticed a lean-to to the left, partially hidden by a cluster of trees. As she drew near, she realized it resembled a structure from where her daughter used to go riding.

Hope propelling her, she peered inside. The air expelled from her lungs as her eyes landed on her daughter, hunkered down in the shadowed corner. She sat rocking on the straw-littered ground, hugging her legs, face buried in her knees.

"Gianna." Charlotte spoke softly as she stepped toward her. "Sweetie, you're okay." Repeating this, she knelt beside her and pulled her into a tight hug, knowing the firm pressure would help her daughter feel safe.

She remained there, holding tight, until Gianna's rhythmic moving stilled and her stiff posture relaxed against her.

After a few more breaths, Charlotte loosened her grip. "Feel better?"

Gianna made eye contact for a brief moment, then looked away. "Yes."

"Are you ready to return to the arena?"

Gianna frowned. "I don't like that dog."

"I understand. But I'm confident he's gone by now." At least, she hoped it was.

Unless the guy and his friends wanted to show off for the girls. Charlotte wanted to believe the teens were too mature to do anything dangerous or destructive, but memories from her high school days left her uneasy. She'd seen guys, and girls, too, for that matter, do some crazy things when they started playing the role of strutting peacock.

How long had she been gone from the arena? In her panic to find Gianna, she'd completely lost track of time.

"Come on, sweetie." She stood and brushed debris from her jeans.

Gianna scraped a stick in the dirt.

"Would you like a turn on the vaulting equipment?"

She nodded.

"All right. Let's go back, then. You can practice your seat."

"What I learned yesterday."

"Correct."

The child's face brightened, and she stood and marched toward the arena. Charlotte fell into step beside her, grateful Gianna was all right.

Next time, she might not be so fortunate. She needed to tell the girls to let their friends know not to bring animals to the arena. Although she hated for her unique parenting challenges to affect her job, and the team, she had to do what was right for her daughter. Nor could she simply leave Gianna with Rachel. She needed the time and space to get their nonprofit up and going. Then, once their pasture returned and they were running their therapy program, they could more easily adapt to Gianna's needs.

Until then, Charlotte needed to find a way to fulfill her responsibilities here without sacrificing her daughter in the process. That meant maintaining an environment free from rambunctious dogs, pulsating music and strutting teenage boys that turned her team into giddy gigglers.

None of which were great for Dolly, either.

She'd make sure to stress that.

They'd nearly reached the arena when Mandi came barreling out, her expression conveying obvious alarm. "Ms. Murphy, Morgan's hurt." Her words erupted in breathless spurts.

"What?" Her legs felt jittery and primed to run. She shot a glance at Gianna, knowing she'd mirror any panic she herself displayed. Inhaling calm into her soul, she quickened her pace. "What happened?"

Half a step ahead of her, Mandi said, "We were goofing around on the mechanical horse." Her break in eye contact verified she knew they'd disobeyed. "She wanted to show the guys her dismount. And she landed hard and hurt her knee. Bad."

She entered the arena to find Morgan on the ground, rocking and clutching her leg. Although she wasn't crying now, her bloodshot eyes and tear-streaked face indicated she had been. The others, guys included, were gathered around her.

As Charlotte drew near, everyone turned and began talking at once.

Potentially triggering Gianna to experience another meltdown.

Grounding herself to remain calm, Charlotte raised a hand, effectively silencing the clamor.

She knelt beside Morgan. "Can you move it?"

"It hurts too much."

Charlotte's next question, could she stand on it, was now unnecessary. That also meant the girl would need help getting up and to her mother's car.

The thought of Mrs. Wolfe arriving any moment to see her daughter incapacitated turned her stomach. Of all the athletes to get hurt, it had to be the one whose mother was most likely to become furious.

But she couldn't think about that now. "You might have sprained it or worse."

"No!" Anguish filled her voice. "What about the Fourth? Will I still be able to perform?"

"I don't know, sweetie. You need to see a doctor." She shot Xavier a quick text, then glanced toward the arena entrance. "Is your mom coming to pick you up?"

Morgan shook her head. "I'm supposed to go to Peyton's after practice."

Would it be better to have her call her mother, or for Charlotte to do so? As much as she longed for the former, she needed to muster her courage and act like a mature coach and not an intimidated child.

CHAPTER ELEVEN

MEETING CONCLUDED, XAVIER was talking with Mayor Pearson and polishing off the remaining doughnuts when his phone rang. Charlotte's number flashed on his screen.

She wouldn't be calling if it wasn't important. Most likely Mrs. Wolfe had shown up and was making a stink. That woman brought vinegar wherever she went.

His cell trilled again. "I've got to take this."

Pearson gave a wave of his hand and tossed his foam cup into the nearby trash. "I best be going, anyway."

Tipping his hat in goodbye, Xavier answered the call. "Hey. Everything all right?"

"Morgan's been hurt." She explained what happened.

"How bad?"

"Not sure, but I worry she might be out for a while."

Closing his eyes, he pinched the bridge of his nose. As if the kid's mom hadn't been riled up enough. "Mrs. Wolfe know?"

"I left her a voice mail, and sent a text asking her to call me."

"Okay. I'm on my way."

He never should've left her to manage practice alone, without him in earshot. Should've asked the planning folks for an afternoon meeting.

Except that he'd hired Charlotte to free up his time for precisely these types of deals. Besides, his being on the ranch wouldn't have prevented Morgan from getting hurt.

Although his presence could help shield Charlotte from whatever flames Mrs. Wolfe hurled her way.

He hurried out of the school and into his truck. Hoping beyond logic to make it to his ranch before Helicopter Mom, he bridled his urge to speed down the highway.

As expected, the woman's car sat parked helter-skelter near the arena entrance. The raised, high-pitched voice that greeted him upon entry verified she was *not* pleased.

Seeing Charlotte's defeated posture challenged his ability to remain calm and levelheaded.

He'd never been one to leave bullies unchallenged. But neither would he allow Mrs. Wolfe's ugly behavior to bring out the worst in him. Especially with his athletes watching.

"All right, y'all." He drew closer and stopped a few feet from Morgan, with Charlotte to his left and Mrs. Helicopter glaring her down to his right. "Let's dial things down a bit." He approached Morgan, who sat, leg extended, on the bench behind her mother. "Heard you hit a hard landing."

She nodded.

"Doing your backward handstand dismount?"

The way she dropped her gaze verified his suspicions. Charlotte hadn't given the girl permission to practice the harder exercise. With the event so close, the team needed to devote all their time to perfecting their routine.

But stating that now would add heat to Mrs. Wolfe's emotional explosion—especially since she was likely the reason her daughter had worked on the move.

Yet, from what he'd learned over the phone, Charlotte hadn't been around to stop her. And that would be enough for Helicopter to cast all blame on Charlotte.

Mrs. Wolfe leveled her scowl on him. "The question is, what are you going to do about this?"

"Listen to what the doctor says."

"I'm talking about your incompetent coach. As you can see" she flung a hand Morgan's direction "—she's a danger to the team."

Crossing his arms, Xavier widened his stance. "This is a challenging sport. Figure someone's bound to get hurt sometime."

"Yeah, but did you expect Ms. Murphy to leave the team unattended?" She hurled the words out. "Seems to me that should be a dismissible offense."

A tendon in his jaw twitched. "And it seems to me that I'll manage my program, and employee, as I see fit." Unblinking, he matched her glare.

"I know why you hired her."

"Yeah? And why's that?" What foolishness had him engaging her in this?

"I heard about you two. And with the way you look at each other now, all gooey eyes, makes one wonder if you're actually making decisions for the good of this team. Or if you're focused on something else."

Heat climbed up his neck. "How about you stop the vinegar and tend to your daughter?"

She stared at him, slack-jawed. Then, muttering under her breath about adults acting like teenagers, she whirled around and helped her daughter to her feet.

Shaking his head, Xavier watched them hobble out, then faced the rest of his team. "Enough gawking. Go get yourselves something to eat, and tomorrow morning, come ready to work. Because we're going to put on the best performance this town's yet seen."

They offered sheepish smiles, probably due to a measure of guilt for their part in what had happened.

As soon as they left, Gianna ran up to Charlotte. "My turn now?"

She turned to him with worry lines etched into her forehead.

The poor woman looked ready to cry. That made him want to pull her close, to once again have her in his arms and her head resting against his chest.

"I remember the deal you two struck. We can talk about this later." They'd also need to adapt the girls' routine as Morgan wasn't only one of his better vaulters. She and Mandi had a jaunt they performed together, pas-de-deux, which happened to be the grand finale of their performance. He wasn't sure any of his other athletes were ready for paired moves. "Over coffee and pie at Wilma's?"

"Okay."

He checked the calendar on his phone, pleased to see an opening where he'd previously scheduled a riding lesson. Yet another example of how the Father was orchestrating things on his behalf? Scripture *did* say He was the God of reconciliation, and He certainly seemed to be working His grace with himself and Charlotte.

"You free tomorrow at two?"

She nodded. "That's when Rachel takes Gianna adventuring."

"I'll pick you up."

If Mrs. Wolfe lobbing this mess their way led to him and Charlotte rebuilding what they'd lost, at least something positive would come from all this.

CHARLOTTE TRIED TO quiet her jittery stomach in anticipation for her meeting with Xavier by sorting through memorabilia she'd not previously taken time to unpack since moving from her parents' five and a half years ago, in fact. But her trip down memory lane, dominated with reminders of the love she and Xavier had shared, only heightened her anxiety.

She couldn't deny that they were rapidly heading in the very direction of which she'd determined to steer clear. Nor that she was completely losing her resolve and allowing the hope she'd once squelched to reemerge.

If only the situation wasn't so complicated.

Rachel popped her head into the bedroom. "Be careful."

Stack of folded notes from Xavier in hand, she straightened. "It's not like he's going to fire me or anything."

"That's not what I'm referring to. I know you and your need to unburden yourself from guilt."

"Like I told you the last time you expressed concerns about us spending time together, I won't say anything."

"Good. Because we both *know* what that would do to Gianna, to find out everything she believed to be true was a lie."

Charlotte sighed. "It's just dessert." Although she couldn't deny that her attraction to him grew with every encounter.

Rachel's frown indicated she'd picked up on that.

Could she sense that Charlotte wanted more?

Despite her sister's assertion to the contrary, she was convinced she and Xavier could restore their relationship without her feeling compelled to divulge the truth.

At least not until she was certain doing so wouldn't destroy their reemerging love or Gianna's world.

The doorbell rang, causing her to jump.

Rachel crossed her arms. "If this little meeting of yours is so platonic, why didn't you just meet him at Wilma's?"

"He passes our place on the way to town anyway. Suggested I save the gas and ride with him."

Her raised eyebrow said she wasn't buying it.

Ignoring her sister's pointed stare, she returned her notes to the box and crossed the room. "Excuse me."

Rachel moved aside and followed her down the hall and into the living room, where Gianna sat cross-legged on the ground, counting her paper dolls as she set them in a line.

Charlotte knelt beside her. "Gianna." She waited for her

daughter to glance up, her eye contact as brief as her breath. "Remember, I'm going into town while you and your mom go exploring."

"I know."

"But I'll be back in time for supper."

"Chicken fingers and green beans. But I only need to eat three bites."

The best compromise they'd found to get vegetables into the child. "Correct. And if you do?"

"I get a Fruit Roll-Up."

"That's right." She ran a hand over her daughter's head. "Have fun."

The doorbell rang again. She answered to find Xavier standing on her stoop wearing his signature easy grin.

He rested a hand on his belt buckle. "You ready?"

Suddenly shy, she swallowed. "For Wilma's peach pie? Always."

"I see how I rate." His teasing tone increased the warmth in her face, making her feel like she'd regressed back to her high school days.

Descending the porch stairs two at a time, he beat her to his truck and opened her door for her.

The interior smelled like an enticing mixture of sawdust, leather and his regular musty-citrus scent. Whether from cologne or aftershave, either suggested he'd intentionally spruced up prior to picking her up.

A gust of cool air flowed from the vents as he started his vehicle and eased down the potholed gravel road toward the country highway. A country song started up on the radio about a dangerous love that demanded too much and left the man trampled in the dust.

Charlotte stiffened, wanting to turn the music off and fill the cab with mindless chatter. Anything to divert his attention from the lyrics traipsing much too close to their story.

The weight in her gut didn't lift when he clicked off the radio.

They'd never talked about how things had ended. Did he hold any bitterness toward her? The day they ran into one another at the hardware store, the way his expression hardened upon seeing her, she would've said yes. Now, she saw no hint of anger.

She still owed him an apology. Maybe that would help appease some of her guilt. Taking a deep breath, she wiped her clammy hands on her shorts. "I'm sorry for how I ended things between us. I was a jerk. And coward." She couldn't offer more explanation than that.

Following the curve of the road, he cast her a sideways glance. The pain in his eyes felt like an elbow to the chest. Refocusing on the asphalt ahead, he gave a casual shrug. "That was a long time ago."

His message rang clear. He wasn't interested in discussing their past. Except she didn't sense any hostility in his response.

But neither did she receive the release for which she'd hoped.

The speed limit dropped to twenty-five once they passed the feedlot. Stopped at a four-way, he waited for a bald man in neon green shorts and matching running shoes to jog through the crosswalk, then turned onto A Street, and then again onto Main. Pedestrians, mostly moms with strollers, flowed up and down the sidewalk and in and out of stores.

Two men in suits sat at one of the wrought iron tables outside the Literary Sweet Spot, a coffeeshop/bookstore down the street from the diner, laptops in front of them both. A rack of colorful scarfs danced in the wind outside a trendy boutique that sold everything from clothing and house décor to jewelry. The sign above them said 75% Off in bold red letters. Further down, vibrant flowers arranged on a three-tiered wooden display reached their faces toward the sun.

"Front-door service." Xavier grinned and eased into an empty parking slot directly in front of Wilma's.

He slipped out of the vehicle and was holding the diner door open before she'd reached the curb.

"Thank you." Stepping inside, she was greeted with '50s music and the scent of fried food, buttery toasted buns, and freshly brewed coffee. The combination created a sense of nostalgia.

"Seat yourself," Sally Jo called out en route to the kitchen with an armload of dirty dishes. "I'll be with you in a minute."

Nodding to an older couple as they passed, Xavier removed his hat and led the way to a back corner booth. "Didn't realize how hungry I was until just now." Depositing his Stetson on the table near the wall, he sank into the orange cushion. "Might have to order me a plate of fried chicken."

She sat across from him. "Missed lunch?" Maybe she wasn't the only one who'd been nervous about their date.

Except this wasn't a date, but it did make her long for one.

"Do protein bars and a thermos of sweet tea count as a meal?"

"If I can claim the same regarding peach cobbler."

"Hey, that's fruit. Add a scoop of ice cream, and you've got dairy."

"And protein."

Laugh lines crinkling around his eyes, he nodded, but then his expression sobered. "How are you feeling, about practice and all?"

She rubbed her collarbone. "Better. I think. I tried calling Morgan last night, to check on her and see what the doctor said. Phoned her mom, too." That had taken courage and significant time spent in prayer asking the Holy Spirit to bind her tongue, should Mrs. Wolfe say something to trigger her defensiveness. "Neither of them answered. Nor did they show up during practice this morning."

"You thought they would?"

"Not Morgan…"

His nod said she needn't say more. "'Spect we'll hear from her mom soon enough."

"That's what I'm afraid of." She smoothed her hands down her temples and grasped the back of her neck. "I get the sense she's used to bullying to get her way. And that she's one to hold a grudge."

"Sounds about right."

She released a heavy breath. "Just how spiteful is she?"

"You mean, will she try to discredit you? Turn folks in the horse community against you?"

She nodded.

"Sadly, that woman's about as mature as a middle school clique. But I've got to believe people have grown immune to her venom."

"I hope so." As nice as everyone had been, in many ways she was still an outsider.

Sally Jo arrived with two glasses of ice water and menus under her arm. "Y'all need a minute?"

"I walked in ready." Xavier chuckled and looked at Charlotte.

She smiled. "Me, too."

They ordered, Sally Jo left and Xavier shifted the conversation. "How's Gianna doing? She seemed relaxed the couple times I popped into the arena this morning."

Although he'd hung back, Charlotte had been aware of his presence and felt calmed by it. "Better."

"I'm glad."

"She really enjoyed getting to ride the mechanical horse. She practiced her seat on the couch armrest while I made lunch."

"Yeah? A vaulter in the making." Looking past her, he frowned, and the conversation stopped.

Charlotte followed his gaze. Her chest tightened to see Mrs. Wolfe standing outside the diner window talking to a slender woman with long blond hair, dressed in a trendy outfit that suggested wealth.

So much for the pleasant date that wasn't officially a date.

Xavier turned back around and shook his head "That woman's like a storm cloud on the Fourth of July."

"Do you know the person she's talking to?" Hopefully, it wasn't anyone in the local horse community, because the lady's body language indicated she was buying whatever Mrs. Wolfe was selling. As much as Charlotte hoped otherwise, she feared Morgan's mom was waist-deep in vengeance.

"Yep. She's the reason my schedule cleared up and I was able to meet with you."

Her confusion must have shown on her face, because he explained what he meant.

Her eyes widened. "Do you think she canceled her lesson because of Mrs. Wolfe?"

"I wouldn't have said that. But I never would've pegged them as buddies, either. Although Marlene's friendly with just about everyone. I'm sure this is just a coincidence."

"I hope you're right. I'd hate to think that I caused problems for your ranch."

"Nah. I wanted to bring you on, and I'm glad I did. Even if I hadn't, I still wouldn't have hired Helicopter. And she still would've been madder than a bull chasing a matador."

"Yesterday didn't help matters." She didn't blame Gianna for what had happened. Of course the poor child had felt overwhelmed. Nor was Charlotte hugely surprised that the girls had used her brief absence to show off. She also couldn't be too upset about the boys showing up blaring their music, as she'd never established boundaries to prevent such behavior.

Considering, it seemed the only one she could rightly feel frustrated with was herself.

"I can tell your inner critic is running on overdrive," he said. "Care to share?"

"That obvious, huh?" He'd always been able to read her. Always made her feel like he cared enough to know how she felt.

"Might help to talk it out."

Dropping her gaze, she rolled her straw wrapper into a tight coil. Would expressing her concerns and insecurities about her coaching role place doubts in his mind?

"I worry about whether I can adequately care for Gianna and lead the team," she said.

"Hey." He placed his hand on hers, sending a soothing rush of warmth through her. "What happened wasn't your fault."

"But I left the girls unattended in the arena."

"With the instructions that they were to stay off the equipment. You're not responsible for their disobedience. As far as tending to your niece—you are amazing with her. Truly."

"Thank you." Although she could easily state a hundred ways she'd failed her daughter, his encouraging words helped disarm some of her guilt. His response also reminded her that he'd make great father, and someone's life partner. "Too bad Mrs. Wolfe doesn't view things that way."

Xavier waved a hand. "That woman was aching for something to get worked up over." He straightened. "Enough fretting over spilled milk that already went sour. Any ideas regarding what to do about our performance?"

"I don't think any of the other girls are ready to fill in for Morgan. Doubles, I mean. But we could easily extend each of their time on the horse without increasing their difficulty level."

"True. Although wouldn't hurt to have an extra cushion. Experience tells me the hullabaloo before us will probably go over."

"Remind me again of the schedule?" He'd forwarded the email, but she'd mainly paid attention to their portion and what directly preceded and followed.

"They've got stuff going on all day. Parade in the morning. Pie eating contest. Local a cappella group will be performing live. Talent show benefiting the veterans center. Mayor Pearson will speak, and then Pastor Roger, who's emceeing the whole deal, is going to give out some awards."

"I saw that. For what?"

"Figure he'll publicly honor our vets, and probably those who've positively impacted our community."

"Do you know how many people he plans to acknowledge?"

"Nope. Nor how long it'll take them to walk onto the stage, get their plaque and move on. Although the planning committee says they've accounted for all that."

"What happens if our team finishes early?"

"Guess that depends on by how much. We are getting paid to entertain folks. But I doubt anyone will get riled up over ten minutes, over or under. My biggest concern—overpromising and underdelivering."

She smiled, hoping to convey more confidence than she felt. "I know the girls will do great, and that the audience will love them."

He grinned. "That attitude is exactly why you, and not Mrs. Vinegar, are leading the team. Among other reasons."

His praise, and the warmth radiating from his eyes, reminiscent of how he used to look at her, touched her deeply.

He ignited emotions within her that she no longer had the strength to suppress.

CHAPTER TWELVE

XAVIER'S THURSDAY WAS packed from sunup to supper, with a handful of free introductory lessons occupying his day. Hopefully, this would earn him at least one additional client. He should probably reach out to a few of his students to ask for recent competition photos to post on his website. God willing, maybe they'd even have some wins he could mention.

Biting into a juicy, cheesy sloppy joe sandwich, he checked the time on the microwave. Thirty minutes until Charlotte and Gianna arrived for Gianna's nightly grooming and horse riding.

That child had captured his heart nearly as completely as her aunt had. Their evenings together had quickly become the best part of his day.

An image of the three of them trotting around the nearby lake triggered a smile. Maybe one day soon he could make that happen, followed by a picnic and paddle-boating across the water.

If he couldn't be a dad, an uncle seemed the next best thing.

Not that he was ruling out fatherhood. In fact, the more time he spent with Charlotte, the more alive that dream became, and all that came with it. Having seen the strain JoEllen had placed upon his parents, he used to worry about the potential of having an autistic child. Folks said the condition was hereditary. If that occurred, he knew his child would need a compassionate and patient mom. The gentle and loving way Charlotte responded to her niece verified she'd fit that role perfectly.

That assured him she'd see their son or daughter as a gift, however God created them.

Treasure them as he did her.

He still couldn't believe Gianna's dad had abandoned her. Did he even pay child support?

Or maybe Rachel was the one hindering the father-child relationship. Not long ago, a buddy of his had experienced something similar. His ex had not only kept him from his kid, but had actually claimed the boy wasn't his.

Nah. He couldn't imagine Rachel being that vindictive.

Regardless, Gianna could use a positive male influence in her life, a role he was more than happy to fill.

Shoving the rest of his supper into his mouth, he pushed back from the table, deposited his dirty dishes in the sink and hurried out to bring in and feed his boarders. Once finished, he brought in Tucker so he'd be ready for Gianna.

She and Charlotte arrived shortly after. Gianna immediately asked about vaulting.

He laughed. "I'm game if y'all are."

Charlotte's appreciative smile lit her green eyes. "Not to be presumptuous or anything, but we adjusted our schedule. Just in case."

He didn't know what he found more alluring—the way her wavy hair framed her delicate face and complemented her peachy complexion, or her nurturing nature.

He grinned. "Glad to hear it!"

Picking up a curry comb, Gianna nodded. "If I work hard and pay attention, I can join the team."

Eyebrows raised, he looked at Charlotte.

A slight frown lengthened her features. "Remember what

I told you in the car? Mr. Xavier already has a set team. And they're older."

The child jutted her chin. "That's not fair."

The hint of distress in Charlotte's eyes suggested she shared his worries—that this conversation could soon turn into a tantrum.

"Tell you what," he said. "How about we focus on developing your skills and see where we're at in a month or so?"

Head angled, the child paused mid brush stroke, then gave one firm nod. "I'm a fast learner. And I like horses. They like me, too."

"I can see that." One glance at Charlotte, and seeing what he could only term adoration in her eyes just about turned his insides to mush.

Standing a mite taller in an attempt to activate his logical side, he came beside her and rested an arm on the stall gate. "How're things going with the nonprofit? Rachel close to finishing her certification?"

"Not exactly, although she can complete most of it online."

"Nice. You planning on joining her?"

Her glance shot to Gianna, and she shook her head. "Maybe later. When I have more time."

And wasn't spending most of her mornings working with his girls?

Part of him wanted to release her from her obligation, so that her focus wouldn't be so divided. Except his team needed her. Plus, he enjoyed having her around. Them both.

Was that selfish? Putting his needs above hers? Sure, she was getting free boarding out of the deal, and a meager salary. Paycheck aside, four horses grazing on his land and occupying an otherwise empty stall didn't cost him anything.

Obviously, Charlotte couldn't say the same.

Scratching his jaw, he gazed toward the pasture and the tree line beyond. What if they merged their endeavors? Charlotte and Rachel could run their program on his property, and he could help train the horses and their volunteers. Maybe he could even form a special needs vaulting team.

Would she and her sister be open to that?

"You okay?"

He looked over to find Charlotte studying him with a furrowed brow. "Yep. Just playing out potential scenarios in my brain."

"Dollar for your thoughts?"

"They're worth that much, huh?"

"Hmm..." She tapped her chin. "I suppose I could go as high as five."

He laughed. "Well, now, that might-could change things." But this was a conversation to have over sweet tea. "Mind if I pop over this evening?"

"It's my turn to read Gianna stories and get her tucked into bed."

"After that, then?"

Her eyes widened, and a beautiful blush colored her cheeks. She cleared her throat and nodded. "Sure."

Her almost shy expression suggested she was looking forward to the prospect as much as he was. The notion made him about want to give a whoop and fist pump the air.

He restrained himself and acted like the grown man that he was. But mentally, he was already imagining sitting beside her on her porch swing, talking about blending their ventures into one united dream.

Maybe even sealing the discussion with a kiss.

Clearly, his emotions were overriding his logic, tempting him to forget the pain he'd felt when she'd shattered his teenage heart. Tempting him to believe things could be different this time.

Normally, he would've been reluctant to see their evening together end. He would've thoroughly enjoyed counting with Gianna as she brushed the horses, then guiding her on the vaulting equipment followed by the three of them trotting across an open field.

Tonight, however, Charlotte and her niece couldn't drive off quickly enough.

Once they left, he tidied up a neglected storage area to keep from incessantly checking his phone for Charlotte's text letting him know he could head her way.

As if he wouldn't hear the notification.

He stacked some spare boards he kept around for unexpected repairs and gathered some rough outs he'd purchased thinking he might try his hand at carving. They'd been growing dust going on three years now, long enough that he should give them to one of his woodworking friends. Either that, or he'd toss them.

As he set them on the other side of the opened door, he received a call, igniting a grin. A glance at his screen elicited an immediate frown.

Strolling toward an overloaded shelf, he answered. "Jason. What's up?"

"Dude. You've been holding out on me."

"How so?" Phone sandwiched between his ear and shoulder, he combined three boxes of mostly empty light bulbs.

"What's up with you and Charlotte?"

"We're just friends. And colleagues." Although he wouldn't deny that he wanted more—and hoped tonight would be a solid step in that direction.

"There's nothing going on between us, Jason."

"Uh-huh. Because you do all your horse training at Wilma's."

"Went there to discuss vaulting stuff. For the Fourth of July event."

"Twice? Whatever, dude."

Had people been talking about him and Charlotte? Then again, it made sense that they would—if they knew their history.

Then again, it was just as likely Mrs. Wolfe was spreading garbage, accusing him of putting his social life above the team. That woman was fouler than a neglected pig trough.

He thought about her conversation with Marlene and frowned. Who would call to cancel their lesson next? Although he wanted to think none of his clients were foolish enough to listen to a lady filled with more vinegar than a gallon of pickles, trusting the truth would come out eventually wouldn't help him keep his business running today.

"Where'd you catch the local gossip chain?" he asked.

"Mama asked me about y'all. Wanted to know if it was serious, and if I thought you'd like her to make your wedding cake."

He about choked on his saliva. "Where'd she get a notion like that?"

"The quilting ladies."

"They've got quite an imagination."

Not that he was opposed to the idea of marrying Charlotte, or taking Jason's mother up on her offer. She was more talented than Sage Creek's baker, and that was saying a lot.

But he and Charlotte were a long way from walking down the aisle.

Although, he'd like to think they were heading that direction.

"Tell your mom if I ever find myself needing such a cake, I'll be sure to let her know."

"As to you and Charlotte… Maybe the four of us—you, Charlotte, Rachel, and me—could hang out sometime."

"Goodbye, Jason."

Shaking his head, he ended the call. When would Jason realize that if Rachel hadn't welcomed his advances after all this time, she wasn't likely to do so?

The poor guy needed to grieve and move on.

There'd been a time Xavier had told himself the same thing.

A twinge of worry, fed by memories from that painful period, bid him to proceed with caution. But he didn't let fear drive his actions in any other area of his life. Otherwise he never would've taken steps to build his ranch or launch his vaulting club. While matters of the heart felt wheelbarrow loads riskier, he wasn't willing to walk away from an opportunity to rebuild a relationship with the only woman he'd ever loved.

Ever *could* love.

Besides, everything pointed to the fact that God had brought her back into his life. Such an example of His love and grace practically guaranteed more to come.

Father, the Bible says every good and perfect gift comes from You, and that You don't add any trouble to it. You know I've experienced my fair share of that, as far as my heart's concerned. I have to trust You're not leading me to a repeat. I'm not sure I could take it. Besides, You were the One that said it wasn't good for folks to be alone. I know I told you that was how I wanted to remain. But that was before You brought Charlotte back.

Seemed time to let his faith lead.

Whistling a hymnal that popped into his head, he tossed an empty container of hoof conditioner and a tattered waterproof sheet into the trash. He was in the middle of stacking sixteen-gallon tubs inside each other when his cell pinged, sending an anticipatory jolt through him.

Grinning like a schoolboy given his first horse, he pulled his phone from his back pocket and tapped the screen. Charlotte.

The fact that she'd ended her message with a smiley face made it impossible to exit the stables and walk to his truck without a noticeable bounce in his steps.

He texted back: Be there in a few.

Climbing into the cab, he eyed the horizon and the vibrant sky. If he hustled, they could enjoy the sunset together, ending their night gazing upon the emerging stars and, God willing, knowing he'd be holding her in his arms for countless nights to follow.

CHARLOTTE HAD JUST finished loading oatmeal raisin cookies, Xavier's favorite, on a plate when the doorbell rang. Ignoring Rachel's disapproving frown, she answered to find him standing on the stoop looking adorably shy in his signature cowboy hat and fresh blue T-shirt that deepened the blue in his eyes and accented his broad, muscular chest.

"Hey." His boyish smile initiated a flutter through her midsection.

"Hey." Suddenly bashful herself, she tucked a lock of hair behind her ear. "Let me grab us some snacks right quick."

He followed her to the kitchen, where she filled a plate with baked goods and two glasses with sweet tea.

"Oatmeal raisin?"

Warmth filling her cheeks, she nodded. "With extra cinnamon."

"Nice." Stepping back onto the porch, he took one and shoved half of it into his mouth, then closed his eyes with a moan. "The best I've had in a while."

It'd only taken him saying that once, back when they were teens, for her to bake him a couple of dozen each week. "If you think that'll get me to keep you supplied..."

"No? You telling me you have greater priorities than baking?"

She laughed. "Just a tad."

He wasn't any less busy, yet he was taking the time to come over after having already spent a chunk of his evening with her and Gianna. Surely that meant something.

And potentially that whatever he wanted to discuss held weight. Was he wanting to cut her loose? Considering the drama her presence had stirred up for him and his team, maybe. Except he'd been nothing but supportive in the aftermath.

The porch swing creaked as he sat in it.

She joined him. "Weather app said it might rain tomorrow. If it does, Gianna won't be happy." Nor would Charlotte.

"We can always take her riding in the arena."

"She'll probably ask about joining the team again."

"'Spect so." He paused. "Speaking of, I had an idea."

"Okay?"

"What if she wore noise-canceling headphones and we made sure not to have flashing lights or anything while she rode? And we kept the horse at a walk?"

His desire to include Gianna reflected his tender heart, and how much Gianna had come to mean to him.

Charlotte angled her head, considering, then nodded. "We could have her do a basic seat."

He grinned. "She'll be stoked."

His enthusiasm was contagious, and deeply touched her, reminding her once again of the wonderful dad he'd make. God willing, one day, when her secret was out and Xavier had processed the truth, her thinking of him as a father would bring praise for all the Lord had done, not guilt for what she hadn't.

Clearing his throat, he set his glass on the porch railing to his left and shifted to face her. "I've been wanting to talk to you about something."

"Okay."

"What would you think about merging our businesses?"

She blinked, a prick of disappointment weighting her shoulders. Was that why he'd asked to come over? Had she completely misread his signs, thinking he actually had feelings for her, when he was simply focused on forming a partnership?

Maybe, if she hadn't built up her expectations so unrealistically, she might find his suggestion appealing. She and Rachel would certainly benefit from the stability he'd bring.

He studied her. "If you're worried I'd turn controlling and stampede all over y'all—"

Clearly, her face had been much too revealing. "No, of course not. It's a generous offer. Rachel and I would definitely appreciate access to a fully functioning facility. Especially since our contractor seems in no hurry to complete our indoor arena."

Drew Mason. Xavier glanced that direction, the build-site hidden by the barn in front of it and the night's lengthening shadows. "Mind if I go take a look?"

She stood. "I'll come, too." The short walk would give her time to school her emotions and recover from hope raised, then doused.

But not shattered entirely. So, he wasn't here to disclose his feelings. At least he wasn't wanting to cut her loose. To the contrary, he was suggesting they spend *more* time together.

It made sense that they take things slow. Especially considering her confusion regarding what to disclose to him and when. Hopefully, by the time she gained her courage, they'd have built a strong enough connection to absorb the blow her news would inflict.

Matching her steps as they strolled past fire-scorched pastures bordered by fence in need of repair, he reached for her hand.

Heat surged up her arm and accelerated her pulse as he twined his fingers with hers. Her heart immediately latched onto the familiarity of his touch, igniting a love that distance and years clearly hadn't diminished.

And making her believe that he felt the same.

Suddenly, his partnership offer took on increased depth—a potential promise of sorts.

When they reached the building site, Xavier asked her a bunch of questions, like how big they wanted their arena and if they planned to run a water line from the house to the structure. He listened, nodding periodically, then stood rubbing his jaw and staring at the posts long enough to sour Charlotte's stomach.

"What is it?" Her voice carried a slight squeak.

"You got a tape measure?"

"Yeah. I'll get it."

She jogged back to a shed adjacent to the house, rummaged through the tools the previous owner had left and returned to Xavier with the requested item.

Then she watched and waited as he inspected the work done by the contractor, which wasn't much.

After a few minutes that felt more like hours, he walked toward her with a frown. "I'd like to ask a buddy of mine to come out to give his professional opinion. But I think y'all might have a problem."

She swallowed, her nausea increasing. "How so?"

"Grade's off, and I don't believe the support posts from the stall to arena are at the proper height for your twenty-four-foot tresses."

Her nausea turned to a deep, dull ache. "What do we do now?"

"Let my buddy take a look. And go from there."

Easy for him to say, considering he wasn't the one slipping further into debt with little more than scorched grass and, apparently, the botched start of an arena to show for it.

Facing her, he took her hands in his, and his expression intensified with an almost protective affection. "You're not alone in this."

Dropping her gaze to keep from crying, she nodded.

But when he gently raised her chin, bidding her to make eye contact, the tears building within her slipped out.

He thumbed them away and cupped her face in his strong, calloused palm. His gaze fell to her mouth, and her breath hitched.

Was he going to kiss her?

A stampede of butterflies chased away her nausea and sent a flutter through her midsection.

But then he withdrew his hand, cleared his throat and took a step back. "I'll give my buddy a call tonight."

She nodded, disoriented from the swirl of emotions that

had swept through her over the course of the evening. Worry regarding Rachel and Gianna. Frustration at her sister's constant reminder of their secret. An almost teenage anticipation as she and Xavier sat, shoulder to shoulder, on the porch swing. Panic upon learning their contractor might be inept, followed by her insides becoming jelly at the prospect of Xavier kissing her.

And the assurance that, although he hadn't, he'd wanted to, a tender affection for which she felt profoundly grateful.

This time, she would *not* let anyone or anything sabotage one of the best gifts God could give her.

Even if that meant disclosing the secret she'd sworn to herself and to her sister to forever keep.

She'd made that promise *before* God brought Xavier back into her life. As knotted as her stomach felt whenever she thought of revealing the truth, she had to believe God wouldn't cost her the man she loved.

CHAPTER THIRTEEN

THE NEXT MORNING, Charlotte was fighting with her uncooperative hair when her sister poked her head into the bathroom.

The look on her face indicated she was *not* happy.

Charlotte set down her curling iron and turned to face her. "Hey. Everything okay?" Had another bill come due that they couldn't pay? Or was she thinking about their problems with the arena and their need to find another contractor—after already having spent a great deal of money.

For shoddy work.

Rachel crossed her arms. "You're sure fussing over your appearance, considering you'll be spending the morning in a dusty horse arena."

Heat rushed to Charlotte's cheeks. Shrugging, she stepped around her sister. "Had some extra time. Figured I'd actually fix my hair for once."

Rachel followed her into her bedroom. "This is precisely why agreeing to his partnership is such a bad idea."

Charlotte had relayed Xavier's suggestion when she'd mentioned the possible problems with the posts and arena grade. Her intent—to cushion the devastating news in hope.

And maybe to decrease Rachel's hostility to the idea.

Charlotte glanced at her earring stand on her dresser, then

thought better of it. Wearing jewelry would only heighten her sister's anxiety. That's all this was.

Taking in a deep breath to keep her tone and body language relaxed, she faced her sister with a warm smile. "I understand your fear, but you have nothing to worry about. I promise."

"You're falling for him."

Charlotte couldn't deny that, nor, apparently, could she hide it. "Rach, this could be a really great opportunity. One we desperately need."

"At what cost?"

"None."

"You're going to tell him."

"And if I did? If I finally had the courage to speak the truth, and we didn't have to live with this ginormous secret hanging over us all the time?"

"Is your relationship with Xavier really worth risking my—*our*—daughter? What if upon learning he's her biological father he fights for custody?"

"He wouldn't do that."

"Why? Because of his love for you?" Rachel huffed. "Would *you* relinquish your daughter for a man?"

Her throat felt tight and scratchy. "He'd never disrupt Gianna's life like that."

"Even if he felt he'd do a better job raising her?"

Rachel's words slammed into her chest, nearly knocking the air from her, but she felt bolstered by memories of Gianna's meltdown and Morgan's injury. Xavier had been nothing but understanding.

Would that change once he learned the truth about Gianna?

These thoughts, and her conversation with Rachel, wouldn't help her get out the door or lead her team through practice.

"What we're doing is wrong—keeping this information from him. We have to trust, if we do the right thing, God will make it all work out."

She was trying to reassure herself as much as she was Rachel.

She grabbed her phone from her bedside table. "I've got to go." She exited the room and walked down the hall.

Once again, Rachel followed. "This conversation isn't over."

She turned around and searched her sister's eyes, her stomach queasy at the pain they revealed. "I know." She took in a slow, deep breath. "I realize how hard all this is, but we can't let it ruin our relationship."

Growing teary, her sister dropped her gaze and picked at her pinky nail.

Father, help us.

Gianna, already dressed and fed, was playing a game in her "cozy corner" in the living room. Squatting to her level, Charlotte spoke her name to get her attention. "We need to leave now."

The child sprang to her feet. "Tucker wants to see me. And Champ and Honey and Whisper. Mr. Xavier wants to see me, too."

Charlotte blinked. The fact that Gianna spoke his name, and looked forward to spending time with him, froze her steps.

Yet another sign from God that she needed to come clean with Xavier?

Her old pastor used to say that truth liberated the burdened soul.

She could only imagine how light her heart would feel, and how much more easily she could enjoy the beauty God was building between her, Gianna and Xavier, once freed from her guilt.

The prospect buoyed her steps as she walked to her car. Her faith that the Lord would bring beauty from a complicated situation bolstered her courage to finally do the hard right thing.

Her determination turned to an undercurrent when they arrived at the stables to find Xavier absent. He probably had an early lesson and would pop by eventually, if not while she and Gianna were grooming their horses, then during practice.

If not? If back-to-back appointments kept her from seeing him?

Then she'd use the time to strengthen her fortitude—and not talk herself into an anxious, self-protecting mess.

Gianna paused mid brush stroke to peer past the stall gate to the aisle. "Where is Mr. Xavier?" She'd already asked that question half a dozen times.

"He's probably working with a student in the arena. Or taking care of something else on the ranch."

Charlotte didn't expect Gianna to accept her answer any more now than she had when she'd offered it previously. All Gianna knew was that Xavier was normally here when they arrived but wasn't today.

She should've realized his presence would create a routine, and therefore, an expectation.

She glanced at the time on her phone. Practice wouldn't start for another thirty minutes. "Tell you what. Once you finish grooming Whisper, we can go see if we can find him."

Presuming he was even on the property and not running errands or something.

Was she setting her daughter up for a letdown?

Gianna smiled. "Yes. I can brush fast. See?" Her strokes and counting accelerated, and she finished with fifteen minutes to spare.

"Nicely done." Charlotte turned Whisper out, set the brush on a hook outside the stall, waited for Gianna to follow, then closed the gate. "Let's check out the arena."

Unfortunately, he wasn't there, although he'd already brought in Dolly. That meant he had to be close.

They exited through the door leading to the pasture, a grin immediately dominating her face. He stood a few paces away, talking with an older gentleman wearing a faded ball cap and a leather apron over his jeans.

Xavier glanced up as they approached and flashed a wide grin. "Hey. Sorry I couldn't join y'all for grooming. Mr. Healy here needed to come earlier than planned to get some of my horses shod. I wanted to send you a text but left my phone back at the house."

Charlotte was touched he'd thought to do so. "No problem."

Turning to the farrier, he introduced her and Gianna, referring to the child as his "little athlete."

Mr. Healy looked between her and Xavier with a furrowed brow.

"Something wrong?" Xavier asked.

"Feel like a clod." He released a sheepish chuckle. "All the times I've been at your ranch and never knew you had a wife and kid."

Charlotte sucked in a sharp breath, her gaze shooting to Xavier.

He stared at the farrier with eyebrows raised so high they practically disappeared beneath his hat. But then he laughed. "Can't claim them. Unfortunately." The wink he gave Charlotte tightened the knot in her gut.

"Now isn't that something." The man eyed Gianna again. "The girl sure resembles you. And your sister."

Xavier's confused expression turned into a frown as he looked at Charlotte. Her face must've revealed her inner turmoil because a tendon in his jaw twitched.

"Gianna?" he asked.

"Yes."

"When's your birthday?"

She proudly recited the day and year.

Sorrow lengthened his features. He addressed Mr. Healy. "You good here?"

"Yes, sir. I can round up the others easy enough."

"Then I'll leave you to it." Shoulders visibly stiff, he walked toward his hay barn, in the opposite direction of the arena or stables.

Charlotte hurried after him. "Xavier, wait."

He paused mid-step, then raised a hand.

She swallowed a sob attempting to wrench through her throat. "Please, let me explain."

He whirled around to face her. "Explain what? That I've got a—" Looking at Gianna, he clamped his mouth shut.

"Gianna?" She forced as much cheerfulness into her voice as her turmoil allowed. "How about you look for butterflies?" She motioned toward the grass bordering the gravel road.

Gianna frowned. "It's not time."

"Just for a few minutes to give Mr. Xavier and me time to talk." Hopefully this change of schedule wouldn't result in a meltdown. But she could leave this relational explosive unaddressed. "I think I saw a zebra longwing."

Her daughter's eyes widened, followed by a grin. With a nod, she hurried off.

"How could you keep something like this from me?"

"It wasn't my choice." At least not initially.

The deepening crevice between his brows said he didn't believe her, but he at least listened to her explanation.

"Back in high school, I'd understand," he said. "But for six years? And not one phone call? Nothing?"

Explaining Rachel's fear only deepened the sorrow in his eyes.

"You really thought that little of me?"

"I'm sorry." Her voice cracked. "I'm so very sorry."

"Yeah, me, too."

Nausea swept over her as she watched him march off.

Father, don't let this destroy our relationship.

Help him forgive me.

Would she him, if the situation were reversed?

XAVIER MARCHED PAST his hay barn to the equipment shed behind it and shoved the door open, releasing a plume of dust into the air. He'd intended to spend the remainder of his morning mucking stalls in between periodic trips to watch Charlotte coaching the girls and talk with Gianna about her game.

Now, he wanted to stay as far away from the woman as possible.

That was why she'd disappeared midway through her senior year, with hardly a goodbye and no forwarding address. And why Rachel's ex showed no interest in the child.

How could Charlotte keep something like this from him? She'd robbed him of holding his infant daughter in his arms, watching her take her first steps or hearing her call him Daddy.

The reality and the precious moments lost felt like a rebar to the chest.

Just when he'd allowed himself to envision a future with her.

What was that cliché about falling into the same trap twice?

He tried to distract himself working on a broken-down ATV collecting dust since he'd purchased this ranch. But not even a wrench and ratchet, nor riding the fence, could keep him from ruminating on the biggest betrayal he'd experienced.

Because she hadn't trusted him with the truth. That hurt almost as deeply.

He felt torn between the love he felt and the anger that made him want to limit his interactions with Charlotte as much as possible, while building a relationship with Gianna.

His daughter. How could someone feel such joy and pain simultaneously?

He pulled his phone from his pocket and called his best friend. The man's nonstop chatter—about sports, the rodeo and all things cowboy—would prove a needed distraction.

Jason answered. "Hey, dude. You calling to rectify that double-date fail we talked about?"

Xavier frowned. "I'm not interested in talking about romance goals." He held back a sigh. He hadn't intended to speak with such bite. "Not trying to be rude. Just ready for some bro time."

"All right. When you thinking?"

"You free now? My first riding lesson isn't until three this afternoon." He'd planned to spend the hours prior working with some of his clients' horses, but the animals were super sensitive to human emotion. Everything felt much too raw right now for him to shove his frustration beneath an appropriate trainer's demeanor.

"Uh… The boss'll be vaccinating his calves today." He paused. "I'll call one of the other ranch hands. See if they can't fill in for me."

"You sure?" The fact that Jason was willing to do so indicated he knew this was more than a random hangout.

That almost made Xavier want to hang up. He might've, if his pastor hadn't spent the last men's breakfast emphasizing how vulnerability was a sign of spiritual maturity.

Besides, Jason had been there for him when Charlotte first stomped on his heart. Not once had he brought up that time when Xavier was rapidly heading toward a repeat, not because his buddy didn't care, but because they respected one another enough to let them make their own decisions.

Even if they landed face down in stable waste.

"I'm always up for fried trout," Jason said.

Xavier chuckled. "You know what they say about heating the oil before you bait your line, right?"

"Can't say I heard that one before."

"Just made it up."

"Show-off."

The light banter felt good. Comforting.

Less than an hour later, they stood on the bank that had become as much a part of their friendship as the poles in their hands and the conversations shared between them.

Jason could act like a cocky goof, but he was as loyal

as men came. And quick to drop his rodeo-king demeanor when necessary.

"You going to tell me what's going on?" Jason cast out his line.

Xavier released a heavy breath and relayed what he'd learned.

Jason stared at him with wide eyes. "You serious?"

He nodded.

"Dude, that's heavy."

Laughter floated toward them from the roped-off swimming area to their left. A hawk circled above them, and a gentle breeze stirred the nearby branches.

"Now what?" Jason asked.

"Think I'd have a shot at getting custody?"

"Wouldn't that pert near knock the child's feet out from under her? Don't know a whole lot about autism, but I remember how change used to send your sister into one of her fits."

"Meltdowns." Which were entirely different from tantrums. The latter stemmed from not getting their way, the other from feeling completely overwhelmed.

"You know what I mean."

He did, and his friend was right. He wouldn't disrupt Gianna's already topsy-turvy world further. But he did intend to build a father-daughter relationship with her, even if she never called it that.

Never called him Dad.

The ache in his chest deepened. "I can't believe she'd keep something like this from me."

"I can."

Xavier glared at his friend. "Explain."

Jason shrugged. "Remember how controlling her parents were, is all. And their obsession with looking respectable. I know I only met them once, but I could tell they hid behind thick plastic. Expected their kids to do the same."

Xavier watched his bobber float on the water, thinking of

all the times Charlotte came to him in tears over a nasty comment or unrealistic demand her mom had made or something hurtful she'd done.

"Can't imagine that was easy on her, being pregnant as a teenager and all. Even if her folks were the supportive type, which obviously..." He flicked a hand. "Not surprised they sent her off to live with her sister, either. Or that they forced them both into this convoluted arrangement where the aunt became the mom and vice versa. Considering Rachel was married and all."

Xavier reeled in his line, then cast it back out. "I get that, but she's a grown woman. She's had five years living out from under her parents' thumb to tell me the truth."

"Maybe she didn't for the same reason you won't fight for custody."

Jason knew him well. Recognized he'd never do anything to hurt his daughter.

Nor would Charlotte.

"She still could've said something," he said. "Should've trusted me enough to know I wouldn't upend Gianna."

"Yet, she's here now." Jason paused. "The question is, can you forgive her for what must've been the most difficult decision she ever made?"

"I don't know."

"Guess that's what you've got to figure out. But as you're thinking things through, ask yourself this—is staying angry worth it, if it means losing the woman you love and the opportunity to raise your daughter, together, united?"

CHAPTER FOURTEEN

SATURDAY AFTERNOON, CHARLOTTE was reading a nonprofit marketing guide while Gianna flipped through her insect encyclopedia when the low rumble of an approaching car grabbed Charlotte's attention. Glancing up, she recognized the vehicle immediately and rose from the porch rocker.

Mandi, one of her vaulters. What was she doing all the way out here? And why hadn't she mentioned anything about wanting to come over during practice?

Had another of the girls gotten hurt somehow?

She descended the steps, reaching the teen as she got out of her vehicle. "Mandi, hello."

"Ma'am." Her furrowed brow deepened and her obvious difficulty maintaining eye contact heightened Charlotte's apprehension.

"What is it?"

"I, um…like…" She shifted. "Morgan's mom called a meeting."

"Okay. What kind?"

She shrugged. "With the other parents, the mayor and a bunch of other people involved with the Fourth of July thing. Pretty sure she's going to try to get you fired. And run Mr. Xavier out of business, too."

Charlotte blinked, her stomach dropping. "I see. When?" As if she hadn't hurt the man enough already.

Rachel had been right about one thing—accepting his collaboration suggestion had been a terrible idea. All that had done was rekindle Charlotte's hopes that things could be different between them, only to leave them worse off than if she'd never come.

"Tonight." Morgan bit a pinkie hangnail. "Seven o'clock, in the high school cafeteria."

"Does Xavier know?"

"Yes, ma'am."

That meant he would be there as well, and likely agreeing with whatever Mrs. Wolfe had to say about her. That'd be his wisest response, and perhaps the only way to neutralize an enemy.

Except he'd never turn on Charlotte like that, regardless of how badly she'd hurt him. It wasn't in his nature, and that only intensified her guilt for the pain she'd caused.

She raised her chin and forced what she hoped looked like a confident smile. "I don't want to sound rude or anything, but why did you tell me this? I mean, I know you're close with Morgan and all."

Mandi dropped her gaze. "Just felt like I should. Considering what happened and all. I told Morgan her falling wasn't your fault."

"And?"

She gave a slight shrug, her face proclaiming her obvious discomfort with the whole conversation.

Poor girl probably felt thrust into the middle of a highly unpleasant—and toxic—situation.

She'd already demonstrated incredible bravery coming out here—potentially risking her friendship with her teammates.

Charlotte offered a gentle smile. "Regardless of Morgan's

response or what happens after tonight's meeting, I appreciate and admire your integrity and courage."

She gave a slight shrug and tucked a lock of hair breeze-stirred hair behind her ear. "I'm glad you're our coach. We all are."

Including Morgan? Then again, the teen hadn't shown any of her mother's hostility, nor was she responsible for her mom's behavior.

This conversation helped soothed her wounded soul. "I like coaching you all as well."

Mandi looked at her for a moment longer, the concern on her face only slightly lessened, then said goodbye, got back in her car and drove away.

Rubbing her temples in an attempt to stanch an emerging headache, Charlotte enticed Gianna with the promise of video games to go inside, then went in search of her sister. She found her in her bedroom, folding a mound of laundry.

Rachel eyed her with a weary look that verged on anger. "Your expression tells me whatever you're about to say I won't want to hear it." She crossed her arms. "But I'll repeat what I told you yesterday, when you came home from Xavier's all distraught. This is exactly what I said would happen when you first mentioned having our horses board there and you taking that coaching position. I love you to death, always will. But if you cost me my—*our*—daughter, I'll never forgive you."

Tears blurred Charlotte's vision, the pain ripping through her heart so intense it hurt to breathe. In under twenty-four hours, she'd gone from feeling like the most blessed woman alive, living with a sister who was more like a best friend and working with the man she loved more than anything, to fearing she'd soon lose them both.

Rachel tossed a pair of socks onto the bed and faced her. "Spill it."

Charlotte took in a slow, deep breath that did nothing to

ease her anxiety over this conversation—or the potential chaos ahead.

Struggling to look her sister in the eye, she relayed what Mandi had told her.

Rachel scoffed. "That's just what we need. God only knows who that woman is gathering against us. People in the horse community. Our future clients."

"She's upset with me, not you."

"If you don't think this will affect us, and our program, you're deceiving yourself."

Charlotte's throat burned. "I'll fix this."

Rachel's scowl deepened. "Yeah? And how's that?"

"I don't know, but I'll figure it out."

"You going to the meeting?"

"I feel I should. If you don't mind handling bedtime tonight."

"Disrupting Gianna's routine. Perfect." She rolled her eyes.

"You think it's better I stay here?"

She huffed. "No. I understand why you need to go. But I'm not happy about it."

"I'm with you there."

Charlotte spent the rest of her day trying to distract herself from her growing anxiety, couched in the deep sadness of feeling completely alone. Tonight would feel uncomfortable, to say the least, but she could handle Mrs. Wolfe and her posse. She could even handle losing her coaching position, or her and Rachel's ranch, should it come to that.

But the thought of potentially losing the three most important people in her world devastated her. Logic assured her Rachel would forgive her eventually. They'd fought and reconciled enough to assure her of that.

Her relationship with Xavier didn't have nearly as strong of a foundation. She feared the wound her deception inflicted might shatter the cracks they'd only just begun to mend.

Potentially, beyond her ability to repair them.

Still, she had to try.

* * *

XAVIER HAD INTENDED to arrive at the high school early so that he could get settled before most everyone else showed up. He didn't want to be forced to choose a spot next to one of Helicopter's allies. He still couldn't believe she had any. He'd expected most folks to have tuned out her entitled rants.

Then again, her family was one of the wealthier in Sage Creek, and her father owned the local quarry, which meant he was one of the town's biggest employers. That was probably why so many people had beaten Xavier to the school cafeteria. Although it hadn't helped that he'd noticed a nasty cut on one of his horses less than an hour before he was planning to leave.

Thankfully, the vet had rushed right over. Otherwise, Xavier would be interrupting the meeting rather than simply strolling past a bunch of folks, half a dozen or so who suddenly avoided eye contact.

Because they'd come with their minds made up, or were ashamed to be here at all? Considering most everyone in here belonged to his church family and had known him all his life, he wanted to believe the latter.

Seeing his buddy Travis and his wife, Whitney, to his left, he nodded hello and meandered over.

He greeted Travis with a handshake and his lady with a tip of his hat. "Ma'am. How'd you both get roped into this little shindig?"

"Figured you could use a friend."

"Appreciate that." He sat with his back to the wall, watching Mrs. Helicopter yak it up with a couple of other vaulting club moms. "How'd you hear about it?"

His wife offered a compassionate smile. "News travels fast."

Xavier gave a half chuckle, half snort. "Isn't that the truth. Still, isn't this about my program?" He fully expected Morgan's mom to have spewed her venom to whoever might listen, and then some. Everyone in here surely had better ways to spend a Saturday evening than listening to someone else's drama.

Travis scratched his jaw. "She's got folks all worked up over the Fourth of July event."

"And insinuated that you're careless with your boarders." Whitney grimaced, as if that hurt her to say.

His jaw went slack. "You can't be serious."

She raised her hands, palms out. "Just telling you what I got from the email."

Exhaling, he shook his head and checked the time on his phone. "Wish they'd get on with it already."

He glanced up, then winced inwardly. Charlotte entered, looking far too beautiful in a peach T-shirt, boots and blue jeans, looking near vulnerable enough to reignite the part of him that, a few days ago, would've done anything in his power to protect her.

Yesterday, he'd wasted hours fretting about ways to avoid her while still honoring the agreement they'd made. But then he'd talked with Jason. The conversation he thought would make him feel better only tangled his thoughts and emotions further.

In a sermon series on conflict, Pastor Roger had encouraged church members to seek to understand before drawing conclusions. Seemed that was what Jason had been doing—nudging Xavier to view the situation from Charlotte's perspective.

He doubted she'd had much choice in leaving, and maybe not with the arrangement she and her sister made, either. But they'd had five years to do the right thing.

A loud whistle quieted everyone's chatter. Standing at the front of the room beside his wife, Mr. Wolfe thanked everyone for coming, adding some garbage about banding together to keep everything "on the up and up."

His wife followed with a brief mention of her the deep "respect" she'd long held for Xavier, and how much she liked him as a person. "That's what makes this whole situation so difficult." Her sorrowful expression looked forced. "But I have to think about what's best for the girls, the horses and our town." She went on to explain the importance of the upcoming Fourth of July event. "As you know, this is one of the most important ways we honor our veterans."

A deep voice to his right blurted, "Amen."

Mrs. Wolfe transitioned to the vaulting club, emphasizing the loss of his former coach. "I was more than happy to step in, at least until Mr. Shaw could find a proper replacement. But he let his romantic feelings for Ms. Murphy, a woman with little equine vaulting experience, drive his decisions. Placing our girls, my daughter included, at risk." She motioned to Morgan, who sat with her leg extended and her knee supported by large, rigid brace.

In her retelling that followed, she failed to mention Charlotte's clear instructions that the girls stay off the vaulting equipment.

A gut-level desire to defend Charlotte propelled him to his feet. Yes, she'd betrayed him and stomped on his barely healed heart. But his sense of integrity wouldn't allow Nadia to spew slander unchallenged—regardless of the target. "You're not telling the full story, and you've exaggerated what you have. The girls weren't sup—"

Glaring, Mrs. Wolfe raised her hand. "No one's interested in your excuses, Mr. Shaw, nor will they help us—" she made a sweeping motion with her arm to indicate everyone in the space "—deliver the quality of event to which we're accustomed and our vets deserve."

Her husband, standing beside her, nodded. "The only thing we want to hear from you is an apology and how you plan to run your program differently."

He scoffed, mouth ready with a retort, but Travis's firm grip on his shoulder stopped his sarcastic counter. The action reminded him of his determination to remain levelheaded, no matter what Mrs. Wolfe hurled at him.

His father used to say that a man's self-control was the best way to make his enemy look the fool.

Charlotte stood and walked to the center of the room. "May I speak, please?"

Mrs. Wolfe snorted. "No one wants to hear from you, either."

"I do," someone said, followed by a "Me, too."

They kept pushing until Mrs. Wolfe, who tried to argue, was forced to concede.

Gaze faltering, Charlotte tucked her hair behind her ears and took in a visible breath. "This wasn't Xavier's fault. I take complete responsibility for what happened. I shouldn't have left the girls alone in the arena."

Facing her, Mrs. Wolfe crossed her arms. "So, you're saying when I file a lawsuit I should make it against you?"

Charlotte raised her chin. "Yes. If you're determined to take legal action, it should solely be against me." The obvious tremble in her voice sliced at his heart.

The fact that she'd tried to publicly exonerate him from all blame, even at risk to her and Rachel's business, left him speechless. Not that he found her behavior uncharacteristic.

Up until the Gianna incident, he would've said she was the most honest and honorable woman he knew. That was one of the reasons her betrayal had cut as deeply as it had.

But maybe he was looking at the situation all wrong. Obviously, she hadn't intended to hurt him. She'd simply been doing her best to protect her daughter.

He didn't need to understand all her thought processes to know that.

Although that didn't mean they could move on as if nothing had happened. She obviously didn't trust him. Without that, how could their relationship possibly survive all of life's challenges, let alone while raising a special needs child? An adorable kid who stirred a deep, fatherly love within him, but one requiring unique care nonetheless.

Giving himself a mental shake, he refocused on the drama in front of him.

"If you're truly sorry," Mrs. Wolfe spat at Charlotte, "put your words in action and resign. Your incompetency is a danger to the girls and put your niece at risk, too."

Charlotte looked like she'd been elbowed in the gut. She stood there, blinking, clearly on the verge of crying. "I'm sorry."

"Enough." Xavier's strong voice silenced the room, his hard gaze zeroed in on Mrs. Wolfe. "You clearly don't know what went down. Yes, Charlotte slipped out of the arena for a minute, but she told the girls, in no uncertain terms, to stay off the equipment while she was gone."

Head ducked, she turned and hurried out. The desire to chase after her and pull her close warred with his urge to leave this whole mess and drown his sorrow with a hard, fast ride across his land.

And pretend like his heart wasn't completely shredded.

Yet again.

TEARS BLURRING HER VISION, Charlotte resisted breaking into a full-on run until the cafeteria doors clanked closed behind her. Nausea swept over her as she dashed through the hall and burst out into the humid, evening air. Seeing the numerous vehicles in the parking lot, evidence of the large number of people Mrs. Wolfe had gathered, added to the heaviness that bid her to crumple to the ground in deep-chested sobs.

She'd lost the man she loved, had seriously damaged her relationship with her sister and had likely destroyed the respect they'd been trying to build within the local horse community. Especially considering the rate at which negativity traveled, particularly when fueled by a woman as spiteful as Mrs. Wolfe.

Would Xavier ask her and Rachel to take their horses elsewhere? They couldn't afford boarding fees. They were barely able to pay their mortgage as it was.

What if she'd cost her and her sister not just their program, but their ranch, as well?

She turned toward her car, then stopped. Morgan sat on the bumper of her mother's vehicle, elbows propped on her knees and her face buried in her hands.

Seeing the child's shoulders quiver beneath the silvery beam of the adjacent streetlight sent a stab through Charlotte's heart. While she didn't know precisely what the girl was crying about, she understood what it felt like to be raised by a Mrs. Wolfe.

She approached. "Morgan?"

The girl looked up with tear-filled eyes.

"Mind if I sit with you?"

She hesitated, then gave a slight shrug. "If you want."

A moment of silence stretched between them.

"This is all my fault." Morgan flicked a hand toward the school.

"I don't blame you for any of this. Or hold any negative feelings toward you."

Yes, the girl had gotten hurt due to her deliberate disobedience, but she was a teenager and therefore expected to make mistakes. Especially when boys were involved.

Charlotte knew from her own wounding, what Morgan needed most right now was grace. She thought of the Bible verse that talked about covering a person's offense with love and could easily remember the people who had done that for her over the years.

"I wasn't honest with my mom." Morgan's voice wobbled. "About what happened."

Charlotte had expected as much. The poor child had probably felt too frightened of her mom's reaction to own her part. And now carried guilt because of that.

Charlotte placed an arm around Morgan's shoulder and gave her a gentle squeeze. "I forgive you."

This released another onslaught of tears and, hopefully, a sense of release and feeling of absolution.

"Now I can't be on the team anymore," Morgan said. "Thanks to my mom. She always ruins everything."

How could Charlotte provide reassurance without speaking badly about her mother? "I'm certain everything will settle down with time."

"Why does my mom have to be so stupid?"

"She loves you." Regardless of how the woman acted, as a mother herself, Charlotte knew it was true.

"Even if my mom lets me come back to practice, Mr. Xavier won't. Not after tonight."

"One thing I can promise you. He doesn't hold grudges." She spoke those words to comfort herself as much as Morgan, although she knew her betrayal had cut much deeper. Potentially, irreparably so. "I guarantee there will be a place for you, should you ever want to return."

Unfortunately, she couldn't say the same regarding herself and her coaching position.

"Yeah, but after the Fourth of July event's over."

Charlotte smoothed the hair out of the child's face. "If your mom is comfortable with it, I know we can find a way for you to stay involved."

"Really?"

"Mmm-hmm." Her maternal side roused as she drew the teen closer and, as Morgan relaxed in her arms, she rested her chin on the teen's head.

Glancing up, she saw Mrs. Wolfe standing just outside the school doors, staring. Anticipating a verbal attack, she tensed and was tempted to pull away.

Instead, maintaining the embrace, she averted her gaze.

She tried not to think of all the times Xavier had responded to her tears in a similar fashion.

The ache of knowing she might never experience that again made it hard to breathe.

CHAPTER FIFTEEN

SUNDAY, XAVIER RUSHED through his morning chores so that he could make it to church in time to listen to the choir's pre-service practice. There was something soothing about sitting in the back of a near-empty sanctuary, letting the words of the familiar hymns flood your soul.

Closing his eyes, he leaned forward and pressed folded hands to his chin. "Father, help me make sense of all my tangled emotions." Anger at Charlotte's betrayal, sorrow for the years lost. Incomprehensible joy for the gift of fatherhood—and to such a precious girl! A nagging feeling of insufficiency for this new, unexpected role.

Thankfully, his parents were great role models, even with how they'd raised JoEllen. They might not have had all the resources today's special needs families had access to, but they'd always loved him and his sister deeply.

Reflecting upon that simplified things for him.

The door behind him creaked open, and Pastor Roger popped his head in. "Morning, Xavier."

"Pastor."

He studied Xavier a moment longer, as if debating whether to enter or leave. He chose the former and paused at the end of the pew. "Mind company?"

Either Xavier's inner angst showed or his pattern of seeking refuge here had become predictable.

He motioned to the space beside him. Pastor accepted the invitation and waited while Xavier wrestled over what to say, if anything. In the end, he simply asked for prayer.

Pastor smiled. "I can do that." Hand on Xavier's shoulder, he bowed his head, asking God to provide wisdom, courage and the strength to move forward.

His words were too fitting for mere coincidence.

"Father, I thank You that Xavier will never encounter anything alone. You will remain with him, leading him toward Your perfect will, at each moment. We hold tight to Your declaration, recorded in Joshua 1:9, which tells us to be strong and courageous, because You are with us, wherever we go."

The verse acted like a flashlight within his soul, revealing the root of his inner struggle. His anger and bitterness toward Charlotte, ultimately, came from fear. Her deception had reopened the wounds and feelings of betrayal from when she'd left years ago. But walking away from her now wouldn't protect him from further pain.

It'd only increase it.

He wasn't sure he'd recover were he to lose her again. Nor was he willing to lose Gianna.

His daughter. The thought brought a smile to his face and balm to his bruised heart. God had given him a wonderful gift he'd not even prayed for, while answering what he had—Charlotte's return.

Lord, show me how I can keep them both. Forever.

First step, making sure Charlotte didn't resign as vaulting coach—even if her staying cost him his entire team.

They could figure out together the best way to handle the situation with Gianna. He didn't want to upset or confuse her, but he did intend to act like a caring father, whether or not she ever called him by those words—although the thought of her doing so filled his chest with warmth.

How might Rachel respond to all this?

If she thought he would try to take Gianna from her, not well.

The doors behind him opened again as churchgoers started streaming in.

"Guess that's my cue." Pastor shook his hand, then stood to greet his parishioners.

Unfortunately, numerous people approached Xavier to talk about what the town meeting meant for him and his program. Were folks asking Charlotte the same questions? He scanned the sanctuary and caught sight of her sitting in the far back pew, as close to the wall as possible. She looked about as comfortable as a city girl who'd stumbled into the bull pen.

She probably felt twice as vulnerable.

Should he go to her? Sit with her, to show support?

Before he could move, a family of six slid into the pew beside him, and others did the same with Charlotte. After opening a hymnal, he tried to focus on the service, but his mind kept rehearsing what he might say to Charlotte when they talked.

For starters, he'd make it clear that he had no intention of cutting her loose, or letting Nadia Wolfe, or anyone else for that matter, dictate how he ran his program. Then, even if she didn't feel the same about him as he did her, he'd still have time to win her heart. Although he wouldn't blame her if she said she wanted to quit.

At least she and Gianna would still be coming over to see their horses.

Once the service ended, he followed a stream of people to the children's area to wait for Charlotte. Upon seeing him standing outside Gianna's classroom, her face flushed and her gaze dropped like she assumed he was still angry.

"Hey." He offered a gentle smile. "Can I talk to you for a minute?"

She lifted sad eyes. "Sure."

They moved to an area free from people at the entrance to the baptismal stairwell.

"That was quite an ordeal last night, huh?" he asked.

She nodded. "I'm sorry for—"

Shaking his head, he pressed a finger to her soft, pink lips. "Like I told you after Morgan's accident, it wasn't your fault."

"I appreciate you saying that. But if I hadn't brought Gianna—"

"I encouraged you to do so."

She gazed past him toward the crowded hall, then turned back with a sigh. "Anyway, I also understand that you have to do what's best for your program and your team. When would you like me to make arrangements for the horses?"

"I wouldn't."

The worry lines faded from her forehead, but sorrow remained in her eyes. "Thank you."

"As to doing what's best for the club, I completely agree. Which is why I hope you'll stay on."

"Are you sure?"

He nodded. "You're an excellent coach, and the girls love you. As do—"

"There you two are!"

He turned to see Bonnie, a member of the church's quilting club, hustling toward them.

"Ma'am." He greeted her with a tip of his hat. "That grin you're wearing tells me you come bearing good news."

"We've finished with the girls' uniforms—and not a moment too soon." She laughed.

"That's fantastic." Grinning, he shot a glance at Charlotte. Her noticeable relief indicated she'd been fretting the ladies might not finish in time. Considering the event was only a few days away, he should've been concerned, as well.

But he'd trusted Charlotte completely.

Did he still?

Yeah. More than her words or her actions, he trusted her heart. She'd never intentionally hurt him or Gianna.

She must've felt so alone when she was pregnant, so frightened. And to a teenage girl, letting her sister and brother-in-law parent the child would've made perfect sense. They were married, owned a home and Rachel's husband held a thriving career.

But holding on to that secret must have about killed her.

Bonnie's mention of his name jolted him back to the conversation before him. "Ma'am?"

"I want you both to know that I'm standing behind y'all. As are most folks here."

Charlotte grew teary and dropped her gaze.

He cleared a lump from his throat. "I appreciate you saying that."

Bonnie shrugged. "We know what Nadia's like."

He thought of a statement his dad used to make about how a person's stink followed them.

"Anyway," Bonnie said, "I can bring the uniforms for the girls to try on tomorrow, if that works for y'all. To make sure they fit and all."

He glanced at Charlotte, and she nodded. "Practice typically ends at eleven thirty." Her gaze faltered. "Although I'll have to leave by noon."

Was she feeling guilty about needing to tend to Gianna? Made sense with how Mrs. Wolfe had used that against her. That woman's very public reproach would've poked at any parenting insecurities Charlotte already held.

And how had she responded? By comforting the teen that had caused the whole mess. Watching Mrs. Wolfe leave less than five minutes after Charlotte, he'd followed, ready to intervene should the woman escalate the situation.

He hadn't prepared himself for the scene he'd encountered, or how deeply it'd impacted him. Seeing Charlotte holding

Morgan beneath the parking lot light had sliced through the last of his bitterness, reminding him of who she was at her core.

CHARLOTTE STUDIED XAVIER—HIS body language and facial expressions. His tone when he spoke to her. The fact that she didn't see any hint of anger or resentment, and that he was willing to honor their boarding-coaching arrangement, proved what she'd already known. He was the most forgiving man she'd ever encountered.

Although there was a big difference between not hating someone and loving them.

She checked the time on her phone, knowing she'd be risking a meltdown should she remain here a moment longer. "I should probably get Gianna."

Bonnie smiled. "I heard she's been doing wonderfully in Sunday school."

Charlotte nodded. "Mrs. Cuevas has been amazing with her." Thanks to the woman's insightful kindness, Gianna had gone from sitting off by herself to interacting with the other students and engaging with activities. This, along with all Gianna continued to learn through her speech therapy program, provided some assurance that she'd adapt well to elementary school.

"She's been doing a lot of reading on how to prevent overstimulation in classroom settings."

That touched Charlotte deeply. "Is that why she bought noise-canceling headphones?"

"Yes, along with those fidget-thingies and some of those porcupine balls."

"It means a lot that she'd go to such effort to help Gianna feel comfortable."

Bonnie shrugged. "She adores the child. We all do."

Charlotte felt that to her bones. The acceptance the people in this church showed her and her daughter helped soothe some of the rejection wounds she'd experienced in childhood.

And confirmed that she and Rachel had made the right choice moving here.

Reflecting upon these little evidences helped counter her incessant fear that Nadia had ruined their reputation and therefore their chance of launching a successful program.

Excusing herself while Xavier and Bonnie continued to talk, she slipped into Gianna's Sunday school to find the child building a structure made from magnetic shapes. She spoke briefly with Mrs. Cuevas, thanked her for serving, then approached her daughter, expecting a battle. Thankfully, her daughter followed her out and to their car with minimal prodding—and the promise of doing a special craft when they got home.

She arrived home to find an unfamiliar vehicle parked beside Rachel's. The personalized license plate read ATTY UP.

Oh. Right. She was meeting with a lawyer this morning to learn how to fire their contractor without winding up with a lien on their ranch. Hopefully they could also recoup some of the money they'd already spent—with nothing but shoddy work to show for it.

Once inside, Gianna headed straight for her "safe area" while Charlotte strolled to the kitchen to learn of their legal options.

The attorney, a short guy with thick, black hair secured in a low-lying man bun, stood as she entered. Rachel made introductions.

Walking toward Charlotte, Mr. Givens initiated a handshake as Rachel made introductions. "Ms. Murphy. Good to meet you."

She set her purse on a nearby counter. "Thank you for coming out." She eyed the documents laid upon the table. The top sheet, which looked like a representation agreement, reminded her that this meeting, and any conversation that followed, was far from free.

"Like I was telling your sister, you've done well to document everything. Keep it up." He went on to explain, in detail and at an exorbitant rate per hour, everything of which they needed to make note.

Someone had said a person needed to spend money to make money. Apparently, they had to save it, as well. But at this point, they'd do about anything to break free from Drew Mason.

Although, she wasn't all that confident they'd be able to hire anyone else, nor was their bank likely to increase their loan amount. All their problems had only highlighted their lack of experience and know-how, which Mrs. Wolfe had no doubt amplified.

"Course, I don't expect your contractor to fight you on this," Mr. Givens said. "Especially now that I'm involved." He returned to the table and went through the lawyer agreement.

Once Charlotte and Rachel had signed, he explained the process and what to expect. "If this goes to court, best-case scenario the judge makes him pay my fees and punitive damages."

Charlotte frowned. "We don't want to be vindictive about this."

He gathered his papers together, placed them in his briefcase, then snapped it shut. "Your decision."

They thanked him again for coming, walked him out, then returned to the kitchen.

Charlotte sank into one of the chairs. "Why does everything have to be so hard? And expensive."

Rachel rubbed her temples. "Whatever happened to having a sense of integrity and being a person of your word? I mean, first the wellness center, then the contractor. Who's to say this lawyer guy is any different?"

"Way to bring the cheer. As if we didn't have enough to feel depressed about already."

"Oh, I'm sorry. Did I pull you out of la-la land?"

She stared at her sister. "What?"

"Am I raining on your rose-colored-glasses parade? Because the real world is full of scammers and cheats. Maybe if you remembered that, you wouldn't constantly be jeopardizing what little we have here."

"That's not fair. Besides, I wasn't the one to hire Drew Mason. *Remember?*" She couldn't remember the last time she and her sister had bickered like this, nor when Rachel had spoken to her with such venom.

Then again, they were beyond stressed. With all they'd been dealing with since arriving in Sage Creek, it made sense they'd act prickly to one another. She'd be grateful when they had all this figured out and could go back to living as friends.

"Frankly, Drew Mason is the least of my—or Gianna's—concerns."

Oh. Right. "You mean Xavier."

She scoffed, as if that should've been obvious. "So? What's the plan?" Did the bite in her tone stem from anger or fear? Probably both.

Charlotte grabbed the fixings for PB and J sandwiches from the pantry and set them on the counter. "Our arrangement stands."

She released a breath. "Okay." She paused, rubbing the back of her arms. "What about…?"

Charlotte hated to see such anguish in her sister's eyes. Hated more that she didn't have any answers for her.

"We didn't talk about his relationship with Gianna." She eyed the apples in the fruit bowl, wondering if she could get their daughter to eat a few slices. "But he won't take her from you. From us."

"How do you know that?"

"I just do." She laid out six slices of bread and began spreading peanut butter on half of them. "Although he'll want to spend time with her."

"That won't trigger his fatherly instincts or anything." Sarcasm weighted her tone. "This is such a mess."

"I understand how unsettling this all has been." For the both of them. "But you're forgetting an important detail."

"What's that?" She flung the words out.

"I'm Gianna's biological mother. I have parental rights." Although they'd discussed years ago the possibility of Rachel and her husband officially adopting Gianna, Charlotte could never bring herself to that point.

"But I don't." Her sister spoke barely above a whisper.

The defeat in Rachel's voice hit Charlotte square in the chest. She now understood. Rachel's deepest fear wasn't that Xavier would fight for custody, but that he and Charlotte would form a family without her.

She turned around to reassure her that she'd always want her in their daughter's life, but she was gone.

Charlotte checked the living room, then her bedroom. "Rachel?" Assured she wasn't in the house, she stepped outside in time to see her sister driving toward the country highway.

She contemplated calling her, but what would she say? Could she really promise that if, by God's grace, she and Xavier got back together, they wouldn't want their daughter with them?

If after all these years the Lord granted her greatest longing, a prayer so deep she'd never had the courage to voice it, she knew she couldn't leave Gianna here, with Rachel.

But she wasn't sure she could take her from her, either.

CHAPTER SIXTEEN

THE NEXT MORNING, with the Fourth of July event mere days away, Xavier reviewed his remaining tasks. He still needed to talk with the lighting and fireworks crews to discuss how to avoid overstimulating Gianna and other autistic spectators while still meeting guest expectations.

Charlotte might have some ideas. Hopefully he'd finish preparing the event arena while she was leading practice.

That meant no dilly-dallying. Grabbing the filled wheelbarrow, he rolled it out of the stall, down the stable aisle and to the compost pile out back. The Herrings, who owned the local peach orchard, would be out to pick up a truckload come week's end. Although he didn't charge much, the new arrangement proved financially helpful while reducing ranch waste.

Quickening his pace, he finished mucking all the stalls fifteen minutes before he needed to leave. Seeing Charlotte pull in, Gianna sitting in the back, brought a grin followed by a twinge of nervousness, similar to how he used to feel whenever he stood on her doorstep, ready to pick her up.

That sensation had never gone away—not back then, even after over a year's worth of dates. Nor now, five, almost six, years later.

He met her at her car as she was gathering her things. "Hey." He smiled.

"Hi." She seemed reluctant to maintain eye contact. Last conversation, he'd assured her that he wasn't upset, and that he wanted her to continue coaching.

He would've said more, if Bonnie hadn't interrupted.

How might Charlotte have responded? What if she'd sensed where he was heading, and his near declaration made her uncomfortable because she didn't feel the same?

What if that was why she seemed so hesitant now?

Dude, you're way overthinking things. Yet one more sign of how deeply he'd fallen for her, only now he was done fighting his emotions.

He turned to Gianna, standing a few feet away, clutching her iPad. "How's my little athlete?" *My.* The word, and all it encompassed, hit him hard. He was a dad. To a precious and adorable child who celebrated the smallest details in God's creation, like the markings on a butterfly's wings or the counterclockwise whorl in Tucker's hair.

His daughter lifted her chin. "I learned a new move."

"Oh?" He walked with her and Charlotte toward the arena.

She nodded. "On my knees."

"Really?" Eyebrows raised, he looked at Charlotte. Her smile radiated maternal pride, reminding him of the connection they shared. Knowing she had birthed their child hit him on a deeper level than he could verbalize or comprehend.

"She's been working really hard," Charlotte said. "And today, she feels ready to try kneeling on the mechanical horse while it moves."

Ah. So Gianna had again been practicing on the furniture at home. He suppressed a chuckle at the image of her kneeling on the arm of her couch, face set with determination.

He led the way into the arena and turned on the large overhead lights. Gianna immediately headed for the bench area.

He turned toward her. "Gianna?" Assured he had her attention, he said, "Think you can show me your kneeling exercise?"

"Yes." She focused on her iPad.

He fought to keep the amusement from his voice. "I meant now. Before practice starts."

She looked up, brow furrowed. Then shook her head. "My turn is after."

"Well, then. I best get going so I can be back in time to watch."

"Where are you going?" Gianna asked.

He explained. "Got to make sure the arena for the Fourth has proper footing depth, smooth out any uneven spots and sprinkle water to control the dust." The space, located on the county fairgrounds, was often used for cattle auctions. A horse could injure himself in the divots bulls left.

"Mom does not like dust, either."

His gaze shot to Charlotte. When she once again avoided eye contact, reality hit him square in the gut. Gianna was referring to Rachel. Did it feel like a blow to the heart every time Charlotte heard her daughter refer to her aunt that way?

Did knowing she could never truly fill that role, without shattering Gianna's world, tear her up inside as much as it did him?

Would Gianna remain with Rachel should he and Charlotte get married? Made sense that she would. And that such a scenario would prevent Charlotte from accepting his proposal. He wouldn't blame her. Regardless of her title, she'd lived with Gianna from the moment she was born.

But that didn't change his mind on proposing. Was that selfish?

Releasing a discouraged breath, he excused himself with a promise to return and headed to the event venue, where he spent the hour and a half hearing every detail of the night's schedule and answering questions.

He made it back to the ranch as a Suburban full of quilting club ladies and driven by Bonnie arrived.

He greeted them with a tip of his hat, then strolled to the rear of the vehicle, grabbing the uniform boxes as soon as Bonnie popped the trunk. "How much do I owe you?"

Bonnie flicked a hand. "Not a dime. My husband's rifle club pitched in for the fabric."

"Wow. That was incredibly thoughtful."

She smiled. "They were happy to do it. Said they loved how Sage Creek is honoring our veterans and that they wanted to play a part."

That was one of the many things he loved about this town. They were always quick to celebrate local heroes. He couldn't help but feel the pressure knowing his team would be presenting the main entertainment, with a new and largely inexperienced coach, and without Morgan, their star athlete. And there'd be no pas-de-deux finale.

He and Charlotte had talked about finding a way to elevate the rest of their routine but decided against it. The girls were nervous enough.

"Y'all go on in." He stacked the uniform boxes on top of each other. "I've got these."

"Thank you, hon." Barbara, an elderly lady with short silver hair that sprang from her head in tight coils, smiled. Hands on her hips, she looked about. "Such a beautiful day."

"Minus the ninety-degree temp, sure." Bonnie laughed and led the way to the arena chattering about it being so hot a person could fry chicken on the sidewalk.

Charlotte must've told the girls about the uniforms, because the moment he and the quilting crew entered, they stopped what they were doing and half jogged, half bounced over.

Bonnie offered a slight smile in response to their repeated "Let me see!"

"I hope you like them. We haven't had much experience working with Lycra."

Placing a hand on the woman's shoulder, Charlotte gave a gentle smile. "I'm sure they're wonderful."

And they were. Perfectly matching, and exactly like the sketches he and Charlotte had agreed upon, without a stitch out of place or crooked seam. Equally thrilled, the girls resumed their bouncing, their excited voices high-pitched and punctuated by giggles.

Their joy was contagious, and his gratitude for these women who had invested so much time and love into his team felt almost overwhelming.

"All right, now," he said. "Go try them on already."

With more enthusiastic chatter, the girls pranced off toward the tack room they sometimes used for changing.

Holding up one last uniform, this one considerably smaller than the others, Bonnie looked at Gianna, who stood a few paces away, watching. Thankfully, she showed no sign of overstimulation, despite the teenagers' increased energy.

"This is for you," Bonnie said.

Gianna's face lit up and she rushed forward. "I am a vaulter, too." The pride in her expression warmed him clear through. "I can do the seat, where you hold your arms out like this."

"I see." Amusement danced in Bonnie's eyes. "I can't wait to see you perform."

Charlotte's eyes widened. "Oh, she won't be—"

Xavier stopped her with a hand on her arm and a look he hoped communicated they'd talk about this later. Because after seeing his daughter's pure joy at being included, and valued as an athlete, he knew he'd do whatever he could to keep her hopes from getting dashed.

A determination magnified when Gianna went straight for the mechanical horse to show the women her moves.

He motioned Charlotte out of earshot. "I think we should let her perform." He explained the arrangements he'd made with the lighting team. "She can wear her noise-canceling headphones, and the fireworks won't go off until after we finish our gig."

She bit her bottom lip, worry lines stretching across her delicate forehead. "I don't know. What if she has a meltdown while on the horse?"

"How about if you ride with her? Then you could use this as a way to promote your program."

She scoffed. "If we ever get it off the ground, you mean?"

"My offer of partnership still stands. Merging could benefit both businesses."

That gave him an idea—a potential solution to all of their concerns, those surrounding Gianna especially.

CHARLOTTE STRUGGLED TO make sense of Xavier's words. Clearly he was no longer upset with her for how she'd deceived him. But dare she also believe that maybe, just maybe, he was open to more? Wasn't that the direction they'd been heading, before the farrier visit?

If so, then what? Were they to merge not just their businesses but their lives as well, she'd had to leave Gianna. That was something she'd never do. And it seemed like a real jerk move to take the child from her sister, especially after all Rachel had done. She'd opened her home when their parents had booted Charlotte out, agreeing to the only parenting arrangement that made sense at the time.

At the cost of her marriage.

Not that any man who could leave a woman because of a special needs child, or who couldn't fall in love with someone as wonderful as Gianna, was worth holding on to.

Still, her sister had been nothing but faithful. How could Charlotte respond to Rachel's loyalty with such betrayal?

Maybe things would be different once Gianna became an adult.

Thirteen years was a horribly long time to wait.

"Hey." Xavier nudged her arm with his. "What's got your brain waves all in a kink?"

"Just thinking."

"Looks to me more like fretting." He offered her the boyish smile that had stolen her heart so long ago, and still did. "You worried about tomorrow night? Because the girls are going to be great. I have no doubt."

"It's not that. It's just..." *I wish I could go back to the day I first learned I was pregnant and do it all over.* She'd thought God was offering her a second chance, but Scripture said His gifts came without trouble attached. From where she stood, her and Xavier's relationship came with a truckload of problems.

But the Bible also said all things were possible with God.

Xavier's phone rang, and he pulled it from his back pocket. Glancing at the screen, he frowned. "My one o'clock. Probably calling to cancel her lesson this afternoon. Then again, gaining an hour won't hurt me none. Catch you later?"

She nodded and turned toward the cardio area, where a couple of the girls were doing planks with Gianna. The teenagers' kindness touched her, as did her daughter's response. Gianna obviously adored the attention, and the sense of inclusion.

Perhaps Xavier was right. Maybe she should allow Gianna to perform with the team.,

So long as Rachel agreed.

But they wouldn't be able to talk about that until this evening, as Charlotte had numerous errands to run. That included making copies of all the text messages between her and Rachel and Drew Mason in their attempts to get him to actually do his job. She also needed to buy groceries and a thank-you card and chocolates for the quilting ladies. She still couldn't believe how beautiful the uniforms had turned out.

Or that they had made one for Gianna.

After dropping off Gianna at speech therapy, Charlotte grabbed a bagel and dashed back into the car. As she was paying for a tank of gas, using money earned through coaching—praise God for that—a snippet of a conversation between two customers caught her attention. From the sounds of it, someone had bought the older woman an edible bouquet to thank her for something kind she had done.

Charlotte should do the same for the quilting crew. She couldn't afford anything fancy, but she could certainly make them something, like those treats in jars she sometimes saw displayed on social media. Gianna could help.

She'd love that, as would the ladies, knowing her daughter had contributed.

Hustling back to the grocery store, she purchased chocolate bars, graham crackers, heavy cream and marshmallows, and found pretty ribbon on clearance at the sewing store.

"What're you making?"

She turned to see Mrs. Cuevas, Gianna's Sunday school teacher, standing behind her. "Hello." She smiled and explained her project.

"What a lovely idea, and such a beautiful way to allow your niece to give back. I must say, I'm really looking forward to watching her in the Fourth of July performance. I mean, all of the girls, of course, but Gianna holds a special place in my heart."

"Oh, I'm not sure if… Who mentioned her involvement?"

"Bonnie," Mrs. Cuevas said. "What a brilliant way to increase her confidence and help her feel included. I know every family must make their own choices, and as you know, every child is different."

Charlotte nodded.

"But I read something in a forum that about broke my heart. The mom was wanting her autistic child to join a soccer team, but her husband refused. I don't think the woman ever specified why, but were I to guess, I'd say the man was acting out of fear. Seems that's always what holds us back when God opens a door of blessing before us."

The woman's statement hit Charlotte on two levels. Mrs. Cuevas was right. Her daughter deserved to feel like a part of a team. And she'd been working so incredibly hard, practicing her seat and, lately, kneeling. Yes, the event could feel overstimulating. As could school, or a visit the stables, or the library. But Xavier was working hard to reduce the visual noise by ensuring the lights stayed low-key. And Gianna's headphones would drown out the crowd.

Besides, what was the worst that could happen? Her daughter might experience a meltdown from which Charlotte could talk her down.

As opposed to being excluded from something she'd longed to participate in and a team to whom she felt she belonged?

She smiled at Mrs. Cuevas. "I appreciate you sharing that story with me." Her statement regarding fear also encouraged Charlotte to boldly follow how God seemed to be leading when it came to Xavier. Yes, their situation was complicated—to say the least. But surely there was a way to hold tight to the man without losing the child.

Mrs. Cuevas took both of Charlotte's hands in hers. "You and your sister are doing a great job with that sweet girl. I hope you know that."

Rachel. The woman Gianna called Mom.

That was the biggest snag Charlotte hadn't yet figured out how to address.

But fretting about all that now would only sour her afternoon with her daughter. Mentally casting her concerns onto God, she parked in front of Gianna's speech therapy center and got out. Ten minutes later, they were singing along with one of her daughter's favorite Southern gospel songs pouring from the radio.

Envisioning a lovely afternoon in the kitchen with Gianna, she turned onto her property.

She blinked, nervous energy bubbling in her gut as her eyes fell on Xavier's truck parked in front of the house. Why was he here? Had Mrs. Wolfe stirred up more trouble? Or had something happened with one of their horses?

She rolled her eyes at her catastrophizing. The man was probably here to talk through last-minute details.

Or, maybe, just maybe, to ask her out on an actual date? Not that either of them had time for that, with the event so close. But a woman could daydream.

"Can I play outside?" Gianna started unfastening herself from her booster seat the moment Charlotte parked.

She looked at the clock on the dash. "For a bit, yes." Some fresh air and butterfly scouting would do her daughter good.

Anticipation provoking a smile, she gathered what she could from her trunk and ascended the porch steps.

The door opened before she could reach for the knob, and Xavier almost walked into her. Rachel stood behind him.

"Oh." He smiled at her, although the gesture appeared muted. "Almost bowled you over."

"No worries." Her gaze shot from him to her sister. Noting the sorrow in Rachel's eyes, she looked back at Xavier. "If you'll give me a minute to unload my groceries..."

He rubbed the back of his neck, and the gaiety in his expression evaporated. "I'll lend a hand."

She nodded and proceeded inside while he headed for her open trunk. Pausing in the living room, she turned to Rachel, who was moving toward the hall. "Is everything all right?"

With a slight shake of her head, her sister shuffled, shoulders hunched, toward her bedroom and closed her door.

Anxiety knotted Charlotte's stomach as realization hit. Rachel's greatest fears were unfolding. Xavier had come to demand custody, if not full, then joint.

Pain stabbed at the back of her throat. How could he?

Then again, how could he not? He wasn't the type of man to abandon his daughter.

But she'd felt so certain that his desire not to disrupt Gianna's world would overpower his paternal drive to assume the role of father.

Obviously, she'd been wrong. While she couldn't blame him, not really, that didn't make this situation hurt any less.

The creak of the front door announced Xavier's entrance. A moment later, he appeared in the kitchen, carrying her remaining packages.

Walking toward her, he peeked into one of the bags. "Looks like y'all are fixin' to make s'mores."

"Sort of." She explained her gift idea.

"A thoughtful way to show your appreciation. Wish I would've come up with something like that."

"You? In the kitchen?" Her former therapist used to suggest that Charlotte covered difficult emotions with sarcasm. Apparently, she hadn't changed much in that regard. Not that this was the time or place to dig into why Xavier had come and why her sister looked like her favorite horse had died.

Worse, like she was about to lose the child she'd always loved as her own.

"Be nice." Xavier set the items on the table. "I'll have you know I fry up a mean omelet."

His teasing banter almost made her wonder if she'd misread the situation when she first arrived. But his expression seemed…cautious?

Enough pitter-pattering around the ginormous question dominating her brain. Inhaling deep, she turned toward him and leaned against the counter. "So, what brought you out to our very humble ranch?"

His gaze faltered. With a slight cough, he widened his stance and began popping his knuckles, a clear sign that something was up. "Had some questions is all."

"About?"

"You done much advertising for your therapy deal yet?"

Was he trying to shift the conversation, or was that why he'd come? He had suggested they use the Fourth event to promote their program. Yet, if that's why he'd come, why had Rachel looked so upset?

Father, can you please untangle this for me? Don't make me choose between my daughter, my sister and the man I love.

CHAPTER SEVENTEEN

THE DAY BEFORE the Fourth of July celebration, Xavier hired a couple of high school boys to tackle ranch chores so he could focus on final event details. He'd already cleared his schedule of riding lessons. While that'd cut into his finances, if all went according to plan tomorrow, the lost income would be more than worth it.

Charlotte was managing the team well, and the girls seemed more than prepared—and excited—for their performance. Thankfully, they and their moms hadn't agreed with Mrs. Wolfe's accusations. Like Bonnie, they'd become accustomed the woman's vinegar. He should've known they'd remain supportive.

Xavier stopped by the arena to offer encouragement, but didn't linger as much as he wanted. Partially, because he simply didn't have the time. But also because Charlotte knew all his tells and would puzzle out his surprise, if given opportunity.

A surprise with one major thread still to unravel.

After parking in the grocery store lot, he grabbed his phone and navigated to Rachel's contact. His finger hovered over the blue phone icon. How he wanted to push! But doing so could easily nudge her in the opposite direction.

He knew he was asking a lot. Hopefully she could see that he had a lot to give, as well. This could be the best scenario for all of them.

Stepping out into the hot midafternoon sun, he pocketed his keys and followed an elderly couple past an outside display of plants and into the produce section. Eighties country music poured from overhead speakers. A blast of cold air carried the scent of melon and fried chicken. Both made his mouth water, reminding him that it was now well past lunch.

And that half of his day was gone—with a long list of to-dos he still needed to tackle.

The store manager offered a smile as Xavier passed.

He tipped his hat in greeting and scanned the signs above the aisles. Coffee and condiments. Bread. Pasta. Baking. He found the office supplies at the far end, with the greeting cards. Following the list Mandi had texted him, he placed markers, large letter stencils and three poster boards in his cart. He grabbed extra for potential oopses.

His phone chimed, and Mandi's number flashed on the screen, along with "Did you get everything?"

He chuckled and responded with a yep, hoping she and the others would keep quiet about everything. All it'd take was for them to tell one person, and his little surprise would sprout wings faster than a cocooned caterpillar.

Thoughts of emerging butterflies reminded him of Gianna and how she'd blossomed in the short time since he'd known her. Crazy to think that less than a month ago he hadn't known she existed. Now, he knew he couldn't imagine life without her.

Or her mother.

At the checkout counter, Mrs. Hendrickson, the cashier, eyed his items with a raised brow. "Crafting, are we?"

Face flushed, he cleared his throat—grateful he'd vetoed the glittery heart stickers the girls had urged him to buy. "Just working on a project."

"Oh. Right. For the festivities tomorrow?"

That was a question he could honestly answer. Nodding, he handed her two crisp bills, asked about her husband and bid her have a great day.

The team—all except for Gianna and Morgan—and two moms were waiting for him at his ranch. And they'd clearly vetoed his veto. They must've had at least five packages of stickers, all red or pink, spread out on his porch.

"It won't be cheesy," Mandi said. "Promise."

Mandi's mom, Mrs. Boyd, took his bag and rummaged through it. Seeing the stencils, she made the most exaggerated frown that he couldn't help but laugh. "We don't need this. We're doing bubble letters. They're way cuter."

He chuckled. "That's the look you're going for?"

"You need balloons," Mandi said. "And flowers."

The other girls squealed and voiced their agreement.

He scratched his jaw, envisioning the moment. "You're right. That'd be a great touch. Guess I'm heading back to the store."

"I'll call the Stoughtons." Mrs. Boyd grabbed her phone. "They grow the most beautiful wildflowers for their honeybees. They'd be thrilled to donate a couple bouquets to the cause."

"At the risk of widening our 'who knows' pool," he said.

"Pshaw." Mrs. Boyd waved off the notion. "They know how to keep a secret."

He scrubbed a hand over his face. How had he gotten roped into this? Or more accurately, how had he lassoed himself and his athletes into this? But they'd been far too perceptive, and insistent, and what began as fairy-tale-like talk between a bunch of teenage girls had turned into, well, this.

"You go on and do whatever you need to." Mandi's mom waved a hand. "We've got this."

Knowing he'd only get in their way, he thanked them, told them to help themselves to anything in the kitchen and ambled off to the stables to see what the teen boys had accomplished. He was in the middle of listening to a story about a horse that dropped his hay in his water barrel before eating it when his phone pinged with a text.

The number flashing on his screen immediately accelerated his pulse.

He was really doing this. About to make the best, or most embarrassing and devastating, move of his life.

He'd sure feel a lot better about all this if he knew Rachel was on board.

And if not? If she told him to pound sand?

If he thought about that now, he'd lose all his nerve.

Some might find him foolish, maybe even childish, letting a group of teenagers play such a big role in one of the most important moments in his life. But his creative skills were near nonexistent, and so he'd follow their lead, praying God would make much of his little. Plus, it just felt right letting them be involved, considering how much they meant to both him and Charlotte.

Whistling a made-up tune, he hustled to make it to the florist before she closed.

A bell chimed above him as he entered the fragrant store, filled with bouquets and greenery of every variety, revolving racks of cards, shelves with candy and candles and soft instrumental music. Heart-shaped, birthday and smiley balloons flanked the counter lining the back wall.

"Well, hello there." Jaycie Opitz, the storeowner, stepped out from behind a display of picture frames and inspirational phrases engraved in wood.

"Ma'am." He tipped his hat. "How's business?"

"Busy." She laughed. "And I'm grateful for it. Let me guess—you're here to buy roses for your team." His confusion must've shown on his face, because she added, "For tomorrow night?"

He frowned. "Is that a thing?"

She nodded. "A lot of people do that for their friends and loved ones after a play, ballet, recital or the like."

"I see." As if his preparations for that night weren't complicated enough. He wanted to honor the girls, especially if that was the customary thing to do, but would that steal the impact of his plans?

He needed to figure out a way to do both.

He eyed a row of vases with pink, peach and red flowers. "Something like this?" He noticed the price tag, multiplied it by ten and winced.

"You could go with that, although most people buy a single rose for each performer."

He smiled. "That'll work." Then, hoping he didn't trigger Jaycie's curiosity, he selected an equal number of balloons.

Eyebrows raised, she slipped behind the cash register. "Your athletes are going to be blown away."

He chuckled. "Good." No need to correct her assumption.

"Although, you might want to pick these up tomorrow. The helium will leak out."

"Oh." He frowned, mentally running through his already very full day. But he'd make it work. "Okay."

"You know, we can always have these delivered. I'm sure you'll be quite busy getting ready for the performance and all."

He smiled. "That would be helpful."

After making the arrangements, he paid and headed to the next stop on his list, grinning like a kid about to mount his first stallion.

Knowing he was about to experience the ride of his life, or land face down in the dirt, he swallowed his fear to make room for hope.

SITTING AT THE kitchen table, Charlotte reviewed the minute-by-minute outline for the Fourth of July event. The schedule was tight. She'd need to make sure the girls were on task and their horse ready to go—and their environment spook-free.

Had Dolly performed in front of a crowd before? With people cheering and lights flashing?

Of course she had. Xavier wouldn't place the girls, or Gianna, on a horse with any degree of unpredictability.

She glanced at the child through the kitchen archway. After spending a good hour practicing her vaulting moves on the couch armrest, she now sat in her "safe area" with her iPad.

Father, thank You for all the ways You have expanded Gianna's world. And for allowing her to get to know her dad. Watching those two together felt bittersweet, a beautiful gift that triggered a longing for more. *Please let this event be a good experience for her.*

Xavier said he'd talked with the venue team to ensure they kept the visual and auditory noise to a minimum. Asking them to delay fireworks would help, as would her weighted lap pad, headphones and the wraparound sunglasses Charlotte had purchased online. Besides, they'd be riding together.

The night could actually turn out quite special, a shared experience she'd always cherish.

Thankfully, the cultural committee had secured a volunteer photographer. Charlotte would pay her to snap a few photos of her and Gianna.

She checked the time on the microwave, then walked into the living room. She squatted to her daughter's level. "Gianna?"

The child glanced up, made eye contact for a brief moment, then looked back at her iPad.

"Ten minutes until you leave for speech therapy." She transitioned best when given timed warnings.

"And then I get to pick a book from the library."

"Correct." Some might call their constant bartering spoiling the child, but she preferred to think of it as training the art of negotiation. And appealing to Gianna's sense of fairness helped ward off potential meltdowns.

She stood and glanced about. Where was Rachel? Last she

heard, she was leaving to weed their relatively nonexistent garden—a sign that she was upset about something.

She'd been acting pensive ever since that day Xavier came out. Whatever they'd discussed had completely thrown her, and the fact that she wasn't talking to Charlotte suggested it had to do with Gianna.

Rachel likely blamed her for whatever he'd requested, and it wasn't hard to figure out what that might be.

With a sigh, she stepped outside to search for her sister to see if she'd changed her mind about taking their daughter to speech therapy. About to round the house, she stopped. Rachel was talking with someone. She peeked around the corner and strained her ears.

On the phone, her sister sat on the back porch, leaning against their siding, and her tone indicated she wasn't happy. Not that she had been lately.

"Can we meet at Wilma's?" she said. "I have some questions, and I really feel like this is something we should discuss in person."

She was probably talking to their lawyer. He, and Drew Mason, could be the cause of Rachel's increased moodiness. That situation increased Charlotte's anxiety as well, which was why she tried hard not to think about it—or all the money they'd spent and would have to pay back to the bank.

"Thanks, Xavier," Rachel said. "I'll see you in about twenty minutes."

Charlotte froze, her chest tight. So her initial suspicion had been correct.

Obviously, whatever they'd been speaking about, now and when he'd come to the house, was serious. Why hadn't they said anything to her?

She could only think of one reason, and it made her feel ill.

Darting back inside before Rachel could catch her eavesdropping, she resisted the urge to pace as she thought of a way to broach the subject.

What if, after her conversation with Xavier, Rachel became so upset, or felt so threatened, she pressured Charlotte to quit coaching and to bring the horses to their ranch?

Once Rachel and Gianna left for Wilma's, and after a lengthy internal debate, Charlotte decided to follow so she could watch their meeting through the diner window. Maybe she could glean some information from their body language, or slip inside, feigning coincidence.

Then they'd have to tell her what was going on.

Standing outside Wilma's thirty minutes later, she strained for a better view of Rachel and Xavier. Unfortunately, she couldn't see their faces, although their postures appeared tense. Should she go in, pretend she came for a midafternoon snack and casually invite herself to join them? And then, offhandedly ask why they were meeting?

Would they be honest? If Xavier truly cared about her, yes.

She moved toward the door, then dropped her hand with a huff. Why was she so nervous?

Probably because she was acting like a spying middle schooler.

Maybe she didn't want to know why Xavier and Rachel were meeting. Not if they were discussing custody issues.

If Xavier took Gianna from Rachel, even part-time, she'd never forgive Charlotte. And he could feel equally resentful toward her if Rachel refused to allow him the parental access he craved.

Their strained conversation could easily turn ugly. And she would land smack in the center between the sister who had always been there for her and the man who'd wanted to be.

Needing a temporary distraction to untangle her knotted emotions, she scanned the storefronts lining Main Street. Directly across from her was the hardware store and next to it a sewing machine and vacuum repair place. An antiques store was to her left, and then the public library, with shelves full of women's fiction and contemporary romance novels.

Inviting her to momentarily lose herself in a world that promised a happily-ever-after.

If only life held the same guarantee.

Proceeding to the library, she moved aside to let two women with strollers pass, then stepped inside one of her favorite spaces in Sage Creek. Apparently, they were hosting some event or club because the tables near the back were filled with women, some she recognized from church.

"Charlotte, hello."

She turned at Elsie's familiar voice with a smile. "Elsie. How are you?"

Elsie shrugged. "Either working hard or hardly working. I haven't decided which."

Charlotte laughed. "Any new books you suggest I read?"

"Girl, don't get me started." Launching into a recap of her top favorites, she led the way to a shelf displaying the staff's top picks, then left Charlotte to peruse in peace.

She was reading the back of a historical set in Amish country when another voice she recognized said her name.

Jaw tight, she faced Mrs. Wolfe with a forced smile. "Nadia. How is Morgan doing?" The question slipped from her mouth before her brain caught up, warning her that she might've poked at the woman's bitterness over the injury.

But Charlotte cared about the teen and truly wanted to know.

Mrs. Wolfe's face was void of its normal edge. She even looked a bit uneasy, almost vulnerable. "Actually, I was hoping to talk to you about her."

"Okay?"

"I saw the way you comforted her, the night of…well, you know." She waved a hand, her gaze faltering. "And she told me how you defended me."

Charlotte frowned. "I did?"

Mrs. Wolfe nodded. "You told her that I love her. When you could've spoken in anger."

In other words, slandered the woman as she had done to her and Xavier. But doing so not only would've dishonored Christ; it would've hurt Morgan as well, a girl that was already wounded enough.

"I understand you want what's best for your daughter," Charlotte said. The woman might have a dysfunctional way of showing it, but beneath her hurtful behavior was a mom who had once held baby Morgan in her arms and dreamed of what she might grow up to become.

That maternal longing was something Charlotte and Mrs. Wolfe shared, and that was the commonality she chose to focus on now, because she trusted God was behind this unexpected encounter.

She felt it deep in her soul.

Glancing at the floor, Mrs. Wolfe rotated the bracelet on her arm. "She also told me what happened, the day she got hurt. That none of the girls were to get on the equipment while you were gone, and how she'd been trying to impress the boys."

Charlotte chuckled softly. "Teenagers."

"Indeed. I'm sorry I blamed you."

The apology loosened the knot in her stomach, allowing her to offer a genuine smile. "I forgive you."

Mrs. Wolfe's face brightened. "You're a gracious woman." She paused. "My daughter also told me that you assured her she could still participate tomorrow, if she chose?"

A burst of joy filled her heart. "Absolutely. Would she like to do that?"

"If there's a way, yes. With her knee in a brace."

"I'm sure we can figure something out." She'd need to talk with Xavier, but she was confident he'd feel the same way. Regardless of how he might feel about Mrs. Wolfe, he cared for her daughter.

His, as well. And just like that, she was back to fretting about his conversation with Rachel and the problems she'd created for them.

She needed to get back to the diner before the two of them finished their conversation and left—and she missed her opportunity to slyly catch Xavier on his way out.

What she'd do then, she didn't know.

She told Mrs. Wolfe she'd call her after deciding the best way to include Morgan in the performance, then politely excused herself to hustle back to the Wilma's. She entered as they were getting up to leave.

She approached with what she hoped was a casual smile. "Hey. What are you two doing here?"

Xavier's face flushed, and he looked to Rachel, then back to Charlotte. "We were just talking business stuff."

"Oh? Such as…?" His body language indicated the conversation went deeper, and that he was hiding something.

He cleared his throat. "Your horses, the stables. That sort of thing." Rubbing the back of his neck, he gazed toward the street. "I best get going. I've got a meeting with the cultural committee to go over last-minute details."

"Speaking of…" Charlotte relayed her conversation with Morgan.

He frowned. "I don't see how she could mount or dismount. Although, Jon and Katey have an old-fashioned carriage we could use."

"That would be great. Decorated with a Fourth of July theme."

His face relaxed into a genuine smile. "Perfect." He scratched his jaw, and once again, glanced around. "I'll catch you tomorrow at the event?"

She nodded. "The girls and I will be there by four thirty. That'll give them time for a brief rehearsal and to get dressed."

"Sounds good." His gaze shot to Rachel, and a hint of nervousness tightened his expression—convincing Charlotte more than ever that the two of them had been talking about a lot more than business.

The fact that neither of them showed any indication of letting Charlotte in stung.

Xavier might've forgiven her for her deception regarding Gianna, but she'd obviously destroyed whatever trust she'd rebuilt.

CHAPTER EIGHTEEN

XAVIER SCANNED THE dozen or so crew members hustling about the indoor arena in preparation for the night's event. A handful of guys were setting up large, portable lights—their supervisor had assured him again that they wouldn't blast them during Gianna's portion of the event. A group of sound technicians were gathered behind a table adorned with patriotic ribbons and miniature flags set in glass containers filled with clear marbles. The bleachers and support beams gleamed with red, white and blue.

A sharp whistle got his attention, followed by the event coordinator's voice booming through the sound system, calling everyone to his booth. The man, Mark Armstead, was affectionately referred to as the refrigerator because he had the frame of a defensive lineman and the appetite to match.

He thanked everyone for being there and for all their hard work, then handed them each a schedule. "Doors open at six ten. Folks will have twenty minutes to buy snacks and find their seats. Then Perry will kick things off with a welcome and what not." He motioned toward the tall, broad-shouldered man standing beside him in a plaid button-up shirt, charcoal cowboy hat and matching boots. He'd graduated high school a couple of years after Xavier. "Unfortunately, Pastor Roger came down with a stomach bug and won't be able to make it."

That had to bum him out. He looked forward to these types of things and the opportunity to make others, the town's veterans especially, feel special and appreciated.

"Then Perry will introduce Sage Creek High's marching band and flag team," Mark said.

Those kids had talent and would be a tough act to follow. Not that this was a competition, by any means, but their precision could amplify any timing mistakes or rough mess-ups made by his team.

The fact that he thought this way, rather than celebrating the students' giftedness, demanded a heart check. *God, may I never become so blinded by my ambition that I begin to see people—kids, no less—as threats.*

It had to be nerves making him feel that way. He focused back on Mark in time to catch his explanation of the slide show presentation honoring each of the town's vets, including those who'd passed. It would be projected on large screens while the band played.

"Then they'll line up along both sides of the arena while Annie Hentz, a local senior, sings the national anthem."

One of the light crew guys gave a low whistle. "That girl's got a voice. Great job looping her in."

Next came Xavier's place in the itinerary. "Your girls will have exactly thirty minutes, after which Annie will come back out, and we'll invite everyone to join her in singing 'America the Beautiful.'"

An older man from the facilities team thumped his chest. "That one gets me every time."

Xavier could relate. There was something deeply touching about reflecting upon the cost for a person's freedom, and the tangible reminder each national hero, alive or dead, provided of the Savior's love. As Scripture said, no one could display a greater love than to lay down their life for another.

After Mark answered remaining questions and led them all in prayer for God's blessings, Xavier dashed out to find Mandi's mom, who had agreed to help coordinate his plans.

He found her and her daughter pacing in the back hallway near the bathrooms.

They glanced up as he approached.

"You're not nervous, are you, kiddo?" He could relate, for the same reasons and then some. Tonight would provide the perfect opportunity to showcase his skills as a trainer, thereby countering whatever nonsense Mrs. Wolfe had tried to spread. Plus, this event could lead to more paid performances to come.

But it was his plans relating to Charlotte that had him feeling as jittery as a yearling worked in the corral for the first time.

Mandi gave a sheepish smile. "Just hoping I don't fall off and do a face-plant in front of everyone."

"Nah," he said. "You're well prepared."

Taking a deep breath, she rubbed the back of her neck with both hands. "When's everyone else getting here?"

"Y'all need to meet me in the cattle barn for warm-ups and a quick run through at five thirty, then be back here, dressed and ready to rock and roll, at six thirty sharp."

He looked at the time on his phone. He'd received a text from Charlotte. Suppressing the schoolboy grin she always seemed to trigger, he clicked on her message.

Did you get a chance to eat yet?

Chuckling, he responded. As in real food? Or do potato chips and a beef jerky stick count?

I'm making sandwiches for Gianna and me. She's used to having supper at 6:00 pm. Figured now wasn't the time to switch things up on her. You like tuna salad?

The fact that she'd thought of him sent a surge of warmth through his chest. And increased his confidence regarding how she might respond at…precisely 7:00 p.m.

His text back, You know I'll never turn down food, earned him two emojis, one a smiling face, the other laughter with tears dropping from each eye.

He started to return his cell to his back pocket when another notification chimed, this one from the florist, letting him know she'd arrived with his balloons. And right on time. He might've given himself more cushion than necessary, but he'd worried Charlotte might arrive early and ruin the surprise.

Although he did have a plausible story to sell, just in case.

He relayed the information to Mrs. Boyd.

Smiling, she shot him a thumbs-up. "On it. Tell her I'll meet her at the east entrance. Mrs. Stoughton's bringing the flowers?"

"Yep."

She'd probably assumed he wanted the bouquets for the performance, and while he did, it wasn't in the way she thought. Although he felt badly for misleading her, the fewer people who knew about his plans, the less likely word would get out prematurely.

With that covered, he called Haiven's mom to make sure she and the others had the poster boards ready.

She answered right away. "Hello, Romeo."

He gave an awkward laugh. "Ma'am."

He only had himself to blame for her teasing, considering that he'd roped her and nearly the entire team into helping him tonight. But he'd desperately needed their creativity. Not to mention, he never would've had the time to pull off even half of what they'd accomplished had he attempted to do it all alone.

"We're walking in now," she said.

They'd arranged to meet in the same place he'd told Mrs. Boyd. "Heading that way."

He arrived as they were entering, Haiven carrying butcher paper rolled around two wooden dowels. "What's this?" He glanced at the other girls who were with them. Dressed in T-shirts and hoodies, they were each carrying duffel bags but not poster board that he could see.

"We wanted our sign to be big enough for people to actually read," Haiven's mom said. "I know the tech crew will show it on the big screen." Brow furrowed, she angled her head. "Won't they?"

He frowned. That was something he hadn't considered. "I don't know. I 'spect so? The tech guys brought video cameras."

She smiled. "Good."

"Want to see what we made?" Haiven bounced in front of him, the other girls copying.

He laughed. His amusement at their enthusiasm helped temper some of his nerves. At least the banner they'd made would do the speaking for him. Otherwise, he'd probably make a fool of himself stumbling over his words—on camera.

Wait. This would all be taped.

What if she rejected him? In front of all of Sage Creek.

"Hey." Haiven gave him a slight shove. "Don't go turning scaredy-cat on us."

The concerned looks on the girls' faces assured him of how disappointed they'd be were he to let his insecurities win. And he'd feel equally frustrated with himself.

He'd never been one to play the coward and he wasn't about to start now. Not when it came to Charlotte Murphy. Nor would he let fears of getting hurt keep him from building a life with her and their daughter.

"I'm psyched," he said. "And grateful for everything you all have done."

"You haven't seen what we made yet," Haiven said. "You could hate it."

"I doubt that." He motioned to the banner. "Show me already."

She glanced behind her as if ensuring Charlotte wasn't approaching, then began unrolling the wooden dowels. When they became wider than her arm span, she handed one side to a teammate. Together they unveiled their purple, pink, red and bubbly lettered creation.

The colorful cardboard *"I-heart-U"* forming a garland dangling from each side reminded him of the way Charlotte used to decorate his locker before football games. The afternoon before, she'd get one of her friends to drive her to his school, and together, they'd tack up posters with lollipops and mini-candy bars taped onto them. Then, they'd head to the football field to watch him practice.

His friends had teased him, but he hadn't cared. He'd figured they were just jealous because they didn't have a girlfriend like Charlotte. She'd always made him feel like her favorite person in the world and frequently assured him he was.

Now it was his turn to make her feel just as special.

To let her know just how much he loved her, and how miserable he'd be without her.

WHEN CHARLOTTE REACHED the cattle barn with Gianna, she was surprised to see the entire team and numerous moms already there.

Then again, this was the biggest event they'd performed at, and not just because the city valued their skills enough to pay them. They were also expecting a packed-out arena, a total of 1,200 people—half the town, and all the space could hold.

The teenagers' giddy excitement, and the way they burst into giggles whenever they looked at Charlotte or Xavier, revealed their delight to make them proud. It felt good to know she'd played a part in building their confidence.

Gianna's as well. She'd never seen her stand so tall, or such joy glimmer in her eyes.

Charlotte handed her daughter her favorite cup, also known as the only one she'd drink from, and filled it with milk from a thermos. Once Gianna sat cross-legged on the ground, she gave her one of the sandwiches, brought another to Xavier and kept one for herself.

"Thanks." He grinned as if she'd provided a rib eye.

"You must really like tuna salad," she teased.

"Made by you, absolutely."

"Right. Because I'm known for my culinary skills." She used to joke that, were they to marry, they'd need to hire a chef, otherwise they'd starve. To which he'd reply, "No one else I'd rather waste away with." She'd roll her eyes as if she'd found his words corny when they'd only increased her love for him.

Back then, she'd felt certain she had the sweetest, most attentive boyfriend in all of Sage Creek. This realization, and all she'd lost and feared she'd never experience again, had led to countless tears.

But now she was here, once again spending nearly every day with the man who had stolen her heart so completely that she knew she could never give it to anyone else.

As much as she longed for more, she was grateful for their friendship and hopeful that given time, he'd forgive her for keeping Gianna secret.

"All right, now." She raised her voice above their silly chatter. "Let's run through warm-ups."

"I'll get Dolly." Xavier jogged off and returned with the horse as the team made their last lap around the barn.

By then, the high school marching band and drill team had arrived and filled half the space. But this still left the girls plenty of room to run through some of their most challenging moves.

While Mandi practiced her dismount, Charlotte stepped closer to Xavier. "Any news on the carriage?"

His phone chimed, and he glanced at the screen. "Matter of fact, Jon and Katey are here now." He read the message, then tapped a response. "What about Morgan?"

"I told her she didn't need to come until six, since she won't have to rehearse."

"Makes sense."

"You nervous?"

"About the performance?" He shrugged. "A bit." His gaze latched onto hers with such intensity she almost thought he was about to kiss her.

Would he have, if not for the barn full of people?

A flutter swept through her as heat flooded her face.

A loud whistle drew everyone's attention to the front, where a massive man in dark jeans and a button-up shirt decorated with numerous flags stood waving his arms. He thanked everyone for coming, reminded them to remain punctual, then called the marching band forward.

Charlotte felt like a thousand centipedes were doing acrobatics in her stomach. She glanced toward the opposite entrance. Where was Morgan? Had her mom decided not to come after all? Although, considering the carriage still hadn't arrived, maybe their delay wasn't so bad.

While Mrs. Wolfe had demonstrated obvious contrition, Charlotte didn't want anything to reignite the woman's anger or sense of injustice. She started to ask Xavier to check on his friend when the guy, Morgan and her mom entered together, already seated in the horse-pulled carriage.

Xavier hurried over. Charlotte followed and listened as he thanked Jon, then relayed the event timeline to Morgan.

The teen's grin was contagious.

Nadia looked from Xavier to Charlotte with teary eyes. "Thank you for this."

"Of course." Xavier's tone radiated warmth. "Couldn't perform without our star athlete." He gave Morgan a high five.

She responded with a sheepish laugh. "Some star." She placed her hands on either side of her braced knee, then looked past them to her teammates. "I need to talk to Mandi's mom." A spark of mischief lit her eyes. Xavier's gaze pinged to Charlotte's with a hint of a smile he was clearly trying to squelch.

He cleared his throat. "No problem." With a quick glance at his phone, he faced Charlotte. "Should we remind Gianna of what to expect tonight?"

Spoken like a protective father.

The thought reminded her of his meeting with Rachel, reviving the swarm of insects in her gut. But she refused to allow her anxiety over whatever he and her sister had talked about to dampen this evening and the joy of seeing her daughter participate in her first-ever performance.

She accompanied Xavier as he approached Gianna, waited while he encouraged her, then reviewed their plans using the arena drawing she'd sketched.

Then came their turn.

Charlotte remained with Gianna as the rest of the team lined up behind Xavier and Dolly.

She pulled her daughter's headphones and wraparound sunglasses from her duffel bag. "You ready?"

Grinning, her daughter sprang to her feet. "Yes. We will ride on Dolly together. I will be in front. I will do my seat with my back straight and my arms out." She demonstrated, and, chin raised, repeated word for word what Charlotte had told her.

"That's right." Her daughter's confidence and the joy radiating from her eyes filled Charlotte's heart.

They followed as Xavier led Dolly and the girls into the

arena entrance. Jayda approached the horse, released a heavy breath and jiggled her arms and legs.

Charlotte wrapped an arm around her waist and gave a gentle squeeze. "Remember, it's just you and Dolly."

Jayda smiled and nodded. "Brownie points for going first, right?"

She laughed. "With ice cream. And sprinkles."

Offering a prayer of blessing, she watched the teen she'd come to love mount and rise to her knees as she entered the arena. When the band, now sitting in a designated section behind the announcer, shifted tempo, Jayda performed a half mill to reverse positions.

Rotating sideways with one arm extended, she knelt, one leg on the saddle, her other foot on Dolly's neck, then bracing with her knee, extended a leg behind her. It was an exciting opening that led to enthusiastic applause.

Standing beside Charlotte, Gianna gave commentary on each move, learned from all the practices and YouTube videos she'd watched.

Charlotte's heart swelled with the joy of living out her passion and connecting with her daughter through it.

She refocused on the arena. *Here it comes.* She tensed as Jayda's most challenging move drew near. Although the teen faced the other way, Charlotte could envision her determined expression as she prepared for the exercise she'd nailed at least a dozen times in practice. *You've got this.*

She held her breath as Jayda grabbed both handles in a partially standing position and extended a leg behind her in a perfect split before performing a wobbly but successful somersault.

"Yes!" Charlotte clapped along with the team's cheers. The proud smile she exchanged with Xavier only deepened her attachment.

Mandi came next, launching into her routine with precision

and artistic flair. The crowd and team hushed as she extended into a handstand before softly rolling onto the horse's back.

"Boom!" Xavier pumped a fist into the air, and he and Charlotte shared a joyous grin.

They turned to Morgan, who sat with her mother in the horse-drawn carriage decorated with red, white and blue ribbon and glittery tulle. Mrs. Wolf's sequined gown complemented her daughter's uniform beautifully.

Tears filled her eyes as they met Charlotte's. "Thank you."

Charlotte smiled. "Of course." She watched, heart full, as the mother and daughter shared an almost sacred moment. Their participation together celebrated not only the event, but the healing God had brought to their relationship, as well.

Then came Charlotte and Gianna's turn.

Xavier's eyes latched onto Charlotte's with a tender affection that flooded her heart with hope.

He squatted to their daughter's eye level. "How's my favorite athlete?" He raised his voice so she could hear through her headphones. "You ready to show those people how it's done?"

Standing taller, expression sober, she nodded.

Five minutes later, utter bliss obliterated Charlotte's anxiety as she sat behind her daughter, circling the arena. Did Xavier feel the same?

She and Gianna were halfway through their third lap when two vaulters pranced out, holding white baskets and scattering stemless flowers upon the ground.

This wasn't part of their routine.

Had Xavier changed things without telling her?

She searched for him among the faces gathered behind the sound booth and near the entrance. Where was he?

Two more of her vaulters trotted out on their personal horses. Each held one side of a rolled sheet of pink butcher paper, Valentine-like garlands dangling from the wooden dowels in their hands.

This wasn't part of their finale or patriotic-themed.

This didn't make sense.

The audience quieted as the girls approached Charlotte. Widening the distance between one another, they slowly unrolled their banner.

Her gasp echoed the crowd as the decorated bubble letters registered in her brain: *Marry me?*

A moment later, Xavier rode out on his black thoroughbred.

Someone whistled, and, with Dolly now stopped, Charlotte instinctively calmed her daughter by tightening her hold on her.

Coming alongside them, Xavier offered a shy smile that squeezed her heart and stole her breath. He was definitely the most handsome man she'd ever met.

And he wanted her.

Tears blurred her vision as he pulled a velvet box from his shirt pocket and opened it to reveal a glimmering oval diamond set in white gold.

"Oh, Xavier."

The intense love radiating from his eyes captivated as he extended his hand, beckoning to hold hers. "What do you say? Will you make me the happiest guy in all of Texas?"

She wanted to say yes, but her thoughts jumped to her sister. "What about Rachel? We can't—" She clamped her mouth shut before verbalizing the words that could upset their daughter.

His grin widened. "Your sister and I worked out an arrangement."

"I don't understand."

"Y'all will move in with me at my ranch. Once we're married, of course."

"All four of us—"

"Yep. One happy family."

She smiled, joy flooding through her. "Sounds like you've taken care of everything."

"Almost." He raised the ring. "Will you marry me, Charlotte Murphy?"

Unable to contain her tears, she nodded. The crowd erupted in one loud cheer that, thankfully, didn't overwhelm Gianna. Perhaps because she was so distracted by the beautiful flowers scattered across the arena ground.

Each was a reminder of Xavier's effort to make his proposal more romantic than she could've imagined.

The celebration they all shared after the event, their hard work come to fruition, the girls bouncing with excitement and the love shared between her and Xavier felt sweeter than anything she'd known.

Back in the barn, he took her hand, intertwined his fingers with hers, pulled her to his side and brushed a feather-light kiss on her cheek. "You did it."

Facing him, she shook her head. "We did it."

He nodded. "We make a great team."

"That we do."

"Um, Ms. Charlotte?"

She turned to see Peyton standing beside her.

"Yes?"

"That guy would like to speak to you." She motioned to where a tall, balding man lingered a few feet away.

He stepped forward as Charlotte turned toward him. "I'm Robert Tolsmon." They shook hands. "President of the All Access Center for Houston, an organization that furthers opportunities for people with disabilities. I'm here visiting my brother. He invited me to the show."

"Thank you for coming."

"I thoroughly enjoyed it. I have an autistic son, and I was deeply moved watching you and your daughter and reading about your equine therapy program in the event brochure. I would like to invest in your mission." He handed her a folded slip of paper.

She unfolded it to reveal a sizable check—enough to more

than compensate for the money she and Rachel had lost to the shady contractor.

Swallowing, she gave her brain a moment to catch up. A lump lodged in her throat. "This is quite generous."

"And well worth the investment." He gave a greeting nod to Xavier, who had joined them. "I meet with the board this month and will suggest we fund your organization, as it aligns well with our vision."

"I don't know what to say."

He offered a playful smile. "Thank you will suffice."

"Thank you!"

Once again, Xavier linked his hand with hers, the spark in his eyes echoing the awe that filled her heart.

Father, You are so, so good. You indeed bring beauty in place of ashes.

EPILOGUE

One year later

CHARLOTTE STOOD IN front of the mirror as Rachel secured a floral and pearl headband in her hair. "I still can't believe you talked Gianna into wearing a dress."

"It helped that we let her pick the fabric. Although I knew not to even attempt formal shoes."

Laughing, Charlotte turned and watched her daughter forming a line on the floor with rose petals from her basket. "I hear sneakers are as bougie as they come." She lifted her foot, revealing matching tennies. "Besides, we are holding the ceremony on a ranch." She sobered. "Did I tell you lately how grateful I am for how supportive you've been? Allowing Gianna to have two moms and a dad." They'd had to introduce the concept to the girl gradually, and patiently answer Gianna's questions—again and again.

So far, she'd adapted well and seemed excited to soon have all her favorite people in one home. Charlotte knew together they could handle Gianna's meltdown, should it occur once their discussion became reality.

Rachel shrugged. "From my perspective, I'm not losing anything. I am gaining a brother-in-law who adores our girl as much as we do, a business partner more knowledgeable about horses than both of us combined and a way out of the money pit we never should've purchased. Praise the Lord that after our closing date on Monday, we'll be free."

And for the full price they'd paid—only by God's grace.

"Where's Xavier's sister?" Rachel asked.

"I'm sure she'll be here soon." Charlotte loved that he'd wanted to include JoEllen in the ceremony. The way her eyes had lit up when he asked her warmed Charlotte's heart just thinking about it.

Rachel excused herself to check that all was going well with the ushers and returned with JoEllen.

Making eye contact, Charlotte smiled. "Your hair looks beautiful." JoEllen had vetoed all the dress options they'd suggested, opting instead for her favorite outfit—leggings and a plain, soft T-shirt. Charlotte wasn't concerned with the attire, so long as her soon-to-be sister-in-law felt comfortable.

JoEllen nodded, looking about, then pulled on her fingertips. "Flowers?"

"Yes, of course." She handed JoEllen her basket filled with silk petals.

Rachel dabbed her forehead, nose and cheeks with a tissue. "When you told me you wanted to get married here, I thought it'd be hokey. But I must say, this may be one of the most precious weddings I've attended. And not just because my baby sister is about to marry the man of her dreams."

Charlotte laughed, thankful for the friendship and mutual respect Rachel and Xavier had developed over the past year.

After considering a few venues, they'd chosen the location that initiated their reconnection—Jon and Katey's farm that had initially boarded their horses. And the place from which she and Xavier had embarked on the horse ride that had reminded them of some of their most romantic moments.

That day gave them both glimpses of why they'd first fallen in love.

Rachel's phone pinged. She glanced at her screen and smiled bigger than a teen at her first dance.

As she typed a response, Charlotte peered over her shoulder. Jason. She raised an eyebrow at her sister's smiling sunshine emoji and cleared her throat. When her sister made eye contact, she said, "Um, when were you going to tell me about you two?"

Rachel's cheeks flushed. "I…"

Charlotte laughed. "Just need to know when we need to start planning another wedding," she teased.

Rachel huffed and busied herself straightening her nonwrinkled dress.

Charlotte wasn't offended. Rachel had always kept private about such things. She was just glad to see her sister moving forward.

Another healing God had brought about.

Someone knocked on the bathroom door a moment before it opened. Mrs. Wolfe, who along with Morgan had overseen all decorations, poked her head in. "You ready? Because Dolly's all snazzed up and set to go."

Charlotte smiled. "I appreciate you." She'd found the woman's enthusiasm, and all her help with planning, comforting.

"Pshaw." Mrs. Wolfe waved a hand. "Gives me practice for when my princess gets married. Which hopefully won't occur until she's at least thirty-five."

Charlotte chuckled.

It stung that her parents had shown zero interest in reconnecting and wouldn't be part of this day. But Charlotte had gained numerous "moms" and friends within Sage Creek's horse community.

They'd become like family to her. For that, she was grateful.

"Gianna and JoEllen?" She waited to receive eye contact. "It's time."

Both of them hurried over.

Gianna quickly gathered her petals and placed them carefully into her basket. Standing, she gave one firm nod and repeated the directions Charlotte had explained half a dozen times prior.

"Correct." Charlotte smoothed a hand over Gianna's hair, kissed her cheek, then watched as she, Rachel and JoEllen exited the makeshift dressing room.

After giving them a good ten-minute head start, Charlotte accompanied Mrs. Wolfe to the stable entrance, where Dolly stood tied to a hitching post. They'd interwoven pink tulle accented with beading in her braided mane and tail.

"That man of yours is going to fall over flat when he gets a look at you." Grinning, Mrs. Wolfe helped Charlotte into the saddle.

Charlotte had chosen a dress with a loose, flowing skirt for easy mounting and riding, and she and Xavier had opted for a simple, nontraditional ceremony. They'd kept their wedding party small. Just Gianna and JoEllen as the flower girl and bridesmaid, guided by Rachel, Jason, Charlotte and Xavier on horseback and Pastor Roger.

Mrs. Wolfe walked alongside Charlotte riding Dolly to where the dirt path met the gravel road. She looked at Charlotte. With tears in her eyes, hand to her chest, Nadia traipsed off to find her seat among the other guests, all of whom had become special to Charlotte and Xavier.

They never would've been able to accomplish all they had with their equine therapy program and vaulting club without the incredible support they'd received from the community—in many ways led by Mrs. Wolfe, whom God had turned from foe to their greatest cheerleader.

The harpist began to play as Charlotte, still on horseback, passed through the tall, flower-covered archway set at the beginning of the grassy aisle lined from beginning to end with petals, each placed precisely by Gianna.

Charlotte loved that about her.

Reaching Xavier, who sat upon his horse and gazed at her with obvious adoration, she felt overwhelmed by all God had orchestrated since her return to Texas. He'd even formed a special connection between Gianna and JoEllen, who now stood, tall and proud, at Rachel's side.

Thank You, Lord, for working all this out so well. What she'd determined irreparably broken—twice!—had simply provided a backdrop to highlight the power of God's healing grace. She thought of the verse that spoke of the Lord doing more than a person could ask or imagine and smiled. He'd made her life a living example of that Scripture, and that flooded her heart with praise.

Pastor Roger addressed the crowd, read a prayer of blessing, then directed them to exchange vows.

Xavier went first. "Charlotte, when you left, years ago, I wasn't sure I could go on—or that I wanted to. It felt like I'd lost everything good and right in my world." His voice turned husky. He cleared his throat. "I was so confused, because I knew in my gut God brought you to me, created you for me, and me for you. For a while, I became bitter and disillusioned—because I got stuck in the middle of the story, forgetting that Jesus writes the most beautiful endings."

Moisture filled his eyes, and a muscle in his jaw flexed—a telltale sign he was fighting to maintain composure. "But it was more than that. I couldn't believe that God would bring you back to me, because I realized, from the moment we met, that you were well out of my league. Women like you deserve the world, wrapped in ribbon, with chocolate. Much more than this cowboy can provide. But I promise you this—I'll spend the rest of my life proving how much I love you." His gaze shifted to Gianna. "And our precious daughter."

Our daughter. How she'd long ached to hear those words. She laughed over the lump expanding in her throat. "I've never wanted anything fancy. Just you."

"Woman, you've got me. All of me, now and forever."

She forgot everything she'd planned to say after that, nor could she have spoken without becoming a blubbering mess.

"That's the best gift you can give one another," Pastor Roger said. "To choose each other, in the good and the hard seasons, and to keep choosing one another again and again, day after day and year after year."

Xavier grinned. "That won't be a problem."

"Then, with the power vested in me, I now pronounce you husband and wife." He looked at Xavier. "My friend, you may now kiss your bride."

He gave a whoop, slid off his horse and came to her side. Extending his hands, he helped her dismount, cupped her face and stared into her eyes with such intense, pure love, she worried her legs might give way.

They did when he pulled her to him and captured her lips in his—and she found his embrace more than strong enough to keep her standing.

*****

His New Companion

Jill Kemerer

MILLS & BOON

Jill Kemerer is a *Publishers Weekly* bestselling author of heartwarming, emotional, small-town romance novels often featuring cowboys. Over three-quarters of a million of her books have sold worldwide. Jill's essentials include coffee, caramels, a stack of books and long walks outdoors. She resides in Ohio with her husband, and they have two adult children. Jill loves connecting with readers. Please visit her website, jillkemerer.com, or contact her at PO Box 2802, Whitehouse, OH 43571.

Books by Jill Kemerer

Wyoming Legacies

The Cowboy's Christmas Compromise
United by the Twins
Training the K-9 Companion
The Cowboy's Christmas Treasures
The Cowboy's Easter Surprise
His New Companion

Wyoming Ranchers

The Prodigal's Holiday Hope
A Cowboy to Rely On
Guarding His Secret
The Mistletoe Favor
Depending on the Cowboy
The Cowboy's Little Secret

Visit the Author Profile page at millsandboon.com.au for more titles.

For I reckon that the sufferings of this present time
are not worthy to be compared with
the glory which shall be revealed in us.
—*Romans* 8:18

To Melissa Endlich, Shana Asaro, Tina James
and Rachel Kent. The Wyoming Legacies series
wouldn't have been published without you.
Thank you for believing in my books and giving me
the opportunity to write them.

To Sophie and Harvey, the inspiration
for Peanut and Fritz. Our late black-and-tan miniature
dachshund and my sister's golden retriever
always got along like peanut butter and jelly.
Sophie, you'll forever be in my heart.

CHAPTER ONE

HE WOULD *NOT* get attached to the dog. After all, this was a temporary gig.

Ty Moulten stood outside the entrance of Howard Service Dogs in Jewel River, Wyoming, after five on Friday and wondered again if fostering a dog on the weekends was wise. Maybe he should wait until next year when he'd have more time to get used to the idea. Or he could try in a few months when the temperature cooled. July had been a scorcher so far, and they were only midway through it.

Either the sun was melting him or he'd worked himself into an actual fever. Why was he so sweaty? Probably didn't help that after he'd finished checking cattle, he'd opted to change into a fresh pair of jeans instead of shorts.

Life made more sense in jeans, cowboy boots and a cowboy hat. And being comfortable would help him keep his head on straight. His heart had been broken once. Shattered, really. Fostering a dog was nothing compared to what he'd had with Zoey, but it didn't change the fact there wasn't enough of his heart left for him to squander the little that remained.

He didn't do love—or people in general—anymore.

Ty opened the glass door, stepped into the small entryway and continued through a second set of glass doors. Inside the warehouse, industrial-sized fans overhead circulated the air, and the large space in front of him had been sectioned into training areas. To the far left, a door led to the kennel room, and to the far right stood the office and a hallway leading to restrooms and storage.

Patrick Howard had moved to Jewel River after purchasing the abandoned warehouse from Ty's older brother, Cade. Patrick's daughter, Mackenzie, had opened her veterinary clinic in the smaller building next door. Their arrival had worked out great for the community as well as for the Moulten family. The area had a veterinarian again, and Mackenzie and Cade had gotten married in January. The training center's renovations had taken the better part of last year.

Ty's mother, Christy Moulten, had been the one to convince Ty to volunteer there. For someone who'd spent the past six years on his ranch avoiding extended interaction with anyone besides his brother and mom, the idea had sounded ludicrous. But then it had grown on him. Helping Patrick meant helping people who needed a service dog. Fostering a dog on weekends for a cause he believed in? Yeah, he could probably handle that.

"You made it." Patrick emerged from his office with his German shepherd, Charger, by his side. The tall, lean man in his early sixties wore athletic shorts, a T-shirt and running shoes. He strode toward Ty. "I appreciate you doing this for me. Hope you don't mind, but there's been a slight change in plans."

Ty didn't like the sound of that. He braced himself as Patrick stopped a few feet in front of him.

"I'm worried about Fritz."

"Who's Fritz?" Ty asked.

"I'll show you." Patrick jerked his thumb toward the kennels. "Let's go."

Ty followed him to the large kennel room. Shuffling noises,

whining and a few barks greeted them. Patrick stopped near a crate that contained a black-and-tan miniature dachshund.

"Fritz is three years old. I brought him here last week. His owner, a retired veteran, passed away, and the family couldn't keep the dog. A dachshund rescuer told me this guy was trained to help his owner with anxiety and depression. Naturally, I hoped to work with him and place him with one of my clients."

"You don't think you'll be able to?" Ty peered down to get a glimpse of the dog, but he was curled up in the rear corner.

"I'm not sure. At this point, no. He's miserable here even when he's out with the other dogs. I think he was attached to his owner and needs one-on-one attention."

Ty could see where this was headed, and panic zipped through him. He'd expected to get a bigger, easygoing dog that didn't need much attention. He'd pictured the two of them walking around his ranch or hanging out in his living room from Friday night through Monday morning.

"Hey, Fritz, come on out." Patrick bent and opened the kennel door. The dog slowly emerged, stretching his legs in front of him. Then he shook his body—ears flapping loudly—and trotted directly to Ty.

Those big brown eyes melted him. Fritz's tail wagged as he sniffed Ty's shoes. Then he began wiggling ecstatically with what appeared to be a smile on his face.

"Well, I'll be." Patrick rubbed his chin. "I haven't seen him this excited since bringing him here. He likes you."

Ty crouched and let the dog sniff the back of his hand before attempting to pet him. Fritz ate up the attention. He was wiggling so much that Ty laughed and picked him up. The dog instantly settled in his arms.

"Would you be willing to take Fritz for the weekend?" Patrick asked.

As if on cue, Fritz turned to stare up at him with eyes full of longing. Stirrings in his heart threw him off balance. This dog liked him. Really liked him. And he couldn't weigh ten pounds. The warm little body with his soft, short fur was evaporating all the arguments warring in Ty's brain.

He promptly set the dog down and rocked back on his heels.

"What would it entail?" Ty had already filled out the necessary paperwork to volunteer. He'd watched the video on understanding a dog's body language. Reviewed training techniques with Patrick and with his mother, who'd trained her Pomeranian, Tulip, to be a therapy dog. But he'd mentally prepared himself to take care of a large dog, not this bitty thing.

"Doxies are energetic, vocal, loving dogs." Patrick picked up Fritz and stroked his back. The dog stared mournfully at Ty. "They're quick learners, always on alert. He'll enjoy being around the horses. Expect him to follow you around all the time. He'll want to be on your lap whenever you're sitting. Fritz is well trained. He'll sleep in a crate. But he'll be your shadow during the day."

Ty liked the idea of having a buddy, but this dog with its take-me-home eyes worried him. How could he avoid getting attached?

"What will happen to him if I don't take him for the weekend?"

Patrick waved as if not to worry. "I've got volunteers coming in tomorrow and Sunday. He'll be taken care of."

That meant the dog would be as gloomy as he was before Ty arrived.

"What dog were you originally going to have me take this weekend?" He eyed the line of kennels.

"Nico." Patrick backed up three steps to a chocolate Lab's kennel. "He's only got three more weeks here, and he'll be off to his new home."

Nico was grooming his paw. The dog looked pretty chill. Fritz, on the other hand, was wriggling to get out of Patrick's arms. The man set him down, and he zoomed to Ty's feet and let out a yip. Then he sat up on his hind legs with his paws in the air.

Ty couldn't ignore that demonstration. Who could? Anticipation built, and he picked up the dog again. Fritz heaved a sigh of contentment.

"Like I said, this is the first I've seen him show any excitement, and I've had him for over a week. Proves my point. He lost his human, and I don't think he'll thrive here, let alone with a client, if I don't do something to help him."

"What's going to happen to him come Monday?" He'd liked the feel of the dog in his arms too much.

"Maybe a weekend with you will snap him out of it. If not, I'll find him a home. A formally trained, well-behaved miniature dachshund like this will be in high demand."

"If you think Fritz would be better off with me this weekend, I guess I can take him."

"It would give me peace of mind, especially seeing how he feels about you. I'm going to be out of town most of the weekend, and I don't like thinking of him all dumpy and depressed here."

"I'll do it." Two minutes. That was all it had taken for him to want this dog. He was already growing too attached.

Maybe this was a bad idea.

Why was he worrying? Patrick would find Fritz a home, and Ty would forget about him. He'd go on to foster other dogs, bigger dogs.

"I really appreciate it. Let's go to my office." Patrick led the way. Ty carried Fritz. Man, he was cute. His ears and tail were black like the rest of his body. Tan eyebrows and long eyelashes topped his expressive brown eyes. The fur on his paws and neck was tan, too. He seemed right at home in Ty's arms. Ty was so taken with the mutt he didn't even realize someone else was in the office until he walked in.

"Ashlinn!" Patrick beamed as he hugged the woman wearing a sundress and slip-on canvas sneakers.

She had long blond hair and big blue eyes. She was thin—very thin—and pretty—very pretty. A golden retriever wearing a service-dog vest sat by her side. She held the handle of the dog's harness. Was it *her* service dog? Or one in training?

"I figured I'd stop by before you locked up for the night." Her soft voice strained as if it took effort to speak.

"Are you all settled in?" Patrick gestured for her to sit, and she lowered herself into the chair.

"I'm getting there. Mom and Dad finished unpacking the kitchen. Everything else is pretty much done. They're driving back on Sunday."

"I'm glad it's working out." Patrick remained standing. "Ashlinn, this is Ty Moulten. He's one of our volunteers fostering dogs on weekends." Patrick addressed Ty. "Ty, this is my new assistant, Ashlinn Burnier. She'll be dealing with the administrative tasks around here from time to time."

"Nice to meet you." He nodded, still holding the dog.

She gave him a shy smile. "You, too."

Patrick addressed Ashlinn again. "Let me get everything for Ty to take Fritz, and then you and I can talk. Just sit tight."

She patted the head of the dog sitting next to her. "No worries. I've got Peanut."

"I'll be giving him a warm welcome, too, in a minute." Patrick went over to a stack of supplies in the corner. "All right, Ty, here's his crate. Easy to put together—like this." He gave a quick demonstration, and it did look simple to assemble. "This bin has his food, treats, toys and harness. Here, I'll show you how to put it on."

Patrick demonstrated how to put on the harness, clipped the leash to it and handed the leash to Ty. Then he explained how the booster seat would work in his truck.

"Anything else I need to know?" Ty asked, holding the leash. Fritz had sniffed his way toward Peanut, but they remained a few feet apart. With his mouth slightly open and tongue panting, Peanut watched the small dog.

"I can't think of anything. Text or call me with any questions or concerns. Mackenzie's always available, too, and I know you have her number." Patrick motioned for the two of them to leave the office. He picked up the crate, while Ty hefted the bag with supplies.

"It was nice to meet you," Ashlinn said.

"You, too. Um, welcome to Jewel River." He didn't mean to stare, but the smile on her face reminded him of last week's fireworks. Dazzling.

"Thanks."

He gave her a nod, then hurried out of there with Fritz trotting next to him. Once they'd loaded everything in his truck and gotten the harness clipped to Fritz's booster seat in the passenger side, Ty waved goodbye to Patrick and drove away.

The dog sat in the doggy seat with his front paws on the top, and he panted eagerly as the truck gained speed.

"You like driving around, huh? I do, too."

A sense of excitement—of actually looking forward to something for once—overcame him. Then, right on cue, anxiety flared. He liked this dog. But it wasn't his. Patrick would find it a home soon, so he'd better not get used to having it around.

His thoughts turned to Ashlinn. The dog wearing the vest must be hers. And that meant…

The beautiful woman needed a service dog. And if she needed one, there was a reason for it. A medical reason.

A lifetime ago, he'd fallen in love with Zoey Daniels, knowing she had cystic fibrosis. He'd asked her to marry him, and she'd accepted. Less than two months before their wedding, she'd died from complications due to the disease.

He had no regrets. He'd do it all again—fall in love with the vibrant girl with long brown hair, freckles on her nose and hazel eyes. He'd known she'd probably die young, but neither of them had thought it would be so soon.

He counted himself blessed to have loved her. But there

could only ever be one Zoey. And he couldn't—wouldn't—go through a loss like that again.

She'd died six years ago, and time hadn't healed his wounds. He'd learned to live with them, and that was about all he could hope for. His dream of having a wife had been buried with Zoey. There would be no other woman in his life.

ASHLINN KEPT HER breathing steady while Patrick helped Ty. Peanut sat on his haunches next to her. The fact he was relaxed boded well. She'd had two fainting spells since arriving last night. Her mother had fussed, and her father had declared moving here was a mistake and they should return to South Dakota where they could keep an eye on her.

Her parents worried about her. With good reason.

But she wasn't moving back to South Dakota. She wasn't moving back in with them, either. Her disease had made her ill for six years, four of which she'd been mostly bedridden in her childhood home. Last year, with the help of various treatments and getting Peanut, her medical alert dog, she'd slowly been able to have something that resembled a life.

When Patrick had offered her this job, the prospect had been a bright light in a murky future. She'd be able to walk to work—a necessity since she might never be able to drive. She could use the business skills she'd learned in college. And best of all, Patrick could train dogs to recognize a variety of symptoms simply by being around her. Other people dealing with blood pressure problems, migraines and fatigue would benefit from the dogs she'd be interacting with at the center.

She couldn't think of a better job if she tried. It wasn't like she could work anywhere else, either. Between the syncope—fainting episodes—and her stomach problems, it was unlikely she'd ever be able to work full-time again. With the help of her parents and medical team, she'd applied and qualified for disability benefits to help pay her living expenses.

"Sorry about that. Now, where were we?" Patrick came

back into the office and took a seat behind the desk. "How's the house? Will it suit your needs?"

"It's perfect." Ashlinn adored the two-bedroom, one-story home built in the 1950s only a block away from the training center. The rooms had been freshly painted before she signed the lease, and it had a fenced-in backyard for Peanut.

"Your folks coming around to the idea of you living here, yet?"

"No." She shook her head, suppressing a grimace. "Every five minutes they remind me I can change my mind at any time and drive back with them. I'm trying to be patient, but I had to get out of there."

"This is hard for them, too." Patrick had a gift for understanding the challenges people like her faced.

"I know." The guilt she'd been grappling with eased slightly. "I appreciate them and all they've done for me."

"I know you do. How have you been holding up? Physically?" His concern reminded her she had someone in her corner here. She wouldn't be alone. Well, she'd mostly be alone, but she had Patrick and Mackenzie looking out for her, and that counted for a lot.

"Decent. As soon as we arrived, I set up a couple of stations for when I pass out. One in the living room and one in the bedroom. Peanut approves."

"Glad to hear it. What are you using for the stations?"

"Weighted blankets, a few pillows. I have an ottoman to elevate my legs if need be."

"Have you had to use them?"

"Yes." She petted the dog. "It was just like at home. This guy licked me and went straight to the blanket in the living room. I chugged some water, got on the floor and had him sit to cover my legs. I wasn't out long. Mom said he stayed right by my side and nudged and nibbled my arm until I recovered. I think she's been worried that the move will affect Peanut's ability to alert me."

"I guess he passed that test with flying colors."

"Exactly."

"Keep in mind, I'm only a minute away if you need anything."

"Thanks. I appreciate it. I think I'll be okay. I talked to the manager of the supermarket, and they'll deliver my groceries once a week. The man mentioned a few retirees who can drive me places if I need a ride somewhere." She didn't anticipate going anywhere besides work. Too risky. And embarrassing. She couldn't bear the thought of passing out in front of people, and she tended to pass out a few times each day.

"Peanut is legally allowed to go most places with you. Don't forget that." Patrick had his stern face on. "According to the ADA, you qualify as disabled. The effects of your autoimmune disease have been debilitating, and if anyone questions you bringing Peanut into church or a store, you can tell them to talk to me. I'll set them straight."

While it was nice of him to offer, she had no plans to get out much. Having her own house and a limited part-time job would be taxing enough.

"You said your folks are heading back on Sunday?" he asked.

She nodded. "I'll come in on Monday."

"Your schedule is entirely up to you. If you can only work for an hour once or twice a week, that's fine. I don't want you overexerting yourself."

"You sound like my dad." She smiled. She and Patrick had discussed appropriate working hours at length. They'd agreed she'd come in for an hour or two on weekdays—but only if she felt up to it. If she didn't, she'd stay home. "Don't worry. I'll listen to my body. Peanut's great at letting me know when my blood pressure's dropping. And I'll play it by ear for a while. Give it a few weeks. I should be settled by then."

They talked for a while longer and said their goodbyes. Outside, the sunshine and slight breeze were such welcome sensations on her skin, she couldn't help raising her face to the sky. *God, You've blessed me with improved health, a dog that knows my body better than I do, a house of my own and a job tailor-made for me. Please bless this new phase in my life.*

"Come on, Peanut. We're going on patrol." They headed across the parking lot. For years, she'd barely been able to go outside, and she certainly hadn't been able to enjoy it when she did. And here she was. Independent-ish. At last.

Peanut walked in a heel beside her, and her thoughts strayed to Ty. What a handsome cowboy. She wasn't sure what to make of him. He seemed quiet. He'd cradled the little dog like he would a baby—protective and gentle.

A pang pinched her heart. No babies for her. No husband or boyfriend, either. Her life had veered off course during her sophomore year of college. As a twenty-year-old, she'd started getting bouts of severe stomach cramping. Then blood in her stools. Occasionally, she'd vomit for no apparent reason. After the doctors had run all their tests and told her stress was causing her health problems, she'd pushed herself to finish the semester. Then, on top of the other health issues, the fainting had started during her junior year of college, and her life had launched off a cliff.

Those had been dark days. Ashlinn tried not to think about them. They were too depressing.

As pleased as she was to move to Jewel River, this wasn't what she'd thought her life would look like at twenty-six. Yes, it would be wonderful to dream about a future with a gorgeous cowboy and a few babies, but that was all it would ever be—a fantasy.

At the stop sign, she checked for traffic, then continued forward with Peanut next to her. There was no use thinking about what she didn't have—what she'd never have. She'd focus on her blessings, instead. She had plenty of those.

A slice of independence. A purpose in life. The best dog in the world. Parents who loved her…a little too much.

Two houses ahead, her mom stood on the front porch and waved. Ashlinn waved back. In no time, she and Peanut had joined her.

"How did it go?" Mom took her arm to lead her inside. Ashlinn tactfully slid it free.

"It went well."

Her mother grabbed for her hand, and this time she yanked it away.

"I'm okay, Mom. You don't need to help me. I'm fine on my own."

Her mother's eyes narrowed as she sighed. "This move is taking a lot out of you. Moving takes a lot out of everyone. I don't want you to fall and crack your head open."

"Peanut would be licking my hand or nudging me if my blood pressure was dipping."

"I know." She shut the door once they were inside. "But I still think you need to be careful."

Ashlinn bent to take off Peanut's service-dog vest. "Good boy. You were awesome out there." She petted his head and scratched behind his ears. As soon as she was done, the dog took off to the kitchen, where her dad praised him. Was probably showering him with treats, too.

"The poor dog is going to miss you guys." Ashlinn sat on the couch and let her head fall back against the cushions. "He didn't know how good he had it living with you."

"We'll miss you both. It's going to be an adjustment for all of us." Her mother's brave face looked dangerously close to cracking. "I hate leaving you here alone. Are you sure this is what you want?"

Irritation grew, but she tamped it down. What had Patrick said? To be patient with them. He was right. They'd done so much for her—putting their lives on hold for years to take care of her—and the least she could do was try to reassure them about her decision to move here.

"I'm sure." She nodded. "This is more than I'd hoped for.

Patrick understands my limitations. I don't have to worry about the fact I can't get a driver's license. And there's a medical clinic less than a mile away."

"But…you'll be alone. What if you fall and hurt yourself? Peanut can't call 911 for help."

"Patrick and his daughter are going to check on me, and if they can't, one of their friends will. They'll both have keys to get in if there's an emergency." Her mom's concerns had been at the top of her list, too, and she'd forever be grateful for Patrick and Mackenzie for offering to help her.

"What if your symptoms get worse? This could be a temporary reprieve."

The doctors weren't sure why her symptoms had improved so drastically over the past couple of years. They'd experimented with numerous treatments, including several sessions of plasmapheresis—a total plasma exchange—which should have only produced short-term results. The treatments had allowed her to stand without passing out, and she'd no longer been bedridden. For reasons no one could explain, she'd continued to improve without additional plasmapheresis sessions. She'd slowly gained strength, and her dad had contacted a company about getting a medical alert dog. Patrick had been the trainer. He'd paired her with Peanut. Her life had improved a million-fold in just a year's time since getting him.

"You're right. My good health might be temporary. And if it is, you'll be the first to know."

Her mother came over and sat next to her, taking her hand in hers. "You'll always have a home with us. You're never a burden. We love you, and if there's any reason at all you need us to come get you, we will."

Tears pricked her eyes. She didn't deserve this kind of love, and it humbled her that her parents had sacrificed so much. They'd been the ones feeding and bathing her, taking her to doctor's appointments. They'd been desperate to find a way to get the nutrition she needed when she struggled to keep food down. They'd stood by helplessly as she fainted every time she attempted to stand up.

"I love you, Mom. Thank you for everything."

Her mom hugged her, and Peanut and her dad came into the room. The golden retriever's smiling face always put her in a good mood.

Dad rubbed his hands together. "I'll go pick up our dinner. We can eat it at the park."

"I'd rather eat it here if you don't mind." Ashlinn didn't want to worry about passing out in full view of anyone at the park. "I can come with you, though, to pick it up if you want company."

"That's okay. Stay here and rest." Her father patted his pockets for his keys. "You'll have your hands full after we leave."

That she would. While it made her nervous, she was looking forward to it. She'd make the most of her life while her health was good. Unless she had no other choice, she wouldn't move back in with her parents. For all their sakes, she hoped she wouldn't have to.

"A WIENER DOG? I didn't have that on my Bingo card for July." Cade handed Ty a large pizza box—still warm—then closed the front door and crouched to let Fritz sniff him. Their mother sailed down the hall ahead of them with her hands full of who knew what. Ty wasn't surprised to see his mom and brother here. For years, they'd been dropping in whenever the mood hit them. "I thought you were fostering a trainee. You know, a big dog."

"Change in plans." The aroma of pepperoni made his stomach growl. Ty carried the pizza to the kitchen and set it on the counter next to a box with a logo he recognized—Annie's Bakery. His mother might be a busybody, a terrible driver and a relentless matchmaker, but she also knew exactly what to bring to cheer him up. His taste buds came to life thinking about the doughnuts and cookies sure to be in the box.

"He's cute." Cade held the dog. Ty checked the pup's body language. Mouth relaxed and slightly opened. Ears alert. Tail wagging. Yep, the dog liked his brother. Not surprising. Everyone liked Cade, even dogs. "What's his name?"

"Fritz." After grabbing a stack of paper plates and some napkins from a cupboard, he set them on the counter. "Where's Mackenzie?"

"She got an emergency call. She had to drive out to the Yances' to check on one of their horses."

Ty admired that about Mackenzie. Her willingness to be on call 24/7. His sister-in-law had made an enormous impact on the surrounding area with her veterinary skills. Plus, she was genuine. No-frills. Ty got along well with her.

"Okay, my hands are free. Let me see your foster dog!" His mother rushed to Cade, who handed her the dog. "Oh, he is precious! Fritz, you said?"

The dog hadn't been here an hour, and Ty had already fallen head over heels for the little guy. The feeling seemed to be mutual, since he'd been following Ty everywhere.

"I'm so glad you're volunteering for Patrick." Mom stroked Fritz's back. "The training center helps so many people in need. And it's not easy for Patrick keeping up with all the expenses. Having you take a dog on the weekend is one less thing he needs to worry about."

Ty slid two slices on a plate and handed it to Cade. Then he dished out a slice for his mom. "Here you go, Ma."

"Thanks, hon. I could hold this sweetie all night long!" She turned to Fritz with the kissy face she reserved for small children and her dog, Tulip. "You are the cutest little thing. You're going to love it here. Don't worry if Ty gets grouchy. There's a softie lurking in those cowboy boots."

Ty and Cade exchanged wide-eyed glances and brought their plates to the kitchen table. A glass sliding door led to a patio, and the green grass of the back lawn ended in the distance at a split-log fence.

Their mother finally set down the dog and joined them at the table. After saying grace, they all dug into their pizza.

"Want anything to drink?" Ty wiped his mouth with a napkin, stood and headed to the door leading to the garage, where he kept a refrigerator for drinks.

"I'll take a diet soda," Mom said.

"I'll have whatever you're having," Cade said.

He opened the refrigerator, stacked three cans of soda and carried them back to the table. Once his mom and brother had their drinks, he returned to his chair, cracked open a Coke and took a long drink. Fritz stared up at him through big, begging eyes.

"No pizza for you, Fritzie." Ty smiled at the dog and patted his little head. He got excited and danced around the chair. "You've got kibble in your bowl."

"He needs a pepperoni." Their mom picked one off her pizza. It dangled between her manicured nails.

"No. Patrick said dachshunds are prone to overeating. I don't want him to become a literal sausage dog."

"Fine." She huffed, setting the pepperoni on her plate. She took a bite of crust. Ty gave it approximately one minute before she slipped the pepperoni to Fritz.

"How many weekends do you think you'll have him?" Cade grabbed a napkin from the holder in the center of the table.

"Probably just the one."

"You're not quitting already?" His mother's anguished tone and expression were as familiar to him as his face in the mirror. In the years since Zoey's death, his mother had been needling him to get out more, to spend time with friends, to join the Jewel River Legacy Club in town, to get a pet and most of all to "dip his toes in the dating pool."

"I'm not quitting. Patrick doesn't think Fritz is meant to be a therapy dog anymore. The dog's been depressed since arriving at the center. He needs a permanent home, not an assignment."

"Little Fritzie's depressed?" His mom's lips wobbled. She wasn't going to cry, was she? "Poor little darling." She blinked a few times. Her chin rose. Alarm bells rang in his mind. "You have to adopt him, Ty."

Funny, he'd been thinking the same thing. But he couldn't. How had he gone from *Don't get attached* to *I want this dog forever* in the matter of an hour? It didn't make sense. And he wasn't ready to discuss it with his mother. He'd better change the subject.

"You mentioned Patrick's expenses with the center." Ty took another sip, watching his mom, who discreetly slid the forbidden pepperoni to the dog. The woman couldn't help herself. He couldn't imagine how badly she'd spoil grandchildren when Cade and Mackenzie started a family. "I thought the people who needed the service dogs paid for them."

"They do. The dogs are expensive. Thousands of dollars. To keep the clients' costs down, Patrick applies for grants. He occasionally gets donations, too."

"Hmm."

"What's that hmm for?" she asked.

"I've been thinking about Zoey—"

"It's time to let her go." Her tone sounded understanding, but something hard had infused it. His muscles tensed.

He'd never let Zoey go. She'd been the love of his life. He'd cherished her, and he would love her until the day he died. Living without her didn't really work. He merely existed. But even he could admit he'd hidden away on his ranch for too long. "I wasn't thinking...never mind."

"What were you thinking?" She brushed crumbs off her hands.

He shouldn't have said anything. Now his mom would get all up in his business—as usual—and he hadn't thought through what he wanted to do.

"Forget I said anything."

"No, go on. I want to hear." She tilted her head encouragingly.

He glanced at Cade, who gave him a look as if to say, *You got yourself into this.*

"I want to honor Zoey's memory."

Ty wasn't sure how he'd expected them to react, but it wasn't with silence. His mother typically filled every conversation gap from here to the next county.

"I think that's a nice idea." She nodded. "What are you thinking of doing?"

"I'm not sure." He turned his attention back to his plate. But with her mentioning how Patrick received funding, he might be able to combine the two.

"You could buy a memorial plaque," she said.

"I could." He didn't want to, though. Too sterile. "I'd like it to be more meaningful."

"Come to the Jewel River Legacy Club meeting. It's Tuesday night. Everyone will have plenty of suggestions for you." She'd asked him to attend one of the meetings no fewer than eight-hundred thousand times. He had a policy of avoiding contact with members of the community as much as possible. That way he could dodge awkward questions or pitying stares. "Or you could always wait until it's over and talk to Erica. With her owning the Winston, she's sure to have ideas."

That sounded more up his alley. Cade and Mackenzie's wedding reception had been at the Winston—a large pole barn converted to a rustic-inspired event center—on Erica Cambridge's ranch.

Wait. Was he actually considering going to the meeting? What was getting into him? Fostering a dog. Going to a meeting. What next—joining his mother's book club? He shuddered at the idea of all those romance novels.

"The meetings don't last long." Cade pushed back his chair and motioned for Ty to hand him his empty paper plate. He added his mom's to the pile and took them over to the trash can.

"Okay. I'll come. But only to talk to Erica."

Cade and Mom exchanged shocked glances.

"Good. And I'm serious about you adopting Fritz," Mom said. "He's happy here. And well behaved. Look."

Ty checked on him, and he was sitting next to his foot. He wagged his tail. The small dog positively tugged at his heart.

"I don't know..." Ty wanted Fritz, but he'd grow attached. And five or ten years down the line, the dog would die, and he'd be left with a broken heart all over again.

"I'll doggy-sit anytime. Tulip will *love* Fritz. Can you picture them together?" Mom brought her hand to the base of her throat. "It will be too adorable."

The Pomeranian *would* probably get along great with Fritz. They were about the same size. And knowing his mom would dog-sit eased his mind. "I'll think about it."

"Good." Her big smile made it seem like the matter was settled. Maybe it was. "Oh, I heard Patrick's new assistant arrived in town. I wonder what she's like."

"I met her." As soon as the words left his mouth, he regretted them. Now his mom would expect a thorough report about the new girl in town.

"You did?" Her voice lilted. "How old is she?"

"I don't know. I didn't ask." He gave Cade a stare that begged for help. But his traitor brother sat there grinning.

"Honestly, Ty, I don't need exact numbers." Exasperation poured from her. "Is she fresh out of high school? Your age? My age?"

"Younger than me." He barely got the words out through his clenched teeth. He knew exactly where this would go, and he wanted to kick himself for saying anything.

"Is she pretty?"

He let out a groan. The questions would be nonstop. Why had he opened his stupid mouth?

He'd better get everything out all at once. Then maybe… just maybe…his mother would leave him alone.

"She has a golden retriever wearing a service-dog vest. She's got blond hair. Blue eyes. She's real thin. Her name's Ashlinn." There. That should cover it.

Mom blinked rapidly.

"Don't ask me anything else. I barely met her." He pushed back his chair to toss his empty can into the recycling bin. Fritz's little toenails clicked rapidly behind him. He crouched to pet the dog. "Hey, buddy, are you keeping tabs on me?"

Those eyes pleaded for Ty to pick him up. Ty obliged, petting him all the way back to the table.

"I wonder if she's single…" Mom tapped a fingernail to her chin as she stared out at the back lawn. Ty held the dog close to his chest. *Here we go.*

Of course she would wonder if Ashlinn was single. Because his mother wasn't only a matchmaker, she was a meddler, too.

He never should have mentioned Ashlinn. It was bad enough he was considering adopting this dog. What would happen if he opened access to what he'd locked down long ago?

He'd be in big trouble. He couldn't let that happen.

No matchmaking. No girlfriends.

He'd be spending his life alone. Fritz licked his wrist. Well, maybe not completely alone. He'd have to do some soul-searching before making a decision about adopting the dog. But there was no soul-searching necessary when it came to love. He'd done it once. He'd never fall in love again.

CHAPTER TWO

WHEN WOULD THIS meeting end? Ty shifted in his seat again. It had been the longest two hours of his life, and the Jewel River Legacy Club members were still talking. His mom sat to his left, and Cade was at his right. If Mary Corning interrupted one more time with another bizarre idea—she'd actually mentioned buying drones to drop candygrams to citizens—he was getting up and leaving.

He'd survived the preview of the upcoming Shakespeare-in-the-Park film. To be fair, the movie, with its explosions and a tornado, appealed to him. Never having read Shakespeare, he doubted the original plays had so many explosions, but he could be wrong.

Ty had briefly considered raising his hand earlier to share his idea of hosting a fundraiser in Zoey's honor, but he'd chickened out. Having everyone hurl suggestions at him would have been horrible.

His mother was right—waiting for this to end so he could ask Erica Cambridge about it was the smart thing to do. And he'd already decided any money raised from the event would be donated to Howard Service Dogs. He couldn't think of a more worthy cause. He'd dropped Fritz off at the center yesterday morning, and he'd been thinking about the little dog constantly.

Did the dog miss him? Was he doing okay?

Everyone began to stand. Ty glanced around. He hadn't realized the meeting had ended. *Finally.*

"I'm getting ice cream with Clem." His mom patted Ty's hand. "Go catch Erica before she leaves."

"I'll see you later, bro." Cade put on his cowboy hat. "Mackenzie's waiting for me."

Ditched by his family. A first. They were the ones constantly harping on him to get out more and attend one of these meetings. He made his way over to Erica, the president of the club, as she slipped papers into a folder.

"Can I talk to you a minute, Erica?" Awkward didn't begin to describe the moment.

"Oh, hey, Ty. It's great to see you here. Are you thinking of joining the legacy club?" She gave him her full attention.

He shook his head. "Um, no. I'm thinking of hosting a fundraiser—"

"A fundraiser? Perfect!" She closed the folder and beamed. Erica was around his age. She'd moved to Jewel River a few years ago and married Dalton Cambridge. She'd been at the helm of helping bring the town back to its former glory. "Do you want to have it at the Winston?"

"I guess. If it's available." He scratched his chin, not sure what he was agreeing to. "I want it to honor Zoey Daniels. She was my fiancée. She died a long time ago." It felt strange saying all that. His throat tightened. Man, he missed her.

Erica's expression was all sympathy. "I know, and I'm sorry. I wish I could have met her."

"You'd have liked her." He knew deep down she would have, too.

"I'm sure."

"I want all the proceeds to go to Howard Service Dogs."

"Great idea!" She brought her hands together in the prayer

position below her chin. "You can host it at the Winston for free. Dalton and I want to help the service dog center as much as possible."

"Really?" He hadn't expected her generous response. "I couldn't let you do it for free. I'll pay to have the event there."

"No, you won't. It's for a good cause. You'll put on a dinner, right? What about hiring Drake Arless? He smokes a good barbecue. Oh! You could have silent auctions. Gift baskets and gift cards and all kinds of stuff. This is going to be amazing!"

Erica had certainly made it into a better idea than he could. "Sounds good."

"Why don't you call me tomorrow, and I'll let you know when the Winston has availability?"

"Okay," he said. "I don't have a date in mind. I'm pretty open."

"Good." She motioned for him to walk with her to the door. The community center had emptied out, and Dalton was waiting near the exit. "We tend to book up quickly, but we get cancellations, too. I'm sure we can find the perfect evening for it."

"All set?" Dalton asked after locking up. Erica filled him in on the fundraiser as the three of them strolled outside and across the parking lot. The sun was beginning to set. Another gorgeous summer evening in Wyoming.

Ty veered left toward his truck, and his mind went to Fritz. Yesterday morning, he'd told Patrick how active and happy Fritz had been all weekend. The doxie had adjusted to life with Ty in one second flat. Patrick thought maybe that was all the dog needed. A reminder that life wasn't over.

As much as he knew he shouldn't adopt the dog, he wanted to. If all it had taken for Fritz to bounce back was a weekend on his ranch, shouldn't he be glad? Then the dog would have a future helping someone else who needed him.

But Ty *wasn't* glad. Because *he* kind of needed him.

Patrick wanted to see how Fritz acted this week before

making a decision. As long as the dog remained upbeat, Patrick would work with him until he could place him with a client.

Ty started the truck. Was it wrong to hope the dog didn't do well in training all week? He already missed him. Maybe he should have said something to Patrick about wanting to adopt Fritz. What if Patrick changed his mind and placed him with someone else before the week was over? Ty wouldn't be able to say goodbye.

On a whim, he turned in the opposite direction of his ranch to drive to the center. Yes, it was closed for the evening, but he didn't have anything else to do. A detour past it wouldn't hurt anyone.

As he neared the center, he noticed Ashlinn sitting on a patch of lawn near the sidewalk. She was petting the golden retriever, whose front legs were across her lap. Seemed odd. Why was she just sitting there? Did she need help?

He slowed the truck, pulled up in front of her and rolled down the window. "Everything okay?"

She blinked those big blue eyes up at him and nodded. "Yeah. Enjoying a walk."

Didn't look like much walking was getting done. "Do you need a ride?"

"No. I live two houses down." She angled her head in the direction of her house.

He wanted to ask why she was sitting on her neighbor's lawn if her house was so close. But it was none of his business. He put the truck in Drive but didn't take his foot off the brake.

"Are you settling in okay?" What was he doing? He'd checked on her. She was fine. That meant he could drive away. But here he was, making small talk.

Ty didn't do small talk. He should leave.

"Yes, Peanut's been a big help."

The dog stretched across her lap did *not* look like he was helping, but what did Ty know?

"I'm glad. Well, I'll see you around."

"See you later." She kept petting the dog. He eased off the brake and drove past the center. When he turned around to head back, Ashlinn was walking the dog up her porch steps.

Good. She seemed fine. No need for him to worry.

But he did worry. A little. Because that dog was wearing a service-dog vest for a reason, and something told him Ashlinn hadn't been sitting in the neighbor's yard on a whim.

SHE'D BEEN DREAMING of having a job—a purpose—and her dream had finally come true. On Thursday afternoon, Ashlinn took a break from entering Patrick's client contact information into a spreadsheet. She'd been at the center for almost two hours. The first hour had involved greeting the dogs and letting them get used to her. The second hour had been working on the paperwork Patrick had let pile up, including organizing client forms and what type of dog they needed. They'd agreed it was a long-term project she would work on only when she felt up to it.

Today she felt up to it—at least she had earlier. Now? She was getting tired. Peanut had curled up on a dog bed in the corner of the office. Every now and then he came over to check on her, and then he'd wander back to the bed. She was thankful he'd only had to alert her twice, and both times, she'd reclined on the floor and hadn't passed out.

Patrick appeared in the doorway. "Question for you."

"What is it?"

"Fritz." He bent down and scooped up the miniature dachshund Ty had fostered last weekend. "I keep hoping he'll come around, but he's not acclimating here. He's mopey again. Tomorrow, I'm going to call around to find him a home. In the meantime, I think Fritz could use a lap to sit on. Are you up for it?"

"Am I up for it?" She beamed and held out her arms. "I would love to have him on my lap."

Peanut woke and, tail wagging, joined them. Patrick set Fritz on the floor. The dogs sniffed each other, and the way their tails were wagging, she assumed they liked each other. Peanut came over to sniff her and sauntered away. She took the opportunity to pick up Fritz. As she petted him, he licked the back of her hand a few times, then settled on her lap and let out an exhausted sigh.

"You're tired, aren't you?" she said to Fritz as she glanced at Patrick, who was taking a binder off a shelf. "I hate to think of him all sad and out of sorts."

"Me, too." He opened the binder and flipped through the pages. "Wish I could place him with a client. From all accounts, he did wonders for his previous owner's depression and anxiety. It's a shame he won't be able to help someone else who needs him."

"At least he helped one person," she said softly. "He could come home with me tonight if you think it would help. I don't like thinking of him here all sad."

"I appreciate the offer, but we don't know how he'd do with Peanut, and you have enough to deal with. I'm going to give Ty a call. Fritz was a completely different dog with him last weekend. I'll see if he'll keep him until I can find someone to adopt him."

Ty. She'd thought about the handsome cowboy too many times over the past few days. She hadn't even been here a week. How could he have taken up so much space in her head already?

Probably because he liked dogs, had volunteered to foster Fritz last weekend and had stopped to check on her the other night when she'd had an episode.

Had she been embarrassed that he'd pulled up to find her sitting on a stranger's patch of grass? Yes. Had she told him the reason why she'd been sitting there? No.

If only she'd been able to make it home before Peanut had started licking her hand…but no. And it wasn't as if she'd had other options. Peanut had broken out of his heel and blocked her from going any farther. The dog had known her blood pressure was plummeting. And when she'd sat on the grass, her shallow breathing and erratic pulse had confirmed it. She'd been dangerously close to passing out. By the time Ty had pulled up, she'd been almost back to normal. Almost.

Seeing his handsome face and hearing the concern in his tone had affected her blood pressure in the opposite way, and it had nothing to do with her autoimmune disease.

She was attracted to the cowboy. Plain and simple. He seemed like a genuine, kind guy.

"I'm going to call him now." Patrick left, and Ashlinn absentmindedly petted the sleeping dog. Peanut came over, wagging his tail, and checked on both of them before going back to the bed. She saved her progress in the spreadsheet and began shutting down the program. Time to call it a day.

Her phone rang, and when she saw who was calling, she answered it. "Hi, Dad."

"How's it going, kiddo?" He and her mom called multiple times each day, and she always tried to answer as soon as she could. Didn't want to worry them.

"I'm good. I'm at the center, typing in a spreadsheet."

"Don't overdo it."

"I'm not. I'm actually wrapping up. Oh, and I've got a mini-doxie on my lap. He's so cute."

"A wiener dog?" His voice grew animated. "I had one of those growing up."

"He's feeling displaced at the moment. Patrick's working on finding him a home."

"Well, it makes me feel better knowing you've got a dog on your lap. Means you're sitting."

She chuckled. "Trust me, I force myself to sit. You don't think I'm over here running laps, do you?"

"I hope not." He laughed. "Any episodes?"

"The usual." She slowly stroked Fritz's back. "Nothing Peanut and I couldn't handle."

"What about getting around? Were your groceries delivered? Did you find a ride to church?"

"I'm getting around fine. And I'm not ready for church." She wasn't ready to be out and about at all. Just living by herself and walking to work a few days a week were massive changes she'd need time to get used to.

"All right. I wanted to make sure you're taking care of yourself and not working too much."

"I know. I'm doing my best."

"Go right back home and get in bed if you need to. Get in bed whenever you need to."

"I will." They'd been over this a thousand times. "But I don't need to be in bed right now. I'm sitting in the office with a sweet little dog on my lap and Peanut in the corner. I'm fine."

"If you need us to come up there, say the word. And if you want to move back home, we'll make it happen."

She rolled her eyes. "Da-a-d."

"You can't blame me for caring."

"I don't. But let me try to be independent, okay?"

"We're trying."

"Listen, Dad, I've got to go."

"Call me when you get home."

She ended the call. She might be living in a different state, but some things never changed. Her parents' concern for her could feel overbearing at times. She tried not to resent it. At least they cared.

Patrick came back into the office. "Ty's on his way."

"You mean I have to give up my lap warmer?" She faked a frown.

He chuckled. "He's at his mother's place here in town, so you've got five or ten minutes with a warm lap. I'm going to start feeding the dogs." He knocked his knuckles on the doorframe and left.

Five or ten minutes. That should give her time to calm the chaos in her tummy. As if on cue, Peanut came over and licked the back of her hand.

"I know, buddy, but trust me, this isn't a fainting thing." She ruffled his fur, and with his tongue lolling, he strolled away. She had enough physical issues. She certainly didn't need to add romantic flutters to the list of things Peanut alerted to.

And anyhow, the cowboy was off-limits. Her life had shrunk six years ago. Sure, it might have gone up a size over the past year, but that didn't mean she could fit a boyfriend into it.

She was too scared to go to church or enter a store. She could only work four or five hours a week—if that. And she'd fainted at least twice every day since moving here.

Ashlinn wasn't in any shape to have a boyfriend, and she wouldn't torture herself into thinking she was. A yawn caught hold, and she took a deep breath. As soon as Ty came for Fritz, she and Peanut were heading home.

CHAPTER THREE

TY MADE IT to the training center in four minutes flat. His mom had been getting on his nerves anyhow. She'd gone on and on about how Ty should invite Ashlinn to church. When he'd grunted to indicate there was no way he was doing that, she'd shoved a book in his hand—some romance novel that he'd dropped faster than the rhinestone-covered cowboy hat she'd handed him while shopping last fall—and basically commanded him to give Ashlinn the book and to tell her about book club.

He'd tap-dance on Broadway before that would happen.

His mother could browbeat Ashlinn into coming to the book club herself. He wanted no part of it. He'd been around more people this week than he had in the previous year. Made him want to pitch a tent in the mountains by his lonesome for a month—with Fritz, of course.

Ty couldn't wait to see the dog again. And this time, he wasn't taking chances. He was coming right out and asking Patrick if he could adopt Fritz. He hoped the man agreed. Ty parked the truck, pocketed his keys and took long strides to the entrance.

Barking from the kennel area grabbed his attention, but he didn't see Patrick over there. Ty strolled to the office and paused in the doorway. Fritz was asleep on Ashlinn's lap. Her tender expression as she petted him reminded him of a young mother with her baby. Punched him right in the gut.

Since when had he gotten so sentimental? Ashlinn must have sensed him there because she smiled at him.

"I suppose I have to give him up, huh?" Her eyes shimmered with good humor. A guy would get lost in those ocean-blue eyes.

Ocean eyes? What was wrong with him? It was that romance novel. The brief contact with it had turned him into a sap. He needed to haul himself back to the ranch. Ride a horse. Rope a calf. Pitch some hay.

"Is Patrick around?" Why did his voice sound like he'd swallowed gravel?

"He's feeding the dogs. Check the kennel room."

He nodded, wanting to say something more, but not trusting himself to say anything coherent. He wandered toward the kennels and found Patrick scratching behind Charger's ears as the rest of the dogs ate their kibble.

"Thanks for coming, Ty. Let's go to the office. Fritz is in there with Ashlinn."

Ty fell in beside him as they crossed the main training area.

"Fritz isn't adjusting here." Patrick gave him a sideways glance. "I'm disappointed, but I've got to do what's right for him. I think it's time to place him in a permanent home—as a pet. I'm wondering if you'd keep him with you on the ranch until I find him a new owner. I don't want him miserable here when he could be enjoying life."

Ty's heart pounded in his chest. "I'll take him. Permanently."

Patrick halted, clearly taken aback. "You want Fritz?"

"Yeah. He fit right into my life last weekend. I like the dog. I think he'll be happy with me."

"I know he'll be happy." Patrick grinned, shaking his head.

"I'm surprised. You were adamant about only wanting a dog on the weekends."

"I know." He shrugged, the corner of his mouth kicking up. "Surprised me, too. Fritz is special, and I hope you'll agree to let me adopt him."

"Of course you can adopt him. Can't think of a better placement for the dog."

Fritz was his! What a fantastic development.

"There's something else I want to run past you, too." He'd been meaning to talk to Patrick about the fundraiser, and now was as good a time as any.

"What is it?"

"I believe in what you're doing here. I admire all the hard work you put into training these dogs. They'll help people lead fuller lives."

"They sure will. And thanks. I love my job."

"It's obvious," Ty said. "A long time ago, I was engaged to a local girl named Zoey Daniels. She passed away from cystic fibrosis before we could get married. She'd appreciate what you're doing here, too."

"I'm sorry for your loss." His sympathetic expression matched his tone.

"I want to host a fundraiser dinner in Zoey's honor with all the proceeds going to Howard Service Dogs."

"You're serious?" Patrick looked stunned, then his face lit up. "I don't know what to say. Thank you. I've been trying to figure out how to purchase a wheelchair-accessible transit van to pick up our clients from the airport. This will jump-start a down payment."

"Any money from the event can go straight toward it." Ty was humbled he could provide something concrete for such a worthy cause. Zoey would approve.

"Three dogs will be fully trained and ready to be placed with their owners this fall. And after Brooke Dewitt gets married to Dean McCaffrey in September, she's going to let my clients rent her house—it's fully accessible for wheelchairs—so they can spend a week here while I train them how to handle their dogs. Getting the clients from the airport to Jewel River was the only problem I hadn't resolved."

"In that case, I'd better make sure the fundraiser is soon. Erica Cambridge offered to host it at the Winston. The earliest opening she has available is the second Friday in September. I'll ask her to save it for me."

"That's great." Patrick shook Ty's hand vigorously. "Wow, I appreciate this, Ty."

They continued to make their way to the office, discussing the type of van Patrick wanted to buy. Barking loudly, Fritz raced out the door to them. Patrick immediately jogged ahead, and Ty picked up the dog. Fritz laser-focused on the office and barked nonstop.

Something must be wrong. When Ty made it inside, his heart dropped to the floor.

Ashlinn was flat on her back near the dog bed, and her golden retriever was nudging her limp hand and licking her palm and wrist. She was clearly unconscious.

"Oh, dear." Patrick kneeled next to her. "Hey, Ashlinn, wake up."

His voice was quiet, calm, whereas Ty had gone straight to panic mode. What should he do? She needed help. He set Fritz on the floor—the dog trotted straight to Peanut and Ashlinn—and grabbed the cell phone from his pocket.

"I'll call 911," he said.

"No need." Patrick stood. "She's coming to."

"But she's on the floor. She fainted or had a heart attack or…" His breath seized in his lungs. He had no idea what had happened.

"She passed out. This happens regularly. She'll be fine."

This happened regularly? Ty tried to make sense of it and couldn't.

Ashlinn came to and groggily started petting the golden

retriever. "Good boy. Good job, Peanut." The dog stayed near her as she reached for a water bottle. She sat up enough to take a long drink. Fritz sniffed her, then turned away to go straight to Ty.

Once again, he picked up the dog, but this time, he cradled him to his chest and petted him. Seeing her on the floor had given him a scare. Fritz licked his forearm as he stroked his back.

Ashlinn slowly rose to a seated position, and it was only then that Ty realized a folded blanket covered her calves, and she'd had her head on a pillow. It was as if she'd prepared ahead of time. She seemed to realize Ty was in the room, and her face flushed.

"You okay, Ash?" Patrick asked in a normal tone. "Need me to get you anything?"

"I'm okay." She shook her head, glancing sideways at Ty. "Sorry you had to see that."

See what? He wanted to know what was going on.

But it was none of his business.

"I don't know if Patrick told you, but I have AAG, Autoimmune Autonomic Ganglionopathy. Say that three times fast." She let out an embarrassed chuckle, still looking exhausted. "It means I pass out often. Among other things."

AAG. An autoimmune disorder. His mind skipped back to when he'd met Zoey. How she'd warned him she had cystic fibrosis, and he'd told her he didn't care, he just wanted to be with her.

Knowing what he knew now, he wouldn't put himself through that with another woman.

"I'm sorry to hear that." He continued petting Fritz, who finally stopped licking him. The tail end of her comment caught up with him. *Among other things.* What other things?

"Peanut alerts me when my blood pressure gets low. He always knows when I'm going to pass out. It gives me time to get to a safe position. That's why I was sitting on the lawn the other day."

"Your blood pressure got low."

"Yep." She moved to stand up, and Patrick thrust his hand out to help her. She took it, and when she was upright, placed her palm on the desk to steady herself.

"Ty's adopting Fritz." Patrick gave her the water bottle. "And he's hosting a fundraiser for this place. The van might not be a wish much longer."

Her face took on a healthy glow. "That's wonderful! Fritz will be happy with you. And a fundraiser—how generous. I'd love to help."

"Um, thank you, I've got it under control." He didn't have it under control at all. Honestly, he had no clue what needed to be done. Erica had mentioned hiring Drake for barbecue and something about an auction, but beyond that he didn't know what was required.

"Oh." Disappointment covered her face. "Okay."

Now he felt like a jerk, turning down her offer.

Patrick opened a file cabinet behind the desk and took out a manilla folder. "Here's everything you need for Fritz. The papers show he's a purebred miniature dachshund. You'll see the list of all his shots, his Canine Good Citizen certificate and notes regarding his previous home."

"Thank you." Ty set Fritz down to leaf through the papers. "What do I need to do?"

"Fill out a form with the county to get him licensed. That's it."

"What about an adoption fee?"

"None for you. Oh, and feel free to take Fritz to the nursing home when you visit your grandmother. Just put a therapy-dog vest on him first." Patrick patted him on the shoulder, then turned to Ashlinn. "Why don't I take you home? Then you won't have to walk. I know it's been a long day."

Ty could see in her expression she was going to decline.

He felt bad for dismissing her help with the fundraiser. "It's on my way. I'll drop you off. And Peanut, of course."

"Great," Patrick said. "Then I can let out the dogs again."

Ty turned to Ashlinn. "Ready?"

"You don't have to do that." He couldn't read her body language. But he knew he'd been the one to dull her glow. And he remembered how Zoey had wished people wouldn't see her as incapable. Regret piled on at dismissing Ashlinn's offer.

"It's on my way. I'll feel better if you'll let me."

She sighed and nodded. "Let me get my things together."

A sense of victory overcame him. And that in itself was disturbing. It seemed no matter what he told himself was the right thing to do, lately, he did the opposite. And with a woman like Ashlinn, that could be costly. But what choice did he have? He couldn't let her walk home after passing out. He'd keep an emotional distance. He'd been perfecting it for six years.

ASHLINN FUMBLED, DROPPING her keys, as she attempted to unlock her front door. Today couldn't get any more embarrassing. Ty stood directly behind her, holding Fritz's leash, and Peanut was by her side. She'd told Ty she didn't need him walking her to the door, but apparently, he'd thought otherwise.

He probably viewed her as an invalid, unable to fend for herself. In some ways, he'd be correct.

She'd been mortified to have him witness her fainting spell earlier. Sure, the incidents barely fazed her after all these years. But she'd never had someone she was attracted to witness her passing out. Until today.

And the fact it had been Ty made her mortification so much worse. What a thoughtful man. Putting on a fundraiser. Adopting Fritz. Insisting on driving her home.

Ty bent and picked up the keys before she had a chance to. His fingers grazed hers as he handed them to her. How could a simple touch make her feel all swoony? "Here you go."

Even his deep voice was giving her junior-high-crush vibes. It had been a long time since she'd been around a cute guy and even longer since she'd dated one. None of her previous dates could hold a candle to Ty, though.

"Thanks." This time the key fit in the lock, and she opened the door.

"About the fundraiser…" he said. She turned back to him. "I *could* use some help. But only if you want to. I mean, you might have offered just to be nice."

He wanted her help? Maybe he didn't see her as an invalid after all.

"I'd love to help." She hesitated. Should she invite him in? This was all new to her—having her own place, being independent in a new town. "Want to talk about it now?"

He checked on Fritz, who stood at his feet smiling up at him with his little tongue panting. "Sure. If you don't mind Fritz being with me."

"Please. I adore him." She headed inside with Peanut, and Ty and Fritz joined her. She promptly got to one knee to remove Peanut's vest. Then she hugged him and scratched behind his ears. Rising, she nodded to the couch. "Make yourself at home. Do you want anything to drink?"

"No thanks." He found a seat. She dropped into her favorite chair and closed her eyes briefly to get her bearings. Peanut went to the kitchen. Fritz took off in his direction. The sound of lapping water reached her.

"I'll make sure he doesn't get into anything." Ty rose and left the room.

Maybe she shouldn't have offered to assist with the fundraiser. She'd put in two hours of work today and felt like she could sleep for a week. She wouldn't be surprised if she had another fainting episode tonight. Moving to a new town and starting a job might not be a big deal for someone else her age, but for her? She was nearing the outer limits of her energy levels—and stress ramped up her symptoms.

What if she relapsed and ended up bedridden again?

"Guess I worried for nothing." Ty returned with Fritz on his heels. Peanut wasn't far behind. "Do you care if he sits up here with me?"

"Of course not. Have at it."

Ty sat down again, this time with Fritz on his lap. The dog circled twice to get comfortable. "About the fundraiser…"

"Right. When is it?" She glanced around for her water bottle. She kept water on hand at all times. It helped her manage the fainting better. "Excuse me. I need to get some water."

"I'll get it," he said.

"No, no. I'm fine." She took her time rising. "Don't want to disturb the tired little puppy."

He chuckled. "He's pretty worn out."

"I'm glad you're adopting him. He's a completely different dog with you than at the center." She left the room and poured water into a drink tumbler, then returned to her seat. She should have grabbed a bag of potato chips. Not only was she getting hungry, the salt helped raise her blood pressure.

"How long have you had AAG?" Ty asked.

She schooled her face, not wanting to reveal her surprise that he remembered what her disease was called.

"Six years."

The way he startled confused her. Was she missing something?

"Six years ago I was supposed to get married, but my fiancée passed away before the big day. Cystic fibrosis."

"I'm so sorry." She brought her hand to her chest. The poor man. "I guess it was a bad year for both of us."

"I guess so." He met her gaze, and the warmth in it made her stomach swirl. "The fundraiser will be in her honor. Her name was Zoey Daniels."

A sinking feeling came over her. Was he still in love with the woman? Zoey?

Of course he was still in love with her. Why else would he host a fundraiser in her name?

"That's a lovely thing to do," she said quietly. Inside, though, her heart hurt. She didn't see herself ever getting to a point where she could have a long-term relationship. Her health problems were too limiting for her to date someone.

No one would ever host a dinner in her memory. No one would get close enough to her to want to.

Shame crushed her. How awful—to be jealous of a dead woman. At least Ashlinn could be thankful she wouldn't be dying anytime soon. "Where are you at with the planning?"

"I'm not far." He had the look of a man in over his head. "I need to call Erica—Erica Cambridge owns the event center—and let her know the twelfth of September works. It's a Friday. That should be okay, right?"

"Friday seems like a good time for a dinner." Her gaze strayed to Peanut. He was lounging in his dog bed and nibbling on one of his back paws. Good. That meant she wasn't having issues.

"She recommended a local who caters barbecue. I guess I need to call him. Beyond that, I don't know."

"Ask Erica if we need to provide tablecloths and paper plates, napkins, that sort of thing. We'll also have to create flyers and find a way to get the word out around town."

"I didn't think of all that." His eyes, deep brown, met hers. "Oh, she mentioned a silent auction."

"Good idea." Ashlinn was beginning to picture the event. She'd helped plan school dances in high school, and she'd been in a sorority before having to drop out of college due to her illness. Planning events was in her blood. "We'll contact local businesses and any groups or clubs to see if they'll donate items for it."

"They'll do that?"

"They sure will." She nodded. "What about an emcee?"

His shoulders climbed to his ears as he shook his head. "I'm not the person to ask."

"Does Zoey have family around?"

"Not here. Her parents moved to Colorado to be near her brother."

"We can figure out an emcee and everything else later. We have plenty of time. Almost two months." She yawned, trying to stifle it with her palm, but failing. "Sorry about that."

"Don't be." He picked up Fritz and stood. "I should get going."

"I wasn't trying to run you off."

"I know." He hesitated. "This is a weird question, but you obviously walk to work. Do you have a car?"

"No. I can't get a driver's license with my health the way it is."

"Oh." He averted his eyes. "If you need a ride to church or wherever, let me know. In fact, if you need anything, holler. I'll give you my number."

There went her tummy again, twirling like batons in a marching band. She'd have to remind herself later that he was offering out of kindness. Best not to read more into it. She swiped her phone. "What's your number?"

He spelled out his full name and his number. Then she texted him: This is Ashlinn Burnier.

Soon, she'd followed him to the front door and said goodbye to Fritz. Then she gripped the door handle.

"You sure you're okay?" His caring voice wiggled into the lonely part of her she tended to ignore. How easy it would be to ask him to stay.

But she couldn't. She'd help with the fundraiser, and by the time September rolled around, Ty would have plenty of opportunities to see she lived a very limited life. She'd never put a man into such a tiny box. But she was thankful for her tiny box, just the same.

"I'm okay." She gave him what she hoped passed for a smile.

He searched her eyes, then glanced down at Fritz. "All right. See you around."

Yes, she'd see him around. And fight the envy that some other girl would get to date this cowboy and have all the things her disease had taken from her.

She'd better get out her Bible. Envy was an ugly look on her. And she didn't intend on wearing it for long.

WHAT A DAY. Ty buckled Fritz into the booster seat, then loped around the front of the truck to climb into the driver's side. He now owned a dog. And he'd agreed to let a beautiful woman with major health problems help him plan the dinner he was hosting in honor of his dead fiancée.

Life was strange.

As he put the truck in Reverse and checked the mirrors, a sense of hope filled him, though. He was doing the right thing, having Ashlinn help him.

She clearly knew what needed to be done, and he didn't. Plus, he'd realized another way he could honor Zoey. She'd always wanted to be treated like everyone else. Ashlinn probably did, too. He regretted treating her like an invalid earlier.

Soon he was speeding down the country road to his ranch. The mountains in the distance always made him feel like he was part of something bigger than his own life. The vast prairies on either side of the road were beautiful in the summer. *He maketh me to lie down in green pastures.* Psalm 23. Funny that one came to mind.

Ashlinn couldn't drive. She fainted on a regular basis.

Among other things.

He didn't know what those other things entailed, but something told him she wouldn't be straying far from home, and it wasn't by choice. Her world was a within-walking-distance one. And since she passed out often, she couldn't be walking far.

He was going to do something about that. He'd invite her to church like his mother suggested. Bring her out to the ranch so she could see the beauty of Wyoming for herself.

Maybe he could expand her within-walking-distance life a little bit.

As long as he protected his heart, he'd be okay. And it wouldn't be difficult. All he had to do was picture Zoey's smiling face. It wasn't possible for him to love anyone else. Not even the new girl in town with pretty blue eyes and a big heart to match.

CHAPTER FOUR

WOULD THE DOGS be able to detect blood pressure abnormalities by being around her? The following Wednesday, Ashlinn sat in the training arena while the two dogs Patrick had acquired over the weekend sniffed her. Bandit, the German shepherd, had a lot of energy. The golden-retriever-basset-hound mix, Candy, had just finished a fourteen-month stint with a puppy trainer and showed promise to be a service dog.

At the beginning of the session, Patrick had swabbed Ashlinn's saliva and allowed both dogs to smell it. Her blood pressure readings remained steady. Surprising, seeing how much she'd been looking forward to this afternoon. Ty was picking her up soon to discuss the plans for the event.

"The more we get them used to your scent when your blood pressure is normal, the easier it will be for them to recognize the chemical reactions altering it when it's low." Patrick allowed them to linger another minute and led them to the corner before commanding them to sit and stay. He came back over to her. "I think that should do it. I know you've got your meeting with Ty. Why don't you get your things together and call it a day?"

"Are you sure? I can stick around a few more minutes. Maybe my blood pressure will change."

"No, go on. We'll have many opportunities over the next months." Patrick turned back to the dogs. She stood, and a whoosh of dizziness came over her. Peanut immediately licked her hand. She sat right back down. "Bring them over, Patrick. I feel lightheaded."

He brought both dogs to her. Bandit's nose traveled from her hand to her thigh and feet. He spun in a circle once. Patrick rewarded him with a treat. Candy barely paid any attention to her. The dog plopped down on the mat, bringing her hind leg up to itch her ear.

"She doesn't seem interested." Ashlinn nodded to Candy.

"That might change."

She checked her blood pressure. Almost back to normal. Good. "I'm going to try this again. Do you want them both near me just in case?"

"Yeah, let's see what happens." He called the dogs to come.

She took her time rising. Peanut moseyed over. Bandit did, too. He smelled her once and walked away, the same as Peanut. That was a good sign. Candy plunked down on the mat, not interested in her at all.

"I think Bandit shows promise. We'll see about Candy. It's too early to tell at this point." Patrick walked out of the training area with her. "Thank you for being patient with them."

"I'm happy to do it. I don't know what my life would look like without Peanut, but I do know this. I wouldn't be here, living on my own. I hope both Bandit and Candy can be trained to help someone else live more independently. You're doing God's work here, Patrick."

"I hope the same, and thank you. I'm blessed to love what I do."

The entrance doors opened, and Ty strolled in with Fritz by his side. The dachshund picked up speed as he saw Patrick, Ashlinn and Peanut.

"Heel, Fritz," Ty said. The dog immediately fell in beside him and stopped straining at the leash. "Good boy."

Ashlinn's heartbeat thumped in anticipation. She'd talked to Ty twice since he'd dropped her off at her house last week, and she'd been looking forward to seeing him tonight. Peanut's nose brushed her hand. She almost chuckled. The dog knew.

"How's Fritz doing?" Patrick checked over his shoulder—Bandit and Candy were fine—and bent to pet Fritz.

"Great. I've been getting him used to the horses and the stables. He might be under the impression he was born to be a herding dog." His eyes shimmered with humor.

"Small in body," Ashlinn said. "Big in personality."

"Exactly." Ty met her gaze, and she almost fanned herself. Peanut stayed close by. She patted his head. Couldn't fault the dog for knowing her inside and out.

"Do you think you'd be up for fostering one of the dogs occasionally on the weekends still? Not this weekend, of course, but maybe in a few weeks." Patrick gave Fritz's back a final stroke and straightened.

"I hadn't thought about it." With his free hand, Ty wiped his forehead beneath his cowboy hat. "I probably could."

"Great. Bandit, especially, could use a break running around your property. He's still a puppy at heart."

"I've got plenty of land for him to explore." Ty glanced at Ashlinn again, and she had to force herself to look away.

She excused herself to get her bag and Peanut's harness from the office. When she returned and got the dog situated, they chatted another minute before saying goodbye. Ty held the door open for her and Peanut, then he and Fritz accompanied her to his truck. He helped her into the passenger seat. After getting Fritz and Peanut settled in the backseat, he started the truck and turned to her. "If you want a change of scenery, we could go to my ranch."

She instantly pictured horses in pastures with mountains behind them. Wouldn't it be something to see his ranch in person? But she wasn't ready. Might never be ready.

"It's about a thirty-minute drive." He waited patiently for her answer.

"Um, I don't think that's a good idea." She didn't want to offend him. "It has nothing to do with your ranch. It's just… I'm safer at home."

He nodded. "I get that. You should come out at some point, though. If you need me to have anything on hand to make it safer for you, let me know. I've got a great view of the mountains, and the prairie spreads for miles. There's no better place to see the sunset than from my front porch."

The way he described it was exactly how she imagined it. While she'd love to visit, it wouldn't be wise. Not now, anyway. "Wyoming sunsets are pretty spectacular."

"They sure are." He didn't seem put out by her refusal. "Your place, then?"

"Yes." As he drove, Ashlinn's thoughts circled around. Ty wasn't a pressure guy. Nothing about the exchange made her feel like she'd disappointed him. But a part of her disappointed herself. She hadn't even realized she wanted to see his ranch until he'd invited her. And she'd turned him down—she'd done the right thing, hadn't she?

He pulled into her driveway and parked. "Wait there. I'll come around."

A chivalrous cowboy. Maybe it was only due to her disease, but something about Ty made her believe he'd open the door for her regardless of her health status.

"Thanks." She took his hand to step down. Calloused skin. His touch sent a tiny thrill through her veins. He let go as soon as she was out of the truck. Truthfully, though, she wouldn't mind if he held her hand all the way inside.

"I'll get the dogs."

Ashlinn waited for Peanut to get out of the truck, then she climbed the porch steps and unlocked the front door. Ty brought Fritz inside. Ashlinn crouched to remove Peanut's harness, giving him a lot of loving as she did. When she straightened, he and Fritz gravitated to each other. Ty had taken off his cowboy hat.

"Want some iced tea?" she asked on her way to the kitchen. "I brewed it myself on the porch."

"Sun tea? I'd love a glass."

"Coming right up." She took two glasses out of the cupboard and filled them with ice from the fridge's dispenser. After pouring the tea, she brought the glasses to the living room and handed one to Ty. "Did you want a snack, too? My groceries were delivered yesterday."

"No, I'm good. Is the delivery working out for you?"

"Yes. They leave everything on my front porch. All I have to do is put it all away. My parents were relieved when I told them it went well. That was one of their biggest concerns about me moving here. How would I get food?"

"Yeah, we aren't like the city where you can have everything delivered. At least we have the supermarket and Cowboy John's for local delivery." He sipped the tea. "This is good. What flavor is it?"

"It's my favorite. Ginger peach." She took a drink and leaned back in her chair.

"Long day?" he asked.

"No. But a good day. Patrick started getting the new dogs used to my scent. We'll be working with them for the foreseeable future to detect when my blood pressure changes. It's exciting, thinking someone like me will have a dog of their own to help them."

"It is," he said so quietly she almost didn't hear it.

She reached into the basket next to her chair and pulled out a notebook and pen. After turning to the page with her notes for the event, she turned her attention back to Ty, who'd lifted Fritz to the couch. The dog was in the process of curling up on his lap. "Why don't you tell me where you're at with the planning?"

"Sure." He set the glass on a coaster. "Erica reserved the

Winston for me on September twelfth. We'll be able to set up the day before, and she gave me the number of a cleanup crew to hire if we don't want to do it ourselves."

"Did you find out if we'll need tablecloths and stuff like that?"

"I did. She'll provide tablecloths, disposable dinnerware, glasses and napkins—all for a fee."

Ashlinn frowned. "Will we be able to afford it?"

"Yes. Erica and Dalton are donating the Winston for the dinner. No charge. I'm covering the costs of everything else."

"And then we'll pay you back from the proceeds." She added bullet points in her notebook.

"No. I don't want repayment. Like I said, this is to help Patrick. Knowing he'll be one step closer to purchasing that van makes me feel good."

His generosity made her hand falter. Throwing a big fundraiser like this would cost thousands of dollars—money Ty could use for any number of things.

"Why?" She stopped writing to stare at him, trying to figure him out. "Besides honoring Zoey?"

He averted his eyes, and his knee began to bounce. Then he met her gaze. "I don't have the expenses a lot of guys my age deal with. No wife or wedding to pay for. No kids and all the costs they entail. I live a simple life. And I don't think God intended for me to hoard His blessings."

She found his contentment refreshing. In many ways, she and Ty were similar. Except she had a solid reason for not having all the things he'd listed. Why didn't he have a wife or children?

"You say that like you don't ever plan on having a wife or kids."

"I don't."

She was taken aback. Maybe she shouldn't press for more information, but she couldn't help herself. "I'm not getting married or having kids, either. I know my reasons. What are yours?"

His face flushed. "There was only one Zoey. And she's gone."

The words pricked her heart. Of course. She'd figured as much. Why a teeny part of her had hoped otherwise, she wouldn't think about. Zoey had been his one true love.

"What about you?" He tilted his head, curiosity written all over his face.

"I'm…this…" she motioned her hand down her body "…is my life. I wouldn't put a husband through it."

"Is your condition terminal?"

"No," she shook her head, "AAG won't cut my days short." It would just make them difficult.

"What all are you dealing with?" His concerned tone didn't demand answers, but she figured it couldn't hurt to be honest.

"The fainting, obviously. Dizziness. I get tired easily. Stomach issues—a lot of stomach issues. Sometimes I struggle with dry mouth. Dry eyes. There are times when I can't sleep. And on rare occasions, I'll get confused. It's like a mental fog. But that's more if I have a migraine."

"I'm sorry. That must be difficult for you."

"I'm much better now than I was a year ago." She kept her tone bright, not wanting him to think she was feeling sorry for herself. "I mean, look at me. I have my own house and a part-time job. Peanut." The dog glanced up from his dog bed. "You're the best dog in the world, aren't you, boy?"

"I'm glad." He leaned back with a tender, understanding expression. "And since you're doing better, I think we should plan a time for you to come out and see my ranch."

"I don't think so." She drew her eyebrows together. "My health…"

"We'll make a fainting station for you."

"But the other things I deal with—"

"If you're having a bad day, we'll reschedule."

She was finding it hard to turn him down. And her earlier vision of endless prairie made her not want to. "Why do you want me there?"

"I know it must be hard being home or at the center all the time."

"Not really. I feel like I'm on vacation compared to the years I spent in bed, only leaving the house to see the doctor."

"I won't push you. I'll drop the subject." He stretched his neck to one side then the other. "I promise I'm not a creeper."

"I didn't peg you for one." She let out a small laugh. It was curious that a man so stuck on his deceased fiancée was insisting she come out to see his ranch. Maybe it was pity, but she didn't think so.

"If you ever change your mind..."

As much as she'd like to see his land, she wasn't changing her mind. This house, her job—they were enough for her. And if she continued to decline his invitations, at some point Ty would give up on her, which would be for the best. She might not like it, but staying in her world gave her the best chance to continue to live independently.

"We should get back to the planning," she said.

"PLANNING. RIGHT." TY'S neck burned. Why had he pressed Ashlinn to visit his ranch? He shouldn't have been so heavy-handed. She clearly didn't want to, and why would she? Her health problems kept her close to home. Going someplace new would probably be too stressful for her.

The fact he'd even invited her would be laughable to anyone who knew him well. He was an expert at avoiding people. He'd been hibernating for six years.

With a quick scan of his list, he got back to the reason he was there. Planning the event.

"I called Drake Arless. He's free that night. He sent me the menu options. I'll read them to you." Ty pulled up the note on his phone and read her the menu items and their prices. "What do you think?"

"The smoked chicken is a firm yes for me. Should we offer both the pulled pork and the ribs, too?"

"You probably know better than I do."

"Let's go with the ribs, the chicken, mac and cheese, cornbread and slaw." Her satisfied nod brought out her dimples. He couldn't look away from them.

"Okay. I'll let him know." Easy enough. On to the next item… "I'm not sure what to do about the flyers and getting raffle baskets."

"Here's what we used to do…" She explained how she'd been in a sorority and the types of baskets they'd gotten from donors. Then they went back and forth over what to include on the flyers. By the time they were finished, Ty's stomach grumbled.

"Why don't we get a pizza?" he asked, rising to retrieve his phone from his pocket. "Unless you're tired. I can leave."

"Pizza sounds good."

"I'll order it. Any requests?" He found the contact info on his phone for Cowboy John's.

"Pepperoni. No onions."

"Meat lovers?" He glanced her way. Her big blue eyes sparkled as she nodded. He called in the order to have it delivered. "Done."

"Tell me about Jewel River." Ashlinn set the notebook in the basket next to her chair and gave him her full attention. "You grew up here, right?"

"I did." He lowered himself to the couch again. "What do you want to know?"

"Everything."

"That narrows it down." He let out a soft chuckle. "Winters are bitterly cold. Beautiful, though. There's something special about riding out to check cattle when the air's so clear and cold it makes your breath crack. Summers can get real hot. This town lives for festivals—there's a Christmas festival, Easter egg hunt, Fourth of July fest, Labor Day parade, harvest festival. Oh, and Shakespeare-in-the-Park—a movie, not a live performance. It's relatively new."

"I thought Shakespeare-in-the-Park events were for plays." She tucked her legs under her body.

"They are. But not in Jewel River. One of the legacy club members has a grandson in high school who reimagines Shakespeare plays and films them with local actors and props."

"Are they any good?" She scrunched her nose as if she couldn't picture it.

"Honestly? I have no idea. I don't go to them. But I did see the preview for this year's film. I have to admit it was entertaining."

"When is it?"

"August, I think. I can't remember the date. Everyone brings lawn chairs and quilts to the park, and they watch it on a big projector screen."

"Why don't you go?"

He shrugged.

"Are you going to attend it this year?"

He winced. Going would mean talking to the people he'd been avoiding. They all meant well, but… "I don't think so."

"Why not?"

"It's not my thing."

"What is your thing?"

Tough question. Did he even know anymore? "I spend a lot of time at my ranch, riding around the pastures, checking the cattle. It's peaceful out there."

"I'm sure it is." Her wistful expression made him wish she'd come out and see it for herself. But she'd said no—more than once—and he needed to take the hint. "What about the other festivals? What happens at them?"

"Honestly? I don't know."

"You told me all the fun things to do around here, but you don't do any of them?" Her incredulous tone caught him off guard.

Put like that… It wouldn't make sense to anyone else, but it did to him. "I guess not."

"That makes me feel better." Her remark confused him.

"Why?"

"Means I'm not the only one staying home." She laughed. How could she have such a good attitude? Ashlinn didn't attend local festivals due to her health. Ty didn't attend them by choice. Something uncomfortable settled in his gut.

Maybe he should change the subject.

"Oh, my mom wants you to join her book club." Why had that come out of his mouth? "They only read romance novels."

There. He'd warned her.

"How kind of her." She glanced away. "It's not a good time. I'll have to pass."

Disappointment warred with relief. "I don't blame you. Not much of a reader myself."

"I like to read."

"Not romance novels, though."

"I like romance novels."

"Oh."

"It's not the books. I'd be embarrassed if I fainted there. And I have Peanut. He's big. I wouldn't want it to be awkward."

"You clearly don't know my mom. No dog is too big for her house. No amount of fainting would deter her."

"Really?" She seemed genuinely surprised.

"Really."

"I'll keep that in mind."

The doorbell rang and Ty answered the door. After paying for the pizza, he brought it to the dining area. Ashlinn went to the kitchen for plates.

He couldn't remember the last time he'd gone to anyone's

house other than Cade's or his mother's. Yet, he felt comfortable at Ashlinn's. She was easy to be with, fun to talk to, and he was glad they were planning the event together. Maybe going to one of those festivals wouldn't be so bad. Should he start taking advantage of what Jewel River had to offer?

Maybe if Ashlinn was by his side.

CHAPTER FIVE

STRETCHED OUT ON the couch with a blanket over her, Ashlinn clicked through television channels. Nothing interested her. What did she expect for a Friday afternoon?

Over two weeks had passed since she and Ty had shared the pizza and discussed the fundraiser. Since then, she'd seen him several times. He dropped by the training center often, and they'd made progress planning for the September event. The flyers were being printed locally and would be ready by the end of next week. She'd been playing around with software to make graphics to share on social media for the event, too.

Unfortunately, every time she got a taste of normal life, she ended up having a health setback. Stomach problems had kept her home for four days. The nausea had been unbearable. The first two days, she hadn't been able to keep much down. Yesterday, she'd turned the corner, but she still felt weak.

Patrick and Mackenzie took turns stopping by each day, and they'd brought her crackers, sports drinks and foods easy to digest. Even Ty's mother, Christy Moulten, had checked on her. She'd also dropped off a romance novel. Ashlinn had thought Ty had been joking about it. She'd been wrong.

Christy was delightful—a force to be reckoned with, for sure—and kind. An older gentleman had driven her, Clem something or other, and scowled at Ashlinn from the driveway where he'd climbed back in his truck rather than come inside. He wasn't someone she expected getting to know very well.

She really should make another cup of tea to stay hydrated.

It took forever to shift her legs over the side of the couch and place her feet on the floor. Were the nausea and vomiting signs her health was regressing? She could *not* become bedridden again. Fear gripped her throat. Had she come this far to only come this far? If the stomach problems persisted, she might be forced to move back home. She shuddered at the thought.

Pushing off the arm of the couch, she stood. Waited for the dizziness to clear. Peanut smelled her hand. "Good boy."

She shuffled to the kitchen and turned on the electric kettle. The stomach problems were temporary—they had to be. Because she wasn't giving up her new life. Helping Patrick's dogs detect her health issues gave her purpose. And she enjoyed typing his clients' information into spreadsheets.

She'd finally gotten a taste of feeling useful. Would her sense of value be snatched away along with her independence?

A knock at the front door startled her.

It was too early for Patrick or Mackenzie to stop by, and she wasn't expecting any packages. With a sigh, she slowly padded to the front door. Ty and Fritz stood on the welcome mat.

"Why are you here?" She opened the door wide, not caring her hair was a mess and she still wore the T-shirt and shorts she'd slept in last night. Peanut wagged his tail next to her, and Fritz lifted his nose to greet him.

"Heard you were under the weather. I brought soup." He held up a plastic bag. "Can I come in?"

"Sure. Don't mind me, though. I know I'm a wreck."

"You could never be a wreck."

Did he not have eyes? He brushed past her, and she closed the door and followed him to the kitchen. After he took off

Fritz's leash, the dogs greeted each other in circles, then Peanut came over. He didn't alert her, thankfully.

"I hope you like chicken noodle." He set the bag on the counter and lifted out plastic containers. Cracked the lid off one.

"I love chicken noodle. I don't know how much I'll be able to eat, though. Still working through some stomach issues. Don't worry—I'm not contagious. I'm just dealing with a flare-up." She saw no point in pretending otherwise.

"If you can't eat it today, it'll be good for a few days in the fridge. Want a bowl now?" The aroma of chicken broth filled the air. She almost declined, but the smell made her hungry.

"A small bowl. And please, help yourself to one, too." A wave of exhaustion overcame her, and she padded to the dining table. Pulled out a chair and sat, resting her elbow on the table with her cheek against her palm. Much better.

"I'll have a biscuit and leave the soup for you." He ladled soup into a bowl and arranged biscuits around a small mound of butter on a plate. Then he set the bowl in front of her. "One sec. I'll get you a spoon."

How she longed to tell him she'd do it herself, but her weary body refused to cooperate. All she could do was sit there, thankful for his help. Fritz trotted over and sat next to her chair. He looked up with big eyes. How could anyone not pet the little darling? She stroked his back.

"It's good to see you, Fritz." Feeling off, she didn't have the energy to bring her hand back up. Fritz nudged her hand with his nose, just like Peanut would. In fact, Peanut came over and stared. Uh-oh. An episode was on the way.

How could standing, opening the door and walking to the kitchen make her feel like she'd run a marathon? Peanut must not be too concerned, though. He left to find Ty with his tail wagging.

"Here you go." Ty placed a spoon and butter knife next to her bowl, then took a seat to her left and reached for a biscuit. He tore one open and slathered it with butter before taking a bite.

She dipped the spoon into the soup and discreetly checked him out. His dark brown eyes and cropped black hair accentuated his tanned face. He'd taken off his straw cowboy hat and wore a dark T-shirt that stretched across his muscles. Although the temperature outside was hot, he was in jeans and cowboy boots. She doubted she'd ever see him in anything else. Wouldn't bother her a bit. He looked good in them.

"Do you need me to take you to the doctor?"

"I'm doing okay. I know the signs of dehydration. I'm not there yet." She turned her attention to the soup and lifted a small bite to her lips. "Mmm. This is good."

"Glad you like it. I've been perfecting the recipe for the past couple of years."

"You made this?" The soup tasted like health in a bowl. The perfect ratio of chicken, vegetables, noodles and broth.

"I did."

The cowboy continued to surprise her. She took another spoonful. The warm broth went down easy.

"Want a biscuit?" He held up the plate.

"I'd better not. The soup isn't bothering me. I'd be pushing it if I tried anything else."

He nodded, and she appreciated that he accepted her answer. Her mother would have gotten increasingly agitated, insisting she try a bite. And Ashlinn would have hated the shrillness in her tone, eventually caving, only to get sick again.

"If you need anything, you can call or text me anytime." Sincerity oozed from him. Hearing those kind words relieved something deep inside her—the awful feeling of being a burden. Her parents weren't perfect, but they'd never made her feel like one.

"Thank you." It would be so nice to have him on speed

dial. Relying on people other than her family was new to her. She wouldn't take advantage of him.

Neither spoke as they continued to eat.

"I hear my mom and Clem stopped by." Ty's amused eyes caught her off guard. He looked younger when he wasn't so serious.

"They did. Clem stayed in the driveway, glaring at me. Is he a serial killer or something?"

Ty barked out a laugh. "Serial killer? No. That's just Clem being Clem. He's actually a good guy."

"If you say so."

"He's brutally honest. Tells it like it is. He and my mom go round and round arguing whenever they're together."

"Are they together a lot? Like a couple?"

"No—oh, no. My mom's driver's license is constantly being revoked. She's a terrible driver. Ever since she moved from the ranch to her house in town, Clem has taken it upon himself to be her driver. I think it keeps them both out of trouble."

"Did she live on your ranch?"

"Actually, she lived on the ranch where I grew up. Cade owns it now. Before our father died, he divided the property. Dad owned a lot of acreage, and it made sense for us to each have our own operations."

"Have you ever lived anywhere else?"

"No. Jewel River is home. Cade lived in New York City for several years, though. He moved back for good after our father died."

"You're close to your brother, aren't you?" She nudged the bowl away.

"Yeah, I am."

"Your mom gave me a romance novel. Told me to keep the first Thursday of the month open for book club."

"What did I tell you? That's my mom. Always trying to get people to join her book club. Are you thinking of going?"

"No," she said with a self-deprecating shrug. "I told her I

don't drive, and she said you would drop me off. I wouldn't want you to do that. I told her it would be too complicated with Peanut and my fainting."

"I'm sure she had a reply for that," he muttered.

"She told me she's used to being around service dogs since she trained Tulip. And she assured me I would have a comfy chair in case I fainted."

"Mom doesn't know how to take no for an answer."

Ashlinn privately agreed. "Then she said no one would even notice if I fainted, since a few of the older members fall asleep on occasion—apparently, I'd fit right in."

His expression blanked. "She didn't."

"She did." Ashlinn's lips twitched. At the time she'd been surprised, but looking back, it was kind of funny.

"I'm sorry. I don't know what to say. She's—"

"Wonderful. Your mom is wonderful." Ashlinn meant it. "But I still told her no."

"Good. You need to do what's right for you." He glanced toward the back door. "The weather's nice. Have you been able to get outside much?"

"No. I haven't been feeling good. I've been in bed or on the couch."

"Why don't we go out back? It's a beautiful day. I'll set up a lawn chair for you."

"I don't have a lawn chair." If she did, though…she wouldn't mind sitting out there in the sunshine.

"You do now." He stood and grinned. "I'll be right back."

What was he talking about? He went to the back door. She wanted to rush over to the window to watch him, but she'd better conserve the little energy she had. Her top priority at the moment was making herself presentable.

She went to her bedroom and changed into a clean shirt and shorts. Peanut followed her. Then she crossed the hall to the bathroom and brushed her hair. She returned to the kitchen. Ty opened the back door and offered her his arm. She was thankful for his strong muscles to lean on as they carefully made their way down the steps. Two loungers and two Adirondack chairs were set up on the lawn. Side tables had been placed between them.

She blinked back tears. “It’s like a tropical oasis in my backyard.”

Peanut was nosing around all the furniture. With his nose to the ground, too, Fritz trotted around the perimeter of the fence, then came over to them in leaps and bounds. Peanut looked up at them with his tongue hanging out.

“See? Even the dogs approve.” Ty helped her sit on one of the loungers, and as she stretched out her legs, she heaved a sigh of relief. He was right. The sun felt amazing.

“How much do I owe you for the chairs?” She glanced over at Ty, who’d taken a seat in the lounger next to her with a content expression on his face.

“Nothing.”

“I have to pay you.”

“No, you don’t. You didn’t ask for them. And I had an ulterior motive.”

“Ulterior motive, huh?” She wasn’t buying it. He kept doing nice things for her, and what did she give him in return? Not a whole lot.

“Yes. I was thinking about buying a set of loungers like this for my place. Now I know they’re comfortable.”

“Then take these with you.” She didn’t want to be in his debt. And she couldn’t really afford the chairs.

“Nope. I got a deal on a four-pack. Two for you, and two for me.” He wiggled his shoulders and closed his eyes with his hands on his washboard abs. “I’m going to string some patio lights over there, too, if you don’t object.”

“Really?” She could picture lights strung overhead, like the ones she secretly wanted whenever she scrolled through her phone. This man was so thoughtful.

“Yes, really. I wouldn’t lie about it.”

"Thank you. That's so generous and thoughtful of you." The sound of birds chirping and the wind gently rustling the leaves in the nearby tree were more relaxing than any music could be. Within moments, drowsiness overtook her.

She must have fallen asleep because when she woke, she sensed that if she tried to get up, she'd pass out. Peanut had noticed, too, because he was sitting next to her chair, staring at her. He began licking her hand. She petted him. "Good boy. Good boy."

"What do you need?" Ty shifted to face her, placing his feet on the ground between their chairs.

"Potato chips. Water." She didn't bother insisting on getting them herself. Her blood pressure was low, and she needed the salt and the fluids. Could kick herself for not bringing them out here. Too in a rush to enjoy the weather. Too excited to be with Ty. She made a mental note to prepare better if she came outside alone.

"Done."

A few minutes later, he handed her a bag of potato chips and her tumbler full of ice water. She thanked him and munched on a few chips.

"You okay?"

She nodded. "It's funny, but I never thought I'd be able to do this with someone other than my parents."

"What do you mean?" He'd shifted to recline on the lounger again but kept his head turned to watch her.

"I don't know." She took a long drink. Nice and cold. "I guess I didn't think I'd feel comfortable having anyone see me like this."

"Getting a suntan?" he teased.

"Ha ha." She threw a potato chip at him. He caught it and grinned. She grinned back. "You're seeing my normal life. Bedhead, weak, on the verge of passing out. It's not something many people have witnessed, and surprisingly, it's not as humiliating as I'd worried it would be."

"Good. It shouldn't be." He popped the chip into his mouth. "Toss me another, would you?"

She handed him the bag, and he took a handful before passing it back.

"What about your friends?" he asked. "You know, before you moved here?"

That brought a pang to her chest. She didn't have the best track record with friends. "They all kind of moved on with their lives. I didn't have a best friend in high school. I hung out with a group of girls, and after graduating, we all went our separate ways. None of my college friends lived nearby, and the ones who made an effort quit coming around after years of me not being able to go anywhere."

He probably thought she was a loser for not having friends.

"I pushed my friends away." His gruff words were not what she was expecting. "They refused to give up on me, though. My brother made it his mission to barge into my life whenever he feels like it. Mom, too. I used to resent it."

"You don't anymore?"

He shook his head, wiping the crumbs from his hands. "I don't. He loves me. Worries about me. And I can honestly say if our roles were reversed, I'd do the same to him."

"He seems nice. He's stopped by the center with Mackenzie a few times. What about the rest of your friends?"

"A couple of guys moved back recently—Dean McCaffrey, he's a builder here in town if you need any work done, and Trent Lloyd, who manages Cade's horse-boarding business. I should drive you over there sometime. I think you'd like the stables."

At that, she directed her attention to the tumbler in her hand. Ty seemed to keep forgetting she couldn't go wherever she pleased. He'd asked her out to his ranch, and now he wanted her to see his brother's stables?

He didn't get it.

For the past four days, she'd barely been able to stand.

How could she possibly leave her house and drive somewhere with him?

She couldn't. And she needed to keep that in mind before she went all gaga over the cowboy sitting next to her.

Still…until yesterday she hadn't even considered spending time in her backyard. Maybe because there wasn't any patio furniture. No safe spot for her to lie down if her blood pressure dropped.

Ty had made this possible. And if he could give her a safe space in her yard, what else could he do?

How many of her *I can'ts* were real, and how many were simply fears?

AN HOUR LATER, Ty knocked on his mom's front door. Figured he'd try to be a better son and make more of an effort with her. She'd never given up on him, and he'd provided her plenty of reasons to in the past couple of years. Gratitude—especially for how she'd reached out to Ashlinn to make her feel welcome—flooded him. His mom was special.

Ashlinn had barely been able to keep her eyes open when he'd taken off. First, he'd made her promise she'd call or text him if she needed anything. He'd also told her he'd be back in the morning with doughnuts from Annie's Bakery. She hadn't seemed enthused about it. Doughnuts might not have been the best suggestion since she was sick. Or was her lack of enthusiasm due to him coming over again?

They'd clicked all afternoon. She'd said she felt comfortable with him, and he felt the same. It hadn't bothered him that she was tired and low on energy. In fact, he'd liked helping her, liked the way her face had lit up when he'd shown her the outdoor furniture. He'd enjoyed their teasing banter. The woman had no idea how beautiful she was, bedhead and all.

"I wasn't expecting you!" His mom's mouth spread into a smile full of wonder. She pulled him in for a hug. "Charlene's here, and Clem's coming over in a bit—we figured the fish fry at Dixie B's was the right move. You'll join us, of course. Four is better than three."

"Char's here?" He retreated a step, but Fritz surged forward at the sight of Tulip, his mother's Pomeranian. "I'll come back another time."

"Yoo-hoo, Ty!" Charlene Parker called from the living room. "Get your cute self in here and give me a hug."

He winced, shifting his jaw. Just one of the reasons he didn't drop by his mother's house very often. There was no telling who'd be visiting. Charlene and his mother together unsettled him. He knew exactly what he was walking into—the latest gossip, endless questions about the fundraiser and not so subtle hints about dating Ashlinn.

These two had been trying to set him up with every single woman in his age range for years. Ew.

His mom took him by the arm and practically dragged him inside. The dogs finished greeting each other, and Ty bent to pet fluffy Tulip. Then he went over to Charlene.

"Hi, Charlene." He gave her a hug and sat at the other end of the couch. She was the director of the small nursing home where his grandmother lived. "How's everything at the nursing home?"

"Good as it can be, hon." She picked up a dainty teacup and took a sip. "Miss Trudy's been sleeping more lately."

Trudy Moulten, his paternal grandmother, had been living at the home for a few years. Her Alzheimer's was getting worse. His mother brought Tulip to see her almost every day. "Is that good or bad?"

"A bit of both. She's confused a lot, so sleeping gives her peace." Charlene's affectionate tone eased his worries. "Now, where is little Fritz?"

Good question. He looked around. "He should be here—oh, there he is." The mini-doxie trotted to Charlene's feet, waiting for her to pick him up. She promptly snuggled the dog to her chest. He gave her cheek a lick, and she laughed. "Sweet Fritzie."

"Did you check on Ashlinn?" Mom settled into an overstuffed chair and propped her feet on the ottoman. "I like her. I might have convinced her to join the book club. I hope she's feeling better soon."

"Stomach bug?" Charlene continued to pet Fritz, who'd taken the opportunity to sit on her lap. The dog seemed to know he'd be pampered there.

"She called it a flare-up," Ty said. "She looked pale. The weakness is due to her autoimmune disease."

"Poor thing." His mom shook her head, making a tsking noise. "So pretty and so young. Doesn't seem fair her life is so limited due to her health."

"At least she's alive." Ty hadn't meant to sound bitter. But it occurred to him that Zoey's life had been limited, too, but she'd died. She'd never have a chance to enjoy afternoons in the backyard anymore.

"True, but I wish she had her health," his mom said. "From what I understand, she's nearly homebound when it comes to activities. It's got to be hard."

"She doesn't see it that way." He propped an ankle on the opposite knee.

"How *does* she see it?" Charlene mindlessly petted Fritz.

He squirmed a little. Why hadn't he kept his mouth shut? Let them do all the talking as usual? They were good at it. Better than he was.

"I gather she's glad to have some freedom again."

"Freedom?" Charlene gave his mom a skeptical glance. "If you say so. We haven't seen her around town at all."

"I do say so." It annoyed him that they weren't giving Ashlinn her due. Fritz stepped off Charlene's lap and came over to his. As the dog licked his forearm, Ty's tension faded slightly.

"She's spent the past six years relying on her parents for everything. And now she's living in a house on her own, and she even has a part-time job. Both were more than she could have hoped for previously."

"You're right." Charlene had a contrite air. "I guess it depends on how you look at things."

"I, for one, hope we all see a lot more of her. I gave her this month's book since *someone* was being a baby and refused to give it to her." Mom gave him serious side-eye.

"I'm not carrying around a book with a dude holding twin babies on the cover."

"What if the man was a cowboy and there were no babies?" Mom asked. "Would you take her a book if it had mountains on it or something?"

"No." He had to be firm. If he agreed to one cowboy or mountains, she'd start pressuring him to deliver books with babies and dogs and guys making googly eyes at some woman. Wasn't happening.

The women exchanged disappointed stares. He willed himself not to squirm.

"It's just a book," Mom said. "I'm not asking for much."

"Why are you mad?" He opened his hands. "The book club is your pride and joy, not mine. I'm not doing your dirty work."

"Dirty work." His mother shook her head as if he'd lost his mind. "I'm asking you to drop off a novel, Ty, not smuggle drugs."

He knew better than to respond.

"So where are you at with the event planning?" Charlene took another sip of tea.

He filled them in on everything, including the flyers and social media graphics Ashlinn had made.

"Did you figure out what you're doing about the silent auction yet?" Mom asked.

"No. I'll ask Ashlinn about it when she's feeling better."

"Why don't you let us handle it?" Her face lit up. "We can go around town and ask for donations. I stop by most of the businesses every week, anyhow."

He opened his mouth to decline her offer, but then he closed it. His mother and Charlene were perfect for the job. They knew everyone in Jewel River and had no problem asking for donations.

"Actually, that would be a big help, Mom."

She blinked a few times. He braced himself for…something.

"You're letting me help?" Her voice sounded strangled, and her eyes shimmered in surprise.

"Yeah. You'll be great at it. Better than me."

She pushed Tulip off her lap, stood and crossed over to him. He rose slightly as she hugged him. Then she kissed his right cheek and nodded, clearly emotional.

What was that all about?

"This is the first time you've accepted an offer of help from me in years."

She was right, and he hadn't realized his dismissal had hurt her. "I'm sorry—"

"No, no. I didn't mention it to make you feel bad. Something's changed with you, Ty, and I like it. I hope you'll continue letting me help."

He ran his finger along the collar of his T-shirt. "Um, sure."

A knock on the door sent his mother in motion. "That must be Clem. Ty, will Fritz be okay here alone with Tulip?"

"I'm not going out to eat."

"Yes, you are," she said on her way to the door. "Look at them." Fritz had jumped up on her chair and smooshed in next to Tulip. "Fritzie will be fine here."

"Come on." Clem's gruff voice filled the room. "We need to leave now if we want to get a table."

Ty waited for Charlene to gather her purse, then followed her to the door, where Clem's eyes widened in surprise.

"Christy didn't tell me you were here. Finally. A man. These two hens will be clucking nonstop. I might be able to eat in peace."

"We are *not* chickens, Clem." His mom hiked her purse strap over her shoulder and marched down the porch steps to his truck. "And we don't cluck."

Clem strode after her. "You two gab so much no one can get a word in."

"Oh, and you're such a talker."

Ty closed the door and followed them to the driveway. His mom waited for Clem to open the back door for her. Ty jogged around the other side and held open the door for Charlene.

Once the women were settled, he gave them a nod. "I'm going home."

"Don't be a ninny." Clem climbed into the truck. "Get in. Time's a wasting."

"Maybe next time."

"Get. In." Clem's steely eyes meant business.

Ty sighed.

"What? You think there's a rattlesnake on the seat, boy?" Clem made a sucking sound with his teeth.

Ty climbed into the passenger seat. Clem backed out of the drive.

"Clem, you'd be bored out of your mind without us around," Charlene said. "We keep things lively."

"Bored? I don't think so."

Panic set in as Ty realized he was voluntarily going to Dixie B's with his mother, her best friend and Clem.

He didn't go out to dinner with people. Not even his family.

Maybe his mother was right. Something *had* changed. He wasn't sure he was ready for this new development.

What would it hurt? His mom and Charlene would do all the talking. And Clem would glower at anyone who stopped by to say hello. Dining with these three was probably the best-case scenario if he ever wanted to start getting out and about town more often. But did he want to? It was too late to back out now.

CHAPTER SIX

THE MAN HAD brought doughnuts, and Ashlinn loved a good pastry.

"I've got crullers, cinnamon rolls, long johns, pumpkin doughnuts—you name it. I hope you don't mind. I know you haven't been feeling great." Ty lifted the lid off the box marked Annie's Bakery in her kitchen the next morning. She'd been ready when he'd arrived a few minutes past ten. She'd even showered and done her hair. Yesterday, both had been impossible.

"Ooh, the cinnamon roll, please." She set two small plates on the counter. Then she straightened the red-and-white checked dish towel hanging from the oven handle. "Want a cup of coffee?"

"Sure." Icing from the cinnamon roll oozed on one plate, and a cruller and pumpkin doughnut were crammed on the other. Sunlight streamed in through the window over the sink. He pointed to the coffeepot. "I can pour if you'd like to sit and rest."

"I'm okay." She took out two mugs from an upper cabinet. "I think the fresh air and soup yesterday helped me turn the corner. I feel much better."

"I'm glad to hear it."

"I have flavored cream in the fridge if you want it."

"No thanks. I take my coffee black."

She poured the coffee and brought the mugs to the table where Ty had carried the plates. Peanut glued himself to her side and licked his doggy lips twice.

"You're not getting any of this, mister." She stroked Peanut's soft, furry head.

"What are you doing today?" Ty sat in the same chair he had yesterday. "Do you need a hand with anything?"

She'd known him less than a month, and he'd continued to go out of his way to help her. She tore off a small chunk of the roll and popped it in her mouth. After chewing, she stared at him. "Actually, I wanted to ask you something."

"What?"

"I've thought about it, and I'd like to see your ranch." Her nerves jittered over what could happen, but excitement rose, too. The more she'd thought about it last night, the more she realized she wanted to expand her world. Little by little. Inch by inch.

"When?" He toyed with the handle of the mug.

"Today?" She cringed a bit. Was she ready? "I'd need to bring supplies. And I might not be able to do much besides sit."

"You want to visit my ranch?" An incredulous grin spread across his face. "Today?"

She nodded. Why was he so happy about it? It wasn't like she could ride horses or rope cows or whatever people did on ranches.

"I don't want you to be nervous." He extended his arm, palm out. "We'll sit on my front porch. I've got a pair of rocking chairs. We'll watch the world go by. It's my favorite thing to do."

A rush of emotion had her blinking away tears. Rocking on a front porch sounded absolutely wonderful. Could he truly want something so simple?

"Good, because that's about all I can do right now," she said. "I don't want you to be disappointed."

"Never." He pushed his chair back and stood. "What do we need to bring?"

She laughed, pointing for him to sit again. "Let's enjoy our coffee first."

He gave her a sheepish grin.

"What did you do last night?" she asked, sipping her coffee.

"Believe it or not, I went out to supper with my mom, her best friend and Clem."

"Why would that be hard to believe?" She assumed he dined with them often.

"I don't go out to eat very often."

"No?"

"I don't get out much in general." He bit into the cruller.

"Why not?"

"After Zoey died, it was too hard."

Zoey. Again. Ashlinn tried not to let the name bother her. She'd ignore the sudden burst of heartburn it produced.

"Is it still hard?" she asked.

"More uncomfortable than hard, I guess."

"Six years, right? Maybe being alone became a habit."

"Maybe." He didn't meet her eyes.

Another thought occurred. "Do you think you've been depressed?"

When he didn't immediately say no, she took it as a yes.

"What's changed?" She lifted her mug to take a sip.

"Nothing." Then he rubbed his chin. "A lot of things."

"Like what?"

"My brother marrying Mackenzie. Mom moving to town. Patrick opening the center. My buddies settling here again. I guess I started to wake up to the world around me."

"I'm glad you did." His honesty touched her.

"Why?"

"Otherwise, you wouldn't have adopted Fritz, and we probably wouldn't have met."

"I think you're right." His thoughtful expression was tinged with sadness. "I wouldn't have wanted to meet you."

Ouch. That comment stung.

"But I would have missed out." His searing gaze and tender tone chased away the sting. "I'm glad we met."

"I am, too." She polished off half of her cinnamon roll and stood. "Let me get a few things together, and we can go."

"What do you need? Let me help."

"The weighted blanket folded next to the couch. I'll grab my blood pressure monitor."

"Don't forget the chips and water." He headed to the living room.

"I won't." Her phone rang on the way to her bedroom. She answered it. "Hey, Mom, what's up?"

"How are you doing? Have you eaten anything? I called the clinic in Jewel River, and they can give you an IV on Monday when they open."

Ashlinn slowed, her good mood crashing. "I'm doing okay. I'm eating again. Yesterday was much better than the rest of the week."

"Can you call Patrick to take you to the doctor on Monday for the IV?" Her voice was shrill.

"It's not necessary."

"Not necessary? The last time you had stomach problems, you were in bed for a week."

"And this time I bounced back more quickly." She suppressed her mounting frustration. "In fact, I feel good enough to go on a small adventure today."

"Adventure? Absolutely not. Please don't tell me you're walking to work."

"It's Saturday. The center's closed." She forced herself to the bedroom, where she located the monitor and grabbed a hoodie in case it got cold.

"What are you doing, then?"

"Ty is taking me to his ranch." She braced herself for a lecture.

"A ranch?" The long pause didn't help her nerves. "What are you thinking? You can't ride horses. What if you faint? How far away is this place?"

Disappointment seeped to her toes. Her mom never gave her any credit. Always saw the downside. "I didn't say I was riding horses."

"This is going to send you right back to a life in bed. Have you forgotten those days?"

"No, Mom. I haven't forgotten. I know what I'm doing."

"I don't think you do. You're playing games with your health, and who will be around to take care of you when it falls apart this time?"

Why did there have to be a "this time?" Ashlinn gripped the phone tightly. "I'm not talking to you when you're in this mood."

"What mood?" Her mom's voice rose. "I don't know what you're talking about."

"Goodbye." She ended the call and perched on the edge of her bed. Her hands were trembling. Was her mom right? Was she playing games with her health? Would she be bedridden if she overdid it by going to the ranch? Her doctors encouraged her to get out if she felt up to it.

"Ashlinn?" Ty called from the living room. She stood and carried the monitor and hoodie down the hallway, where Ty held up the tote. "Oh, there you are. I've got the blanket, chips and water. Do you need anything else?"

"Peanut." She tried to smile, but she was pretty sure her face was cracking.

"Hey, are you okay?" He put his hand on her shoulder, and she almost burst into tears. "If you're not feeling good—"

"I feel good." She lifted her chin and looked into his eyes. "Let's get out of here."

Questions lingered in his eyes, but he gave her a nod. She helped Peanut into his vest. Took a deep breath.

God, I don't know if this is the right decision or not, but I know You'll be with me today, and that's all I really need.

Ty held the door open, and she and the dog headed outside. Something told her she had nothing to worry about as long as Ty was at her side. A taste of life—an afternoon somewhere new—was exactly what she needed. And if her health fell apart? Her mom could tell her, "I told you so."

"WAIT RIGHT THERE." Ty got out of the truck and jogged around the front to open the passenger door for Ashlinn. She'd been quiet during the half-hour ride. He'd turned the radio to a country station and watched the world go by. When she'd told him she wanted to see his ranch, he'd been shocked—and excited. And in his haste to make it happen, he'd overlooked one important question. Could he handle it if anything went wrong?

What if she had a medical emergency? His ranch was thirty minutes from town, and the nearest hospital was a good hour and a half away.

Ashlinn might look fine, but she was still recovering from her flare-up. He should have told her they could come out next weekend. But he hadn't. Selfishly, he'd wanted to bring her here today. Probably because he feared she'd change her mind in a week.

Being around Ashlinn made him feel alive. And he hadn't felt alive in a long time.

"Are you ready for this?" He took her hand and helped her climb out. Then he let Peanut out of the backseat. The dog always appeared to be smiling. Ty grabbed the tote from the floor and offered Ashlinn his arm. Together, they strolled to his front porch. He ignored the way his heartbeat pounded at the feel of her small hand in the crook of his arm.

"Wow, Ty." She turned to him. "All this is yours?"

His chest expanded. He was proud of his home and property. "Yes. The house, outbuildings, corrals, pastures—all of it. My land stops at those trees." He pointed to a forest in the far distance. "Come on. I'll show you around inside."

The front door led directly into his living room. Hardwood floors, dark brown furniture and white walls—suited him just fine. The place had never had a woman's touch.

"It's lovely." She let go of his arm and drifted over to the picture window. "I can't get over your view." Beyond the lawn, the prairie rolled out for miles.

"I could stare at it all day." Although, at the moment, the only thing he was staring at was her.

"Me, too." She turned to him with a soft smile, and he couldn't help wondering what it would be like to kiss her. *Slow down, cowboy. You're not kissing anyone.*

"I'll, uh, set everything right here." He put her tote next to the coffee table on the rug. "Can I get you something to drink?"

"No, I'm fine. Oh, there you are, Fritz." Fritz bypassed Ty to run straight to her, and she bent to pet him. Ty didn't blame the dog. He was drawn to her, too.

When she straightened, she thrust her hand out to steady herself, but all it met with was air. She began to sway. Peanut hurried over, and Ty sprang into action, putting his arm around her waist.

"Whoa, there. You okay?" He guided her to the couch and helped her sit. Peanut stayed by her side, staring at her. "Do you want to lie down?"

"I'd better sit on the floor. I could faint and fall off the couch. I try to stay on the ground when Peanut alerts me. Could you put a pillow and the weighted blanket down there?" She pointed to the area rug. "I'll drink some water. Maybe this will pass."

"Do you feel like you're going to faint?" He brought over

her weighted blanket and set a throw pillow on the rug. Peanut put his paw on the blanket.

"Peanut wants me on the floor. When he acts like this, I usually pass out within minutes. See how he's focused on the blanket? He wants me down there." She scooted forward, and Ty assisted her to the floor. Peanut lay next to her, licking her hand. Fritz bounced over and tried to sit on her lap, but Ty scooped up the mutt and cradled him to his chest.

"Leave Ashlinn alone. She's not feeling good, buddy." The dog licked his chin and wiggled to get down. Ty set him on all fours but commanded him to sit. Fritz obeyed. Anxiety began rising within him.

"I need the blood pressure cuff." Her voice faded.

"I'll get it." He set her tumbler of water next to her and rooted through the tote to find the blood pressure monitor. His fingers shook as he carried it over.

"Thanks." She stretched out her legs and placed the weighted blanket over her shins. Peanut sat upright next to her. She wrapped her arm around him. "You know it's coming, don't you, boy?"

"Want me to put this on?" Ty held up the cuff, hating how helpless he felt.

"Cover." Her voice grew weaker as she pointed to her lap. Panting, Peanut draped his body over her thighs. "Good boy."

"Ashlinn?" Ty's nerves frayed. What should he do? Fritz came over and whined. Ashlinn's breathing grew shallow and her eyes closed as she stroked Peanut's fur. The dog licked her forearm and hand.

"Cuff." Without opening her eyes, she touched her left wrist. He ripped the Velcro and wrapped the cuff around it. Then he pressed the start button. Peanut continued licking her hand, and she kept praising him. She shifted from sitting to lying on the rug with her head on the pillow.

Ty knelt beside her with no clue what to do. On her other side, Peanut licked and nibbled her fingers and wrist.

She'd passed out. Her arm was limp. She was unresponsive.

Fear spread through his core. Peanut wouldn't stop licking her arm, and Fritz came over, clearly aware something was happening, and put his front paws on Ty's thighs.

Should he check her blood pressure? Shake her?

What if she didn't wake up?

Get yourself together. Fritz licked his hand. Great. The dog was copying Peanut, and Ty was pretty sure he wasn't the one with the medical problems.

He checked the monitor on her wrist. Her blood pressure was low. Too low. Another wave of anxiety crested. Fritz licked his hand again, and he picked up the dog, hugging him to his chest. He began to feel calmer.

"Good boy," she whispered.

Ty inhaled sharply. She was conscious! *Thank You, Lord. Thank You!*

Peanut no longer licked her hand. Instead, he softly panted and stayed beside her. She opened her eyes and closed them again. A few moments later, she moved her arms slightly. Peanut licked her fingers again. Her face was pale. She looked exhausted.

As Ty sat there watching her, he was thankful for Fritz's warm body in his arms.

What seemed like a lifetime later but was probably only a few minutes, Ashlinn turned her head and stared at him through unfocused eyes. "I'm okay."

She didn't sound okay.

"Stay where you are, Ash. Can I get you anything? Do anything?"

"Legs." Her hand flopped as she pointed to her lower legs.

He moved the weighted blanket, not sure what she was asking him to do. Then she made a scrunching motion with her fingers. He set Fritz on the floor and gently massaged her lower legs. Fritz joined Peanut, sniffing Ashlinn's arm.

Ty continued to compress her calves, grateful to be doing something—anything—to take his mind off his helplessness.

"Almost there." She turned her head. "Thank you."

He nodded, touched by her gratitude. He'd done next to nothing. Wished he could have prevented it. She reached for her tumbler of water, and he put it in her hand. "Can I help you sit up?"

"Not yet. Give me a few minutes."

"Sure." Peanut ambled away with Fritz. Either the dog wasn't concerned or he was distracted by the wiener dog. Something told him Peanut wasn't easily distracted.

True to her word, Ashlinn shifted to her side and dragged the weighted blanket over her legs once more. Peanut was off doing his own thing, and Fritz came over wagging his tail. She caressed the little dog. "You're worried about me, aren't you?"

"He's not the only one."

She met his gaze, understanding emanating from her eyes. "I know. It's not easy watching me have an episode."

"How long are you usually out?"

Resting her cheek on her arm, she frowned. "It depends. Sometimes only a few seconds. Sometimes longer. If Peanut was still here licking me, I'd probably pass out again, but he's moved on with his life."

"Should he have moved on?" He wanted to know more about what to expect.

"Yes." She looked cute lying there on her side with her cheek on her upper arm and her blond hair spilling out across the rug. "It means my body's returning to normal. Speaking of which, I'd better check the monitor again."

After reading the number, she began to sit up. She scooted so her back was against the couch. Ty found the bag of potato chips. As soon as he gave it to her, he went to the kitchen, braced his palms against the counter, and let his head drop.

Witnessing a full-blown faint had scared him more than he wanted to admit. Lifting his head, he clenched his jaw.

Maybe he shouldn't have asked her to come. Had the drive caused her to faint?

What if she hadn't woken up? What would he have done then?

He had to stop that line of thinking. She *had* recovered. She'd been able to prepare for it. She'd known what to do, and Peanut had, too.

After centering himself, he returned to the living room and fount Ashlinn attempting to stand. He rushed over and helped her sit on the couch.

"Thank you." She crunched on a chip. "Regret inviting me yet?" Her tone was teasing, but worry ran deep within her eyes.

"Of course not." He wanted her there. He just didn't want to make her sick. Wished she could enjoy it. "I'm glad you're here."

"Me, too." She ate another chip.

"I wasn't sure what to do. What if you didn't wake up?" He hoped she wouldn't be offended by his question.

"I always wake up. That's one thing you don't have to worry about. The danger is when I'm not able to get to a safe position before fainting. I could fall and hit my head—that sort of thing."

An image of her on the ground with a pool of blood spreading through her hair made him pace. Fritz came over and let out a yip. He stared down at the dog.

"He knows when you're nervous." Ashlinn continued eating chips.

"What do you mean?"

"He's alerting you."

"What?" Was it possible?

She nodded, finishing her bite. "He was trained to alert his previous owner, a veteran with anxiety and depression. He's good at picking up on moods."

Huh. Ty hadn't put two and two together. Ashlinn could be

right. Fritz always zoomed over when he was stressed. Licked his hand. Demanded attention. Even yipped on occasion.

"I never thought I'd be getting alerted by a service dog." He let out a soft snort, looking at the tiny dog through new eyes.

"Now you know." She took a long drink of water. "I'm feeling much better. And I believe you promised me a rocking chair on the front porch."

"I did." He offered her his hand. Her small fingers felt delicate in his, strengthening his desire to protect her. "You're sure you want to go outside?"

"I'm sure."

"The dogs should be okay out there with us." They made their way to the door. "Or do you think they need leashes?"

"Peanut never strays far from me."

"Fritz doesn't like to be more than ten feet from me." His worries began to fade. "He's always by my side."

Out on the porch, Ty helped her into a rocking chair. Peanut and Fritz jogged down the steps and played with each other on the front lawn. Then Ty went back inside to get her water, the weighted blanket and the blood pressure cuff. Just in case.

The serenity on her face as she rocked and took in the view stole his breath. He'd never have guessed she'd spent the past fifteen minutes dealing with a fainting spell and its aftermath.

"It's beautiful out here, Ty." She sighed in contentment. "I saw a hawk flying overhead."

"You'll see a lot of them." He set everything beside her on the porch, then lowered his frame into the other rocking chair. "In the evenings, you'll see pronghorns and deer."

"This is like something out of a picture book. I'm not used to having such a wide-open view. No neighbors. No houses. Just all this glorious land."

"I feel the same." Except the things she listed could be a liability, too—not for him—but for her.

What happened if she was all alone out here and fainted? Hit her head and was hurt?

"Is it only you running this place?" she asked. Peanut checked on her, then he and Fritz sprawled out on the porch.

"No, I have a full-time ranch hand and a part-timer, too."

"Tell me about what you do here. How does your day begin?"

"Mornings start before dawn. We take care of the horses, in the winter we feed the cattle..." He gave her an overview of his life as a rancher, answering each question that came up.

"I'd take you on a tour—"

Her laugh cut him off. "No, I don't want to chance it. Right here is perfect."

He gave her a searching stare, then turned his attention to the land before him. Right here was perfect for him, too. Always had been. The fact she felt the same filled him with satisfaction.

And then he remembered Zoey.

Zoey had been the one to suggest he buy two rocking chairs so they'd be able to enjoy the good weather "like a couple of old folks." But she'd died before she could enjoy sitting out there with him.

What would she think of him out here with another woman in her chair?

He stood abruptly. "I'll be right back."

He hurried into the house and marched straight to the bathroom. Splashed water on his face and glanced up at his reflection in the mirror. What was he doing?

Ashlinn wasn't supposed to be part of his life. No woman was.

But he couldn't pretend he wasn't drawn to her. And he'd better get back out there in case she had another fainting spell.

Lighting matches around dry tinder. That was what he was doing. And he'd be the one getting torched if he didn't start guarding his heart.

CHAPTER SEVEN

"YOU SHOULD COME with us to the Shakespeare-in-the-Park movie." Mackenzie Moulten sat across from Ashlinn at the desk in Patrick's office on Thursday afternoon. Peanut was grooming himself on the dog bed in the corner. Mackenzie had arrived twenty minutes ago telling Ashlinn all about the various ranches she'd been to for herd health visits over the past couple of weeks. Her mobile vet trailer allowed her to treat large animals on-site. With her long blond hair, athletic style and fresh-faced beauty, Mackenzie was as authentic a person as she'd ever met.

Could she say the same for herself? Probably not. She wasn't sure who she was anymore. Hadn't known for years. And lately, she wanted to find out exactly what Ashlinn Burnier was all about.

"When is the movie thing?" Ashlinn acted like she was actually considering it. She wasn't.

"This Saturday." Mackenzie clasped her hands and stretched them over her head. "Ugh. My shoulders have been so tight lately. Anyway, Cade and I are getting there early to help Erica and Dalton set up the screen and make sure the food vendors park in the right area. I hope Lindsey doesn't spring any wild animals on us this go-round. It was pandemonium when the critters got loose last year."

Ashlinn chuckled softly. She'd heard all about the raccoon incident from the previous summer.

"It's at Memorial Park, right?" Before Mackenzie had arrived, Ashlinn had finished entering information into the spreadsheet. No more work was getting done today, so she saved it and closed the program. She'd made it through two hours of work without a single alert from Peanut. Felt like a victory.

"Yes. Cade and I will gladly pick you up. Everyone sits on the lawn. Brooke and Dean are leaving the twins with her mom—the girls' father was killed in a training mission shortly after they were born. When Dean moved back to town last November, Brooke reconnected with him. Their wedding should be a good time. Have you met her brother, Marc Young?"

"Not yet."

"Their mom owns Annie's Bakery. Marc's wife, Reagan, isn't sure about bringing the baby, so I don't know if they'll be there. Do you know Trent Lloyd and Gracie French?"

"Gracie stopped by the center with the girls."

"Aren't they adorable? Gracie was worried Noelle would get scared from the special effects, but the older two girls insisted they were all attending. Everyone loves this event. The entire town shows up for it."

Ashlinn swallowed the fear and insecurity lodged in her throat. That was what she was afraid of. The entire town would witness her flat on her back, passed out for who knew how long. No thanks.

"I don't know. Last week was pretty rough. I don't want to overdo it."

Patrick appeared in the doorway. "I didn't hear you come in, Mackenzie. Would you check Candy for me? She's favoring her left paw. I didn't feel anything out of the ordinary in her right foreleg. Maybe you'll know what's wrong."

"Sure." Mackenzie stood and turned back to Ashlinn. "Text or call me if you change your mind. I'll come get you and Peanut right before the movie starts."

"Are you going to the Shakespeare thing, Ashlinn?" Patrick's eyebrows arched.

"Um, probably not. I'm trying to take it easy." She gathered her tote and tumbler of water. "I'm taking off. I'll let you know tomorrow if I'm coming in or not."

"Thanks. If you do, I'll have Bandit continue working with you like he did earlier. I feel good about his progress."

"Me, too." She went over to Peanut, helping him into the harness. Then she grabbed the handle. "You ready, boy?"

Out in the sunshine, she adjusted her grip on his harness before telling him they were going on patrol. The command let him know he was supposed to heel unless her blood pressure plunged. If that happened, he'd block her path until she sat on the ground. They crossed the parking lot.

The Shakespeare movie would have appealed to her in college before her health had collapsed. She'd loved going to community events—summer concerts in the park, farmers markets, festivals. Last fall, she'd mentioned to her mom she'd like to go to an apple fest in a nearby town. The woman had acted like she'd requested to skydive without a parachute. And, truthfully, Ashlinn had been somewhat relieved to stay home. Who knew what might happen if she tried to navigate crowds?

At the stop sign, she checked for traffic, and she and Peanut crossed the road. Her mom and dad still called a few times each day, but lately, they hadn't sounded as panicky. Yes, her mother had overreacted to her visiting Ty's ranch, and the following day Ashlinn had had to listen to a ten-minute lecture on knowing her limits. Then, her mom had gone off on a new tangent, worrying about what Ashlinn would do come winter.

Ashlinn and Patrick had already discussed it. He would pick up her and Peanut and take them home on the days she came in. When she'd told her mother winter wouldn't be a big deal, she'd been met with a long, cold silence.

Dad hadn't been much better. He'd thrown out what-if scenarios and none of them had been good. What if Patrick got sick or was out of town? What if her house lost power? What if Peanut slipped on ice and took her down with him?

Just thinking about it made her grimace. As soon as she got inside her house, she removed Peanut's harness. The weather was perfect to sit out back in one of the chairs Ty had brought over.

This time she'd be smarter about it. She strapped on the monitor, grabbed a half-eaten bag of chips and her tumbler of water. Swiped the novel Christy had given her and called for Peanut.

As soon as she'd stretched out on the lounger, she closed her eyes, savoring the warm sun on her skin. Minutes ticked by as she relaxed. This was living.

"Knock, knock." Ty's low voice made her eyelids fly open. What was he doing here? And why was her heartbeat going thump, thump?

"Come in." She waved him to open the fence gate. He entered the yard, closing the gate behind him and took a seat on the lounger next to her. He had a package in his hand.

"I've never seen you in shorts." She grinned, pointing to his attire.

"I don't wear them often." He gave her a self-deprecating smile as he extended his legs on the lounger. The T-shirt, athletic shorts and running shoes looked good on him, as did the baseball hat. "Feels weird without my cowboy boots and hat."

"I'm sure." She nodded to the box he'd set on the side table. "What's that?"

"The flyers. Thought you'd like to see them." He passed it to her. She adjusted the back of the lounger upright and lifted the lid, taking the top flyer out.

The colors and layout looked amazing. “It’s perfect. Exactly what we ordered.”

“Yeah. I’m happy with how they turned out.”

“Now what?” She placed the box on the grass between the chairs.

“Mom’s been all over town this week asking for donations for the silent auction. She volunteered to drop these off to all the local businesses, too.”

“That’s really nice of her.” Peanut came over but not to alert her. She wrapped her arm around him and kissed the top of his head. “You’re a good boy.”

Ty tilted his head slightly. “You been okay this week?”

“Yep. Back to normal.” She nodded. “Well, my normal.”

“That’s good.”

“I suppose you’re going to the Shakespeare movie.” She took a drink of water. “Mackenzie asked me to join them.”

“Are you going?” He frowned. At the thought of her at the film? Or that she might be attending with Cade and Mackenzie?

“No. I don’t think so.”

“I’m not going, either.”

“Why not?”

He shrugged. “Not my thing.”

“Liar,” she teased. “You told me you liked the special effects in the movie trailer.”

“You remembered that?”

“Of course.” Did the man have any clue that she’d hung on his every word since meeting him? “You should go.”

“If I go, you should go, too.”

“I couldn’t.”

“Same here.”

“Ty…” She dragged out his name.

“Ashlinn…” He matched her tone. She laughed. “I’ll go if you go.”

“That’s not fair,” she said.

"Why not?"

"You don't have to worry about strangers seeing you pass out."

"You don't have to worry about everyone in town coming up to you and acting like you've been living in a cave for six years."

"Is that what's holding you back?"

"I don't know." He plucked a blade of grass from the ground and twirled it between his fingers. "I guess I don't get out all that much."

"Why not?" She shouldn't be surprised, but she was. Yet here he was. Hanging out with her. She was flattered.

"I like to cook at home or grab takeout. I'm not a recluse or anything. I go to church. Groceries. The feedstore. I hang out at Cade's sometimes, and I visit my grandma at the nursing home once a week."

She studied his handsome face, those solemn eyes. It seemed a shame he wasn't enjoying life to the fullest. Ty was missing out on all his hometown had to offer. From their previous conversations, she was certain he'd get a kick out of the local festivals and events. Maybe he needed a good excuse to get out more. Could she be that excuse? But if she was, could she handle being out and about?

"I tell you what, Ty Moulten. I think you and I *should* go to the movie this weekend."

"What?" He clearly hadn't been expecting her to suggest it. "No. It's too much for you."

She'd ignore that comment. Reminded her a little too much of her parents. "We'll spread out a quilt, bring the dogs. It'll be fun." Fun? More like stressful. And exhausting. Her stomach churned. While she would like to look forward to it, her anxiety wouldn't let her.

"But what if you faint? What if you get sick?"

"I'll lie on the quilt like I do at home." Maybe it wouldn't be as bad as she thought. The movie wouldn't start until it was getting dark out. And they'd be on the lawn. She could simply rest on a blanket if Peanut alerted her. Her nerves started to settle. "I don't think anyone would even notice me fainting if what Mackenzie said is true."

"About what?"

"Everyone sits on the lawn facing the screen. No one will be paying me any attention." She hoped they wouldn't be, anyway.

Was she being naive thinking she could handle a movie in the park?

"Okay. You talked me into it. We'll go. I'll get everything set up beforehand, then I'll pick up you and Peanut. But you need to prepare yourself for one thing."

"What?"

"Everyone *will* pay attention to us. It's a small town. They'll notice."

"Oh." She wasn't sure she liked the sound of that. "So if I pass out, people will talk?"

He nodded.

"Maybe it's for the best. Get it out of the way. I'm sure most of them know about my condition at this point."

"Are you sure you want to chance it?" he asked.

No. But she'd do it for him. "Yeah. I'm sure."

"Could anything trigger you to get worse?" He tossed the blade of grass behind him.

"Permanently?"

"Yeah."

"I'm not sure. Right now I'm managing the fainting and stomach problems."

"What made you bedridden back when you lived with your folks?"

"I wasn't able to keep food down, and without Peanut, I had no warning when I fainted. Every time I tried to stand I would pass out. Eating was impossible—I missed most meals. I was so weak I couldn't do much of anything. I lived on meal replacement drinks, and I relied on my parents for everything. The health I'm enjoying now? I'm not guaranteed it will last."

He nodded as if he understood. "I want to make sure I'm prepared. Is there anything else I should be concerned about?"

"Like what?" She'd told him her symptoms. What more did he need to know?

"Your blood pressure—could you have a heart attack? What about seizures?"

"My heart's fine. I've never had a seizure."

His expression cleared in relief. She hadn't realized he worried about all that. Had he built up her disease to be more dangerous than it was?

"Right now, passing out and injuring myself in the process are my only real threats. Everything else I can manage."

"What if it gets worse again? What if you can't get out of bed or keep food down?"

"Don't say that." She winced in a playful manner, trying to lighten the mood. "I don't know what will happen. I could get worse, and I suppose I'd have to move back in with my parents."

"I don't want you to."

"I don't want to, either."

What had started out as a light conversation had shifted to something deeper. She realized he cared about her—and not as a friend—as something more.

Ty knelt next to her. Then he tenderly ran the edge of his finger down the hair framing her face. She could only stare wide-eyed at him, sensations firing her nerve endings.

"You're so beautiful, Ashlinn. I want to kiss you."

He thought she was beautiful? Wanted to kiss her? She couldn't think of a single reason to object. "Then kiss me."

His hand slipped behind her neck, and he cradled the back of her head as he brought his mouth to hers. She tentatively touched his cheek, smooth from shaving, warm from the heat of the day, and gasped at the feel of his lips on hers. He smelled like leather and bodywash. Tasted like mint. She kissed him back, feeling more alive than she had in years. Maybe ever.

Then he drew back. His dark eyes brooded as they glimmered with unspoken words—he liked her. A lot.

The feeling was mutual.

He rose and backed up a step. Regrets crashed over her. She shouldn't be flirting with Ty. Shouldn't be kissing him or leading him on.

He didn't see marriage in his future, and neither did she, in hers.

But if their circumstances were different…

She knew better than to saddle this cowboy with her health problems. He'd been devastated when he lost Zoey. He deserved someone who didn't need constant care—a woman who could sit next to him at church and go to a local festival and be a true partner to him. She'd never be that woman.

HE NEVER SHOULD have kissed her.

Saturday evening, Ty adjusted the quilt on the lawn of Memorial Park. He'd brought a cooler full of ice and beverages, two camping chairs and a bag with an assortment of snacks. All he had to do was drive to her place and bring her here. And he would. Soon.

But he wasn't ready just yet.

He'd spent all day yesterday and today thinking about how soft her lips had been against his. How sweet she'd tasted. How her fingers had touched his cheek so tenderly. How she made him feel like a strong man instead of a weak hermit.

But he wasn't strong. He was scared. Too caught up in his own problems to leave his house and socialize. Too insecure to face the town's questions and pity. Even now, he worried more about how people would react to seeing him than if Ashlinn would be safe.

He gave their spot a final once-over. Cade strode his way. "Good, you're set up next to us."

Like he'd had a choice in the matter.

"Mom's going to be up there with Charlene, Mary and some other ladies." Cade pointed ahead to where an entire row of camping chairs had been set up. "And I told Trent to sit on the other side of us."

Ty tried not to wince. Trent's three nieces were cute and all, but Ty hadn't been around kids much. Would they be running around, bothering Ashlinn?

"What about the twins?" he asked, bracing himself for Brooke and Dean and her two-year-old identical twin girls.

"Anne's babysitting them. Reagan and Marc might bring baby Elizabeth."

"Don't tell me. Next to us." He gulped.

Cade let out a guffaw. "No, dummy. They're up there next to Erica, Dalton and the boys."

"Then who's sitting here?" he asked.

"How should I know? Snoop around. Maybe there's a name." Cade nodded to the neat stack of supplies—a camping chair, cooler, rolled-up blanket. "I hope the weather holds."

"Me, too." Ty's phone alarm went off. "I've got to pick up Ashlinn."

"You bringing Fritz?"

"Yeah. He's with her now."

"All right, man. See you in a little while."

Ty kept his chin down as he strode to his truck. The park was filling up, and he didn't want to be stopped by anyone who had a bunch of questions.

As soon as he drove away, regrets filled him. Maybe he wasn't cut out for this. Too many things could go wrong. He was bound to get questions like, "Haven't seen you in years, where have you been?" and sympathetic smiles practically shouting, "He's finally getting over Zoey."

He wasn't getting over Zoey.

He'd never get over Zoey.

His hands strangled the steering wheel. He forced himself to loosen his grip. *Think about Ashlinn. She deserves a good time tonight.*

He half hoped she'd call the whole thing off. They could stay at her place, share a pizza, enjoy a summer night under the lights he'd strung in her backyard—just them and the dogs. No people. No questions. No worries.

As soon as Ashlinn opened the door, all his objections galloped away. She had on a pink sundress, and her hair was pulled back into a half ponytail with the rest of her hair flowing down her back. To say she glowed would be an understatement. He forced himself to breathe. Man, she was stunning.

"You look pretty." He kept his hands by his sides. All he wanted to do was touch her.

Her cheeks flushed. "Thank you."

The urge to take her into his arms and kiss her again was overwhelming. Instead, he followed her inside and glanced around for the dogs. Both zoomed to him with their tails wagging. "Hey, guys. Ready to go to the park?"

"I know I am." She began getting Peanut's harness on him. "Unlike these two, I'm a little nervous."

"Yeah, me, too." His fingertips tapped like drumsticks against his thighs. Although the weather was warm, he'd opted for jeans and cowboy boots. Had to be as comfortable as possible. He found Fritz's leash and attached it.

"I think I'm all set."

"What else do you need? Do you have your blood pressure cuff?"

She patted the tote bag she'd slung over her shoulder. "Right here."

He hesitated as he stared into her eyes. "We don't have to do this, you know. Say the word. We can stay home."

"Part of me wants to stay here." She blinked up at him.

"All right, then, no problem. We stay." It was what he wanted, so why did he feel let down?

"I don't think so." A smiled flirted in the corners of her mouth. "A bigger part of me wants to go."

He couldn't argue with that. "Okay. Then it's a yes. Let's go."

Five minutes later, he'd parked on a side street and held Fritz's leash in one hand and Ashlinn's tote in the other. She stayed close to him, keeping a firm grip on the handle of Peanut's harness.

"I've never been to the park before."

"It's a nice park. The legacy club enlists volunteers to plant flowers each summer, and one of the high school teachers started a program for students to keep the gazebo and sign painted."

"Everyone works together to make Jewel River nice. That's pretty amazing."

"It wasn't always this way. To be honest, the town had gotten run-down over the years. When Erica Cambridge moved to town, she started the Jewel River Legacy Club. The members identified the areas where the town could use improvement, and that's how Patrick and Mackenzie ended up here. My brother was in charge of calling several veterinarians, and he talked Mackenzie into moving."

"And now they're married."

"Yeah, it worked out great."

"It sure did."

They turned the corner and joined the crowd finding spots on the lawn. Dusk was falling. Ty pointed ahead. "We're over there. How are you feeling? Need to rest or anything?"

"I don't think so. Peanut would let me know if I did."

A couple spotted him and waved. "Well, look who's here! Ty Moulten. It's been forever since we've seen you."

He inwardly groaned. He'd graduated from high school

with Katie Smith. He believed her husband's name was Bryce. He gave them both a nod. "Good to see you."

If he thought that would suffice, he was mistaken.

Katie, a short, full-figured brunette, blocked their path. "Who's your friend?"

Why couldn't she let them go in peace? He forced himself to be polite. "Katie, this is Ashlinn. Ashlinn, Katie. And Bryce, right?"

The guy nodded. Weighed down with camping chairs, a cooler and a few large bags, Bryce didn't attempt to shake hands. Oblivious to her husband's burden, Katie took in the situation. "Oh, you have a service dog."

"I do." Ashlinn's serene tone lowered Ty's stress a tad.

"What's it for?"

Ty wanted to snap that it was none of her business, but Ashlinn merely gave Peanut a loving glance. "I have a disease that makes me faint a lot. Peanut keeps me safe."

"Peanut? What a cute name. He's adorable." Katie turned to Bryce. "Look at his face. We need to get a golden retriever."

"We need to find a place to sit," Bryce said dryly. "The movie's going to be starting soon."

"Fine." She addressed Ty and Ashlinn. "It was good to see you."

Ty grunted, not caring if she thought he was rude. They slowly picked their way around people to get to their spot. After setting the tote next to one of the camping chairs, Ty offered Ashlinn his arm to help steady her as she sat. She smiled up at him in gratitude, and his heartbeat pounded. When she looked at him like that, he'd probably do anything for her.

"You made it!" Mackenzie got up to hug Ashlinn. Cade scooped up Fritz and lavished the dog with attention. Then Mackenzie turned to Ty. "Cade told me you were coming, and I said I'd believe it when I saw it."

"Ty!" His mom spotted him. She and her posse of middle-aged and retired women got out of their seats to bustle over to them. Soon, he and Ashlinn were surrounded. A cold sweat broke out on his forehead.

There was no way out. He had a recurring nightmare where a serial killer strangled him and tossed his body in a creek to drown. This was worse.

"Your mother told me you were coming, and I didn't believe her." Mary Corning shook her head in wonder. "Look at you, Ty Moulten. At the Shakespeare movie. I never thought I'd see the day."

He didn't know what to say. He stood there like a trapped animal.

With both hands reaching out, Mary motioned for him to give her a hug. "Get over here."

He made the mistake of glancing at his brother as he stepped into her embrace. Cade's shoulders were shaking in silent laughter. Ty shot him a lethal glare, then gave into Mary's aggressive hug.

One of the other women shouted, "Dorothy, look! Ty left his ranch."

Charlene came over, making a fuss, and his mother took the opportunity to trap Ashlinn in conversation.

That did it. He was sweeping Ashlinn in his arms, calling the dogs, marching to the truck and driving straight back to her house.

"Ty!" Dorothy wrapped him into a bear hug before he could escape. She placed her palms against both his cheeks like he was two years old. "Your mother said you were getting out more, but I thought it was wishful thinking. I knew time would heal your wounds. I told her, 'You wait, he'll get back to himself, it just takes time,' more than once, didn't I, Christy?"

"Leave the man alone. He's not a stuffed toy." Clem appeared to his left. "He's got better things to do than get fussed over by you biddies."

Saved by… Clem? Ty flashed him a stare full of thanks. Clem gave him a firm nod.

"I haven't seen him anywhere other than church in years." Mary popped a fist on her hip. "I've got a lot of hugs to catch up on. Ty, honey, you've always been one of my favorite cowboys."

Would it be blasphemous to pray that God would make him disappear? That he could vanish into thin air?

"Hey, Ty?" Cade's voice came from behind him.

Ty turned. "What?"

Mackenzie was helping Ashlinn sit down on the quilt as Peanut licked Ashlinn's hand. Ignoring his mother's friends, he crossed over and got down on one knee. Was she okay? Everyone was too close.

"Give us some space, will you?" he said gruffly.

"Come on, let's get back to our seats," his mother said, extending her arms to herd everyone away. "The movie is about to start."

"Cover." Ashlinn patted her lap for Peanut to sit on her legs. The dog did and panted up at her. She stroked his fur. "Good boy."

"You okay, Ash?" Ty fumbled opening the tote and rooted around for her blood pressure monitor. Once he found it, he attached it to her wrist. Then he reached across her for her tumbler of water and handed it to her. She stared at him through grateful eyes and took a long drink.

"What do you need me to do?" Cade asked.

Ty glanced up at him. "Keep Fritz for me for now, would you?"

He nodded, taking the leash. Cade and Mackenzie went to their camping chairs next to them, and Cade lifted Fritz onto his lap. Ty shifted to sit next to Ashlinn, slipping his hand around her lower back to keep her steady.

"Whatever you need, I'm here," he whispered. A hint of flowers and vanilla teased his senses.

"Thanks, Ty." She leaned her head against his shoulder.

He clenched his jaw, honored at her trust, wishing he could cure her.

He'd do anything to keep this woman safe. Even if it meant enduring another hugging session from his mom's friends. He'd still prefer to be strangled by a serial killer and tossed in a creek, though.

"Welcome, everyone!" Near the huge projector screen set up on the lawn, Erica Cambridge held a microphone. "Thank you all for coming. Tonight is our third annual Shakespeare-in-the-Park film, and we have Joey Zane and Lindsey Parker to thank for it. So find yourself a seat and get ready for *Taming of the Shrew: Throw Her into Jewel River*."

"Still doing okay?" Ty asked Ashlinn. Peanut had gotten off her lap and was sitting next to her.

"Much better."

"Want to stay on the quilt or move to the chair?" He tenderly brushed a lock of hair behind her ear.

"I want to stay right here." She glanced at him, and her shining eyes stole his breath.

"Here, you can lean against me." He moved to sit behind her so she could lean back against his chest. He wrapped his arms around her, struck by how right it felt to have her in his arms. The ends of her hair lifted in the breeze, and Peanut lowered himself to rest his chin on his paws.

As the sun disappeared on the horizon, the movie began.

An overhead view of the prairie and the river appeared on the screen. A low male voice began narrating. "Beautiful, gentle Bianca can't get married until her sharp-tongued sister, Katherina, lands herself a husband. Their daddy, Baptista Minola, turns away the cowboys who pine for Bianca. Local rancher, Hortensio, convinces his friend Petruchio to overlook Katherina's mean ways. If he does, he'll get a wad of cash to marry her. And so our story begins..."

Lars Denton, in old-timey clothes and a cowboy hat, entered a log cabin where Henry Zane, Joey's grandfather, was sitting at a table.

"Ahh, rancher Baptista, rumor has it your daughter Katherina is quite a catch." Lars—Petruchio—took off his hat and sat across from him.

"Katherina?" He spat on the floor. "She ain't for you, boy."

Ashlinn turned back to look at him with a confused expression. "This is more of a loose adaptation, huh?"

"Very loose."

Ty kept his arms around her as the movie progressed. Ashlinn startled when a tornado chased Petruchio and Katherina riding horseback across the prairie, and she tensed when Katherina argued with Petruchio, causing him to toss her over his shoulder and march to Jewel River. But he didn't throw her in.

The movie was choppy and strange, and Ty enjoyed every minute of it.

Finally, after a well-placed martial-arts kick to his shins, Petruchio pulled Katherina into his arms.

"Kiss me, Kate."

"Here?" Katherina asked. "In the middle of this dusty street? After I just kicked you?"

"Yes." Fireworks exploded over the couple as they kissed, and the words *The End* covered the screen.

Everyone on the lawn burst into applause and whistles. As they gathered their things, Ty realized Ashlinn hadn't fainted, and he'd survived the fussing by his mother's friends.

It had been the best night he'd had in a long time. All because of Ashlinn.

CHAPTER EIGHT

"SURPRISE!"

What were her mom and dad doing on her front porch? It had been exactly one week since the movie in the park, and Ashlinn couldn't stop thinking about Ty. And now her parents were here? She opened the door wider to give them both a hug. "You drove all the way from South Dakota?"

"We missed you, sweetheart." Carrying two large bags, her mother swept inside. Peanut wagged his tail for her to pet him. "Oh, and darling Peanut. Look at you." She set the bags down to scratch behind his ears.

"I'll bring everything in. Be right back." Dad winked and pivoted to go back down the porch steps. Ashlinn joined her mother in the living room.

Her parents had shown up on a Saturday afternoon. With no warning.

She should be happy. But…they'd assumed she didn't have plans. Not that she blamed them—what plans could she possibly have? She had no car. Of course she'd be home. But why not give her a heads-up? Then she could have cleaned—which was probably why they hadn't called. Mom wouldn't have wanted her to clean. Too worried it would take the wind out of her sails.

"The spare room is exactly the way you left it if you want to put your things in there." Ashlinn tried to keep her tone cheery, but it upset her that they hadn't called in advance.

Her mother gave Peanut a final pat, then made her way to the kitchen and began removing items from one of the bags. "I picked up some of those crackers you liked so much when you were living with us."

"I didn't like them." The words came out clipped, and she couldn't seem to mask her irritation. "They were the only thing I could keep down."

"Oh, well, I figured you'd want them on hand. Especially after your recent stomach problems. Dad's bringing in a case of the nutrition drinks, too. Can't be too careful."

A wave of sadness crushed her. She took a seat at the table, not wanting to get emotional and hurt her mom's feelings. But really—what was she thinking? Bringing in supplies that only reminded her of a time she'd rather forget?

"What's wrong?" Her mom came over and placed the back of her hand against Ashlinn's forehead. She swatted the hand away. Her mother let out a huff. "What was that for?"

"I don't have a fever. I'm not sick. I don't need—" she waved to the bags "—crackers and gross nutrition drinks. I'm doing fine."

"For now." Her mother pulled out the chair kitty-corner to her and gave her a pointed stare. "You need to be prepared for when you're not well."

"Wow. You haven't seen me in a month, and the first thing you do is assume I'm getting worse. I'm not, Mom. If anything, I'm getting better."

The last part was a lie. She couldn't in good faith claim she was getting better. More like staying the same. She still passed out two to three times a day. On Tuesday, she'd been nauseous and had survived on broth and tea. But by Wednesday, she'd bounced back. And she'd gone into the training center twice this week. That had to count for something.

The front door opened with a creak, and the stomp of her dad's heavy footsteps faded down the hall to the spare room.

"I know you *want* to be better." Condescension dripped from her mother's tone. "It's natural to feel that way."

"Why are you talking to me like I'm twelve?"

Her mom straightened as she pursed her lips. "I'm not. Honestly, Ashlinn, I'm starting to wonder if you're even happy we came."

Guilt slid down her spine. "Of course I'm happy. You simply caught me off guard."

"Don't tell me you had big plans." Her mother shook her head, seeming to laugh at her own joke. That one hurt.

"Last weekend I did."

"What do you mean?"

"Jewel River hosted a movie in the park, and I went." She hadn't told her parents about it, knowing if she did, she'd get lectured.

The rapid blinking had Ashlinn girding herself for the speech sure to be on its way. "How on earth did you get there?"

"There. Everything's inside." Her father entered the room and took a seat across the table from her mom. His smile faded as he picked up on the tension. "What's wrong, Paula?"

At her mother's pinched face, Ashlinn spoke up. "I was just telling Mom about the movie in the park I went to last weekend."

"Oh yeah?" His forearms rested on the table. "What was the movie? Anything we've seen?"

"Oh no. Definitely not." Her spirits lifted at the memory. "A couple of local teens filmed it. They adapted a Shakespeare play."

"Which one?"

"*Taming of the Shrew.* Except they added a subtitle: *Throw Her into Jewel River.*"

Her dad's baffled expression lowered her tension.

"How did you get to the park?" Mom's tongue unraveled, and each word could have been chipped from ice.

"Ty brought me."

"The cowboy you've been hanging around?" Why did it sound like she was accusing Ashlinn of something?

"Yes. I'm helping him plan the fundraiser I told you about. It's in honor of his fiancée. She died a long time ago."

"Sounds like he's still in love with her if he's planning a dinner in her honor." She folded her hands primly. She'd said the same words more than once on the phone.

"He probably is." Ashlinn hated admitting it. Wanted to tell her mom that Ty had kissed her. But a kiss was just a kiss. It wasn't love. Wasn't an engagement ring. Wasn't forever. He didn't want forever. And she didn't think she could have it, anyway.

"And he's the one who took you to his ranch?"

"Yes."

An odd, strangled sound erupted from her mother's throat. And her father rapped his knuckles on the table. "When can we meet him?"

"They aren't dating, Dave." The woman got those words out rapid-fire.

"I didn't say they were." He gave her mom an annoyed glance. "I'd like to thank him for helping keep an eye on Ashlinn."

Did they think she was completely incapable of surviving on her own? Well…they might have a point.

Mom widened her eyes sarcastically. "Don't say that, Dave, or she'll accuse you of asking him to babysit her."

"Am I missing something?" her father asked.

Ashlinn inhaled and counted to three. Would have counted to five, but Peanut started licking her hand.

"Great. Now you're upset. This is what I was afraid of."

Her mother stood and held out her hand. "I'll help you get to your fainting station."

"I can do it myself," she said quietly.

"Oh, yes, Miss Do-it-Herself." Her mother crossed her arms over her chest.

Ashlinn ignored her and brought the tumbler of water to the living room. Once she was on the floor, she dragged her weighted blanket over her lower legs.

Her parents joined her and sat on the couch. Peanut plopped down beside her.

"Maybe we should have a word with Patrick." Her mother tapped her chin. "Let him know you need to come in less often."

"You will do no such thing," Ashlinn said. Her mother had been here for all of ten minutes and had already pushed every one of her buttons. "I know my limits."

"But you don't need to work." Now her mother had shifted to concerned mode. The one that made Ashlinn want to grind her teeth and leave the room.

She petted Peanut and took another drink of water. "I like working. Bandit, a German shepherd Patrick's training, has been showing a lot of promise sensing my blood pressure spikes and dips. When I'm there, it helps him get better at recognizing the signs."

"Save your strength, honey. You can tell us about it later."

"I'm fine now. I'm on the floor. I think I know when I can talk." Maybe they needed a change in subject. "How is the dental office, Mom?" *Please take the hint and stop talking about my limitations.*

"Dr. Garrah broke his collarbone last month, and we've had to find another dentist to fill in until he's healed. It's caused a lot of headaches with scheduling..."

As her mother shifted to talk about her challenges as a dental hygienist, Ashlinn tuned out to focus on trying to prevent a faint. Peanut wandered over to his doggy bed, and Ashlinn realized her mom had stopped speaking.

"I would have expected you to faint by now." She looked puzzled.

"Sometimes my blood pressure goes back to normal without me passing out."

"You don't faint?" Her mom sounded baffled.

"Not every time. Most of the time, I do." Maybe she shouldn't have admitted the last part. Confusion was clouding her judgment. She loved her parents. She should be happy they were here. But so far, her nerves had been grated raw.

"Why don't I order some food for us?" Dad pulled out his phone and began swiping. "What sounds good?"

"How long are you staying?" Ashlinn hadn't meant for it to come out so quickly.

"Just tonight." Her mother's face seemed to age ten years. "We'll be on our way home tomorrow. We both have to work on Monday."

Twenty-four hours. She could do a day. "How about pizza?"

"I'll order two." Dad glanced at her. "You can call Ty and ask him to come over and join us. I'd like to meet him."

"Really?" She wasn't sure how she felt about it.

"Dave, don't put her on the spot. It's not like they're dating."

But they could be dating. Not now…but…someday. Yeah, right. She was stuck with AAG. This was her life.

"He's already lost one fiancée," her mom said. "Why would he want to get involved with someone who has ongoing health problems? I shudder to think about how tough life was for you only a few years ago, Ash. I don't want you getting hurt. Think about how hard it would be if you grew close to him only to have him leave you when your health gets worse."

"Who said my health was going to get worse?" And who said Ty would leave her if it did?

"Don't act like I'm the bad guy. We all know it could."

"Leave her be, Paula." Her dad shook his head in exasperation. "I'll call in the order. You call your cowboy."

Her cowboy. She wished.

No matter how much her mom's words hurt, Ashlinn recognized the truth in them. Ty *had* already lost a fiancée. Ashlinn's health *could* take a turn for the worse. And it *would* be devastating to get close to him only to have him walk away.

"Hand me my phone. I'll see if he's free."

TY SHOULDN'T HAVE agreed to come over to meet her parents. Should have given her an excuse like he'd been doing with his mom and brother for years, not that they'd ever listened. But, no, he'd heard the strain in her voice when she'd invited him, and he'd known he couldn't decline. Not when she needed some moral support.

He parked on the street and cut the engine. All week his mom had been raving about how her friends had been glad to see him getting out again and how pleased they were he was getting back to life. Like he'd been in a coma for the past six years or something. To be fair, they had a point.

Ty got out of the truck and shut the door with a bit too much force. His mother meant well. She'd wanted to encourage him, to help him see that people cared about him. But she'd failed.

Her calls and texts only served to highlight the reason he'd stayed away from town. Now that he was getting out more, it was obvious his devotion to Zoey was fading. He shouldn't be spending time with Ashlinn when he'd told himself he'd never get close to a woman again.

He'd lost too much. And he didn't want to lose again.

Taking long strides, he headed up the porch steps and knocked on the door. Voices argued inside. He couldn't make out what they were saying. The door opened, and a middle-aged man with a receding hairline and slight paunch appeared.

"You must be Ty." The man grinned and held out his hand. "Dave Burnier."

"Glad to meet you, sir." He shook his hand and followed him into the living room.

"This is Paula, Ashlinn's mother." Dave motioned to a pretty woman he assumed was in her late fifties. She nodded. Ty detected skepticism in her stare. Or maybe it was suspicion. Hesitation? Whatever it was, she didn't seem to like him much.

"Thanks for coming." Ashlinn came over and gave him a quick hug. He fought the urge to hold her close and whisper it would all be okay.

"Thanks for inviting me."

"We ordered a couple of pizzas. Why don't you and I go pick them up?" Dave held up a key fob. "I'll drive."

"He doesn't have to go with you, Dad."

"No, it's fine," Ty said. "I'll go."

Her father grinned. "We'll be right back. Why don't you two pick out a movie or something?"

Ty suppressed a grimace. This wasn't how he'd planned on spending his Saturday night. All day he'd forced himself to not call Ashlinn. They'd already spent three evenings together this week to work on the fundraiser. The planning could have been wrapped up in one short session. He couldn't seem to stay away from her.

Ashlinn had picked out decorations and ordered inexpensive centerpieces for the tables. She'd also updated him on the guest list. They were expecting it to grow next Friday when they got a final head count. And he'd briefed her on all the donations his mom and Charlene had gotten from local businesses.

"So you've lived here your entire life, huh?" Dave asked as they climbed into his SUV. Green leaves rustled in the trees overhead. The hot weather spelled trouble. Ty wouldn't be surprised if a lightning storm brewed.

"Yes, I grew up on a ranch east of town."

"You still work there? Ashlinn mentioned visiting your ranch."

Ty explained how he came to own the ranch as her father drove to town.

"Sounds like you're a real cowboy."

"You could say that." Ty tried to stay relaxed. "I refuse to ride bulls, though. I'm not getting myself killed."

Dave chuckled.

"What do you do for a living?" Ty asked.

"I'm surrounded by numbers. I work for a financial company. Mostly detail work."

"Do you like it?" Ty couldn't imagine sitting in an office dealing with numbers all day. Every morning, he looked forward to taking a thermos of coffee out to the stables while the sun rose. After a briefing with his ranch hands, he'd saddle his horse or hop in the UTV, and they'd all set off to take care of the cattle.

"I can't complain." Her father shrugged as he pulled up to the pizza place. "Pays the bills."

Can't complain. Echoes of Ty's father saying those exact words pierced him. He didn't think about his father very often anymore. He missed him, though.

What would his dad think of Ashlinn? He'd probably love her. Who wouldn't?

The pizzas were ready, and Ty offered to pay, but Dave insisted. Within a few minutes, they were back in the SUV.

"How is Ashlinn? Really?" He waited for a truck to pass before pulling out on the road.

"Good." Where was he going with this?

"The fainting spells. They're under control?" He glanced sideways at Ty.

"Um, yes? I guess." His shoulders tensed. He didn't know if they were or not. "I don't know what under control means."

Dave sighed. "I worry about her."

"I do, too." He hadn't meant to admit it out loud.

"I'm glad." He nodded, then shot a sheepish stare his way. "I mean, I'm glad she has people here to help."

"She does. Me. Patrick, Mackenzie, my mom, any of our friends. We look out for her."

They drove in silence for a while. Then Dave sighed. "It's only fair to warn you this is the best her life has been in years. We don't know if it will last."

The words hit his gut like a water balloon on concrete. "What do you think is going to happen?"

"I'm not sure. But I stood by helpless for years when she couldn't stand up without passing out. Couldn't eat without getting sick. Couldn't make it to another room without our help because she was so weak. I don't want her hurt if you're on the fence because of her disease. Her current health *is* the best-case scenario we prayed for. It's not perfect, and it might not last."

"I understand." He did. Her dad didn't want her stuck in Jewel River with all her health problems *and* a broken heart. "We're friends. And friends look out for each other."

"Yes, they do. We're thankful she has friends." He parked in Ashlinn's driveway. "We also know that when things tip to more than friends, there's a greater chance of getting hurt."

Ty bristled, not enjoying the implications behind the warning.

"I've been honest with Ashlinn. We're friends. Just friends." If that didn't close the topic, he didn't know what would. But was it true? He'd been crossing the friendship line for a while now. And last he'd heard—friends didn't kiss each other.

"Good to know." Dave nodded. "Let's get in there and eat."

Ty grabbed the pizzas from the backseat. As he and Dave entered the living room, he gave Ashlinn a slight nod to ease the concern in her eyes. After they'd gotten settled around the table, they said grace.

Paula addressed Ty. "Your ranch—it's nearby?"

The slice of pizza in his hand hovered near his mouth. His gut clenched, and he put the pizza back on the plate without taking a bite. It appeared the interrogation wasn't over. In fact, it was probably just beginning.

"Depends on how you define nearby. It's about thirty minutes from town."

"Oh." The word managed to simultaneously convey disappointment and judgment. Ty had a new appreciation for his own mother. Sure, she meddled nonstop, but she would genuinely welcome anyone off the street if he told her they were friends—she wouldn't view them with suspicion. "Not many neighbors around, I gather?"

"No. Just me and my herd. My brother is a short drive away. I have a few ranch hands. They don't live on my property, though."

"I see."

"You should come out and see it sometime." Had he really said that? He didn't invite people over. And these people didn't seem to like him.

Ashlinn's face lit up. "It's beautiful. All that prairie. And you can see the mountains in the distance. It's so relaxing out there."

"I'm sure it is." Paula's smile didn't reach her eyes. "Awfully far away if something were to happen, though."

"Like what?" Ashlinn's voice had a jagged edge.

"You know." Her mother's eyes glinted as she stared at her.

The tension in the air made his toes curl.

Dave cleared his throat. "Maybe next time we come, we can all take a drive out and see your ranch, Ty."

"I'd like that." He'd hate that. But what else could he say? These were Ashlinn's parents.

Their assumptions were backing him into a corner.

They didn't trust him.

"Ashlinn mentioned you live in a small town, too." Ty took a bite, determined to get out of the spotlight.

"Yes, not quite as small as Jewel River, but it suits us." Paula's face softened. "I've never been one for the city."

"Me neither," Ty said.

"I don't know if I'd like the city or not," Ashlinn said. "I've never spent much time in one."

"They're okay." Dave shrugged. "I travel for work sometimes, and I'm always glad to come home."

"I guess we all have that in common," Ty said. At least they had something in common.

When they finished eating, they sat in her living room and talked for a few hours. Then Ty excused himself, telling them he had to get back for Fritz. On the porch, Ashlinn gave him a quick hug.

"I'll see you in a day or two." More than ever, he wanted to hug her, to hold her, to kiss her again. The way her parents acted around him had brought up his defenses, though.

Ashlinn's eyes were shining as she nodded. Worry rippled through them. "Thanks for coming."

"Of course."

As he drove home, things he'd been pushing away reared up. His dad, for one. Pete Moulten had been gone for a decade. His father—his hero. And that brought to mind how close he'd been to Zoey's parents. They'd welcomed him into their family, too.

In the end, what had it mattered? He no longer had a relationship with them. They'd vanished from his life the same as Zoey had.

Would it be the same with Ashlinn? With her parents?

Her parents didn't like him. That much was obvious. If he lived closer to town, maybe they'd consider accepting him. But he wasn't living in town. Ever. His ranch was his life.

The hornet's nest of emotions from experiences he'd suppressed stung him. He needed some advice. Needed a way to make sense of everything.

Tomorrow, after church, he was going to pull the pastor

aside and make an appointment to talk to him. Pastor Bracken had counseled him after Zoey died. Maybe he could help him now. Ty had a feeling he needed all the help he could get.

CHAPTER NINE

"THANKS FOR TAKING time out to talk." Ty sat in Pastor Bracken's office Sunday afternoon.

"Anytime, Ty." The white-haired man behind the desk had an easygoing manner. "What's on your mind?"

Where to start? He didn't know. "Everything's jumbled. I'm not sure where to begin."

"Is everything okay at the ranch?"

"Yes, the cattle are in their summer pasture. They should be able to graze all winter without me having to supplement their feed too much."

"The rain we had this spring helped."

"It sure did." His anxiety unraveled bit by bit. "I just finished cutting hay. Still fixing fences."

"Never-ending job." The pastor leaned back with a kind smile. "Work doesn't seem to be the issue."

"No, it's personal," Ty said. "I don't think about my father too much, but yesterday he came to mind. And when I thought about him, I couldn't help but think about Zoey's family. When I was part of it. It's like my dad and the Daniels family are intertwined."

The pastor nodded encouragingly.

"I get this kind of bubble in my throat. Hurts. I don't understand it."

"You were close to your dad. You were close to Zoey's family, too."

"I guess I miss them. It's strange, though. Why would I miss them now? I mean, I've been making an effort to spend more time in town. I'm around more people now than I have been in years. What gives?"

"Grief can be funny that way."

"But Zoey's parents are alive. I'm not grieving them."

"Do you ever talk to them anymore?"

Ty shook his head.

"Another loss." The grooves in the pastor's forehead deepened. "Why do you think they've been on your mind?"

"I don't know." Maybe he did. "The fundraiser?"

"You say that like it's a question."

"I've been spending time with Ashlinn Burnier. Her parents are in town. I wasn't expecting to meet them, and it didn't go all that well."

"Are you two getting close?"

"Not like that," he said hastily. "We're friends. She's helping me plan the fundraiser."

"Marjorie and I have tickets. Should be a fun evening. And for a good cause."

"I appreciate your support." Ty took a moment to process his thoughts. The beige walls of the office held framed photos of the pastor and his family. Three sons, two daughters, lots of grandkids. They all looked so happy up there. "After meeting her parents, I was driving home and got kind of upset thinking about my dad. Thinking about Zoey."

"You've lost people who were important to you. Your father. Your fiancée. Her parents. Getting close to new people puts us in a vulnerable position. You don't know—you might lose them the same as you lost the others."

Ty clenched his hands. Was that what was going on? Was he afraid to lose again?

"I think there's room for more people in your heart. I hope you'll pray about it. I'll pray for you, too."

"Would it be wrong to pray that God doesn't let more people into my heart?"

The pastor leaned forward, sympathy radiating from him. "God is love, Ty. As John 13:34 tells us, 'A new commandment I give unto you, that ye love one another; as I have loved you, that ye also love one another.'"

"But God's talking about general love. Loving your neighbor. Not *love* love."

"Are you talking about *love* love?" He tilted his head, and Ty squirmed at the scrutiny.

"No. I'm not." He almost convinced himself. Almost.

"Well, there you go." He opened his hands. "Nothing to worry about."

"Thanks, Pastor." He rose. The pastor stood as well and walked him to the door.

"Come back anytime. I'm here for you, Ty."

"Thank you."

They shook hands, and Ty strode down the hall and out to the parking lot. While the truck idled, he pondered over the conversation. The pastor made sense. He was supposed to love people. And he *had* lost his dad and Zoey and, in some ways, her parents. Maybe his memories were warning him not to get hurt.

He drove away, and as he left town, one thing pressed against his heart. He wasn't as against romantic love as he'd been before Ashlinn arrived. But he should be. He couldn't go getting attached to her. He wouldn't add another set of people who'd no longer be in his life a few years down the road.

The pastor wanted him to pray about adding more people into his heart. It had taken him years to tiptoe into a somewhat normal life. Adding more people to his life was scary. What if he lost them and ended up retreating to his ranch again? All the progress of the past weeks would be lost.

God, I need Your help moving forward. I don't want to get hurt again.

The green prairie grass waved in the breeze as he drove. He'd keep praying. And hope his attraction to Ashlinn would end quickly. He couldn't afford another loss.

All he wanted to do was get home to Fritz.

"NOT GOING TO LIE, Patrick, that was a rough visit." Tuesday morning, Ashlinn sat on the floor of the training arena while Patrick worked with Bandit. Peanut was gnawing on a dental chew in the corner.

"They didn't call ahead, huh?"

"No, and Mom treated me like I was a toddler made of porcelain." She hugged her knees to her chest.

"What about your dad?"

"He seemed fine." Had he been, though? He'd acted kind of weird Saturday when Ty had been there. Her father wasn't one to grill strangers with personal questions, and he'd come awfully close to interrogating Ty.

"Did the stress wear you out?"

"What do you mean?"

"Did it make your symptoms worse?"

"No, I felt the same. I mean, I definitely had to bite my tongue more than once, and I forced myself to take deep breaths when I got annoyed." She'd gotten annoyed several times. That alone bothered her. "I feel bad. Mom and Dad did everything for me—they sacrificed so much for so long. I hate to come off as ungrateful."

"You're not. You're moving on. They will, too." His kind tone eased her guilt.

"They *are* moving on. I mean, their lives are back to normal. Now that they don't have to help me, they can do the things they used to. Focus on their jobs, go to the farmers market on Saturday mornings, plan trips."

"They can. But sometimes it's easier said than done. It's hard to trust it."

"Trust what?" She rested her chin on her knees.

"That it won't happen again. And I'm sure they're worried that if it does they won't be around to help you. They're in another state."

"I know. But I can't help it. What do they want me to do? Move back in with them on the off chance my health deteriorates? No thanks."

"No parent wants that." He winced. "If you moved back, you'd resent them."

"Resentment is the right word." She pondered her mother's attitude and all the things she'd said. "I think my mom resents me for not falling apart. It's like she expected my health to collapse and is disappointed I'm fine."

She hadn't put her impressions into words, and now that she had, they unnerved her. Peanut ambled over, sat next to her and stared. Patrick commanded Bandit over, too. The German shepherd loped straight to him.

"Ashlinn, will you have Peanut check you? Then you can command Bandit to do the same."

She nodded, petting Peanut. She held out her arm. "Check." He sniffed her hand, licked it lightly and remained sitting. "Good boy."

Then she held her other arm out to Bandit. "Check."

The dog smelled from her wrist to her elbow. "Good boy. Good job, Bandit." She stroked his back, and Patrick gave him a treat and praised him.

"Let's see if Candy shows any interest. Do you mind sitting tight while I get her?"

"I'm not going anywhere. I don't have much choice with Peanut staring me down." It was funny. The dog always knew when her blood pressure was changing, but he detected the signs long before she felt anything. She ruffled Peanut's fur. "You take care of me, huh, bud?"

Maybe she was being too hard on her mom. Her parents had been as helpless as she'd been when it came to her fainting, and it had been scary. Peanut had given them all peace of mind.

Patrick returned with Candy. Ashlinn repeated the process. Peanut licked her hand and hunkered down next to her. Candy didn't seem to know what to do when Ashlinn commanded her to check, but she sat on her haunches nearby.

"I don't think this is her specialty." Patrick watched the dog with a thoughtful expression. "She's well behaved. Patient. She might be good with an autistic client."

"Not all dogs share the same talents." Ashlinn stroked Peanut's back with her right hand and Candy's with her left. "She's calm and comforting me right now."

"Want me to get your water?" Patrick asked.

"Yes, please." As he walked away, she lightly shook out her arms and hands to keep her blood flowing. Patrick returned with her tumbler of water. "Could you bring the chair over?"

He set a folding chair in front of her. She lay back and put her legs on the seat. Peanut got up and went over to Patrick. Candy, on the other hand, lowered her body to the ground and stared at Ashlinn.

"You're obsessed with me like Peanut before I faint." She petted the dog's head. "Maybe you know more than you're letting on."

"You're good at this." Patrick watched them.

"At being flat on my back, waiting to pass out?" she teased.

"No. You're good with the dogs. They trust you. You're patient with them."

"I don't think of myself as patient."

"You should. You're a patient person."

"Tell that to my mom." Again, the guilt crept in. She wished their visit had gone better.

"Maybe you can remind yourself of your patience next time she's here." Patrick turned away. "I'm bringing Bandit over again. It will be good for him to repeat the checks and see you through the entire process."

Patrick was right. She could do a better job of controlling her emotions around her mother. She just didn't know if she had it in her. Maybe she needed to practice like the dogs with their training here.

Bandit zoomed to Peanut's spot, and for some reason, it tickled her funny bone. Surrounded by dogs. She loved it.

"See? He's got it. You're making my job easy," Patrick said. "I'm grateful you're here. There's nothing like real-life experience to train these dogs."

"They're getting plenty of that."

"Oh, I forgot to tell you—I think I've found a van to buy. It's four years old, low mileage and has a rear entry with an automatic lift. It's got everything I'm looking for."

"That's great!" She wished she could sit up, but she knew better than to attempt it. "I hope you'll have enough for a down payment after the fundraiser. I can hardly believe it's only two weeks away."

"Yeah. I sure appreciate Ty doing this. I hope the van will still be for sale."

"Do you think it won't be?"

"If it isn't, God will have something else for me."

"You have a lot of faith."

"God's been faithful. I'm blessed."

God had been faithful to her, too. She was blessed. Yet the desire for more—for something better—kept creeping up on her. Not a better house. Not even a driver's license or a car.

She wanted a future that included a husband. A baby or two. A quiet cowboy to hang out with in her backyard on a sunny day.

Closing her eyes, she shook her head slightly.

God, You've been faithful to me. Forgive me for wanting more.

TY HELPED FRITZ into his therapy-dog vest as he waited for Cade in the nursing home's parking lot. They had a standing date every Friday afternoon to visit their grandmother. Her Alzheimer's had been worsening for a few years. Some days she recognized them, and others she didn't. Ty struggled with these visits, though not because of Nana. The smell of harsh chemical cleaners and the moans of the patients got to him. If it wasn't for Cade, Ty doubted he'd ever come here. He appreciated the chance to catch up with his brother, though.

Cade's truck pulled into the spot next to his.

"You're early." He pocketed his keys and, grinning, gave Ty a half hug with Fritz between them. "How's this little guy?"

"He's good. I will never understand how a dog can burrow under a blanket in the heat of summer. Refuses to settle unless there's a blanket over him."

Cade chuckled. "That's a wiener dog for you. Mackenzie says they're all like that. I see he's wearing his vest today."

"Yeah, I asked Charlene if I could bring him. Showed her his Canine Good Citizen certificate. She agreed as long as he's wearing the vest." The dog's big brown eyes stared up at him, and the easy way his tongue panted told Ty the dog was perfectly content to be in his arms.

"It helps him know he's on duty," Cade said. "Does for Tulip, anyhow."

Neither of them made a move to head to the entrance. Puffy white clouds chugged across the blue sky. These were the days Ty longed for in January when ice storms blew in and the subzero temperature could shatter glass.

"How is the fundraiser shaping up? Need anything from me at this point?"

"Actually, yes, I could use something." He'd brought supper to Ashlinn yesterday, and he'd realized he still didn't have an emcee. "We don't have an emcee. You're good at public speaking."

Cade's chest puffed out. "Got that right."

"We both know I'm not." He didn't bother deflating his brother's ego, not when he needed a favor. "Would you do it?"

"What's involved?"

Fritz squirmed to be let down, and Ty lowered him to the asphalt. With the leash in hand, he began strolling toward the entrance of the one-story, brick building.

"Thank everyone for coming. Ask them to get seated. Announce updates on the silent auction. That sort of thing."

Cade opened one of the glass double doors, and Ty and Fritz entered the hallway. "I'll be the emcee on one condition."

Narrowing his eyes, Ty turned to him. Whatever Cade suggested, Ty could guarantee he wouldn't like it. "What is it?"

"You need to be the one to open the event. Welcome everyone. Tell them about Zoey. Talk about Howard Training Center. Introduce them to Ashlinn, so they can see how the dogs help real people. This is your baby—they'll appreciate hearing from you directly."

Cade spoke the truth. Still scared him to death, though.

"I'm no good at public speaking. I failed every oral book report I had to give in school."

Cade slung his arm over Ty's shoulders. "That was a million years ago. You're older now. You can handle it."

"I don't think I can." They approached the desk, where Charlene stood in her scrubs.

"You can. You will." Cade dropped his arm by his side. "Hello, Charlene. How is Nana today?"

"Well, look at you two. A sight for sore eyes, I tell you. If more single gals knew Jewel River had such handsome cowboys around, they'd move here in a heartbeat."

Ty was used to Charlene's flattery and ignored it.

"Too bad I'm taken." Cade pretended to dust his knuckles on his shoulder. "But Ty here could use a lady."

"I don't need a lady."

"Not anymore, you don't." Charlene beamed. "You and Ashlinn looked cozy together at the movie in the park."

That was not what he meant, but he didn't have the energy to argue.

"Here's our Fritzie!" Charlene clapped her hands as she came around the desk. She crouched in front of Fritz, who was sitting like the good dog he was. "How's our little man? You're looking handsome in your spiffy vest."

When she'd finished lavishing Fritz with attention, she straightened and hitched her chin toward the hall. "Miss Trudy's been pretty tired today."

Pretty tired meant lethargic and unlikely to recognize them. Ty had gotten used to it. Seemed Nana had more bad days than good lately.

"Thanks, Charlene." They headed to her room, pausing to knock on the open door. Cade led the way inside, and Nana turned her head. Her bed was inclined so she could sit up.

"Hi, Nana." Cade hugged her first, then stepped away so Ty could give her a light embrace.

"I brought you a visitor." Ty scooped up the dog. "This is Fritz."

"My, my, he's a cute puppy." She smiled and held her arms out to take him.

"I'll set him on your lap."

"That's fine." She petted the dog as he stared up at her through understanding doggy eyes. "He's soft."

Ty and Cade sat in the chairs next to her bed.

"Where's Pete?" Nana continued to caress Fritz's back.

Ty glanced at Cade. His stomach always lurched when their grandmother acted like their dad was still alive. They'd talked to Charlene and the doctor about how to handle situations like this without upsetting her. Nana couldn't help the changes in her brain. It was best to go along with whatever she said and not argue with her. Would only agitate the woman.

"He's not around," Cade said.

"No?" Her forehead creased as she glanced their way. "Yesterday he told me he was going to the auction to buy some cattle. I thought he was supposed to be back today."

"Must have taken him longer than he expected." Cade made it look easy, handling her dementia. "What did you have for lunch?"

Confusion clouded her eyes. The paper-thin skin of her hand showed the veins as it stilled on Fritz's back. "I don't remember."

"Chicken?" Ty asked. Why would he assume she'd had chicken?

"Yes." Her face cleared as she nodded. "I should have saved a few bites for the doggy. He'd like it."

"He would," Ty said.

"Did Christy get Ty signed up for the mutton bustin' contest?"

Ty met Cade's confused gaze. His brother took pity on him. "Um, I'm not sure."

"Ask her next time you see her. Better yet, have her call me. I sewed him a special shirt to wear. That boy sure can ride a sheep for being so young. Barely five years old, and I guarantee he'll win. I wish his grandpa had lived to see it."

He'd forgotten about riding that sheep. It had been the summer he'd competed in his first rodeo. And he'd been proud to wear the Western shirt Nana had made him. Needless to say, she'd been right. He'd won first place and gotten a big trophy with a sheep on top.

"Christy worries about him being quiet, and I told her the boy might not talk much, but he is fearless. He'll turn out to be a good, strong man."

Fearless? Him?

Ty stood abruptly and went to the door, so neither of them would see his emotions. Fritz let out a yip. With his heart in his throat, Ty went over to the bed and picked up the dog. "I'll bring him right back." The words came out strangled. He couldn't help it. Carried Fritz against his chest out to the hall. Fritz licked his forearm as he tried to get himself under control.

Nana thought he was fearless. She thought he'd turn out to be a good, strong man.

Maybe as a kid he'd been fearless, but now?

Tears threatened, and he squeezed his eyes shut.

A good, strong man. He scoffed. Try a closed-off loner who couldn't even bring himself to give a short speech at the fundraiser he was hosting in honor of the love of his life.

Zoey's face didn't come to mind.

Ashlinn's did.

And that made it all worse.

Fritz licked his arm again and again. He kept the dog close, dropping a kiss on the top of his little head. Ashlinn had been right—the dog knew how to comfort him.

"Everything okay?" Cade stepped into the hall.

"I'm fine." He set Fritz on the floor. "The mutton bustin' contest brought back memories."

"Yeah, I remember being jealous of your trophy. I was too old to compete and too young for any of the other events. You'd have clung to that sheep all the way to Texas if necessary."

He stretched his neck side to side. Why was he so emotional about a good memory?

"She's right, you know." Cade's voice had a far-off quality. "You're fearless. You're a good, strong man."

"Me?" He shook his head. "No, that describes you."

"Duh. I know." He grinned, clamping his hand on Ty's shoulder. "Of course I'm a good, strong man. You are, too."

"Modest as always."

"Come on. Let's go back in there."

"You go on ahead. I—I have something I need to do. I've got to pay someone a visit."

His brother's eyes questioned him, then he nodded. Ty led Fritz down the hall. Charlene wasn't at the desk—a mercy—

and he turned the corner and strode straight out the door to his truck. Blasting the AC, he backed out of the spot and drove through town to the cemetery near the banks of Jewel River. After parking, he led Fritz down the lane to the row of headstones where they'd laid family members to rest.

He stopped at the one marked Peter Moulten. He'd helped Mom pick out Dad's headstone. One corner had a flying eagle etched into it. The opposite corner featured a horse against a mountain backdrop.

Seemed like a lifetime ago they'd stood at this spot. Cade on one side of Mom, and him on the other. Cade had been living in New York City, and after the funeral had moved back to Jewel River permanently. In the years his brother had been away, Ty had grown even closer to their father. Losing him had been devastating.

Fritz stuck his nose in the flowers his mom had planted. Ty looked around to make sure no one else was about. He had the cemetery to himself.

"I miss you, Dad." He dropped to one knee and took off his cowboy hat. "I wish you were here to give me some advice."

His father had never been one to tell him what to do unless he was clearly in the wrong, and then his dad had plenty to say. Ty had hung on his every word, good or bad.

"This is harder than I expected." The man would tell him to be more specific. He struggled to put his feelings into words. "I don't know. I miss you. I could use your wisdom right now. About Ashlinn. Nana. Zoey. All of them. I know Cade's right about me giving a short speech. I don't want to do it. I don't want to stand up there and have everyone staring at me."

It would only take a few minutes, then Cade would handle the rest. What was really bothering him?

"The whole point of planning the fundraiser was to honor Zoey's memory. And I'm a hypocrite. I said I'd love her forever, yet here I am—drawn to Ashlinn. Everyone will see me up there talking about Zoey, and they'll know I'm falling for someone else. How can I ask them to donate to a cause in her memory when I'm not keeping her memory the way I should?"

And there it was. The thing he'd been fighting.

He'd believed he'd never get over Zoey. And he'd broken his own promise.

Even if he ended up being alone forever, he couldn't pretend he hadn't moved on.

"I'm sorry, Dad. I'm not the man you raised me to be."

A blast of wind cooled his neck, and he pushed against his knee to stand. Fritz danced at his feet, waiting to be picked up. Ty lifted him into his arms.

The event was in exactly two weeks. He couldn't call it off because he felt guilty. Too many people had put a lot of time and effort into it. Erica, Mom, Charlene, Cade. And, of course, Ashlinn. Not to mention, Patrick was relying on using the money they raised to buy a van.

Ty had already let himself down. He couldn't let all of them down, too.

He knew what he had to do. But he didn't want to do it.

He needed to prepare a speech for the event.

And it was time to call Zoey's parents.

God, I'm not ready.

He wished he could discuss all this with Ashlinn. He appreciated her insightful thoughts. But how could he? It wouldn't be fair to her.

Neither of them could handle forever. Why complicate things more than they already were?

CHAPTER TEN

"I'LL BE FINE." Ashlinn tried to reassure Ty with a smile the following Thursday afternoon. "I want to tour the Winston with you. We need to figure out the layout—where to have all the tables set up for people to eat. Plus the food, desserts—all of it. We'll also need a few long tables for the silent auction items."

"I can probably do it myself." He rubbed the back of his neck, tipping his cowboy hat in the process. "Maybe."

"I know you can figure it out, but I want to be with you." She shoved her bare feet into sandals and grabbed Peanut's harness from the basket. "We only have one week left."

"Erica can give me tips."

Ashlinn frowned. Why was he pushing back on this when he'd been the one to ask her if she wanted to join him today?

"If you don't want me there, say the word." She put her hands on her hips, all too aware that if she got worked up, she'd be getting a stare-down from Peanut soon.

"I want you there." His imploring eyes spoke the truth. So, what was his problem? "I don't want to push you. You've only been out to my ranch and to the park. I want you to feel safe and comfortable."

She relaxed. He wasn't trying to push her away. He was looking out for her. As usual.

"No one will be around besides Erica to see me faint if it comes to that. I should be okay. Let's go."

Ty went to her kitchen and came back with a bag of potato chips. Stowed them in the tote bag next to the front door. She jiggled her tumbler. Full enough. Ty helped Peanut into the harness as Fritz trotted from her to Peanut to Ty, clearly excited about whatever was happening.

Soon, they were driving past endless prairies. Cattle and the occasional stand of trees broke up the landscape, and blue sky met mountains in the distance.

"It's beautiful."

"I agree." He glanced at her with an intensity that made her skin flush. Was he talking about the landscape…or about her?

They'd gotten together twice this week, but Ty had been quieter than usual. Something had been on his mind. Still was, as far as she could tell. And he didn't seem to want to share it.

"You called the caterer with the final head count?" she asked.

"Yes."

"And your mom's collecting the final auction items?"

"Most people dropped them off to her house. Clem drove her around to pick up the others. When I stopped by yesterday, I couldn't believe how much everyone had donated. There has to be over fifty baskets full of stuff."

"People around here sure are generous. This is for such a great cause."

She sensed him stiffen. Now what had she said?

"What are you going to wear?" she asked.

"My best Western shirt. Dress jeans. Cowboy boots. What about you?"

"Me?" She was taken aback. "I'm not going." Did he honestly think she'd be attending?

"You have to go with me." He gave her a sideways glance.

"I want everyone to know how much work you put into it. They'll be able to see for themselves how important service dogs are to their owners."

Disappointment slammed into her. Her hopes had soared at the words *with me*. She'd thought he meant as a date. But he didn't. He wanted to share the credit with her. Wanted everyone to see her with her service dog.

He had a point about letting people see Peanut. What if she fainted, though? What if she got sick? She couldn't exactly set up a fainting station in the middle of a crowded banquet floor.

"It might help people to see Peanut," she said softly. "But I don't need any credit for the event. I barely helped."

"That's not true. You designed the flyers and the social media stuff. I never would have known what to do about tablecloths and centerpieces and music."

"You'd have figured it out."

"No. I needed you."

He'd needed her. Past tense. This conversation was killing her. If she'd had any illusions about Ty changing his mind about dating or marriage, she no longer did. She'd pretend they were just friends, and maybe her heart would believe it. He'd been honest with her from day one.

"Have you written what you're going to say?" He'd told her about Cade suggesting he welcome everyone, to tell them about Zoey and to highlight Howard Service Dogs. Ashlinn had assured him it was a good idea.

"Um, I'm still working on it." He tapped his fingertips against the steering wheel.

"What's wrong?" she asked.

"Nothing." The tapping stopped. "I don't want to pressure you, but I really want you to go to the event. I know I'm asking a lot, but I talked to Erica. She said they have empty rooms used by bridal parties. I figure we could set up a fainting station in one of them. Peanut will be by your side. I will, too, except for the speech. What do you think? Will you be my date?"

Her pulse took off faster than a lightning bolt. His date. Ty Moulten's guest. Hadn't she been dreaming about dating him for weeks?

But were they just friends? Or more? Was God answering her prayer? Or was she hoping for something not meant for her?

She was so confused.

Her parents had warned her not to get too close to him. He'd warned her himself that he didn't see marriage in his future—he'd already loved Zoey and wasn't falling in love again.

But maybe…they could have one date. She could wear a pretty dress. The one in her closet she'd never had a chance to wear before. With Peanut by her side and a special room where she could go if her blood pressure took a dive…

"Yes, I'll be your date." Her fears skyrocketed as soon as the words left her mouth. She should have taken some time to think about it. Should have weighed the pros and cons. Probably should have prayed about it first.

He took her hand and squeezed. "Thank you."

Pros. Cons. Who cared? Ty was holding her hand. Whatever happened would be worth it.

They listened to the radio, and Ashlinn admired the open land before her. She hadn't seen much of Wyoming, and the bareness of it spoke to her soul. Out here everything had room to breathe. Including her.

They arrived at Winston Ranch, and Ty parked in front of a large pole barn with fancy doors. Erica greeted them inside.

"Hey, Ty, glad you could make it." The woman smiled broadly, shook his hand and turned to Ashlinn. "And you must be Ashlinn. I've heard so much about you. I'm sorry I didn't get a chance to meet you at the movie in the park. I'm Erica Cambridge."

"You were in charge of the event—no need to apologize." Ashlinn shook her hand. "It's nice to meet you."

"You brought Fritz." Erica crouched to pet the dog, then rose and nodded to Peanut. "And who is this handsome fellow?"

"Peanut." Ashlinn kept a tight grip on the harness's handle. "He's my service dog."

"I love golden retrievers. I mean, look at that happy face. I'd spoil him rotten." Erica pointed to the large open area. "Come on. I'll give you a tour."

Ty held up Ashlinn's tote. "Mind if we see one of those rooms first? Just in case?"

"Of course." She waved for them to follow her. "This way."

Erica led them to a hallway, then strode briskly past restrooms to a door. She opened it for them to enter and switched on the lights. Ashlinn made note of how far the room was from the banquet hall. If she was attending this dinner, she needed to make sure her table was close by.

The first thing that came to mind as she took in the room was rustic chic. Twinkling chandeliers overhead made the room bright. Two large area rugs covered the hardwood floors, and couches and overstuffed chairs were arranged around coffee tables to make two seating areas. A counter lined a portion of the far wall. Stools and light-up mirrors had been stationed along the counter for bridesmaids to get ready.

Ashlinn closed her eyes briefly. *I want to get married and have my reception here.*

But she wasn't getting married.

The thought lodged like a stone in her heart. What would it be like to have a room full of bridesmaids getting ready at those mirrors?

"If you need to come in here at any time, the room will be all yours." Erica placed her hand on Ashlinn's arm, and she fought the urge to cover it with her own hand. Erica's generosity, caring nature and overall enthusiasm added up to one impressive woman.

"Okay if I leave this here for now, Ash?" Ty motioned to the tote he set near one of the couches.

"Yes."

Fritz sniffed around and returned to Ty's side.

"Let me grab my tablet, and we'll do a walk-through. You can let me know how you want everything set up. Give me one sec." Erica held up an index finger and left the room.

"You doing okay?" Ty took her free hand in his, looking into her eyes.

"I'm okay." She was perplexed by this new desire for a wedding. It seemed the more time she spent with Ty, the more she wanted things she couldn't have.

Her parents had definitely been right to warn her to guard her heart.

"Here. Want a drink?" He handed her the tumbler of water.

"Thanks." She took a drink, spilling a few drops on her shirt. Trying to lighten the mood, she glanced down, then met Ty's eyes. "Can't take me anywhere."

"I disagree." His lazy smile made her heart thump.

Erica popped her head through the doorway. "Are you ready?"

He arched his eyebrows to Ashlinn, and she nodded. The sooner she left this room, the sooner she could stop thinking about weddings. She and Peanut joined Erica in the hallway with Ty and Fritz behind them.

In the main area, Erica swiped her tablet. "Okay, Ty, we're doing round tables, correct?"

"Yes."

"White tablecloths. You'll have the centerpieces. Will you provide a program for each place setting?"

He glanced at Ashlinn. She nodded. "Yes, they should be arriving by Wednesday."

She and Ty had put the program together and, after some back-and-forth, had agreed on the colors and layout.

"How will the tables be set up?" Ty asked.

"See up there?" Erica pointed to the kitchen. "The food will be in warming trays on the counters for a buffet-style meal. And over there—" she gestured to a large open space near the kitchen "—will be the drink station."

Ashlinn could picture it all.

"The podium and microphone will be set up on a platform here." Erica pointed behind them. "It's the best location for everyone to see you, plus it's tucked against the wall."

"I'll only be up there for a minute," Ty said. "Cade's doing most of the talking."

"That's fine." Erica nodded. "So the tables will be in this area." She made a circling motion with her hand. "I was thinking the silent auction would work in the far corner."

Ty and Ashlinn turned to where she indicated.

"What do you think?" Erica asked.

"Against the wall?" Ashlinn brought her finger to her chin. "Or will guests be able to walk on either side?"

"It depends. How many tables will you need?"

Ty shrugged. "I'm not sure. Mom has everything at her place. There are a lot of donations."

"What if we set up a few rows? That way people will have room to stroll around and see everything?"

"I like the idea," Ashlinn said. "Three long tables in each row, and two long tables against the wall to make it shaped like a U."

"That should work perfectly." Erica tapped out a note on the tablet. "What about sign-up sheets for the auction items?" They discussed trivial matters, went over the timeline and when the hall would be available to bring in everything.

"Now, Ty." Erica grew serious. "What about Zoey?"

Ashlinn halted. Zoey? The name was like a knife to her heart.

"I'm not following." Ty looked down at Fritz, standing near his feet.

"Are you going to have a display with photographs? Something you'll need an easel for? Or do you want a small table? We can cover it with a tablecloth and put a framed picture of her on it."

He wiped his palm down his cheek. "I don't know."

"I thought since you wanted the dinner to be in her memory, you'd have something to commemorate her with. It would help the people who didn't know her well put a face with her name."

"Yeah, that makes sense." His cheeks had lost a shade of color. Fritz let out a yip and danced at his feet. He picked up the dog and petted him absentmindedly.

"Let me know what you come up with. I'll save a spot near the entrance for people to see when they arrive."

He nodded, and Ashlinn noted Fritz licking his arm. Ty was stressed. And so was she.

Peanut licked her hand. "Okay, buddy. Ty? I'm going to the bridal room."

"I'll come with you."

"I think we've covered everything. Let yourselves out whenever you're ready." Erica gave them both a smile. "Call me if you need anything else."

Ty and Ashlinn made their way in silence to the room. She lowered herself to one of the area rugs and told Peanut to cover her thighs. Ty handed her the tumbler, and he sat on one of the couches with Fritz on his lap.

The past hour had cemented a few things in her mind. This event was sure to be a special night. And she regretted agreeing to be Ty's date.

The night would only remind him of Zoey and everything he'd lost. It would solidify his stance on remaining single.

Even if she was wrong, it wouldn't matter. She'd be flat on her back in a bridal suite meant for other people, not for her.

Or she'd be sitting at a table, listening to stories about Zoey and how tragic it was that Ty had lost the love of his life.

No matter what, she'd be faced with the truth. Neither she nor Ty had the emotional tools necessary to move forward. She had no future with Ty Moulten, and she'd better get used to it.

MAYBE HIS MOM would know what to do.

Ty had spent the past two days pushing away thoughts of Zoey and the fundraiser. He still hadn't reached out to her parents, and he couldn't bring himself to go through the box of Zoey's items he'd stored in his closet.

He'd removed all the photos of Zoey from his phone years ago. For months after her death, he'd been stuck in a loop of scrolling through them throughout the day. He'd finally had to limit his access to them by storing them all on a flash drive. He wasn't sure he was ready to open the flash drive again and see her smiling face or remember all he'd lost.

It seemed particularly foolish at the moment. He was finally opening up to someone other than his mom or brother. Ashlinn had become important to him, and he hadn't talked to her since dropping her off Thursday evening. She'd been quiet all the way home. He'd assumed the Winston tour had tired her out. But now he wasn't sure. Maybe she was avoiding him.

Her replies to his texts had been emojis or one or two words. Not like her. He'd asked if she was feeling okay, and she'd assured him she was.

Maybe he should stop by her place. Check on her. No, Ashlinn clearly needed some space, and he knew all about needing space.

After parking on the street in front of his mother's house, he loped up the driveway and knocked on the door. She opened it and drew him in for a hug. Tulip sniffed his cowboy boots, and Ty picked her up to pet her.

"Want a glass of iced tea?" His mother retreated down the hall.

"No, thanks."

"Coffee? Cookie?"

"I'm fine, Ma." He made himself comfortable on her couch, and Tulip jumped down.

"How's Ashlinn?" Mom asked, sitting on her favorite chair and placing Tulip on her lap.

"Good." He hoped so, at least. What if she was going through a flare-up? Did she need supplies? Maybe he *should* have stopped by.

"Is she going to the fundraiser?"

"Yes. I asked her to join me." He prepared himself for his mother's reaction. Her eyebrows rose, and her lips formed an O. "But that's not why I'm here."

Her face fell. "What's wrong?"

"I need some advice."

"From me?" She placed her palm against her chest.

"Yes. Erica thinks I should have a small table near the entrance with pictures of Zoey."

His mom tapped her chin. "Smart thinking. A framed photo would be lovely. Or we could create a collage. Set it up behind the table. Yes." She nodded to herself. "Erica doesn't miss a beat."

"I don't know."

"About what?"

"I feel funny about it."

"Honey, you're hosting this dinner in honor of her. Don't you think a few pictures would be appropriate?"

"I'm sure they would be. But I don't want to pick them out. I'm not even sure I can face her."

"Her?" She scoffed, petting the dog. "Don't you mean a photograph?"

"Yes." The word came out harsh. They were one and the same in his mind.

"Why?" Her expression was genuinely confused.

Now he had to explain himself. Bile rose in his throat. "I thought I'd never get over her. And we're hosting this dinner, and I—" He couldn't say it out loud.

"You're over her," she said quietly.

He nodded, shame crushing him.

"You're afraid of being a hypocrite. Going to all these lengths to honor her memory when you're not mourning her anymore."

How his mother had gotten so smart he'd never know.

"The two things can coexist, you know."

"How?"

"You can honor her memory without pining for her. You can move on with your life and still regret she's no longer in it. It's not paralyzing you anymore. That's a good thing."

"It doesn't feel good."

"Only because it's new."

"So you're saying I should bring pictures? Have them framed or something?"

"Yes. You aren't the only one who loved her, you know. She had a lot of friends in this town. They'll want to see her face again, and they'll also be glad that you're honoring her memory."

"What if they aren't glad? What if they realize I'm not the guy they thought I was?"

"How many of them have you talked to in the past six years?" She was treating him gently, and for that he was thankful.

"None."

"Then you couldn't possibly know what any of them think of you. If they're like most people, they'll want to see you move on with your life."

He massaged the back of his neck. "Move on? Zoey died. Her life was cut short. What gives me the right to be happy and have a life?"

"Is that what you think? That you need to hide away because your fiancée died a long time ago? Life goes on. You might not like it, but it keeps moving no matter what. You need to keep living."

"I've been living."

"Have you? I mean, I guess it's true. Somewhat." Her tone warned him she was wrestling with how much to say. "Until recently, you haven't been enjoying life, though. It's okay to enjoy it, Ty."

He shook his head.

"I lost your dad and thought I'd never be happy again." She stared down at the fluffball on her lap. "Around six months after he died, I forced myself to have lunch with my friends. We made it a weekly date. As time wore on, I got back to living. I found myself smiling again. I'd feel guilty about it—like how can I enjoy anything without Pete here?"

"That's different," he said gruffly. He wasn't sure how it was different, though.

"Maybe. Maybe not. I made a choice. To live. To enjoy life. I still miss your father. Oh, boy, do I miss him. But I don't think anyone, especially you boys, wanted me to fall apart and be miserable the rest of my life."

"Of course we don't."

"My situation was different, though. And I'm different. You're introverted and needed to stay home. I like being around people. Depression can put a damper on life."

"Who said anything about depression?" He'd never been diagnosed, but then, he'd never gone to a doctor, either.

"Ty, the signs were there. I tried to help."

For years she'd hounded him about seeing a doctor. Seemed like every other month, she was calling or texting him about it. He'd ignored her.

"I don't know what's going on in your head right now, but I think hosting this fundraiser, adopting Fritz and getting close to Ashlinn have all forced you to do things out of your comfort zone. You're changing, and change can be scary."

He pondered her words for a few moments. "You make it look easy. Grieving. Getting back to life."

"Me?" She half snorted, half laughed. "No. It's not easy. I pray each morning for guidance, for discernment. And I think more changes are coming for me."

"What do you mean?" He didn't like the sound of that.

"Believe it or not, I've been getting close to Clem."

"Clem Buckley?" He couldn't wrap his head around what she was saying. Sure, Clem had been acting as her unofficial driver after his attempts at improving her driving skills had failed. But getting close? To steely-eyed Clem?

"Yes." A soft smile played on her lips. "I know it's strange. I never in a million years would have thought… Never mind. You didn't come here to discuss me. What can I do to help you finalize the fundraiser?"

"Oh, no, you don't. You can't toss out Clem's name and change the subject." He stood and began to pace. "Are you two dating?"

"No. I mean, obviously, he drives me around. All of his attempts at teaching me road etiquette have failed. I've pretty much accepted the fact I'll never be able to keep my license. But he doesn't mind driving me. In fact, I think he prefers it when he's behind the wheel and I'm the passenger."

"But that's just being friendly, right?" He couldn't fathom anything beyond that at this point.

"It started out that way. But we've also been spending time doing fun things together. Like last week, he took me fishing on his property. I didn't catch a thing. I got to wear waders, though, and that was fun. And the week before that, I made him drive me to Buffalo, and he didn't hate the artsy stores we visited. He even bought a handcrafted mug with a horseshoe on it."

"I'm surprised you haven't killed each other by now." What else didn't he know about his mother?

"Shocking, I know. And yes, we're both still alive. I like that I can argue with him. He speaks what's on his mind. There are no misunderstandings."

Ty thought of Ashlinn. Up until Thursday, he'd have said the same about her. But now? He definitely needed to get to the bottom of what was wrong.

"Don't go thinking we're getting married or anything." Fear and excitement mingled in his mom's eyes. "I'm growing close to him, that's all."

"Married?" Now, that was crossing a line. Or was it? He studied his mom and noted how time had been changing her. More wrinkles, more joy in her wise face. She was beautiful—inside and out.

"Don't ask me to call Clem Dad," he said with a straight face to see how she'd react.

"Ty! No one is calling anyone dad." She shook her head with a huff. "My word. You'd think I'd announced an engagement."

"Calm down. I'm just teasing you."

She threw a pillow at him. It bounced off his head. He laughed. Hadn't seen her this riled up in a while.

"Does Cade know about this?" he asked.

"I haven't told him."

"Are you going to?"

She sighed. "Yes. When the time is right."

"Wish I could see the look on his face when you do." He went over and hugged her. "You could do worse than Clem."

"You think so?" Her vulnerability touched him.

"Clem's a stand-up guy. Kind of scary, too. But someone you can depend on." He stepped back. "I'm going to take off. I've got some pictures to go through."

"If you need moral support..."

"I'll be okay." He sounded confident, but he wasn't.

"Oh, and tell Ashlinn if she needs any help getting ready—her hair, nails, that sort of thing—I'd be tickled pink to come over." Mom tucked Tulip under her arm as she got up.

From Zoey to Ashlinn. Ty was pretty sure he'd gotten whiplash. "Why don't you tell her? You've got her number."

"You don't think she'd mind?"

"No. I think she'd appreciate it."

"I will." She beamed.

And on that note, he prepared to make his escape. "I'm going to take off."

She walked him to the door, and he hugged her again. All the way to his truck, his resolve hardened. He was checking on Ashlinn. And after he verified she was okay, he needed to give himself a pep talk to get the courage to call Zoey's parents. As for going through her pictures, he wasn't ready. He hoped he wouldn't fall apart when the time came to do it.

CHAPTER ELEVEN

ASHLINN COULDN'T THINK of a more miserable Saturday than this one. Oh, the weather was fine. The problem was her. She was a nervous wreck and probably would be passing out soon. She'd been blowing off Ty's texts since Thursday, and while she felt horrible for doing it, she didn't have much choice.

She could *not* be his date to the fundraiser.

And she needed to break the news to him soon.

Was it smart to be tying herself into knots over how to tell him? She hated breaking her word and letting him down. Had she built up what they had to be something more than what it was?

Peanut had been staring at her for over a minute. She was sitting on the floor with her back against the couch. Blood pressure monitor on. Weighted blanket over her legs.

She'd been in a constant state of anxiety for the past two days.

Not good.

Her stress levels were too high, and if she wasn't careful, she'd pay the price with a flare-up like she'd had when she couldn't keep food down a few weeks ago.

What if her health reverted to something worse? The fear of being bedridden for months on end filled her mind.

A knock on the door made her groan. It could only be Patrick, Mackenzie or Ty, and Patrick had already checked on her today, so Mackenzie wouldn't. That left Ty.

With slow, deliberate moves, she hauled herself up to a standing position. Then she shuffled to the door, opened it and immediately turned to resume her position on the floor.

"Hey, are you all right?" Ty closed the door and followed her to the couch.

"I'm good." She was far from good, but what else could she say? That she was falling so hard for him she thought she might shatter? That he clearly still loved a dead woman, and he'd been honest with her about it, but she'd ignored it?

"You don't look good."

"Thanks a lot," she said under her breath.

"Sorry. That's not what I meant."

"I know." She took a drink of water. Wished he'd leave. Wanted him to stay.

"What's been going on? Your texts have been…short."

"Oh?" Her chest tightened. She wasn't ready for this conversation. Not on the floor. Not when she was about to pass out.

"I'm worried about you."

"You sound like my mother." She shouldn't accuse him of that—it wasn't fair to him.

He plunked down on the floor, sitting directly in front of her with Peanut lying at her side.

"I'm sorry for being nosy, Ash. I…care about you."

"I appreciate it." She met his eyes then. Big mistake. Because he did care about her. "I'm fine. Really. Nothing I can't handle."

"Why don't I make supper?" he asked. "It's a little early, but I can put together sandwiches."

Oh, how she wanted this to last. She liked having supper with him. Loved when he made something simple for them to eat and they'd talk about their days.

"I've got plans."

The way he was blinking, she'd surprised him.

"What plans?" His tone was guarded.

Why was she dragging this out? He'd done her a favor by coming over here. Now she could tell him in person.

"I'm not going to the fundraiser with you, Ty." The words pierced the air between them, leaving her relieved and disappointed.

"You really aren't feeling good, are you?"

"It has nothing to do with my health."

"Then why?"

She stroked Peanut's fur, thankful he wasn't alerting her. She might be able to get everything she needed to say out before she fainted.

"I don't want to mislead you. You were quite clear when we met that you'd already lost someone you'd loved and you're not getting married or having kids. I've been conveniently forgetting that—or ignoring it—I'm not sure. At the Winston it sank in that you'd spoken the truth."

"I meant what I'd said when we met." The words came out so quiet she almost missed them. "But I don't know anymore."

"I like you, Ty, I like you a lot. But this—" she gestured to the dog, to the cuff on his wrist, to the tumbler "—is my life. It's not likely to get better from here on out, and it could get worse. Much worse."

He shifted his jaw. "You told me what you have isn't fatal."

"It's not. I'll live with the disease and manage it as best I can until I grow old."

"Then what's the problem?"

She could see it clearly now. The way he fussed over her and cared for her? She'd put him in the same position as she'd put her parents. He felt responsible for her, and it wasn't fair to him. "I'm someone to take care of. Not a partner to spend your life with."

"What does this have to do with the fundraiser?" His face

grew hard. "We're talking about one date. To an event we both planned. No one said anything about forever."

Maybe that was the problem. She wanted forever. One date wouldn't be enough. She'd want another and another…

"I'm sorry, Ty. I'm not going."

His face clouded over, and she held her breath, waiting for him to argue. Peanut licked her hand, and she tried to breathe normally.

"Maybe we're both scared, Ash." He stood up. "I'm going to sit in that chair until Peanut stops alerting you. And I'm asking you to keep an open mind. On Thursday, if you still don't want to come with me, I'll accept it. Fair?"

None of this was fair. She'd told him she wasn't going. But a part of her clung to the idea of having a few more days to decide.

"I'm not going to change my mind."

"Then you can turn me down again when I stop by on Thursday."

"Don't come over Thursday." Why couldn't he accept what she was saying? "I've gotten too close to you. Maybe it was inevitable. I've been isolated for six years. And here you are—this kind, amazing cowboy. Who wouldn't fall for you? I never should have gotten close. I'm sorry. But I can't be your date now or ever."

"You're falling for me?"

Leave it to him to latch on to the one thing she shouldn't have admitted.

She nodded, dangerously close to tears.

"I'm falling for you, too."

"Fall for someone else. All I do is faint or get sick and have to stay in bed. You lost Zoey. You deserve someone who can love you well. Someone who doesn't need a service dog to get through life. Someone who won't embarrass you when you go out."

"You could never embarrass me." His face gave nothing away. Not relief, not pain.

"*I* embarrass me. Okay? And I'm not going to be your burden. Find someone who can ride horses around your ranch and give you ten babies and fly to a tropical island for your honeymoon. I want you to have a full life, and you won't with me."

Exhaustion and mortification sapped her energy. Why had she blabbed on as if he'd proposed?

"I'm fine riding solo around the ranch." He started to rise. "I never thought I'd have babies—even with Zoey. And I'm not a tropical island kind of guy. But I can see you're not in a state to talk. I don't want to rile you up. But I *will* be back Thursday afternoon, and you can tell me to my face if you're still not coming with me. I'll leave you alone after that. You have my word."

"You're never going to be over her." She hadn't meant to say it.

The color drained from his face.

She looked away, closed her eyes tightly, willing him to leave. She wanted to shout at him to get out of there. But he didn't deserve that—didn't deserve any of what she'd just said. She'd spewed out way too much and hurt his feelings. Her lungs felt like two rocks in her chest.

She couldn't have Ty Moulten. She never should have pretended otherwise.

NOTHING WAS GOING right today. Two hours later, Ty sat on his couch and stared at the phone in his hand. Fritz had claimed his lap and was softly snoring.

Every time he thought of Ashlinn, he forced his attention elsewhere. Had briefly considered saddling up and riding around the ranch. It was how he'd gotten through life after Zoey died. But something had stopped him.

He needed to sit with this. To deal with it.

And he didn't want to.

He hung his head and closed his eyes.

God, I don't know what to do.

Ashlinn was right. He'd told her he wasn't getting married or having kids. He'd grown close to her—not just as friends. She'd admitted she was falling for him. Was she? Really?

From the minute they'd met, he'd known he couldn't offer her his heart. At the time, he'd thought it was because he didn't have one to offer. But now? His heart had been healing. Would always be scarred. He didn't know if he was brave enough to risk having it broken again.

Six years of riding around his ranch, avoiding anything that required the most basic interaction with people around town. Six years of numbness and misery and convincing himself it was the way it had to be.

Six years.

Wasn't it about time to get out of this limbo? Was he going to live in a state of nothingness forever?

He glanced at his phone, swiped it and found the contact he'd been avoiding. Pressed it. And waited. His pulse throbbed in his neck.

"Hello?"

"Hi, Mrs. Daniels. It's Ty Moulten." His throat clogged with fear. Would she be upset with him for not keeping in touch? Would this call cause her pain? Remind her of losing their daughter? He didn't want to hurt her any more than she'd already suffered. Maybe calling was a mistake.

"Ty!" The surprise in her tone was upbeat. "How are you? It's been a long time—I hope you're doing well."

It *had* been a long time. Her voice triggered so many emotions and memories. She'd been kind to him. Zoey's dad, Mike, had, too. They'd treated him like a son. And how had he repaid them? With silence.

"I am. And you?" He couldn't get out any more words. Guilt and sadness choked him.

"Doing just fine." Did he detect a trace of wistfulness in

her tone? "Rob got married a few years ago, and we found out they're expecting another baby."

Rob was married? He remembered him being fresh out of high school. "Congratulations. You're a grandma now, huh?"

"And proud of it. Trinity just turned eighteen months. She's a busy girl. I quit my job at the bank to babysit her while they work. Best decision I ever made." She went on to tell him that Mike planned on retiring in ten years. A sense of incredulity mounted as she talked.

Mr. and Mrs. Daniels were doing okay. They didn't seem to be pining for their loss.

What had he expected? Tears? A guilt trip for not staying in touch with them? Mournful reminiscences of Zoey?

"Listen to me going on and on. I'm sorry, Ty. Tell me about yourself. How are you getting on?" Her cheery voice only highlighted the difference between them. She was busy living. And he wasn't. Just like his mom had said.

"Doing okay." He tried to keep it light. "Still ranching."

"Of course you are. Born in a saddle—that's what I always told Mike."

He chuckled out of politeness. "That's me. I adopted a dog recently. He's a fun little guy."

"Good for you."

"In fact, I adopted him from a local trainer. He opened Howard Service Dogs in Jewel River, and I'm hosting a fundraising dinner this Friday night. It's in Zoey's honor, and all the proceeds are going to the training center. I'm sorry I didn't tell you about it sooner. I just… I don't know."

"What a thoughtful thing to do." She went from happy to somber. "You're the son-in-law I always wanted. I hate that Zoey died before you two could get married. And I'm sorry we moved away and didn't keep up with you."

"*You're* sorry?" It didn't make sense. "I should be apologizing to you. I could have called. At least sent a Christmas card or something."

"It was hard. Too hard." Her voice sounded a million miles away. "For all of us."

"Yes." The emotions roared back—this time bringing tears to the backs of his eyes. "There isn't a day I don't think about her. I loved her."

"I know. We all know. It was never in question."

Neither spoke for a while. He sensed they both needed space to work through their feelings.

"Ty, I hope you find someone to share your life with. Maybe you already have. If not, though, open your heart. You'll see Zoey again in the next life. Until then, make the most of the one you've got."

They spoke for a few more minutes and ended the call.

Ty's head reeled. Mrs. Daniels had told him to move on and make the most of his life. To open his heart. And she'd meant it.

From all appearances, their family *had* moved on.

He placed Fritz on the floor and stood, pocketing his phone. An irrational tension hummed through his body.

In the mudroom, he swiped his cowboy hat off the hook and planted in on his head. Then he shoved his feet into cowboy boots and went outside, slamming the door behind him. His pace quickened as he approached the stables.

Everyone was moving on.

Mom had created a new life without Dad as if their years together had never happened. When she'd mentioned having feelings for Clem, it hadn't bothered him much, but the more he thought about it? Yuck.

And then there was the Daniels family. By all accounts living their best lives in another state as if their years in Wyoming—and the life they'd had with their daughter—had never happened. Like she'd never mattered.

Zoey had happened. She'd mattered.

She'd been the sweetest person he'd ever met. She'd gotten him. Liked things simple—the same as he did.

He'd loved her so much. And she'd died anyway.

Why had she died? And why had everyone moved on?

He went straight to the tack room, grabbed everything he needed and got his horse from the paddock. Methodically saddled it and hoisted himself up. Didn't take long to reach the lane leading to the creek, where he nudged the horse to go faster, concentrating on the wind blowing against his face and the thud of the hooves on the ground.

"You're never going to be over her." Ashlinn's voice cut through the jumbled thoughts in his head.

He'd gotten over Zoey. But he'd promised he never would.

"I'm the only one who refuses to forget her," he yelled to the air. "I loved her. I love her. What am I supposed to do? It's not fair. It was never fair!"

The horse galloped along the creek until he slowed the horse to a trot, then a walk.

A red-tailed hawk soared overhead in the blue sky. The subtle change in the temperature told him summer was ending. Autumn would be in full swing soon. He could make out pops of yellow and red in the trees up ahead.

He dismounted. Took a stone from the water and let the coolness of it seep into his palm, then clenched his fist around it. Couldn't believe he'd gotten himself into this situation. He never should have spent so much time with Ashlinn.

If Zoey could see him now…

She'd be hurt. Stunned. Disappointed. Shocked he'd gotten close to another woman after the promises he'd made her.

She'd be…

He stared off toward the horizon.

Dead.

Still dead. Always dead. That part never went away.

The future he and Zoey had planned in those weeks before she'd gotten sick and died would never happen. She'd sat in his arms on his couch and dreamed about their life after marriage.

"We'll have a boy and a girl. Two dogs. And a screened-

in porch. I've always wanted one of those." She'd shifted to smile up at him.

"A screened-in porch, huh? I can start building one. The kids will have to wait until after we're married, though." He'd kissed the top of her head, pained to play pretend. Zoey wasn't ever having kids. They'd both known it. "You can pick out the dogs anytime."

The stone fell out of his hand and rolled to a stop in the prairie grass at the edge of the creek. He took off his cowboy hat, letting it dangle near his thigh, and stared ahead at the land.

He hadn't been able to save her. His love hadn't been enough. He'd never thought she'd die before the wedding. Had always assumed they'd have a couple of years together. That, at the very least, he'd have time to build her that screened-in porch.

"God, can't You rewind it? Make it all make sense?" Tears flowed down his cheeks. He raised his face and shook his fist to the sky. "I'll always love you, Zoey Daniels!"

His hand fell, his shoulders shook, and he took big, gulping breaths. He wiped his face with the handkerchief from his back pocket.

"But I'm not in love with you anymore," he whispered.

It had happened over time. He hadn't realized he was moving on. He should have tried harder to prevent it.

For reasons he didn't want to examine, confessing everything out loud in the Wyoming air was necessary. Felt right. "The truth is—and it seems I'm spilling everything today, even the things I won't admit to myself—I'm in love with someone else. And I'm sorry about that, Zoey. I don't expect you to forgive me."

Could he forgive himself?

"I failed you. I didn't keep my promise. And I'm sorry."

When the sun began to set, he got back in the saddle and took his time returning to the stables.

Zoey was gone.

Ashlinn didn't want him. He didn't blame her.

He'd always have the ranch, but it didn't have the same draw as it had before Ashlinn had arrived in Jewel River.

His future looked as bleak as it had since the day Zoey died. Maybe Ashlinn cutting him out of her life was for the best. Then he wouldn't have another imaginary future ripped out of his grasp.

CHAPTER TWELVE

SHE'D PASSED OUT AGAIN.

Ashlinn's eyelids fluttered open. She tried to recall where she was. The living room window revealed a black sky. The television was off. Middle of the night? Peanut licked and nibbled her hand. "Good boy."

She felt around the floor until she grasped her phone. Checked the time. After midnight. She wished she had a girlfriend who was a night owl. One she could call and tell all her problems.

Lately, she had a lot of problems.

In the three days since she'd told Ty she couldn't be his date, she'd fainted over twice as many times as she typically did. The stress of pushing him away—and of him staying away—was ramping up her AAG symptoms. And this added more stress, causing her to be nauseous.

Worry was eating away at her, robbing her of her improved health.

On Sunday, she'd watched a church service on her laptop, and she'd felt so sorry for herself afterward, she'd broken down in tears. Her mom called three times a day, and every conversation was the same. How many times had she fainted? How was her stomach? Did they need to make a doctor appointment? Was she keeping her blood pressure monitor nearby?

Yesterday, Ashlinn had let all calls go to voice mail. She hadn't had it in her to go through the drill again. She'd texted her mom that she was fine, just busy.

She was neither.

She was heartbroken.

She'd told Ty she was falling for him, but she'd lied. She wasn't falling for him. She'd already gone and done it. She'd fallen for him. Past tense.

Propping herself on her elbows, she debated trying to stand to go to bed. Too soon. She'd pass out if she attempted it now. Petting Peanut, she ignored the awful ache in her chest.

Ty hadn't called or texted her. And she missed him. Missed what they'd had. She'd grown comfortable with him. Enjoyed having him around. He made her feel…normal.

She missed her mother, too—the one she'd been before Ashlinn had gotten sick. Sure, the woman had always been overprotective, but she'd also cared about Ashlinn's hopes, dreams and problems.

Ashlinn wished her mom was capable of viewing her as a mature adult instead of an invalid incapable of making a rational decision.

Had cutting off Ty's friendship been rational?

Didn't matter. She'd made her choice. There was no going back.

Peanut licked her hand. Not again. She didn't want to pass out again. The unbearableness of it all made her want to sob.

With Ty gone, her life felt empty. She closed her eyes, tired of fighting tears. Tired of second-guessing herself. Tired of fainting. Tired of resenting her mother. Tired of telling herself she was good enough to live independently and work with Patrick, but she wasn't good enough to date a kind, patient, incredibly gorgeous cowboy.

She began to shiver. Curling up on her side, she was brutally aware of the hard floor beneath the rug. All she wanted to do was crawl into bed. But she couldn't. Because she'd pass out before she got there.

God, I need You. I feel so low.

As she huddled there, memories chased each other in her mind. Her first kiss—junior year in high school. They'd dated through senior year and had gone their separate ways after graduation. She didn't miss him. Never had. And the friends from high school and college that she hadn't remained close with? Not their fault. Not hers either.

But Ty…

She'd miss him. She already did.

The man wore sadness like she wore her blood pressure cuff. Never out of reach for long.

God, I want him to smile. I want him to be happy. I want...

She wanted to be his. Forever. She wanted to live on his pretty ranch and listen to him talk about the land and cattle. She wanted to rock on that front porch with Fritz on her lap and Peanut sitting next to her.

She wanted it all.

Carefully, she rose and made her way to the bedroom with Peanut trailing her. After climbing into bed, she pulled her Bible onto her lap and opened it to the bookmark. Romans 8:18, "For I reckon that the sufferings of this present time are not worthy to be compared with the glory which shall be revealed in us."

The passage gave peace to her weary soul. *God, I can trust You. You promise that my current sufferings will end in glory. I believe it. Help me get through this.*

She didn't feel so alone. The Bible closed, and she fell into a restless sleep.

IF ONE MORE person called needing advice on what to do for something involving the fundraiser, he was saddling his horse and riding to the next county. He wasn't meant for phone calls and decisions regarding playlists and how much ice to have on hand. The event was in two days, which meant he had to face Ashlinn tomorrow.

He wasn't looking forward to hearing her reject him all over again.

Ty tossed a bale of hay to the ground then kicked it for good measure. His phone rang. Raising his face to the barn rafters high above, he contemplated grinding the phone under his boot. He sighed. Ignoring it made more sense than totally destroying it.

Fritz trotted over from his water bowl as the phone continued to ring. Ty kicked the hay one more time.

"What did that bale do to you?" His brother's voice startled him. Earlier, Ty had opened up both sets of double doors in the barn to let the warm air circulate.

"Didn't hear you drive up." He turned back to the stack of bales, gripped the twine on one with his suede work gloves and tossed it to the ground.

"You gonna kick that one, too?" Cade bent to pick up Fritz. The dog wriggled excitedly.

"I might. Unless you want to."

"Nah. I'll leave that to you." He stroked Fritz's back as he held him. "Need any help?"

"Grab another bale." Ty nodded to the stack he was working on.

"Not with the hay. With the fundraiser. You can take care of your own cattle."

"Good, because I'd rather take care of cattle than deal with all these phone calls. I don't know why anyone thinks I have a clue if we should have instrumental or bluegrass music playing through dinner. And I don't care if the cupcakes or the lemon bars are the first thing people see on the dessert table. What does it matter? None of it is important. People won't notice the music, and not a lick of desserts will be left by the end anyhow."

"Whoa." Cade set Fritz down. "You're worked up. Take a break. Let's go for a walk."

"Fine." He stripped off the gloves and strode to the corner where he kept supplies. Tossed them on the counter and continued outside. The sun felt good on his face. Not as hot as it had been a few weeks back. "Where to?"

"Doesn't matter to me."

"I'm thirsty. Let's grab a soda from the house. We can sit on the patio." He headed down the lane, not caring if Cade was following or not. Fritz bounded ahead of him.

"What's got you all worked up? Besides the phone calls?" Cade jogged up next to him.

"I don't want to talk about it."

"Ashlinn?"

Was he that transparent? "Zoey."

"Zoey?"

"Yeah. It feels like everyone's moved on. Like she never existed." The anger grew all over again. Why couldn't he let this go?

"Life does go on. Whether you want it to or not. Doesn't mean they don't miss her."

"I know. Do you think I don't know that?" Ty shook his head. "What do you think I've been doing all these years?"

"Whatever it was, it wasn't living."

Leave it to his brother to spit out the brutal truth. "I've been living. Working cattle, taking care of this place. What more do you want from me?"

"Let me ask you something."

He rolled his eyes, his adrenaline speeding out of control. "Go ahead."

"What do you want everyone to do? Give a speech about her at church every week? Light candles and cry at night?"

"No!"

"Dying is part of life. I hate it. I hate that you lost her. But I, for one, have been glad to see you get out more. Adopting

Fritz—the dog's good for you—was a smart move. Helping Ashlinn has softened something inside you, too. So forgive me if I'm confused why you're so angry and uptight right now. I'd expect you'd be happy."

"Happy?" He stopped, turning to face Cade. "Why on earth would I be happy?"

Frowning, he tilted his head. "Why wouldn't you be? You have this ranch. Healthy cattle. A great little dog. Mom. Me. You should be grateful for me." His toothy grin didn't amuse Ty.

"I don't have Zoey. I'll never have her again." He resumed walking, and Cade did, too.

"That's right. You'll never have her. But there are people alive—here and now—who want to be with you. Mom. Mackenzie. Me. Ashlinn. Don't push us away."

"I'm not."

"You are."

The crunch of gravel under his boots couldn't drown out his brother's words.

"Seriously, Ty, I worry about you. It's taken a load off my mind to see you getting out more these past couple of months. And hosting the fundraiser? I'm proud of you, man. In fact, that's one of the reasons I came over."

"What are you talking about?"

"Mackenzie and I discussed it—we're going to match all the donations tomorrow night. We want her dad to have that van."

The words were so unexpected, Ty rocked back on his heels. He studied Cade's face, and knew he spoke the truth. Like Cade would lie? Never.

"Really? You'd do that?" He blinked rapidly, stunned at his brother's generosity. Cade's wealth wasn't a secret or anything, but still.

"Yeah. I wish I'd thought to plan something to help him out. I'm sure it worked out better with you in charge."

"I disagree with you on that."

"I'm glad you're honoring Zoey's memory. Everyone around here is. You're not the only one who misses her, Ty. She was well liked. Her family was, too. And, believe it or not, you're well liked around here as well. I can't tell you how many people have said how nice it's been to see you around town lately."

"They're probably going to be seeing a lot less of me." He struggled to accept Cade's words.

"I hope not. I think you and Ashlinn have a good friendship going—"

"It's more than friendship." He ducked his chin. "I love her. I fell in love with her even though I told Zoey I'd love her forever."

A hand on his arm made him look up. "You can do both, you know. You can love Ashlinn and love Zoey."

He wanted to yank his arm away, but he didn't. "And how would that work, Cade? I feel like I'm cheating. Neither of them deserves a divided man."

"Neither?" He scoffed, shaking his head. "You speak as if Zoey is still here. She's gone, man. Sooner or later, you're going to have to accept it!"

"I don't want to accept it!" He did jerk his arm away then. "And Ashlinn's complicated. I can't win. Maybe I'm supposed to be alone."

"Ashlinn's *health* is complicated. Mackenzie's talked to me about it. But it sure looks to me like that doesn't bother you."

"It doesn't. I've been around her enough to know how to help her."

"What's the problem, then?"

Ty's shoulders slumped. Fritz danced around his feet, and he picked him up. "She thinks she'd be a burden. And she thinks I'll never get over Zoey."

"I have to agree with her on the last point. I don't know what it's going to take for you to acknowledge that Zoey's not coming back. She's not suffering anymore. She's in heaven. And you're here. No matter how much you punish yourself by hiding out on this ranch or avoiding Ashlinn, that's not going to change."

"I didn't want to get over Zoey!"

"Too bad." Cade shifted his jaw. "That fearless kid who rode a sheep longer than anyone else at the rodeo is still in there somewhere, Ty. I suggest you find him, or life is going to pass you by."

Fearless? What a joke. He wasn't fearless. Probably never had been. What Cade didn't understand was that was exactly what he wanted—for life to pass him by. Get it over with. He didn't deserve to be happy.

Cade shook his head in annoyance. "I still think you should give a short speech to welcome everyone, but I have one prepared if you decide not to."

He hadn't prepared a speech, and he didn't see that changing. His phone dinged. He checked the text—it was from Ashlinn.

I don't want you to come over tomorrow. I'm not going to the fundraiser.

Disappointment stabbed his heart. She really was done with him. What had he expected? He hadn't reached out to her at all since Saturday. Should he even respond?

Okay.

As soon as he sent it, regrets crashed down. He wanted to wipe his hands down his cheeks and grind his teeth together and yell until he was out of breath. But he kept his emotions locked tight.

He didn't have a future with Ashlinn. The sooner he accepted it, the sooner he could resume his loner life on the ranch. Cade thought it was a punishment. It wasn't. It was the only way he knew how to survive.

Fritz licked his arm. *"He's alerting you."* He petted the dog. At least he wouldn't be completely alone. He had the best dog in the world. Too bad he couldn't have the best woman, too.

CHAPTER THIRTEEN

THURSDAY EVENING ASHLINN did something she hadn't done in a long time. She voluntarily called her mother. "Do you have time to talk, Mom?"

"Why? What's wrong?" Her mother sounded agitated, and Ashlinn could hear pots banging around in the background. "Are you having trouble keeping food down again?"

"No." Closing her eyes, she reached down from where she sat on the couch and petted Peanut. "I'm not calling about my health."

"Oh." The word lilted at the end. The sound of chopping filtered through. "What's going on?"

"Ty asked me to go with him to the fundraiser tomorrow night, and before you freak out, I told him no."

Chop, chop, chop.

"I'm glad you recognized your limits. I like Ty, but a crowded dinner would be too much for you."

Ashlinn thought of the room for the bridal party. How she could easily slip away with Peanut if he alerted her. She'd have time. She typically had a few minutes from the first alert. The room was quiet and comfortable, ideal for her to make it through an episode of low blood pressure.

"Did he ask you to be his date?" Her mother sounded curious.

"Yes." She hadn't thought she'd ever get close enough to a man to be turning down dates. The knowledge was bittersweet. "That's what I wanted to talk about."

The streaming of the faucet running made up for the silence. For once, her mother didn't have anything to say.

"Remember when we used to talk?" Ashlinn kept her tone light. "Back when I first went away to college? Every Sunday night, we had a standing phone date."

"I remember," she said softly. "I looked forward to your call all week."

"I want to get back to that."

"But we talk every day."

"No, I mean, I want to talk about things other than if I fainted, if my stomach is upset or how I slept."

"Like what?"

"Like you can tell me what's going on with work, or I can update you on the dogs Patrick is training."

Her mom sighed. "You want to pretend you don't have AAG."

The words were like a machete to her heart. She closed her eyes, trying to adjust to the pain. Her mother was determined to put her in a box labeled Sick and leave her there forever. A sarcastic reply hovered on the tip of her tongue, but she buried it.

Be patient with her.

"I don't want to pretend anything. I want my life to be more than my disease. Does it have to define every minute of my day?" Silence stretched. No chopping. No faucet running. "Mom?"

"I'm sorry. You're right." She let out a deep sigh. "I've been struggling lately. It's been hard having you move so far away."

"I know you worry, and I understand that it's hard."

"The house got so quiet after you left. I think it kind of hit me how stressful the past years have been. Last week I went to lunch with the new gal at work, and she said something that surprised me. She said I've been surviving on fear-fueled adrenaline all this time. I hadn't realized the toll it took on me. Don't get me wrong, your health improving was an answer to many prayers. I guess I worry that it won't last. That what you're going through is merely a good phase, and a bad one will be coming."

Ashlinn accepted the truth of her statement. "If it did, you'd be back in stress mode. Surviving on fear-fueled adrenaline again."

"I would do it in a heartbeat. I love you, Ashlinn. You know I love you. I hope you know I love you."

"Of course, Mom. I love you, too. I've always known that. You've been so good to me. I appreciate all the sacrifices you and Dad have made for me. I guess I want to be more to you than someone you worry about."

"I did my best, Ashlinn. I don't know what you want me to say."

"I know. I'm not trying to sound ungrateful. I guess I could use a shoulder to lean on. Someone to talk to."

"About what?"

"I told Ty I wasn't going to the fundraiser, and I also told him I can't spend time with him anymore."

"Why would you tell him that?"

The truth pained her. She didn't want to admit it, but she couldn't deny it any longer. "Because I love him. And you were right. He lost the woman he loved, and I won't put him through a lifetime with my health problems, even if he did feel the same about me. He doesn't. He's not over Zoey."

"A few days ago, I probably would have told you that you were being smart."

"And now?" Hope and fear battled.

"I don't know, Ashlinn. I saw how he was with you. He cares about you. Glances at you when you're not looking. Anticipates your needs before you do. How many times did he hand you your tumbler of water when we were together? I didn't want to admit it, but he's the kind of guy you can trust. Your dad and I already trust him from another state. I think he is over Zoey."

Could her mother be right? Ashlinn wasn't so sure. "I don't know what to do."

Her mom hesitated. "Pray."

"That's it?" She'd fully expected step-by-step instructions from her. She'd been getting them on most topics for years.

"Yes. Prayer is all you really need. Put it in God's hands, and He'll work it out for your good."

"I guess it can't hurt to try."

They talked for several more minutes, and Ashlinn promised she'd FaceTime her on Sunday night. They were reinstating their weekly call, this time with video. "I love you, Mom. Thanks for listening."

"I love you, too."

After the call ended, Ashlinn got to her feet with one destination in mind. The backyard. Her mom was right—she needed to pray. Ever since Ty had brought over the outdoor furniture, she'd taken to sitting there in the evenings—a nice change of pace from her living room or the training center.

"Come on, Peanut. Let's go outside."

She didn't have to tell him twice. The dog loved the backyard as much as she did. After grabbing her water and shoving the weighted blanket and blood pressure cuff into the tote, she and Peanut went out the back door. She kicked off her flip-flops. The grass was cool under her bare feet. She sat on one of the Adirondack chairs, placed the water on the table next to her, closed her eyes and let her folded hands rest on her stomach.

Lord, Mom made some good points. Ty is attentive and caring. But that doesn't mean he's ready for a relationship. I don't know if I am either. What if he gets tired of me fainting all the time? What if he resents me for not going to church with him or being able to get groceries on my own? God, I need You. I need discernment.

"Yoo-hoo!" A woman's voice startled her. Ashlinn's eyes opened, and her heartbeat pounded. Christy Moulten opened the fence gate and joined her in the backyard. "I hope it's okay for me to stop by."

"Of course." Ashlinn gestured to the chair next to her. "Have a seat."

"Thank you." Ty's mom took in the yard. "I love what you've done back here. Those lights add a festive touch."

"Ty brought them over and installed them for me."

"He did?" Christy, wearing jeans, sandals and a flowy top, settled into the other Adirondack chair. "I'm surprised."

"You are?" She shifted to see her better. "Why?"

"I didn't think he noticed things like that. He's been a bachelor for a long time."

Ashlinn didn't know how to respond, so she remained silent.

"Rumor has it you're not going to the fundraiser tomorrow."

"I'm not." Saying it brought a fresh batch of pain.

Christy nodded. "You know what's best for you. Char and Mackenzie and I can lend you a hand if you change your mind. We reserved a seat for you close to the hallway where the bridal room is located."

Her kindness took Ashlinn by surprise. "That's so thoughtful."

"It's the least I can do. I can't tell you how much of a difference you've made since arriving in Jewel River."

Ashlinn was taken aback. "Um, I think you have me mixed up with someone else."

Christy shook her head and laughed. "You're too modest. Patrick has told me all about how Bandit is well on his way to being a medical alert dog because of you. And all the help you gave Ty planning this fundraiser? It means a lot to everyone involved. He's not the most event-planner-type of person."

"I didn't do much."

Christy stretched her arm out to cover Ashlinn's hand. "You did. I've been mentally going through checklists of things Ty needed to take care of for the event, and I'm telling you it was hard not to ask for updates. But you helped him with all of it. Filled him in on the little things that easily slip through the cracks."

"He would have figured it out."

"Maybe. But you made it easy for him. And it's been a long time since I've seen my son leaving that ranch of his for anything other than filling up his gas tank, picking up groceries or going to church. I'm glad you've given him a reason to think of something other than cattle."

"I'm sure I haven't—"

"You have." Christy's expression was dead serious. "It takes a special person to do all that you're doing. I admire you. Life deals us with blows, and yours have been particularly harsh. You don't let them stop you. You're a strong woman, and my son would be blessed to have you in his life. I know I'm not supposed to say anything like that. You'll both tell me you're not dating or you're just friends or whatever fibs help you sleep at night. But I know. I know Ty. You're the one who helped get him out more, and I thank you for it. You're the one who brought his smile back." She pushed herself to stand. "And now I'll leave you. Please let me know if you change your mind about tomorrow night. I'd love to help you get ready, and we'll get you to the Winston."

Christy bent to give her a hug. Then she scratched behind Peanut's ears, waved goodbye and let herself out through the gate.

Ashlinn wasn't sure what had just happened, but the hope flooding her told her she had some thinking to do.

She'd blamed her mother for treating her like her disease defined her. But hadn't she been doing the same? Acting like she had little value? Assuming all she'd bring to a relationship was a lifetime of fainting spells and uncertainty?

Maybe she'd been cheating herself, too. What did she want out of life?

Closing her eyes, she could envision exactly what she wanted.

Ty. She wanted Ty. Rocking on his front porch with Peanut and Fritz. Days like these—helping Patrick at the training center—and more.

More than her current situation, too. She wanted to try new things. Go to church, even if she fainted. Attend one of Christy's book club meetings.

She wouldn't even mind going to the fundraiser—but she wasn't making that decision right now. And she didn't know if she could bear to see the look on Ty's face when he gave his speech. It would only remind her how much he loved Zoey, and how he'd never love Ashlinn as much.

Christy's words came back to her about being the one who brought back his smile.

Could she be wrong about the fundraiser? Lying to herself to protect her heart?

She'd see how she felt tomorrow. Then she'd decide if she could handle going or not. Her health was one thing—but her heart was another. She couldn't watch Ty mourn another woman. But then again, it might give her the closure she needed to survive life without him.

TY STRETCHED AS high as he could for the box in his bedroom closet Thursday night. His fingertips shifted it a little. He was able to edge it forward enough to grasp it. Once he'd gotten it down, he stared at the cover for a few moments before padding out of the closet. The clock glowed 11:07 from the nightstand. Could he face the contents of the box?

He blew dust off the top, then sat on the bed and placed it next to him. Fritz danced around his feet, so he put him on the bed, too. After Fritz inspected the pillows, he came over and stuck his nose near the box, sniffing loudly.

"No, Fritz. These aren't treats." He caressed the dog's back, thankful for the distraction. He lifted the cover. Scattered photos and notes greeted him along with the memorial from Zoey's funeral.

God, I'm not ready for this. I should have chucked this box in the trash years ago.

He was finding it hard to swallow. He didn't want to face these memories. He should throw it away now. Better late than never.

"That fearless kid who rode a sheep..." Cade's voice ran through his head. *Fine.*

He selected a photo on top. One of those mini-Polaroids Zoey had loved. They'd smooshed their faces together. Her smile was wider than the big sky above. He brought it close to his eyes to study it. Man, she'd looked happy. And he had, too.

They'd both been young. The Ty staring back at him didn't have a wrinkle, and his current face showed the passage of time.

He placed the photo on the bed and selected a paper. Didn't have to open it to know what it was. Zoey's first love note to him. They'd dated for a few months before he'd asked her to officially be his girlfriend. The following week, she'd handed him this note when he'd driven her to his ranch.

Opening it, he read it, and he frowned as he realized it didn't crush him the way he'd expected. Rather, it brought him back to a special time.

He went through every picture, every memento, until the box sat empty. Fritz had fallen asleep. Ty had expected hot, scalding tears at the pain of missing her. But they hadn't come.

After placing everything back in the box, he set it on the dresser and reclined on the bed with his back resting against the pillows. For years, Ty had pictured Zoey here in his house. She'd been here many times before she'd passed away.

But there was only one woman he could picture here now.

Ashlinn. Her long blond hair and big blue eyes, her radiant face. A golden retriever who helped keep her safe.

Ty wanted to help keep her safe, too. He wanted to hear about her day and listen to her advice. He enjoyed her companionship.

She'd made him like himself again.

Swinging his legs over the side of the bed, he picked out several photos from the box and walked them to the kitchen counter. Then he found a notepad and pen, and returned to the bed where Fritz snored. And he wrote out exactly what he wanted to tell everyone who came to the fundraiser.

When he finished, he read through it, scratching out words and adding new ones in the margins.

Dare he go through with this? Could he really admit everything he'd written? To the entire town?

Yeah. He wanted fearless Ty back. And this would be a good place to start.

CHAPTER FOURTEEN

TY CHECKED HIS appearance in the full-length mirror of the bridal room at the Winston. He'd decided to wear a suit. After all, this shindig had been his idea. He adjusted his tie, shook out his sleeves and got closer to the mirror to make sure he hadn't missed any spots shaving. Guests would be arriving soon, and Erica had told him he could use this room to practice his speech. He'd practiced it twice, and both times he'd barely gotten through it. He'd had to cough and clear his throat. He doubted he'd make it through the entire thing tonight.

Fearless? Yeah, right.

For the past hour, his mom and Charlene had been fussing about the placement of the auction items. Thankfully, Cade was out there smoothing things over. The aroma of barbecue and smoked chicken filled the air, and every now and then, he'd hear, "Check. Check. Hot mic."

The staff they'd hired had been setting the programs on each table when he'd slipped away to this room. He only had a few minutes before he'd be forced to do the unthinkable—greet everyone and give a speech in front of a hundred and fifty people.

Fritz let out a yip near his feet. Ty had talked to his mom

and Patrick, and they'd urged him to bring Fritz and tell everyone how he'd helped a veteran. Mackenzie had agreed to keep the dog with her while Ty was giving his speech.

"Hey, there, buddy." Ty bent to pick up the dog. "You look pretty good in that vest. I guess we're both as ready as can be expected, huh?"

"Yip!"

"Right back atcha." Ty ruffled the fur on his neck.

The door opened, and Cade, Mackenzie, Charlene and his mom entered the room.

"How are you feeling, Ty?" Mom came over and straightened his lapel.

"Good," he said. "A little nervous." Okay, a lot nervous.

"I would be, too." Charlene patted his arm. "You clean up good, cowboy."

"Thanks, Char." He nodded to her. She'd been his mom's best friend for as long as he could remember and had been like a second mom to him all these years. If he was being vulnerable, he might as well go all the way. He kissed her cheek. "Thanks for always being there for me."

"Oh, you!" She blushed, swatting her hand at the air.

"You did a good job with the table for Zoey." His mom studied him. "You sure you're okay?"

"I'm okay." His cheeks puffed as he blew out a breath.

"Want me to give the speech?" Cade asked. He had a sheepish air about him.

"No. I'm giving it. You were right." Ty stood taller. "About that and the other stuff, too."

To his shock, Cade put his arms around him and gave him a full hug. "I'm proud of you."

His chest swelled at all their support. He'd taken it for granted for a long time. Not anymore.

Mackenzie stepped forward. "Why don't I take Fritz so you can greet people as they come in? Unless you'd prefer Christy greet them."

"No, I'll greet people." He met Cade's eyes. His brother mouthed, "Fearless."

For some reason that made him smile.

"Thank you—all of you." These were his people. They'd stuck by him, pushed him when he'd needed pushing and let him figure out his own path after Zoey died. "I haven't been easy to deal with for many years. I don't know if I ever will be, but I appreciate you all sticking by me. And I really appreciate all the help with this event. Now, I'd better get out there."

"We love you. We're proud of you. You're going to be great!" Mom clapped, and her eyes were suspiciously damp.

"Come on." Cade gestured to the door. "It's go time."

They all chattered as they left the room. Ty was the last to leave. But first, he paused to pray. *God, I need Your help tonight. Help me be fearless.*

And with that, he strode out the door with his head held high.

Tonight, he'd honor Zoey. Help Patrick's training center. And before the night was over, he was going to tell Ashlinn exactly what she meant to him.

He needed her. He loved her. And he wasn't letting anything stand in his way any longer.

ASHLINN PEEKED OVER at Clem as he drove her to the Winston. He gave her a sideways glance and a slight nod. "Your dog okay back there?"

She checked over her shoulder. Peanut sat in the middle of the backseat, and his panting smile assured her he was fine.

"He's great. He actually loves riding in vehicles."

Clem grunted.

Her nerves were wound tighter than a ball of yarn, and riding to the fundraiser with Clem wasn't helping them. When she'd called Christy an hour ago, she'd thought maybe Mackenzie or Cade would drive her. But they'd all headed to the Winston early to help set up. So… Clem had volunteered.

He'd picked her up in his late-model truck, which, admittedly, was a smooth ride.

"You about to faint? Is that why your hands are fidgeting?"

She hadn't realized she was wringing her hands. She pressed them flat on her lap. "No. I'm a little nervous."

"About what?" He kept his eyes on the road ahead.

How was she supposed to answer that? About possibly fainting in front of the entire town? Or witnessing Ty mourn the love of his life? A toss-up.

"I haven't been out in public like this since before my diagnosis."

"I'm not surprised." He grunted. Then he glanced at her and appeared to be genuinely curious. "What causes your problems? Christy said something about A&P or AARP, I can't remember."

She suppressed a snort. No, a grocery store or a membership to the senior citizen organization wasn't causing her problems. "I have AAG. It's an autoimmune disease that attacks my autonomic nervous system."

"Give it to me in English, girlie," he said sternly.

"The things we take for granted—our heart beating, how we digest food—my body doesn't handle them correctly."

"The dog back there helps?"

"He does. I mean, he can't do much when I have stomach problems, but he knows when my blood pressure dips, and his alerts give me time to get to a safe position before I faint."

"And you faint a lot?" He didn't sound as gruff. "How often? Once an hour? Twice?"

She almost laughed, but then reality hit her. At one point, she had fainted that often and more.

"Sometimes only a few times each day."

"So two or three times a day?" His gray eyes widened as he shot her a look.

"Yeah, it's much better now. I used to faint almost every time I stood. I was basically bedridden for years. The doctors wanted me to try a plasma treatment, and it helped me. Then I got Peanut. Life is much better now."

She admired the beauty of Wyoming for a few miles, thankful for the silence.

"You sure you want to go to this dinner?" he asked.

"I'm sure."

"The food will be good—Drake Arless knows how to smoke meat—but I've got to warn you, the ladies are going to descend on you like a flock of starving ravens in the dead of winter."

She scrunched her nose, confused. "What do you mean?"

"You're single. And you have a dog. They'll have you married off to one of the locals in no time."

"I'm not sure how Peanut factors into it." She started to feel lightheaded at the thought of all that attention even if Clem was dead wrong.

"A golden retriever? Pshaw." He shook his head. "The cowboys around here would date you just for the dog, but you're pretty, too."

She relaxed a bit at the compliment.

"If you need me to carry you in, say the word. I still rope calves, and these old shoulders can haul a heavy load."

"Um, thank you, but that won't be necessary." She would tuck away the offer to examine later. Did he think he'd haul her into the Winston like a side of beef?

"Fine, but the offer stands. Although, you'd be better off with Ty carrying you. He's a good man. A fine cowboy. Quiet. That's a point in his favor. You could do a lot worse than settling down with a man who keeps to himself like Ty."

Where had that come from? This conversation was zigzagging out of control.

"Of course, he probably still thinks he's in love with that brown-haired girl he'd been ready to marry. We all felt bad when she died. If you ask me, he needs to pull up his britches and move on. When I saw you two at that ridiculous Shakespeare movie—I hope to never sit through one of those again—I was glad. Figured you two would make a good couple. But he's been hiding away again, and I don't like it."

"I don't like it either," she said softly.

He nodded in agreement. "Well, here we are. Don't go getting out of the seat until I open the door for you. Christy would beat me over the head with a wooden spoon if you hurt yourself before I get you inside." Clem parked the truck and got out.

She giggled, which turned into laughing, and she couldn't stop. Maybe she was growing hysterical. The past twenty-four hours had been odd, to say the least.

Clem took her tote and let Peanut out of the backseat, and she'd gotten herself under control by the time he opened her door. When he offered her his hand, she accepted, and he helped her down with a gentleness she'd never thought possible. She took hold of the handle of Peanut's harness. Then Clem held out his arm, and she took it, too.

"Ready?" he asked.

"Ready. Can we go in through the side door? That way I can set up a station in the bridal room in case I faint."

"A station? What are we talking about?"

She explained about the weighted blanket as they crossed the lot to the side door. Getting through the dinner would probably be the easy part. The difficulty would be in figuring out how to pull Ty aside. She had to tell him how she really felt about him.

She loved him. And she was ready to take a chance on love. She just hoped tonight didn't prove what he'd been telling her all along—that he preferred a dead woman to her.

CHAPTER FIFTEEN

"THANK YOU ALL for coming." Ty had spent almost thirty minutes shaking hands and accepting hugs from the members of the community who'd come out tonight. He'd noticed a common theme. They all thanked him for putting on the event, raved about how the service dog training center was a wonderful cause, and then they'd shared a personal story about Zoey.

How she'd babysat their kids when she was in high school, or the time she'd messed up her piece at the piano recital and gave a little curtsy that everyone thought was the cutest thing ever. Throughout the process, Ty realized she hadn't only mattered to him. She'd touched many people's lives. And they all spoke of her fondly.

No one had forgotten her.

He wouldn't either.

As everyone got settled at their tables and turned their attention to him, he smoothed out the paper where he'd written his speech. He took a moment to get his nerves settled.

"When I first had the idea of doing something to honor Zoey's memory, I didn't dare dream this many people would respond. You have other things to do on a Friday night, and I appreciate you joining me here. First, special thanks to

Erica and Dalton Cambridge for supplying the Winston free of charge."

Everyone applauded. Ty studied the crowd until he found Erica and Dalton sitting a few tables back. He nodded to them. Erica clasped her hands over her heart as she beamed.

"Thank you to my family and everyone who volunteered to put this on. As most of you know, Zoey and I were engaged, but God had other plans for her." Could he say the next part out loud? "Most of you haven't seen me much since she passed. I've struggled with grief. Life lost its color. When Patrick Howard moved to town and opened Howard Service Dogs, my dear mother—" he pointed to her table "—told me all about the work he was doing to help people with illnesses and other problems affecting their daily lives. Mom mentioned him needing volunteers. I ignored her."

Titters of laughter circled the room.

"Once again, God had other plans. See Mackenzie over there?" He pointed to her and Cade. Fritz sat on her lap. "She's holding Fritz, a miniature dachshund who used to be a therapy dog for a veteran. When his owner passed, Fritz came to live with me. I didn't know I needed him. I do. He recognizes when I'm feeling down and comforts me."

At the table in front of him, Clem slipped into the chair next to his mother, and to her left, Charlene was dabbing at her eyes with a tissue. "One of Jewel River's newest residents, Ashlinn Burnier, is helping Patrick train dogs to detect medical issues. Ashlinn's medical alert dog, Peanut, allows her to live independently. Training the dogs, housing them, and helping clients learn how to work with their dogs takes money. Every penny we raise tonight will go to Howard Service Dogs."

He could end the speech there. But he was ready to be that fearless kid again.

"Ashlinn helped me plan this event. I couldn't have done it without her. She isn't here, and I wish she was. I'd tell her thank you. Thank you for getting me out of my rut. Thank you for generously giving your time to an event honoring a woman I loved long ago. Thank you for allowing me to see life through a lens of gratitude, rather than one of self-pity."

He glanced at his mom, and her eyes shined brightly as she nodded.

"I'd tell Ashlinn a few other things, too. I'd tell her that Zoey was a beautiful woman inside and out, and I've been ready to let her go for a while. Yes, I've been fighting it, but I'm ready. I'll always have good memories of her. And I'm ready to make new memories. With another woman who is beautiful inside and out. I fell in love with Ashlinn Burnier, and I'm going to hand the mic to my brother so I can drive to her house and tell her myself."

The crowd rose to their feet, clapping, whooping and whistling.

Ty set the microphone in the stand and strode away from the podium. His chest felt tight to bursting in the best possible way.

He was going to win Ashlinn back no matter what it took. Tonight.

ASHLINN HAD BEEN holding Peanut's harness in the doorway of the bridal room as Ty gave his speech. As soon as she heard, "I've been ready to let her go for a while," she hurried down the hall and emerged into the main area. Her gaze landed on Ty as he jogged in the opposite direction.

What if he left before she could catch him?

With everyone on their feet whooping and hollering, she had no shot at catching his attention. Her heart pounded, her pulse raced, and Peanut licked her hand. She ignored the dog to move forward through the crush of people. But Peanut blocked her path.

Tears pressed against her eyes. Not now. Not when she had a million things to say to Ty.

"Quiet everyone." Clem's stern voice filled the room. Ashlinn jerked her attention to the podium. The room went silent. "Ty Moulten, get your buns back in here."

Ashlinn had no idea if Ty obeyed or not. Peanut continued to block her path. Either she retreated to the bridal room now, or she'd pass out here.

"Ashlinn's here. Her dog is, too. You made a smart choice with that woman, Ty. Who cares if she faints now and then? Could be worse. We all remember when Walt, may he rest in peace, coughed up blood at church or when Betty Jane had flatulence through no fault of her own—"

Christy grabbed the mic from him. "No need to go down memory lane, Clem. Ty, hon, Ashlinn's over there." She pointed the mic to Ashlinn. "Now, who's ready to eat? It's past time we dug into this delicious barbecue. I'm starving."

Clem and Christy to the rescue. Another round of applause went up, and Ashlinn, lightheaded, made her way back to the bridal room. Peanut licked her hand and blocked her path again before she got inside. She didn't know if she should laugh or cry. She'd finally gotten the courage to come here, and her body was threatening to thwart her plans.

A strong arm curved below her knees, and Ty swept her into his arms, carried her into the room and kicked the door closed behind him. She leaned her cheek against his shoulder.

Her strong cowboy.

He sat on the couch with her on his lap. She turned to look at him. She'd never seen him so intense. His brown eyes gleamed with appreciation for her.

"You came," he said.

"I did."

"You look…" his gaze took her in from head to toe "…absolutely stunning. This dress—" he shook his head, awe in his expression "—wow."

"This old thing?" The pale aqua dress had been sitting in her closet for years, never worn. "You did good up there, Ty."

Peanut sat on the floor next to them, rested his chin on the couch and stared at her. She petted his head. Ty handed her the tumbler of water. She took a drink.

"Do you need to get on the floor?" He caressed her bare arm.

"The only place I need to be is right here in your arms."

He searched her eyes, then turned his attention to her lips. Taking his sweet time, he lowered his mouth to hers. The kiss started out slow, tender. Then it grew insistent. She kissed him back, wanting him to know how much he meant to her. How his speech—in front of all of Jewel River, no less—had made her feel like the most loved woman on earth.

Peanut jumped on the couch and set his paws on her lower legs. Ashlinn's arms were wrapped around Ty's neck, and she dragged one down to pet the big guy. "Good boy."

"Let's get you on the floor." He helped her down and sat next to her, keeping his arm around her shoulders.

"You meant everything you said, didn't you?"

"I did. Every word."

"I have things to say to you, too. I might mangle this or faint during it, but please hear me out."

"You don't have to—"

"Oh, but I do. You make me feel normal. When I'm with you, I'm not merely an invalid. I'm your friend who happens to pass out a lot. Did you know your mom stopped by last night?" His muscles tensed, and she patted his chest. "Don't worry. She told me something I needed to hear."

"What did she say?"

"She told me that I'm making a difference in people's lives, and that I'm strong."

"You do make a difference, and you are strong."

"I have a hard time seeing it." Her heart no longer pounded, and her pulse had slowed. Peanut wandered around the room. "All I could see was my limitations. But here's the thing. I called my mother. We had a good talk. I explained how I wanted us to have actual conversations. She admitted it's been difficult to return to normal life after the stress of the previous years."

"Makes sense."

"Afterward, it kind of hit me that in some ways I do the same thing as she does. I don't always see myself beyond my illness. I let it stop me from doing things I want to do."

"You have a good reason." With the softest touch, he stroked her hair.

"Maybe before Peanut, I did. But I'm ready to expand my horizons. I'd like to go to church with you."

"You mean it?" A smile spread across his face.

"And I think I could go to the grocery store."

"There wouldn't be a place for you to sit if you fainted." His forehead creased in worry.

"I've thought of that. What if I used a wheelchair?"

"Yes. Then you wouldn't get injured if you did pass out." He kissed her forehead. "What else do you want to do?"

She twined her fingers in his. "I want to go back to your ranch and rock on your front porch. Watch the world go by."

"It's my favorite place to be." He brought their joined hands to his lips, kissing her knuckles. "I love you, Ashlinn. I want you to know I *am* over Zoey. I talked to her parents, went through old photos and letters, and I wasn't devastated. I've been holding on to guilt over her death for years. Afraid to move past it. Afraid I'll forget her. Afraid to try again and lose again."

"Are you still afraid?" She stilled, not quite trusting he could handle being with her.

"I'll always be afraid of losing you. I think that's part of love. The highs and the lows. But I'm not letting it stop me. I don't want to miss out on another minute with you. I love you, Ashlinn, and I'm bound and determined to be a man worthy of you."

"Oh, Ty!" She was getting emotional and didn't care.

"You're worthy. Don't ever think you're not worthy. If I get to be too much for you—"

"Never. Don't even say it."

"But I have to. My health could get worse. I could be bedridden again."

"My love isn't conditional on your health. I love you now. I'll love you through anything. You're the one for me."

"And you're the one for me."

CHAPTER SIXTEEN

"CAN WE COME IN?"

Half an hour had passed since Ty had brought Ashlinn to the couch. He stared into her pretty blue eyes, and she nodded.

"Come in," he yelled.

The door to the bridal room opened, and Fritz raced to them. After helping Ashlinn to her feet, Ty picked up the dog and slid his arm around her waist. Cade, Mackenzie, Patrick, Mom, Clem and Charlene piled into the room.

"So?" His mother clearly couldn't take the suspense. She looked like a balloon ready to pop. Fritz wiggled, and Ty set him on the floor. He immediately trotted to Peanut.

Ty pressed Ashlinn closer to his side. "I love her."

"And I love him." She bit her lower lip, glancing up at him.

"Shouldn't you be on that rug, girlie?" Clem gave a pointed stare to her, then to the rug where they'd put her folded weighted blanket.

"I'm not going to faint. Not at the moment, anyhow."

"Right. That dog of yours isn't licking your hand." The man rubbed his chin. "Proceed."

Cade surged forward to clap Ty on the back, and Mackenzie drew Ashlinn into a big hug. Then Mom hugged her and

Charlene. The women were talking a mile a minute, and he didn't even attempt to decipher what they were saying.

"Fearless," Cade said. "That speech. Whew. People will be talking about that one for years."

"We might not even discuss the book this month at book club. We'll rehash your speech instead. You made me tear up." Mom came in for a hug. "I didn't know you could be so romantic."

"I see you came to your senses." Clem hooked his thumbs in his belt loops and rocked back on his heels. "I expect to see more of you around town."

"I don't know about that." Ty grimaced. "I'm not a social butterfly."

"Is she?" Clem hitched his head to Ashlinn.

"Not really," she said. "A quiet, simple life is what I want."

"Well, there you go."

His mom turned to Ashlinn. "Now will you come to book club?"

Ashlinn met Ty's gaze. He shrugged.

"I'll think about it."

"Good." His mother took Ashlinn's hands in hers and squeezed. "We'd love to have you. And like I said, no one will care if you faint. Mary fell asleep with a cookie in her hand last month. She startled and that cookie went flying."

"Christy." Clem sidled next to her.

"Yes?" She turned to him with an expectant expression.

"What do you think?"

"About what?"

"About making it official."

"I told you I'm not getting married." She huffed.

"No one said a thing about marriage, woman. I'm talking about dating. You and me. I know I'm old and mean. And you're spry and beautiful and fun. You make me feel alive."

"You think I'm fun?" His mom blinked in surprise. "But all I do is yell at you."

"Pshaw." He waved in dismissal. "I need a little yelling at me."

Ty met Cade's gaze—as confused and stricken as his own surely was.

"Then, yes, Clem. I'll be your girlfriend. If that's what you're asking."

"That's what I'm asking. Didn't you hear a word I said? Cheese and biscuits."

"I heard you! See? This is what I was talking about last week. You miss social cues and come across as rude. You are the most exasperating man."

Clem took her hand and tugged her close. "And you're cute when you're upset."

"I am?"

Cade threw his hands in the air. "Okay, what is going on?"

"Well, honey, Clem and I have been getting close—"

"Understood." Cade held up a palm. "I can handle you two dating—at least I think I can—but I draw the line at you two kissing. Take it somewhere else."

Mom gave the biggest eye roll Ty had ever seen, and Clem scoffed. "We're old. We ain't dead."

"I'd rather be dead than watch you kiss my mother." Cade took a step closer to Clem. The older man narrowed his eyes, standing steady and tall. The room had grown quiet, and everyone watched them through wide eyes.

Then Clem smiled—Ty wasn't sure he'd ever seen the man smile—and gave Cade a nod. "That's why I like you, Cade. Your brother, too. You don't shy away from speaking your mind."

"We all know you never shy away from it either." Their mother elbowed Clem's side. "Let's get back to the dinner." She turned to Ashlinn. "You're probably starving. Want us to bring some food back here for you?"

"No, thanks." Ashlinn beamed at Ty. "I'd like to eat out there with Ty."

"You're sure?" He didn't want her to feel embarrassed or push herself too hard. "People are going to come over to meet you. They might have a lot of questions."

"I hope they do. It's time I met my neighbors. I have a feeling I'm going to be living in Jewel River for a long time."

Ty pulled her into his arms and hugged her tightly, then whispered near her ear. "If I have anything to say about it, you'll be living here forever."

EPILOGUE

THE LAST TIME Ty had attended one of these meetings, he'd been a different person—a man afraid of interacting with people around town. He still enjoyed the solitude of riding horseback around his ranch. Still preferred being home to going out. But he no longer avoided people.

Ashlinn brought out the best in him.

He glanced at her and gave her hand a squeeze. Three months had passed since the fundraiser, and she still made his heart do cartwheels. With the money the dinner had raised and Cade and Mackenzie's matching donation, Patrick had been able to purchase the van he'd wanted. He'd already used it a few times to bring clients to the center and teach them how to handle their dogs.

Ashlinn still loved working there. A new dog had arrived last week that showed promise as a medical alert dog. Ty sure was proud of her. With Christmas only two weeks away, the weather was too cold for her to walk to work. Patrick or Mackenzie picked her up and dropped her off on the days she felt up to it. Her health remained about the same as when she'd arrived in the summer.

"Oh, Erica?" Angela Zane waved her hand frantically. Erica

Cambridge stood at the podium. Ty might be mistaken, but was she pretending not to see the waving hand? "Erica!"

"Yes, Angela." Erica turned to the woman.

"Joey asked me to announce that he won't be making the Shakespeare film this year. He was accepted into a fancy film school in Boston. We're so proud of him. But I have to admit, I'm sad our Shakespeare-in-the-Park films will be ending."

"Good for Joey!" Erica beamed. "We're very proud of him. We'll miss his movies, too. They've become a tradition."

"I know. That's what I told him." Angela wore the face of a proud grandma. "He wanted to share a little something tonight. Can you get the audio-visual equipment ready?"

Erica's gaze found Dalton, and she struck the air with her index finger. He nodded, pulling down the screen, while Cade went over to the light switches on the wall.

"What's going on?" Ashlinn whispered. Peanut sat by her side.

"I'm not sure. I'm guessing Joey made a video."

A few minutes later, Cade cut the lights, and the video began with flames burning in the center and expanding outward. A low male voice began to narrate.

"Joseph Zane would like to thank the Jewel River Legacy Club for giving him an outlet to use his digital graphics skills." A plunger detonated dynamite, and explosives roared, blowing up the screen. "If not for the Shakespeare-in-the-Park movies, he wouldn't have gotten accepted into Boston University's VFX, Animation and Interactive Media program. Don't worry. He won't forget where he came from. Jewel River will always be home."

The film cut to Joey typing at a computer and waving to the camera. A rocket flew across the screen, leaving words written from the exhaust. *This isn't the end. It's the beginning.*

Cade turned on the lights, and everyone got to their feet and clapped. When the applause died down, Angela was wiping tears as she smiled.

"We're so proud of him and all he's done for our community, Angela," Erica said. "Tell him he's welcome to put on another film anytime. He's blessed us with his talents."

The phrase stuck with Ty as the meeting continued. *He's blessed us with his talents.*

When the meeting ended, Ty stood. "Just a minute, everyone. I have an announcement."

The members turned to him with curious expressions.

"Over the weekend, I asked this beautiful woman to marry me. To my relief, Ashlinn Burnier said yes."

Cheers rose. People came over to congratulate them. Mary, his mother and Angela surrounded Ashlinn for several minutes. He was proud that she'd gotten the courage to get out more. Sure, she'd passed out at church twice. No one batted an eye when she and Peanut came into stores. They all liked her. How could anyone not like Ashlinn?

Soon everyone trickled out. He and Ashlinn, Clem and his mom, and Cade and Mackenzie left together. Out in the parking lot, Cade and Mackenzie said goodbye to them. Clem took his mother's hand, and they walked ahead, chatting, then arguing. Ty put his arm around Ashlinn's shoulders. The dark sky was full of twinkling stars. Snowflakes began to fall.

"That went better than I expected," Ty said.

"I'm so happy for Joey."

"Me, too." He squeezed her shoulder. "And I'm happy for us. What Angela said back there, 'He blessed us with his talents.' I feel the same about you. You bless us with your talents, Ash. You're patient and kind and the best person I know."

"See? This is why I love you. You only see the good in me. Never the bad."

He kissed her temple. "You're all good. Through and through."

"I'm not, and you know it. You, on the other hand, are about as perfect a cowboy as has ever lived."

"Me?" He pretended to be surprised. "I know better, but you keep thinking that."

"Are we going back to my place to watch the Christmas movie I recorded?"

"Yes."

"What about going with me to your mother's book club in January?"

"I draw the line there."

"I don't blame you." She nestled into his side. "You're still my cowboy."

"I'll forever be your cowboy."

* * * * *